M L N

SHE CAN HIDE

ALSO BY MELINDA LEIGH

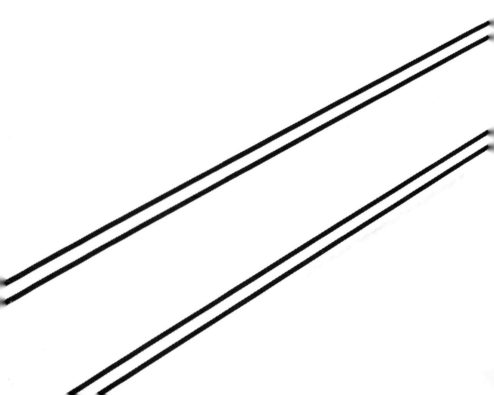

MELINDA LEIGH

SHE CAN HIDE

Montlake
Romance

Text copyright © 2014 Melinda Leigh
All rights reserved.

Published by Montlake Romance, Seattle

www.apub.com

ISBN-13: 9781477849828
ISBN-10: 1477849823

Cover design by Inkd Inc

Library of Congress Control Number: 2013913289

Printed in the United States of America

For Linda
We miss you

CHAPTER ONE

A whoosh and soft impact jolted Abby's body. She slid forward. The seat belt caught her and snapped her back. Pain ripped through her temple. What happened? Her vision blurred, and she rubbed her eyes to clear it.

The steering wheel and dashboard came into focus. She was sitting in the front seat of her Subaru sedan. Ice pellets bounced off her windshield. When had it started to sleet? Blinking hard, she stared through the glass. Water splashed over the hood.

Oh my God.

She swiveled her head to get her bearings. A thin sheet of ice edged the opposite bank twenty feet ahead. Water bubbled over rocks down the center of the flow. Behind the car, fifteen feet of water stretched to an inclined embankment. Her car was door-deep in a river.

The Subaru bobbed for a couple of seconds. The front end tilted down, and water swished over the floor mat. This had to be a nightmare. But her personal horror didn't usually involve water. Abby's bad dreams were all dark all the time. But a minute ago she'd been in the parking lot of the high school where she taught math. How did she get here?

Water swirled around her feet and seeped through her running shoes. Cold. No, beyond cold. Liquid ice. Shocking pain washed over her ankle and jolted her from her dreamlike state.

This was real.

Terror swept through her confusion and jerked her from numb disbelief into panic. Fear, bitter and acidic, bubbled into her throat. Her lungs pumped like pistons, forcing air in and out at dizzying speed. Tiny dots flashed in her vision. Out the window, water rushed past the car, the surface level with the hood and rising.

The interior closed in on her, claustrophobia overwhelming her senses.

The water was going to rise. She was going to be trapped, and then she was going to drown. She was going to die.

A chunk of ice scraped across the windshield. The noise jolted her.

She had to get out of the car. She fumbled for the seat belt release, the frigid temperature and horror destroying her dexterity. Frantic fingers yanked at the nylon. Her thumb found and depressed the button. The strap loosened and recoiled with a snap. Abby reached for the door handle and pulled, but she couldn't budge it. Water pressure held the door closed. Until the pressure was equalized . . .

No! She couldn't sit here and wait for water to fill the car. She'd drown. She had to get out now. Water inched up the glass. The sense of confinement suffocated her. Her heart catapulted blood through her veins.

The window.

She pressed the lever. Nothing happened.

Oh no. It had to open!

Did electric windows work underwater? The car shifted again, the hood dropping thirty degrees. Sliding forward, Abby braced her upper body on the steering wheel.

Water advanced beyond her calves to her thighs. Two layers of winter running pants were designed to facilitate moisture evaporation, not keep water out. The cold bit into her skin like the teeth of a saw. Pain and numbness spread up her legs and reached for her body with a greedy splash.

Tears leaked down her cheeks, and terror sprinted through her heart as she pressed the window button harder. The glass lowered. Yes! Her flash of relief was cut off by the flow of water. It poured through the opening and washed over her torso in an icy fall. She had an exit, but now the car was flooding even faster.

With a groan, the car tipped as water displaced air and the weight of the engine pulled the vehicle deeper into the eddying river. Abby fell forward as the car went vertical. She lost her grip on the wheel. Her world tilted. Her forehead slammed into the dashboard. Blood spattered, but she felt nothing.

The water rose, swallowing her pelvis and chest in the span of two panting breaths. She twisted her body sideways to fit through the opening, but the force of the water pouring through the window pushed her back into the vehicle.

Frigid liquid enveloped her neck and face. The shock seized her muscles. Her breathing sped up in a reflex to the agonizing cold. She pressed her face to the ceiling to suck in a last lungful of air. But the car dropped again, turning as it sank. Her body tumbled like clothes in a washing machine.

Where was the window?

Disoriented by the car's shift, she searched with frantic desperation. Freezing water stabbed her eyeballs. In the murky underwater scene, she saw the opening.

There!

Her arms tangled in her heavy wool coat. She shrugged out of it and pushed her shoulders through the opening. Once her hips cleared the window, the current pulled her free. The surface was a bright layer just above the car roof. Lungs burning, she stroked upward, toward the light, away from the darkness below. Her head burst free of the water and she gasped. Oxygen flooded her brain. With the infusion of air into her body, her limbs went from cold to numb to dead weight in an instant.

She could barely move to keep her head above the surface. Dirty water flooded her throat, choking her. She looked for the bank, but the water carried her farther from the vehicle, toward the center of the rapids that bubbled white down the center of the waterway. With one final desperate lunge, she grabbed the bumper of her Subaru protruding from the surface. She'd never make it to shore. She'd escaped the car only to drown anyway.

Acceptance washed over her, as numbing as the temperature, then sadness. Her poor high school students would grieve. Her only friend and fellow teacher, Brooke, and the young neighbor Abby tutored would be devastated. Zeus would be too, for as long as his dog memory would allow. That was it. She hadn't let many people get close. Her mother was dead, and she hadn't seen her father in three years, since the last time she'd come close to dying, when he'd made his lack of interest clear.

Loneliness rivaled fear in her heart as the current tugged harder. For the second time, she was facing death alone. But if she could do it over again, would she change?

Could she change?

It didn't matter. She wasn't going to get another chance. Her frozen fingers faltered, then slipped. The wet metal slid out of her grip. Frigid water closed over her head.

Two hours earlier
Sleet pinged off the police cruiser's windshield as Ethan slowed

to read the number on a rusted mailbox. The painted numerals were too faded to read, but his GPS told him he had the right address. Besides, there wasn't another farm in sight. Snow-crusted fields stretched out on both sides of the road. On the other side of the flat plateau, the Endless Mountains of Northeastern Pennsylvania jutted into the sky.

He turned into the driveway. The vehicle bounced down the rutted lane. Weather-beaten to a dull gray, a used-to-be-white farmhouse squatted on the right. Porch boards sagged. The roof dipped. To the left, a cluster of ramshackle sheds leaned at precarious angles. Around the supposed barnyard, six inches of frozen snowpack covered three barbwire enclosures. Combined, the corral areas totaled roughly a quarter acre.

Did animals live in those? Ethan knew the answer. This wasn't his first call to provide backup on an animal cruelty call.

He checked in with dispatch and parked behind the Pennsylvania SPCA truck. Three more official vehicles, including a long stock trailer, crowded the yard. A caravan wasn't a good sign. The humane officers had come prepared for seizure.

He grabbed his hat from the passenger seat. Shoving it firmly on his head, he got out of the vehicle and flipped up the collar of his Westbury PD jacket. Under the brim, an icy wind pelted his face with sleet. He opened his trunk and changed into heavy waterproof boots. Then he followed a group of footprints to the center of the compound. Bracing himself, he peered inside the first shed.

His gaze locked on a group of wretched animals huddling in the miserable weather. Sleet and wind cut through the huge gaps in the roof and walls in their pathetic excuse for a shelter. The horses bent heads and closed eyes against the precipitation. Bones protruded through ragged wet fur.

Son of a bitch. Anger seared through the cold.

"Ethan." His cousin, humane society police officer Veronica Hale, trudged toward him, partially frozen mud sucking at her boots. A navy blue watch cap pulled low over her forehead covered hair that was as jet-black as his. The ends poked out and lay wet against the shoulders of her bulky parka. She held a compact camera in one gloved hand and a clipboard in the other.

"What's the story, Ronnie?"

Ronnie tucked her clipboard under her arm and shoved both hands in the pockets of her coat. She hunched her shoulders against the wind. At thirty-one, she was two years Ethan's senior. Both were the oldest in their respective families and shared a lifetime bond created by decades of harassment at the hands of their younger siblings.

Her cheeks were blistered red from the cold. She'd been out here awhile. "We got a call from a utility worker concerned about the condition of a few horses. We did a ride-by, saw three animals in bad condition in the front paddock, and got a search warrant for the premises. When we got here, we found nine more horses. The whole dozen of them are emaciated. The living conditions are beyond unsanitary." Ronnie swiped a knuckle under a watery blue eye. "We're seizing all of these animals today."

"Have you told the owner yet?"

Ronnie gave him a tired smile. "I was waiting for backup. Mr. Smith is agitated and confrontational. The vet is finishing his assessment of the animals. Smith keeps getting in his way."

"Where is he?"

Ronnie squinted against the precipitation. "Inside the third lean-to."

"Let's get it done." Ethan followed her, taking stock of the conditions. Water buckets frozen over. Despite the cold, ammonia

6

burned his nostrils, a sure sign of urine overload from animals confined too long in untended close quarters. As they stepped inside, angry voices dimmed the patter of sleet hitting corrugated metal. A nervous bay horse huddled in the corner. The hips of the roan pony closest to Ethan were sharp as ax blades. The pony turned and gave him a friendly nose bump. Ethan rubbed the bony neck.

"There ain't nothing wrong with these animals." In the center of the space, a skinny man dressed in jeans, heavy boots, and an olive green canvas coat crossed his arms over his chest and glared at the vet. Ethan categorized him automatically. Five-foot-eight. A hungry one-thirty. Gray hair. Gray eyes. Belligerent attitude. "None of them is starving. They get fed twice a day."

Scraggly whiskers and an arthritic posture suggested he was at least seventy and not in the physical condition to care for this many animals even if he cared, which Ethan doubted.

He scrutinized the space. No feed buckets in sight. The only wisps of hay in the frozen muck were mingled with manure. Twice a day his ass. These horses hadn't seen a decent meal in a long time, so long that their bodies had run out of fat for fuel and moved on to burning muscle. The extreme cold weather of the last couple of weeks had sped up the process.

"Where do you keep your feed?" Ronnie clicked a pen over her clipboard.

The old man's eyes drifted left. "I'm due for a delivery tomorrow."

Ronnie paused. "So you have no feed for these animals?"

"I got some. Price of feed is steep. Sometimes I gotta ration." The old man zeroed in on Ethan. "Who's he?"

Ronnie gestured with her pen. "Officer Ethan Hale, Dennis Smith."

"How long is this going to take?" Smith puffed his chest out rooster-style. "I have things to do."

Six and a half feet of no-nonsense large animal veterinarian in insulated brown coveralls and steel-toed boots, Doc White ignored the conversation and focused on the three emaciated horses crowded in the corner of the fifteen-by-fifteen space. He leaned over to get a look at the horses' feet. But inside the shed, the top few inches of frozen muck was trampled soft. Mud and manure buried the animals' feet to the ankles.

Doc approached a filthy chestnut gelding. The horse didn't protest as the vet took hold of its halter and opened its mouth. The poor beast probably didn't have the energy.

"When was the farrier out last?" Ronnie asked.

"I see to my horses' hooves myself." The lie flickered in Smith's beady eyes. He pulled a pack of cigarettes from his chest pocket. He put a filter in his mouth and lit up with a Zippo. Snapping the lighter closed, he took a long drag. The tip flared angry red.

Ethan opened his mouth to reprimand him for smoking in a barn. But what the hell was going to catch fire? Mud? Besides, it wouldn't matter much. These animals weren't going to be here much longer. Ronnie had already started the process. Smith should be prohibited from owning any more large animals. His cousin was known for brick-house-solid cases.

Doc patted the thin neck, slid a hand down the animal's shoulder, and lifted a hoof for inspection. He gently set the foot back on the ground. He gave Ethan a nod of recognition and caught Ronnie's eye. "Same as the others."

Doc gave the red horse a final pat and moved back out into the sleet. Smith intercepted him. "Where are you going?"

Ronnie stepped between the men. The gigantic vet's mouth twitched. He probably had a hundred pounds on Ronnie. But

Ethan knew his cousin. She was the cop. She'd called the vet, and it was her job to protect him, regardless of their respective sizes.

Nearly six feet tall in her socks, Ronnie straightened to take advantage of her height. "Doc is here to assess all the animals. We have a search warrant, Mr. Smith."

Mr. Smith pinched the filter of his cigarette to his lips and sucked in a furious drag.

Ethan tensed. Ronnie could handle herself. She'd been able to beat the snot out of him until he was twelve, but Smith was ignorant and angry, an unpredictable combination. Unpredictable equaled dangerous, and Ethan didn't like Ronnie on the receiving end of the guy's ire.

Ethan stepped up. "Let the vet do his thing."

"These animals are my property." Smith flicked ashes and avoided Ethan's gaze. The guy was hiding something.

"If you care about these animals, you should be glad the vet is here," Ethan said, mostly to keep the guy's attention off Ronnie. His cousin ducked out into the sleet.

Smith clamped his lips around his cigarette tight enough to crimp it.

"Oh no." From outside, Ronnie's voice echoed with sadness.

Smith crossed his arms over his chest. His eyes shut down. Ronnie had just found whatever he'd been hiding.

Ethan kept his eyes on the man's hands as he called out to his cousin, "What is it?"

Ronnie came back in. She stomped across the muddy ground to face Smith. "There's a dead horse in the back of the yard. It's hidden behind some underbrush. When did the horse die, Mr. Smith?"

So much for keeping Smith's attention on Ethan.

"Yesterday." Smith's teeth ground back and forth.

Ronnie pressed. "Had it been sick?"

"No." The lie shone in Smith's eyes. "Just keeled over. It was old."

The last straw snapped in his cousin's eyes. Ronnie stepped forward. "Mr. Smith, we are taking all of these horses right now."

Radiating anger, Smith bristled and leaned closer to Ronnie. "These animals are my property. You ain't got the right to steal them from me."

Ronnie held her ground. "Mr. Smith, these animals are in immediate physical danger. They are starving. They have no water or proper shelter. The weather is bad and getting worse. One has already died from lack of care. All of these horses are going with us today."

Still keeping watch on Smith's hands, Ethan moved closer.

Smith's gaze, mean and flat, flickered to Ethan. The old man backed off. "This ain't over."

"No, it isn't." Ronnie wrote something on her clipboard. "We'll be seeing you in court, Mr. Smith."

Tramping toward his house, Smith's hand moved toward his pocket. Ethan tensed, his palm on the gun at his hip. Smith yanked a cell phone from his jeans. Ethan lowered his hand.

Ronnie turned to one of her assistants. "We didn't plan on this many horses. We'll need another trailer."

The college-age kid nodded. "I'm on it."

"Shit." Ronnie rubbed the crease between her brows. "The county shelter is two stalls short. We had another large rescue last week. What shape is your barn in?"

Ethan hesitated. He didn't have the time or money for a couple of horses. Paying his brothers' tuition and keeping his mom in her house commandeered all of his take-home pay. He looked back to the first shelter. The roan pony stuck its nose over the door and bleated out a thin whinny. "It's solid. How long would you need me to keep them?"

"Soon as the weather clears and they're stabilized, I can move them to foster farms." Ronnie lowered her voice. "I know your budget's tight. Don't worry. We'll take care of the cost."

Ethan's gaze swept over visible rib cages, filthy coats, and defeated eyes. What else could he do? "OK. My brothers are still home for winter break. I'll call and get them to prepare a couple of stalls. We haven't had a horse in years."

"Thanks." His cousin whipped out her cell and punched numbers. "I don't want to have to transport them a distance in this weather and in their current condition if I don't have to. Plus, they'll need to be thoroughly vetted and dewormed before they can be with other horses. Your place is empty. It's perfect."

"Not a problem." Ethan made the call, then spent the next ninety minutes helping Ronnie's team gather evidence and load the animals. The nervous bay alone took twenty minutes to get on the trailer. By the time Ethan changed back into his shoes and settled back in his cruiser, his uniform pants were soaked through, and his feet were ice blocks ready to snap off at the toes. Thankfully, his shift was nearly over.

He cranked the heat on full, pulled off his gloves, and held his red hands to the vents. His skin burned as the air flow warmed. The horse trailers made a right out of the driveway. Ethan turned left toward the police station. As idiotic as his younger brothers could be, he could count on them when it mattered. They'd settle the horses if Ethan wasn't home first.

At four in the afternoon, daylight was dimming fast, solid cloud cover bringing an early twilight. Early January days were short. Snowflakes mixed with the sleet. Ethan switched the heat to defrost as the wipers iced up. Twenty feet to his right, Packman

Creek flowed parallel to the road. What the . . . ? He slowed the cruiser. Muddy tire tracks cut through the roadside grass and led down the embankment.

Ethan stopped his vehicle on the shoulder and got out. He looked over the side. The rear end of a car protruded from the water. The edges of the creek were iced over. But in the center, water flowed white over boulders. Ethan raced back to his vehicle and called for an ambulance and rescue backup. He jumped out and ran to the riverbank. Was anyone inside?

The creek fed into the north branch of the Susquehanna River. In some spots, the stream was barely more than a trickle. Unfortunately, this section was deep and wide, more of a river than a creek despite its name.

Movement next to the submerged car jolted him into action. A head broke the surface and flailed for the car bumper. A woman. Ethan shed his coat and belt on the bank and waded in. The cold hit his skin like a slap.

Her head disappeared under the water.

"No!" Ethan plunged forward. The frigid water enveloped his legs in shocking pain. She popped up again. Up to his thighs in the creek, Ethan's muscles protested. His breaths quickened as the alarming temperature threatened to shut down his body. Seconds. He had seconds to save her.

He trudged. Water lapped over his hips and froze his balls. Teeth chattering, he reached for her, but she sank again. His feet slipped. The current swept his legs from under him. Water closed over his head, and the icy plunge cut off his next breath. His heart stuttered as he surfaced.

The creek bottom had dropped off. Ethan was forced to breaststroke the remaining few feet toward the woman, his body armor making the movement awkward. Training and running in a bulletproof vest was one thing. Swimming in it was quite another. But he had to get her on the next try. His body was slowing down. She'd been in the frigid water longer.

Shit. They were probably both going to die.

Ethan grabbed the car's bumper to prevent the current from dragging him away. Thankfully, the vehicle had stopped sinking, the front end likely hitting bottom. He grabbed for the woman, but she went under. Ethan stuck his hand into the river where she disappeared.

His fingers brushed her face. He reached farther. His fingers closed around fabric, and he pulled her above the surface by her collar. He tightened his grip, wrapping his frozen fingers tightly in her shirt. He was not losing his hold on her.

"Is there anyone else in the car?" he shouted.

"No," she gasped. Her eyes opened wide, bottomless pools of deep brown against skin as pale and fragile-looking as an eggshell. Her sopping hair molded to her head and emphasized her striking beauty and delicate bone structure. Blood trickled down her temple. She tried to swim, her movements sluggish and uncoordinated. Ethan hauled her through the water toward the shore. Fifteen feet seemed like a mile.

He stumbled into the shallow water. Thin sheets of ice snapped under his feet as he hauled her onto the snow-covered reeds that lined the river. His legs gave out on the frozen bank. Ice crackled as he fell to his knees. She lay beside him, still and limp as a corpse.

He tried to speak, but his lips didn't cooperate. A few words came out as a jumble of stuttering gibberish. He glanced up at the car. His cruiser was warm, but he'd have to get her up the steep riverbank to get to it.

The air was as cold as the water. The woman's body temperature was still falling. Running on sheer willpower, he scooped her off the ground, carried her to the road, and stuffed her into the backseat of his car. He climbed into the front and started the engine. Warm air blasted from the vents.

Back out in the cold, Ethan grabbed a blanket from his trunk, then returned to the backseat. He pressed his fingers to her neck, but his skin was too numb to feel her pulse. How long had she been in the water?

Was she breathing?

He pressed his ear to her chest.

CHAPTER TWO

Abby coughed and sputtered. Hands rolled her onto her side. Water poured from her nose and mouth, burning her sinuses and throat. A violent quake rattled her bones.

She'd never been so cold. She felt like she'd slept in a snowbank.

"Thank God," a deep male voice said.

She opened her eyes. Brilliant blue eyes focused on her with laser intensity. She squeezed her lids shut for a second. When she opened them, the rest of his lean features sharpened. Rivulets of water ran from his short black hair down his face. His teeth rattled behind blue-tinted lips, and his body shivered in a drenched police uniform.

"I'm Officer Ethan Hale." His broad shoulders hunched over her. One hip perched on the edge of the large backseat of his police car, the cramped space creating a few square inches of body contact. Ignoring his own shakes, he spread a blanket over her and tucked it around her torso. "What's your name?"

She could hear the whoosh of the car heater on full, but the blowing air wasn't enough to penetrate multiple layers of wet cloth. She harnessed her strength to control her shuddering jaw and spit out a few stuttered words. "Th-thank you. I'm Abby Foster."

Thank you seemed inadequate, but what else could she say to a man who'd waded into a frozen river to save her?

"Can you tell me what happened? Did you slide off the road?"

It seemed like a reasonable assumption to her, but her molars were clacking too hard for her to answer. A vision of water rising to the roof of her car filled her head. Nausea and creek water churned in her belly as she revisited her panic. Her breaths quickened.

"Easy." He pulled the blanket up to her chin. "It's OK. You're safe."

Gratitude, suspicion, and a thousand other conflicting emotions crowded Abby's throat. His soaking wet uniform was a reminder he was a cop. Yes, he'd risked his life to save her, but she'd learned the hard way that the police could never be fully trusted. Most people couldn't be trusted.

Scratch that. She'd moved to Westbury specifically to leave everything about her past behind. Horrible memories invaded her former home every night when darkness fell. She'd tired of the pitying glances from everyone who knew her story, or thought they knew what had happened to her. The whole story never went public. Most people yearned for excitement, but all Abby wanted was a quiet, normal life.

A complete transformation was necessary to achieve her goal, inside as well as out. Changing her address wasn't enough. Her suspicious attitude didn't apply to her new life either. Ordinary law-abiding citizens trusted the police, and Abby was determined to be normal.

A siren approached, saving her from further scrutiny. The cop eased back. He opened the car door. Abby nearly cried as frigid air swept over her freezing body. Her muscles cramped, and her bones and teeth ached. He withdrew from the vehicle to flag down the rescue vehicles.

In short order, she was bundled into the ambulance and wrapped in warm blankets. The paramedic started an IV, the heated liquid warming her from the inside out.

Truthfully, she'd love to answer the policeman's questions. What had happened? How did she end up in a river? And why couldn't she remember?

———————————

While the paramedics took charge of Ms. Foster, Ethan retrieved his coat and belt from the riverbank. The fact that she was still shivering was a good sign. Conscious and talking, she seemed as if she'd be all right. He stopped at his cruiser to change his soaked shoes for the boots in his trunk. Then he walked toward the waiting ambulance and perched on the rear bumper while the medics settled Ms. Foster inside. One of the EMTs wrapped a blanket around Ethan's shoulders and gave him a quick assessment.

A dark-blue SUV parked on the shoulder, and Police Chief Mike O'Connell got out. Ethan's boss swept a knit cap off his red hair and zipped his coat to his chin as he walked over. A slight limp was the only sign of the knife wound that nearly killed him three months before. After several months of recuperation, the chief was nearly back to his collegiate wrestler shape. O'Connell handed Ethan the cap and crossed his arms over his massive chest. Worried pale blue eyes scanned Ethan from head to toe. "Are you all right?"

"Soon as I change I'll be fine." Ethan's teeth chattered, making the words hard to enunciate. "That water is damned cold, though."

With a relieved sigh, the chief nodded toward the river. "Any idea what happened?"

"No. I'll have to get her statement at the hospital." Shivering, Ethan summarized the event while the medic took his vital signs.

The chief scanned the scene. "I don't see any skid marks."

"Road's slippery." Ethan dug a toe at the asphalt. The surface was more than wet. "Black ice."

"If she applied the brakes, there should be some sign of a skid." The chief walked to the shoulder of the road. His critical gaze swept from the snow-dusted road to the car bumper sticking out of the river. He squatted to inspect the tire tracks in the mud and frowned. The car had left twin furrows in the roadside muck. The ruts were too neat and smooth. There were no signs that the vehicle had swerved or slid on its descent down the embankment. "I don't like it."

Suspicion slid down Ethan's back, along with a drop of melted sleet.

The paramedic nudged Ethan toward the open ambulance door at his back.

"Whatever happened, she's lucky you were passing." The chief's eyes snapped back to Ethan. "Go."

"I'll get her statement while I'm at the hospital."

The chief raised a doubtful eyebrow. "Are you sure? I can get Pete to do it. He's coming on shift now."

Now that was tempting. Ethan had enough problems of his own. But the accident bugged him, and there was something about Abby Foster. . . . He stood and looked over his shoulder into the ambulance. Her slim body was encased in thick blankets, her big brown eyes glassy with shock. "Yeah, I'm sure."

The chief lowered his voice and leaned closer. "OK. While you're there, get her to consent to a blood alcohol test." Straightening, he turned toward the tow truck pulling onto the shoulder. "Good work today, Ethan. I'm damned glad you're not dead."

"Me too." Ethan climbed inside and sat on a bench, grateful Ms. Foster hadn't died either. His mind conjured up an image of her body floating lifeless in the freezing current. Ethan pushed it away. There was no point in torturing himself with what-ifs. He'd gotten to her in time. End of story.

An hour later, the ER physician, satisfied that Ethan's body temperature and vital signs were normal, declared him fit. Dressed in a borrowed pair of scrubs and drinking a scalding cup of coffee, Ethan left the curtained ER cubicle. His teeth had finally stopped chattering, but he could still feel the chill in his bone marrow. A nurse directed him to his accident victim. Through the clear glass wall, he saw her reclining in a cubicle. Her eyes were closed. A Styrofoam cup steamed on a tray table next to her. An IV line trailed from a bag of fluids into her hand.

He knocked on the doorframe. She startled, then recovered with a slow blink of doe eyes that warmed Ethan better than any cup of coffee.

"Ms. Foster, how are you feeling?" He stepped up next to the gurney.

Her fresh face and blonde hair poked out of a heap of blankets. She looked sweet and young and vulnerable. A small bump swelled on her forehead, the skin around it reddening. Just below it, a small Band-Aid covered the cut above her eyebrow. She'd have a nice bruise tomorrow. Ethan stamped down his stirring emotions. More than the average amount of sympathy was swirling around in his chest. This was police business. There was no room in the job or in his life for a pretty blonde.

"I'm alive, thanks to you. Please call me Abby. You saved my life."

Ethan's face heated. He sipped his coffee to clear his throat. "I have to ask you some questions."

"Of course." But she looked sick at the thought.

Ethan pulled his notebook from his pocket and took her personal information. She squinted as if the bright light was painful. "Does your head hurt?"

"A little." She touched her temple and winced.

He eyed the lump. "Were you wearing your seat belt?"

"Yes." She nodded. "I unfastened it to get out, but the car kept moving." The small amount of color her face had recovered drained away, leaving her skin pale and smooth as river ice. "It was disorienting."

"I imagine it was." Empathy filled Ethan. He'd been in the open creek, and that had been bad enough. He couldn't comprehend the terror of being trapped in a submerged car with bone-numbing water rising all around. "Tell me about the accident. Where were you going?"

"To the park." Her tone was unsure. Her brows drew together in a confused V.

Ethan's pen hovered over the page. "Which park?"

"I run at the park behind the township athletic fields. I knew I'd be stuck with the treadmill for the next few days, so I wanted to get a good run in before the storm hit." She closed her eyes for a few seconds.

That couldn't be right. "The sleet started hours ago."

"I don't remember driving into the water. I don't even remember leaving the school. I teach math at Westbury High." Her voice trembled, and her slender throat moved as she swallowed.

Ethan checked the Styrofoam cup on the table. Full. "Do you want some of your hot chocolate?"

She shook her head. "I wish I remembered."

"Let's talk about what you do recall," Ethan said. "How did you get out of the vehicle?"

Her eyes filled with moisture. With a brave sniff, she pulled a hand free of the blankets to swipe a stray tear from her cheek. "Through the window. I didn't know the button would work underwater."

"They're supposed to, but they don't always." If the windows hadn't worked or if he hadn't stayed at that farm all afternoon, Ethan would've been diving for her remains. Navy SEALs aside, not many people can keep their cool to wait for a vehicle to fill with water, then calmly open the door and swim to safety, especially if the vehicle doesn't stay horizontal.

"What do you remember about your day?" How hard had she hit her head?

"I was at the high school getting ready for my run. I changed my clothes in the locker room. A second later I was sitting in my car in the river."

"What time did you leave the school?"

"Two thirty."

Ethan glanced at the clock. "What did you do for two hours?"

"Excuse me?"

"By the time I spotted you, it was four forty-five."

Her color shifted from pale to sickly gray.

Concussion? Blackout? Seizure? Possibilities rolled through Ethan's head. If she'd been using drugs, she'd likely be less cooperative. "Did you tell the doctor you couldn't remember?"

Her lips flattened out, and she gave him a quick, short nod. "They're going to do a CAT scan."

Damn.

The chief's request echoed in Ethan's mind. "I'd like you to consent to a blood alcohol test."

"Why?" Her eyes went wide, then darkened.

"So we can eliminate that as a cause of the accident."

Something flashed in her eyes. Fear? "I haven't had as much as a glass of wine since last weekend."

"Then there shouldn't be any problem."

"All right." She nodded, but distrust lingered, along with something else Ethan couldn't identify. Reluctance?

Ethan looked down at his notebook. So far, all he'd written was *doesn't remember two hours before accident.* Some interview. He jotted down a few more notes. Abby Foster and her problems were damned distracting. "How long have you worked at the high school?"

She pressed a hand to her mouth and mumbled, "I'm sorry."

Ethan reached for a pink plastic tub sitting on the tray table. She grabbed it from him. Embarrassment radiated from her watering eyes.

"I'll just step out." Ethan ducked into the hall. A familiar slender brunette in her late thirties rushed toward him.

"Ethan!" Brooke Davenport shoved her keys into her coat pocket. A red tote bag was draped over her arm. "Is Abby in there?"

Ethan nodded. "Is she a friend?"

"Yes. Is she OK?" At the sound of retching, Brooke pushed past him. "Excuse me."

Ethan had known Brooke for years. She taught self-defense classes for women at the local community center. The Westbury officers took turns donning a protective suit and acting as attackers so her young female students could practice their techniques. As the youngest officer on the small force, Ethan was "volunteered" often. He'd taken more than his share of well-placed kicks.

He watched through the glass. Brooke took charge of the plastic tub and was stroking Abby's hair away from her face. Feeling like he was invading Abby's privacy, he turned away. He wasn't going to get anything out of her tonight. He'd leave the poor woman alone. On a positive note, she'd consented to alcohol testing, which saved him a huge hassle. Technically, Pennsylvania had implied consent laws regarding alcohol testing and driving, but Ethan had no desire to play hard-ass or jump through legal hoops.

He bummed a ride from an EMT back to the police station parking lot where his pickup waited. The wintry mix had changed over to light snow. He started his truck and called the chief.

"Did you get her statement?"

"Partially. I'll have to get the rest tomorrow." Ethan transferred the call to hands-free and set his phone on the bench seat beside him.

"What happened?" the chief asked. "Were her injuries more serious than they looked?"

"Maybe. She must have hit her head pretty hard." Turning onto Main Street, Ethan relayed his brief conversation with Abby. "First I made her cry. Then I made her throw up."

"I'm sure none of that was your fault." The chief's voice was sympathetic. "Try again tomorrow. Maybe she'll remember more in the morning."

"Yes, sir." Ethan steered toward home, but Abby's response still nagged him. Despite her evasiveness, his instincts told him she wasn't lying about the accident. She didn't remember what happened. If he were in her place, would he be shocked at a request for alcohol testing?

Maybe. Her life had been flipped on its back this afternoon.

"You had a hell of a day. I can have someone cover for you tomorrow if you're not up to working."

"No, I'll be in." Ethan needed the hours. Plus, he didn't want anyone else to question Abby Foster. Under her seemingly honest, girl-next-door persona, he couldn't shake the feeling that she was hiding something.

CHAPTER THREE

"I'm sorry." Abby covered her mouth. Her humiliation was complete.

Brooke patted her arm. "Don't be silly. I've raised two kids. It takes more than a little puke to faze me."

Over her best friend's shoulder, Abby watched the policeman walk away.

Brooke grinned. "He's an eyeful, isn't he?"

Abby coughed. "I guess."

"You guess?" Brooke lifted her *girlfriend* eyebrow in disbelief. "Honey, Ethan is the total package. He's just as nice as he is hot."

"Do you mind? I'm throwing up here." Abby wiped her mouth.

"I was just saying." Brooke raised a hand in mock innocence. Abby knew her friend was trying to distract her from the awful afternoon.

Her head fell back on the hard plastic pillow. Unfortunately, Brooke was right. Why couldn't Abby have been rescued by a middle-aged cop with a receding hairline and a three-doughnut-a-day paunch? No, fate had to toss a man at Abby who made her hormones wave a foam finger—which was saying a lot given everything she'd been through today. Thirtyish, clean-cut, and boy-band handsome, Ethan Hale had the kind of chiseled good looks that drove young girls to hang posters on ceilings and throw underwear onto stages. And this gorgeous man had handed Abby a basin to barf in.

Ugh. Well played, fate.

The truth was that the whole package, as Brooke put it, had thrown her off kilter. Her new normal life demanded she act like the average person, someone without a traumatic past, someone who would give a police officer a statement and trust he'd do the right thing. But something about her accident was setting off her internal alarms and bringing out her natural defense mechanism. Her instincts forced her into turtle mode. Was she just paranoid? Maybe, but God knew those missing hours had her on edge, and she had her reasons for distrusting the legal system.

The cop had taken pity on her and given up for tonight. But that wouldn't last. Tomorrow he'd be back with his notebook. What if she didn't have the answers? What if she never remembered?

"What on earth happened today?" Brooke asked.

Good question. Now that the nasty water was out of her stomach, the queasiness was fading. "I don't know. The last thing I remember is changing in the locker room."

"Do you remember teaching all day?"

Abby searched her memories again. Pain thumped in her temple. "I do. Right up until the end of school. Then I blank out for two solid hours. Why can't I remember something as important as driving my car into a creek? And what did I do all afternoon?"

Brooke squeezed Abby's hand. "You have a concussion, right?"

"That's what the doctor thinks." Tears and the details of the interview with the cop spilled out in a messy jumble. "The policeman thinks I was drinking."

"That's probably just a routine test these days," Brooke said. "You don't have anything to worry about. The only thing you drink on running days is Gatorade. Maybe you stopped at the dry cleaner's or Walmart. Did you look for receipts?"

"My purse is in my car." Abby fingered the lump and bandage on her forehead. A dull ache drummed behind her eyes. The accident site was on the route between the school and the park. Was she freaking out about nothing? *Did* she run some errands after school?

"Give the police some time." Brooke offered her a breath mint.

Abby popped the peppermint into her mouth. The hole in her memory disturbed her on a primitive level. Two hours didn't seem like much time, unless they were a total blank that nearly killed her.

———————

Ethan drove his truck behind the house and parked. Lights glowed in the barn windows. He glanced at the house, where a hot shower and a meal waited. Getting out of the car, he walked through the fresh dusting to the barn. Flurries drifted onto his head as he crossed the yard. Once he went in for the night, going out into the cold again would be harder.

He rolled the barn door open and closed it behind him to keep the wind out. It was a small structure, with two stalls on each side capped by a feed room on the left and a small tack room on the right. The aisle was swept clean. A few bales of fresh hay were stacked on a pallet in the aisle. Other than a few cobwebs up high, Cam and Bryce had done a stellar job getting the place together in a rush.

A snort drew his attention to the first stall. He leaned over the half door. Clean straw covered the dirt floor. A full water bucket hung by the door. The roan pony stood in the center, dozing. A navy blanket covered the ribs and bony frame. The pony turned its head toward Ethan and shuffled over.

"Hey. You don't have to inspect our work, big brother." Clean-cut Cam came out of the tack room, a green plaid horse blanket in his arms and an annoyed quirk on his lips. Bryce was right behind him. His shoulder-length hair was tied back with a leather thong, and a hoop gleamed from one ear. Like Ethan, they were both just over six feet tall, with the Hale black hair and blue eyes. Ten years his junior, Cam and Bryce were college-student lean, despite the vast quantity of food they packed away every day. His younger brothers were identical twins, but even before Bryce went pirate, Ethan could tell them apart. Cam was born with an up-to-something gleam in his eye. Bryce was the straight man in their duo.

"Where did you get the blankets?" Ethan ignored Cam's protest and scratched the pony behind its ear. On the large size for a pony, between thirteen and fourteen hands high, the roan had a body that should have been stocky. The fuzzy head just reached over the stall door.

"You know Mom. She keeps everything." Cam stopped at the stall next door. "The roan is super friendly and doesn't seem to be afraid of anything, which is amazing considering how he's been treated. We had a hell of a time with the bay quarter horse. He's a wild one."

Ethan gave the roan a final pat and moved on to get a look at the second horse. The body was a muddy brown color, with black legs and a black mane and tail. Nose in the far corner, it turned its head and gave the three men a worried eye roll. "His halter is too small. It's rubbing his nose raw."

"Already on it." Bryce sighed and held up the halter in his hand. He cracked the door and slipped inside.

Ethan watched his brother ease up to the horse. "Easy, Captain."

"What did you call him?"

"Captain." The bay showed Bryce the whites of his eyes. "We named them Captain and Morgan."

"We are not naming horses after booze." Ethan pointed at Bryce. "In fact, we are not naming them at all. If we name them, we keep them."

Next to Ethan, Cam snickered. "Who are you kidding? Every animal that has ever set foot on this property has stayed for the duration of its natural life."

Ethan ran a hand through his damp hair. Snowflakes drifted down around him. "Sorry, guys. You're going back to school next week, Mom's going on vacation, and I don't have the time or money for two horses. In case you don't remember, horses are pricey pets and needy as needy gets. We can't keep them."

"If you say so." Cam nodded with a grin. He draped the horse blanket over the stall door.

"I mean it." Frustrated, Ethan watched the horse's muscles tense. "Careful."

The bay turned its rump to Bryce.

"You need to be patient." Ethan slipped into the stall. "You're going to get kicked."

Ethan stood opposite the horse's shoulder and waited. The animal sniffed and turned toward him. He had the halter changed a minute later.

Bryce's mouth tightened in frustration. "*I* need to be patient. How about giving me three minutes before you step in?"

"You're right. I'm sorry." Ethan held the horse still while Bryce backtracked to pick up the blanket. He handed the old halter to Cam, who dropped it in the garbage can. "What did Ronnie say?"

Bryce kept his voice soft as he eased the blanket over its back. "We should give them small amounts of hay. The vet and farrier will be out tomorrow. That's about it."

Ethan rubbed the bay's neck. The animal nuzzled his jacket. All the Hales had a way with animals matched only by their weakness regarding the same. Cam was right. Every creature that had managed to wander, crawl, or limp onto the property over the decades had found a forever home. But things were different now.

"We have to call them something." Cam opened a bale of hay. "How about Google and Bing?"

Ethan left the stall. "How about Roan and Bay?"

"Those are lame names." Cam gave each horse a scant few handfuls of hay.

"They don't need awesome names because they aren't staying." As Ethan walked away, his brothers were still arguing—and ignoring him.

"Cinnamon and Spice."

"Oreo and Cookie."

"We are not naming these horses," Ethan said over his shoulder and rolled the heavy wooden door closed. The firm thud of wood on wood punctuated his statement.

Before going into the house, he retrieved his soaked uniform from the truck and salted the walkway and the steps that led up to the deck. If his mother went out to feed the birds in the morning, he didn't want her to slip.

He left his coat, boots, and wet clothes in the mudroom. The Christmas tree glittered as he passed the living room. He stepped into the kitchen and salivated at the thick, rich scent of Yankee pot roast. The big meal was a sign his mom's new rheumatoid arthritis medication was working. She pulled a plate from the oven. Dressed in slim jeans and a bulky blue sweater, she looked almost frail. The weight she'd lost when his dad died had stayed gone. But her shoulders were straight, her chin high, and her beige-blonde hair never showed a strand of gray. Nothing short of a natural disaster would cause his mother to miss her monthly appointment at the beauty salon.

Ethan leaned down to kiss her cheek. "Christmas was three weeks ago. Don't you think it's time we took the decorations down?"

"I suppose."

But Ethan knew he'd be doing it alone after she left for her sister's house next week. His dad had suffered his massive heart attack while dragging the tree out five years before.

She waved him toward the round oak table. "How are those poor animals settling in?"

"Fine." Ethan's butt hit the chair hard, his leg muscles suddenly deciding they were exhausted.

"I saw Ronnie unload them earlier." One-handed, Mom slid a dish in front of him. Joint damage permanently curled the fingers on her left hand. A cleaning service came in once a week to do the heavy housework, but his mom loved to cook for her sons. "Be careful, dear, that plate is hot."

"Cam and Bryce took care of them." Ethan shoveled meat, potatoes, and carrots into his mouth while his mom chattered about the animals' arrival. "You didn't go out in this weather, did you?"

"Just for a minute." She set a basket of biscuits at his elbow. "Do you need more gravy?"

"No, thanks." Ethan slathered butter on a biscuit. "How's the packing going?"

"Fine."

"I bet you can't wait to see Aunt Julie."

Mom smiled. She hadn't seen her sister since last winter. "You're right. I'm excited, but I hope we get those ponies straightened out before I go."

Uh-oh. He had to keep her away from the horses until she left. A week was more than enough time for her to get attached.

"Chances are Ronnie will move them before that."

Her eyes dimmed. "Probably for the best."

But didn't Ethan feel like crap? His mother loved nothing more than to care for an animal in need. Bring on the injured dogs, starving cats, and birds with broken wings. Their barn had served as a wildlife rehab center for most of his childhood.

"It'd be nice for them to have a family with kids," he pointed out.

"You're right." She nodded, watching him with patient blue eyes. "What else happened today?"

As if she didn't already know about the accident. The chief's secretary, Nancy, would have called his mom to let her know that Ethan was all right. A few other details likely slipped out during the conversation, but Ethan told her about the river rescue anyway. She used to be active. Now the disease kept her in and slowed her down.

His mom stirred honey into her tea. "I heard she's a math teacher at the high school."

"You know I can't talk about the details of the case." Even though his mother probably knew as much—or more—as he did.

His mother's blue eyes sparkled, a sight guaranteed to give Ethan indigestion. "I heard she's pretty too."

Pretty was an understatement, but Ethan gave her a pointed look. "Mom, this is a case. I'm a professional."

"Of course you are." She put a hand on his forearm. "I didn't mean to suggest you would be anything else. But if that were me, and a handsome young man came to my rescue . . ." His mother sighed, and Ethan knew she was thinking about his father. Dad had only saved his mother from a thunderstorm and a flat tire, but when she told the story, Dad was her white knight. "Well, he'd be my hero."

Ethan covered her hand with his palm. "I was just doing my job."

"You're a good man, Ethan. Your father would be proud." His mom sniffed and stood up to clear the table. "I'd love to see you with your own family instead of getting stuck taking care of me. I'm sorry I'm such a burden."

"You're hardly a burden, Mom." And Ethan could hardly think about having another family when he was still taking care of this one.

She smiled and patted his hand. A scraggly gray tomcat sauntered into the kitchen and wound around her legs. "Would you like some roast beef, Sweetums?" She bent down to scratch behind the torn ear of her latest rescue.

"Sweetums is a ridiculous name for that cat. You should call him Scarface or Reaper." Ethan could hear the feline purring from across the room. He emptied his milk glass and crossed the tile floor. Sweetums raised his back and hissed. Ethan gave the feline a wide berth. Sweetums might be old and missing an eye, but those claws were Wolverine sharp. A fact Sweetums liked to remind Ethan of every once in a while. Apparently, Sweetums never got the memo about all animals liking Ethan. The old cat trusted Lorraine and no one else.

"Nonsense. He's very affectionate." His mom minced some meat and gravy on a saucer and set it at her feet. She stroked the old cat's head. "That's a good boy."

Not.

Still purring and pointedly ignoring Ethan, Sweetums attacked his food like a cat who didn't know when his next meal was coming, which was exactly what he'd been until last summer. His throaty rumble sputtered as if his transmission had dropped a gear.

Ethan tossed his wet uniform in the washer. His shoes weren't salvageable. He headed for the master bedroom on the second floor. His mom's arthritis made climbing stairs painful. Ethan had converted the downstairs den into a bedroom and handicapped-accessible bath, complete with grab bars and every other piece of safety equipment available.

Separate floors gave them the privacy they both appreciated. Thirty-year-old men weren't supposed to live with their mothers, but with the twins' college tuition on top of the farm upkeep, Ethan wasn't moving out anytime soon. His mom had suffered so much, he'd be damned if she'd lose the house she loved on top of it all.

His muscles relaxed as he stepped under the hot spray, his thoughts turning toward the intriguing woman he'd rescued earlier. Was Abby Foster at home? Had she warmed her skin with a hot shower? And how the hell had she ended up in the creek this afternoon? Images of the pretty blonde losing her struggle with the frigid water sent pot roast tumbling through his gut and eliminated all his woe-is-me thoughts.

He left the shower and dressed in thick sweats, then stretched out on his bed and grabbed his electronic tablet from the nightstand. He'd get the official reports on Abby Foster tomorrow at the station, but everyone was on the Internet. Or so he'd thought.

Foster was a common name. He found a few results in this geographical area: mentions of her name in a local newspaper when the high school track team she helped coach won a big meet. A couple of school photographs came up with Abby and Brooke flanking the kids. There were no other pictures or mentions. He couldn't find a single social media account that fit *his* Abby Foster—correction—the Abigail Foster he was seeking. Frustrated with the scant results, Ethan shut down his device.

How could a thirty-year-old avoid the Internet to that extent?

Fatigue seeped through his muscles. Despite his exhaustion, sleep was fitful, disturbed by visions of a beautiful woman sinking beneath the surface of the water. This time Ethan didn't reach her in time. Her brown eyes pleaded with him to save her while ice crystallized over her face. Ethan hammered on the thickening ice, but she sank deeper until she completely disappeared.

CHAPTER FOUR

The crystal paperweight shattered against the wall, but Ryland got no satisfaction from its destruction. It was just one more beautiful object acquired, then ruined by his hand.

Damn it. What was he going to do?

He spun his chair to face the floor-to-ceiling window of the penthouse office suite. The overcast night sky loomed over a white-topped expanse of ocean. Below, lights illuminated the windswept Atlantic City boardwalk. In winter, both beach and boardwalk were empty, the stark beauty of the New Jersey shoreline unmarred by tourists. Ryland had mixed feelings about winter in Atlantic City. On one hand, summer tourists brought revenue to his casino. On the other, they littered the beaches and destroyed his view.

As usual, money won the debate. This wasn't Vegas, with the glitter of a high-priced call girl. Atlantic City had to spend a lot more time on her back to pay her bills. The Jersey Shore lived and breathed for summer. Packing a year's worth of business into three short months took work. Unlike the smaller businesses, the casinos had off-season traffic, but the place came alive from June through August.

Swiveling his chair from the dark and turbulent seascape, he read the alert on his computer screen again: PENNSYLVANIA HIGH SCHOOL TEACHER BARELY SURVIVES PLUNGE INTO ICY RIVER.

For the second time that evening, a measure of anger rolled through his gut with a momentum that rivaled the ocean.

His hand sought another heavy object to break, but he resisted, finding his last thread of self-control.

He'd been keeping track of Abigail Foster from a distance, but this new development could not be ignored. A decision must be made. Truth be told, he'd let the situation with her go on much too long. He should have taken care of her three years ago. But he'd failed, and as a result, loose ends fluttered all over his life.

It was time to see this through to the end, as painful as it might be to all involved.

His decision both relieved and distressed him, but everything gained came at a cost.

He turned away from the laptop on his desk and pressed the intercom button on his phone. "Kenneth, I need to see you."

Ryland's assistant opened the door that separated their offices.

"Yes, Mr. Valentine." Tall, slim, and impeccably dressed in a European-cut suit, Kenneth looked more like a gay urban lawyer than a killer.

Actually, Ryland had no idea if the thirtysomething was straight or gay, but he suspected his assistant got off more on violence than sex and might not be all that choosy when it came to the gender of his partners.

"There's been a development." He pointed to the laptop.

Kenneth crossed the plush carpeting. He leaned over and silently scanned the article.

"I need you to fix this," Ryland said. He aimed for authoritative, but instead, his voice rang with a needy plea that grated against his pride.

Kenneth looked up. Nothing flickered in his pale gray eyes. Absolutely nothing. As a teen in Sarajevo during the Bosnian War, he'd witnessed atrocities that short-circuited the empathetic part of his brain. A section of Kenneth's soul had been severed as neatly as pruning shears snipped off fingertips. Some things, once seen, could never be unseen.

"Yes, sir." Kenneth straightened. "Consider it handled."

"I should have let you handle it three years ago."

"I agree." Kenneth sliced through bullshit as smoothly as one of the knives concealed under his custom-tailored suit. One of his best attributes was his ability to be faithful without cowing. In Ryland's opinion, a sniveler could never be trusted. After twenty years in Ryland's service, his assistant was the only person who knew everything. "Is there anything else?"

"No," Ryland said. He wanted 100 percent of Kenneth's hyper focus on this task. Abigail Foster was a factor he'd long neglected. But that couldn't continue. Three years ago he'd gotten a pass. Now events were unfolding that required him to clean up his past, and she was part of the mess. Why had he let it go this long? "Only you this time. I can't trust anyone else with it."

Kenneth's head tilted in a small, acknowledging nod. Another man might puff up in vanity at such a compliment, but not him. He was a man of careful thought and, once he'd considered his options and chosen one, definitive action.

"Keep me apprised of your progress." Ryland's problem would disappear in a methodical and orderly fashion, as if his assistant was following a precise recipe or a chemical equation.

Unlike the rest of Ryland's employees, Kenneth's trustworthiness was absolute. Ryland had given the lost and broken young man a job as a favor to a dead friend. He'd given Kenneth purpose, and in doing so had given him new life. His assistant had repaid him with nearly medieval fealty, and like an ancient knight, he had no issue with mowing down Ryland's enemies like stalks of wheat. He handled the most sensitive tasks with admirable completion and discretion. Ryland had to admit, the skills Kenneth learned in Bosnia had come in handy on a number of occasions.

"I'll be on my way then." Kenneth withdrew from the room. In some ways, Ryland was closer to his assistant than his own family. He liked to keep his personal and business lives separate. Only Kenneth knew all the facts about both.

Ryland's phone buzzed. He glanced at the display. Marlene. He ignored his wife's call. She'd be pissed, but he needed a few minutes to compose himself before he spoke with her. The decisions he made tonight would change the lives of everyone he loved. He glanced at his watch. Tonight was their oldest grandson's fifth birthday party. They'd be a few minutes late, but nothing short of death would induce Ryland to miss it.

Did Marlene know he'd cheated on her? Probably. She was a smart woman.

Ryland reached for the china cup at his elbow. He sipped his coffee, now cold, and spun his chair back to the view. The churning sea stretched black to the horizon, seemingly endless. As CEO, president, and major stockholder of Valentine Entertainment Group, he controlled the casino that occupied the fifty-story building below him, in addition to several resort hotels and a few residential towers. Last year he'd bought a golf course. Someday his sons would take over. Between now and then, there were other loose ends that needed to be severed or tied. He'd built his business with decades of scratching and clawing, fighting his way to the top of the dog pile. He'd done the dirty work so his sons wouldn't have to. When the time was at hand, Ryland would pass down a legitimate business. His legacy wouldn't come with strings. His children wouldn't be burdened with the consequences of decisions Ryland had made decades ago.

And neither should his wife.

Ryland hadn't always been a good husband. Like in his business, he'd taken what he wanted without regard for the repercussions. Success built ego. Once a man's head swelled, he thought he was entitled to everything.

Would pride be his downfall?

For thirty-five years, Marlene had been an excellent wife and mother. She'd married him before his success was realized. She didn't deserve to have Abby Foster rubbed in her face. In fact, how long had it been since he'd bought Marlene a gift? If he couldn't remember, it had been too long. He'd stop at the jewelers on the way home. It seemed to him that the mother of his children should be rewarded at the celebration of the grandchild's birthday, though no bracelet could make up for his breach of their marital vows. He couldn't undo his past mistakes.

Unlocking his phone, he returned his wife's call, confident that Kenneth would handle the situation with Abby Foster.

Ryland had made some mistakes in his sixty-five years. Unfortunately, many of his transgressions were of a most permanent nature that couldn't be undone.

But this was a problem he could fix, though the solution might cost him everything.

CHAPTER FIVE

Sunlight sparkled on fresh snow. On the cement apron in front of the hospital, Abby squinted at the glare. She zipped up her jacket against the midmorning chill.

"Are you all right?" Brooke stopped next to her car, parked at the curb in the pickup zone. "Do I need to take you back inside?"

"No." Abby lifted her head and inhaled. Crisp winter air filled her lungs. "I'm fine. I just want to go home."

"OK."

They settled in the car. Brooke drove slowly out of the parking lot and headed toward town. Early traffic on a post-storm Saturday was light. The road had been plowed, but a thin film of white still dusted the surface. Patches of black ice lurked underneath. The shiny areas and the fuzzy throb in Abby's head were a reminder to drive carefully in bad weather.

Brooke turned onto Main Street. Stately Colonials and Victorians on large lots lined the road, some converted to offices, apartments, or stores. Fresh snow, plowed after last night's storm, edged the road. Dwellings shrank in size as they drove away from the business district. By the time they reached Abby's development, tired houses crowded together on tiny lots. With some of the lowest-priced homes in town, the neighborhood was a mixed bag of senior citizens who'd lived there forever and young owners willing to renovate, like Abby.

"I dropped Zeus off earlier." Brooke had kept Abby's dog overnight. They pulled up in front of Abby's narrow house.

"Thanks." Relief swept through Abby. Security systems could be breached, not that she could afford one, but no criminal could fool her dog's senses. As long as Zeus was there, she knew the house was safe. No one was in the closet. Ready to—

Stop it.

There was zero similarity between yesterday's accident and what happened to her three years ago. She remembered every single second of *that* nightmare. If only she could rid herself of those memories instead of yesterday's.

"Thanks for shoveling." Abby's mind was still racing with missing time as she trudged up the cleared walk.

"Wasn't me," Brooke said. "The snow was gone when I got here this morning."

Abby glanced at the Tanners' house next door. Twelve-year-old Derek must have shoveled both properties this morning. Today was Saturday. He'd be off from school. A rusted sedan pulled into the driveway. Derek's mother, Krista, got out. She wore a thin jacket unzipped over a black polyester waitress uniform. She must have worked the breakfast shift.

Abby waved. "Thank Derek for shoveling my walk, will you?"

"Sure." Krista smiled through an exhausted face, turned, and went into a house that looked as tired as its owner. Or was Krista hungover? The new boyfriend's pickup wasn't at the curb. For Derek's sake Abby hoped the guy had moved on. Krista had crappy taste in men, and she invariably started drinking whenever she picked up a new loser. Her affairs didn't usually last long, but Derek would spend a lot of time at Abby's house for the duration. Worry churned in Abby's still unsettled stomach, but there wasn't anything she could do about the situation. Derek was street smart. He'd gotten by long before Abby moved in.

Brooke stayed close as Abby slipped her key in the lock. The familiar smell of damp dog greeted her nostrils as she stepped over the threshold. The mastiff greeted her with a high-pitched whine and rubbed against her legs like an enormous cat. Abby's knees buckled, and she grabbed for the hall table to steady herself. "Hello, Zeus."

"He missed you," Brooke laughed.

Abby didn't have to lean down to scratch his massive square head, but today, she knelt and wrapped both arms around his neck. Burrowing her face in his fur, she sighed. Abby didn't trust many things, but Zeus made the short list. "I missed you too. How about a cookie?"

She released him, straightened, and walked to the kitchen in the back of the house. Zeus padded at her side. Abby fished in the cookie jar for an extra-large dog biscuit, which Zeus took with care from her hand.

Brooke tilted the blinds. Sunlight flooded the small room. "I'm told I'm not the best cook, but can I make you some toast?"

"No, thanks." Abby dropped into a chair. Small aches in her body transmitted faint warnings of developing bruises. Her head still pounded. "I'm not hungry. I'd love some coffee, though."

"That I can do." Brooke reached for the canister.

Zeus padded to his bowl. He looked back at them and cocked his head hopefully.

"I fed you breakfast earlier, buddy." Brooke filled his sink-sized stainless steel water bowl and set it in front of him. Zeus drank endlessly. With a sloppy snort, he wiped his mouth against Abby's leg and lay down on the rug next to her feet with a grunt, a sigh, and the *thunk* of dense bones hitting hardwood. He rested his broad chin on her foot and closed his eyes. His head was as big as a Thanksgiving turkey. The weight of it would put Abby's foot to sleep within fifteen minutes, but she found the dog's touch comforting. For his uncomplicated companionship, she could deal with the lack of blood flow to her toes.

Brooke flipped the coffeepot switch. Turning, she leveled Abby with a hard stare. "Now, you want to tell me what the doctor said this morning?"

"The gap in my memory is probably a symptom of the concussion. The CAT scan and blood work all came back normal." Fear and helplessness spread cold through Abby's belly. Tears burned the corners of her eyes. Her lack of emotional control and impulsive sharing were nearly as disturbing as the memory loss. "I don't understand. What did I do all afternoon?"

"Ethan will figure it out." Brooke grabbed mugs from the cabinet.

"I hope so." The neurologist had also said it was possible she'd remember everything with rest and time. Or she wouldn't.

The coffee machine beeped, and Brooke poured. She dumped a packet of sweetener in each mug, gave them a quick stir, and carried them to the table. She set one in front of Abby. "It'll be all right."

Abby sipped her coffee, hoping the hot brew would wash away the haze of helplessness she couldn't shake.

Zeus's head popped up. He leaped to his feet and trotted out of the room with a deep woof. Either someone was at the door, or the cat from up the street was taunting him at the window again.

Panic inched up Abby's throat. "The cop said he'd be here this morning. He keeps asking questions I can't answer."

"It'll be fine," Brooke soothed. "Just be honest. The police are there to help."

"How do I know I can trust them?"

"Why wouldn't you?" Brooke gave her a quizzical look. She opened the fridge and shook a quart of milk.

Abby glanced out the back window. Zeus's giant paw prints already obliterated the clean layer of snow. The yard was small, the house old, and the neighborhood not the best, but the place was hers. She'd bought it cheaply and renovated it with her own sweat. There were no bad memories here. Not yet.

She'd moved to Westbury for a fresh start. She was no doubt just being paranoid. Yesterday's accident was just that. An accident. Why did she have to make it complicated?

"What's wrong?" Brooke's voice went serious. "Talk to me, Abby."

But Abby couldn't share her horror story. Talking about it brought on a panic attack every time. Plus, there were other aspects about her that no one in her new life knew, and she wanted to keep it that way. Her fresh start depended on a blank slate. She'd scraped the scars from her life with the same ruthlessness she'd applied to the wood floors and molding. Every inch was stripped to its core and refinished until it barely resembled its original state. But lying to Brooke gave her a lump behind her solar plexus. "You're right. The concussion must be affecting my mood. The neurologist said it could do that."

Brooke smiled, but her eyes weren't convinced. Fifteen years of teaching high school math had honed Brooke's bullshit detector. "I've known Ethan for years. You can trust him."

"I don't know." Abby's experience with the police wasn't as rosy. Her rushing nerves drove her to her feet. Zeus raised his head and watched her pace the kitchen. The blood alcohol request made her leery.

"Honey, I'm sure you haven't done anything wrong, but you

don't remember what happened. The police have to cover their bases. They don't know you like I do."

"How do you know?" Abby whirled, the sudden motion jarring her head. Pain spiked across her temples. "I can't even say that for sure. I don't know what I did."

"I know you."

Guilt welled inside Abby. Brooke only thought she knew her.

She walked across the kitchen and took Abby by the shoulders. "You could never do anything illegal. You never speed. You count to three at stop signs. Remember that time the clerk at the mall gave you an extra five dollars in change? You made me drive all the way back so she wouldn't get in trouble. You are probably the most law-abiding person in the state of Pennsylvania."

"I'm scared." The statement slipped out before Abby could stop it.

"I know," Brooke said.

Zeus barked again. Abby went to the front of the house. She separated the mini blinds with a forefinger. A police cruiser pulled up to the curb and parked.

———

Ethan parked his cruiser in front of Abby Foster's narrow house. She had obviously put some work into her home. Wooden clapboards were painted a gleaming, clean white. Bright sunshine reflected off glossy maroon shutters and sparkling windows. The harsh winter sun highlighted her well-kept home but emphasized the sad condition of the house next door. Overgrown shrubs and peeling paint gave the place a vacant look.

A brisk wind sliced through his uniform pants as he climbed out of his vehicle. He recognized Brooke Davenport's small SUV parked in the driveway in front of the narrow garage. Ethan climbed the front steps. Inside the house, a large body moved from the front window to the door and back again.

What the hell was that?

The deep woof sounded from the other side of the front door. It opened as Ethan tapped the snow from his boots on the porch post.

"Officer Hale." Abby gestured toward the inside of her home. "Come in."

In slim yoga pants, an oversized sweater, and thick socks, Abby could've passed for a teenager. Her blonde hair was pulled back in a ponytail, leaving those big brown eyes to dominate her fine features. The sadness pooled in their depths made Ethan want to fix everything.

A whine diverted his attention to the giant animal at her side. Ethan did not step backward, but he was tempted. With her free hand, Abby held the collar of a gigantic dog, but the gesture was symbolic. There was no way she could hold that animal back if it wanted a piece of Ethan. It wasn't that much smaller than the roan pony in his barn. But the pony didn't have canines big enough to rip off a limb. The dog was as tall as a Great Dane and had similar markings, but instead of the lean Dane body, Abby's dog was massive. His broad, heavily muscled body was covered with short, fawn-colored fur. A square head ended in a black muzzle. Large folds of skin hung loosely from his powerful jowls.

"Is it a bear or a lion?" Ethan scanned for signs of aggression but saw none.

"Neither. This is Zeus. Are you afraid of dogs?"

Ethan's masculine pride recoiled at the implication. "No," he said louder than he'd intended.

Abby released the dog. Zeus sniffed Ethan's shoes and wagged his thin tail. "He's a mastiff. Shock is the typical response to meeting him for the first time, and sometimes the second."

Her eyes were clearer than the previous evening. The bruise and Band-Aid on her forehead highlighted her pallor. Darkness underscored the exhaustion in her eyes. His desire to protect and care for her disturbed him. There were too many unknown factors around Abby for Ethan to contemplate a personal relationship. His father's death had ended Ethan's career with the NYPD. He couldn't afford to jeopardize his job in Westbury. Too many people depended on him. Not that Chief O'Connell would fire him over getting personally involved with the subject of an investigation. The chief's fiancée had once been a case. But that wasn't the point. Ethan had enough people under his watch.

He held his hand out to the dog.

"He's friendly." Abby smiled, catapulting her from pretty to gorgeous. She had the kind of warm smile a man could wake up next to for a few decades.

"Good thing." He patted the broad head. A string of saliva dripped from the hanging jowls of Zeus's black muzzle and landed on Ethan's shoe.

"Sorry about that, Officer Hale."

"Ethan, please." Yeah. That's the way to maintain his professional status. In reality, though, he'd grown up in Westbury. Most of the townspeople called him by his first name. "That's OK. I grew up on a farm. I'm used to animals."

The front door opened directly into the living room. He wiped his feet on the doormat before stepping on the gleaming hardwood floor. The walls were painted a soft yellow, set off with bright white trim. A worn sofa and chair faced the fireplace and small flat-screen TV. Stairs against the living room wall led upstairs. "And I'm glad to see you have a big dog."

"Zeus is better than any alarm. There is no security system in the world that will tell me if someone is standing on the sidewalk thinking about breaking into my house."

"An alarm system still wouldn't hurt. Security is all about layers." Ethan followed her through the dining room, checking out a few pictures on a sideboard as he passed. Abby with Brooke and the track team at a big celebration. Several photos of Abby at various ages with a blonde woman who had to be her mother. She looked to be a generation older, with the same delicate features but with a hard edge to the set of her mouth that said her life had been a disappointment. "Dogs can be poisoned or shot."

Abby's face paled, and he regretted his last comment.

"Not that it happens often," he said. "Dogs are a good deterrent for the average criminal."

The house was built shotgun style. Rooms were stacked one behind the other, with just an archway in between. The second story would be slightly larger as it extended over the garage. She led him into a tiny square kitchen. A table for two was nestled under the window. One empty mug sat on a yellow placemat. Yellow curtains framed a view of a yard fenced with chain-link.

"Good morning, Ethan." Brooke stood at the sink washing a mug. She placed it upside down on a drain rack and turned to Abby. "I'm going to run to the grocery store. You're out of bread, and the milk is low. Do you need anything else?"

Abby shook her head. "You don't have to bother."

"It's no trouble." Brooke grabbed her purse from the counter. "You don't have a car, remember? And I was going to come back and check on you again later anyway. You don't think I would just drop and leave you alone with a concussion?"

"Thanks, but—" Abby protested.

"No buts." Brooke fished her keys from her bag. "Call me on my cell if you need anything."

"All right. Thank you."

"That's what friends are for." Brooke's eyes darted back and forth between Abby and the cop. "Bye, Ethan."

Ethan waited for the sound of Brooke closing the front door behind her.

Uh-oh. They were alone.

Abby stood in the middle of her kitchen floor and studied her thick socks. Ethan had checked her police records this morning. Before moving to Pennsylvania a little over two years ago, Abby had lived and taught high school in a middle-class suburb in southern New Jersey. She'd never received as much as a parking ticket. She was thirty years old but looked as lost and vulnerable as a child.

Her eyes lifted to his. Hers were full of uncertainty. "Do you want some coffee?"

"Sure." Ethan took off his coat and hung it on the back of a chair. He stuffed his knit hat in his sleeve.

"I can't seem to get warm." She pulled a mug from the overhead cabinet.

"Me either."

The dog settled at Abby's feet, but his attention was on Ethan. "I've never seen a dog that big."

"I didn't know how big he was going to be when I adopted him from the pound. The woman who worked there was a little misleading with her estimate of Zeus's age and size." Abby poured coffee.

A wry smile softened her face. Their gazes met, the brown of her eyes warming. The heat that flared in Ethan's body was significantly lower. She blinked in surprise. Yeah. Whoa. It was way too soon for that kind of reaction, and given the circumstances of his visit, inappropriate. What were they talking about? The dog. That was it. Thank God for the dog.

Ethan cleared his throat. "He seems like a great watchdog."

"He's a big baby."

But the dog kept a wary watch on Ethan. He suspected if he made a move toward Abby, her *baby* would change its attitude.

Dog tags jingled. Zeus lifted his heavy head and stared at the back door. His tail thumped lightly on the floor. Ethan tracked his gaze. A skinny boy loped into the kitchen, eyes bright and cheeks red from the cold. Shaggy brown hair and cautious eyes, the kid skidded to a stop when he saw Ethan. An impassive mask slid over his happiness. He wasn't wearing a hat, and he was dressed in a worn jacket that was not nearly warm enough for the middle of winter. His sock showed through a hole in the toe of his sneaker.

Abby stood. "Derek, this is Officer Hale."

The kid shrank back and pokered up, wiping his expression as clean as an undisturbed snowdrift. But he couldn't control the innate wariness in his eyes. Was he apprehensive of strangers or cops?

Ethan stood up and held out his hand. "Nice to meet you, Derek."

The boy, who looked to be around ten, stared down at Ethan's hand but made no move to accept the shake. Zeus shoved his body between them and broke the awkward tension.

"Derek lives next door." Abby's smile didn't touch her eyes. "He's my dog walker. He and Zeus are buddies."

"What grade are you in, Derek?" Ethan shoved his left-hanging hand into his jacket pocket.

"Eighth," Derek mumbled as he backed away.

"Did you need something?" Abby asked.

"Nothing important." Derek jerked a cold-reddened thumb toward the back door. "I'll catch you later."

"OK," Abby said in a too-bright voice.

With a quick nod, the kid bolted for the exit. Wet sneaker soles squeaked on hardwood, and the back door slammed.

The kid was small for an eighth-grader, Ethan thought. "Guess he isn't a fan of cops."

"Don't take offense. He's shy. He warmed up to Zeus long before he talked to me."

But the forced ease in Abby's voice put Ethan on guard. Something was up with her young neighbor. Her eyes shut down like emotional storm shutters. Any warmth he'd felt when they'd been discussing her dog earlier dissipated.

She was hiding something. The boy had troubles that Abby didn't want Ethan to know about. Why not?

Abby poured two mugs of coffee. "Cream or sugar?"

"Black is fine. Thanks."

She set two cups on the table and sat across from him. "I assume you're here to discuss the accident?"

And the kid was officially removed from the discussion. "Yes. Have you remembered anything?"

"No."

"I talked to your principal and a couple of your coworkers this morning. They all corroborated that you left immediately after school, but no one remembered anything useful." Everyone had been concerned about Abby. Not one had complained about being disturbed on a Saturday morning. The kids and parents loved Abby. No one had anything negative to say about her. Everything he found out told him she was exactly what she appeared to be. It was only her attitude toward him that made him suspect otherwise. "I want you to give me a list of the places in town you frequent: your dry cleaner, coffee shop, anywhere you might have stopped between school and the park. Someone must have seen you."

"I hope so." Abby picked up her empty cup and went to the coffee machine. Why was she so reluctant to help him?

He should leave and let her get some rest. Instead, he stood and followed her to the counter and set his mug in the sink.

She replaced the carafe on the warmer and turned.

Their bodies were only inches apart. "Why are you so nervous? You know I only want to help, right?"

Nodding, Abby retreated as far as she could. Her eyes widened as she bumped into the counter that formed an L behind her. He crowded her, leaning in and catching a whiff of peaches. Her shampoo?

Her eyes darkened. Desire?

Ugh. That didn't help with his plan to keep his professional distance. Neither did the way her eyes showed the emotions she worked so hard to hide. "Can you write that list now?"

"Yes." Abby lifted a shoulder. The neck of her sweatshirt shifted, giving Ethan a view of creamy skin and delicate collarbone. He didn't stare. Not long anyway.

Why was he spending so much time investigating her accident? Yes, there were too many inconsistencies for his comfort. But those anomalies *could* be explained. So was his interest really in the case? Or was he fixated with the woman involved?

She wrapped her arms around her body. The pure vulnerability in her posture ignited an instinct to comfort and protect her that nearly overwhelmed him. Regardless of his personal situation or professional impropriety, there was no way he was letting her case go just yet.

CHAPTER SIX

Abby gathered her thoughts. The accident and missing hours had muddled her brain. Plus, Ethan was way too close, and the proximity with his body wasn't helping her to think clearly. She could see the tiny flecks of silver in his piercing blue eyes and feel the heat that rose from his skin. The need to connect unfurled inside her. She should tell him to back off, but part of her wanted the opposite: to trust him, to hide, to let him take care of everything. There was more to him than bone-melting good looks. Ethan exuded integrity and honesty. But she'd known him for a day, not nearly long enough to place her future in his hands.

She nodded toward the table. "Let me get a paper and pencil."

Ethan took a step backward and gave her room to pass. She carried her coffee to the table, grabbed a tablet, and started writing. The list was longer than she'd anticipated.

"You don't remember stopping at any of these places?" He frowned at the paper she handed him.

"No." Abby's stomach turned. She set the coffee mug down. Toast would've been the smarter option.

Ethan surveyed her with a doubtful gaze. Could she blame him? The whole amnesia thing sounded like a daytime soap plot. All she needed was an evil twin to round out the details. Still, despite the skepticism in the set of his mouth, he tucked the list into his pocket.

"I'll run by these places. Maybe we'll get lucky and someone will remember you came by."

Unease rolled through Abby. He'd questioned her fellow teachers and her boss. Now he was going to ask questions at every other place she frequented. "This is a small town. By Monday, everyone will be talking about me."

"I know." Empathy flashed in the deep blue of his eyes. "But don't you want to know what happened?"

Sort of.

"Yes." Unless it was really bad, in which case she already had enough nightmares. But the unaccounted time chipped away at her peace. It was a big, black hole that threatened to swallow her new life. How could she ever relax without knowing?

"The chief and I are going over your car this morning, and I'm going to pull the security tapes at the school." He ripped a piece of paper out of his notebook and wrote down an address. "Your car is at the impound garage. You'll want to notify your insurance company." He pulled a card from his pocket. "Here's my card. They'll want a copy of the accident report too."

He slid the papers across the table.

"Thank you." Abby didn't reach for them. "I assume they'll total the car."

"Probably. It's old. Frankly, you're better off getting another one. Once a vehicle's been submerged . . ."

She nodded. She'd have to dip into her savings to replace it. Another chink in the independence and security she'd worked hard to build.

He stood and shrugged into his coat. Despite her determination to act like an ordinary citizen, her experience with cops wasn't positive. What was it about this one that caught her off guard? Ethan Hale was a complicated man. He'd risked his life to save her, and he was determined to find out what happened to her. Was he an honest, by-the-book cop? Or was there a dark side to him? In her experience, no one was that bright and shiny.

"Call me if you remember more." He stood. "I'll let you know if my investigation turns up anything else. I'll probably have more questions."

"All right." She walked him to the front of the house. "Thank you."

"It's my job." He replaced his hat.

How deeply would he dig into her life? If he found out what really happened yesterday, could she live with the truth? Or would she have to reboot her life all over again? Pain squeezed her heart as she looked around her house, every inch of it remade with her hands. God, it would hurt to leave it all behind.

The cop car pulled away from Abby's house. Derek peered around the corner of the house. Crusted snow crunched under tires as the cop drove away. Were the police asking about him? Or did something bad happen to Abby? The bruise on her face looked painful.

Guilt tumbled in his belly when he realized he was hoping the cop's visit wasn't about him. He was a shit. How could he wish anything bad on Abby? She was the one person who totally got him. She tried to help Derek on his terms, not like that stupid social worker who had no idea what it was like to live his life. Sure, take him from here and put him in an even worse situation.

No, thanks. He didn't need any more of that kind of help. He could manage just fine on his own.

The cop had left without even looking at Derek's house.

Good. He didn't want to be on any official radar. The social worker's periodic visits were hard enough to fake his way through. With several satisfactory inspections and a heavy case load, he doubted she'd be by anytime soon without cause. So the last thing he needed was a cop poking around. Especially now.

He glanced back at his house. No blue pickup hunkered at the curb yet, but his mom's new boyfriend would be back to-night. So Derek's be-invisible policy was still in effect, and a home visit was on his list of things to be avoided at all cost.

He wasn't ever going into the system again. People who had never been in the foster system had no idea how random it was. A lucky kid could end up in a nice place with people who cared. Or so he'd heard. On the other hand, look what had happened to Derek.

His stomach curled like a useless fist at the memory.

No, thank you, to anyone who wanted to *save* him. At twelve, Derek had already experienced enough of being *saved*. His foster parents had had good intentions, but they'd been clueless about what the two older boys they'd taken in were up to. The brothers had both been bigger than Derek, and there'd been two of them. If he hadn't gotten away—

He shook off the memory and retraced his footsteps in the snow to the backyard. Cold water seeped into his sneakers. Was Abby OK? He chewed on his thumbnail. God, he was such a cow-ard, slinking through the shadows when maybe she needed help.

Her back door opened, and Zeus padded out onto the ce-ment patio. The giant head swiveled. The dog wagged his tail and *woofed* at him. Putting a toe in the chain-link, Derek hoisted himself over the fence. The big dog greeted him with a sloppy snort. Derek didn't mind the slobber. He threw his arms around the thick neck.

"Derek?" Abby called through the open door. "You can come in. It's clear."

A dozen steps carried him across the yard. Zeus followed him inside. Stepping over the threshold, he closed the door behind them. He grabbed the towel hanging from the doorknob and wiped Zeus's feet. Abby's kitchen was warm and clean. He took off his shoes, leaving them to dry on the mat.

Abby was standing in front of the open fridge door. "Are you hungry?"

"What happened to your face?" Anger sprung up inside him, hot and sharp and shocking in its intensity. If someone had hit her . . . He would do what? He was a weakling, powerless to help himself let alone Abby. The only thing Derek had going for him were quick feet. Running away from trouble was what he did best. Hiding was a close second.

Abby smiled at him, but her eyes were sad and tired. "My car slid off the road into the Packman Creek yesterday."

"Oh." Derek hung the towel to dry. Relief flooded him. "You're OK?"

"Just a little banged up." She sighed. "My car didn't fare as well."

"That sucks."

Abby pulled a deli bag out of a plastic drawer and closed the refrigerator. "Do you want a grilled cheese?"

"You sit." Derek stretched a hand toward her shoulder but pulled it back at the last second. Touching people wasn't his thing. "I got it."

Abby eased into a chair, propped her elbows on the table, and dropped her chin into her hands. "How's your mom?"

"Fine." He figured Abby already knew about his mom's latest binge, but he wasn't supplying any details. Men and booze were

Mom's downfall. Fortunately, she didn't fall often. But this latest boyfriend . . . Something was different about this guy. Something that made Derek want to steer way clear. Derek tossed a square of butter into the hot frying pan. He assembled cheese and bread and laid them in the melted butter. He glanced back at Abby. She was squinting in the bright sunlight that streamed in the window. "You're sure you're all right?"

"I'm fine."

"You could catch a nap if you want. I'll hang out with Zeus." He lifted a shoulder. She shouldn't be alone right out of the hospital, and the less time he spent at his house the better. Joe was due back anytime. Luckily, his mom's boyfriends didn't usually last long. Once he figured out Mom didn't have any money, he'd move on. Derek hoped.

Abby fed the dog a corner of her grilled cheese. Indecision clouded her face. "Maybe I will. Thanks." She stood up and walked toward the doorway. A quick flash of apprehension in her eyes set Derek on edge. "Would you wake me if anything unusual happens? Anything at all."

"Sure."

Their gazes locked. Abby never talked about her past, but he recognized wariness. He bet Abby knew plenty about running and hiding.

"I appreciate it." Smoothing her features, Abby picked at the sleeve of her sweater. "Wake me before you leave, OK?"

Derek's nerves stirred. Something was wrong. Abby was afraid. Usually fear was his territory.

He went into the living room and switched on the TV. The extent of her injuries wasn't the only thing Abby wasn't sharing. Derek checked the locks on the front and back doors, then each window on the first floor. Satisfied the house was as secure as possible, he settled on the sofa. He turned the volume down low.

Zeus stretched out on the floor next to the couch. Derek flipped channels until he found an action movie. He settled in to keep watch.

CHAPTER SEVEN

The late-morning sun was thin and weak as Ethan pulled up to the garage where Abby's car was impounded. Parking next to the chief's SUV, Ethan grabbed a cardboard box from the backseat of his patrol car and went inside. Chief O'Connell was walking around Abby's Subaru. The vehicle hadn't been submerged long, but mud, scratches, and small dents coated its exterior.

The chief stopped and snapped pictures from every angle. Wind whipped through the wide-open garage door. Ethan turned his collar up against it and tugged his cap down lower on his forehead. Inside the metal and concrete building, the temperature felt colder than outside. Since yesterday's polar plunge, he couldn't get warm.

"No major dents to indicate she hit a deer or other animal." Chief O'Connell circled the waterlogged Subaru. He took a photo of the front bumper. "Most of the damage is from river rocks."

"I checked her phone records. No texts or calls at the time of her accident. She could have swerved to avoid an animal," Ethan suggested. "The ice on the road could account for lack of skid marks."

The chief sent him an assessing glance. "It's possible, but I wish she remembered."

"Yeah. Me too." Ethan brought the chief up to speed on Abby's case. "I'm coming up empty so far. No one saw her yesterday after school."

"I don't like it." The chief bent low, turned the camera, and snapped a close-up of the Subaru's tire.

Ethan opened the driver's side door with a latex-gloved hand and stuck his upper body inside. Jammed under the dashboard was a black leather woman's purse. He grabbed it by the shoulder strap. He set it in the box he'd placed on the cement floor. "Wonder what's salvageable in here."

The chief moved to the back of the vehicle. "Pop the trunk."

Ethan pulled a tarp from his box and draped it over the driver's seat. He leaned across the vehicle and opened the glove compartment. The trunk released with a push of the button. He emptied the glove compartment item by item. A black vinyl envelope contained the vehicle's documents and owner's manual. Crammed beneath it were a tire pressure gauge, a flashlight, and a silver emergency blanket. The center console held another assortment of innocuous items: a small container of hand sanitizer, a soggy travel pack of tissues, an MP3 player the size of a stick of gum, and a tube of cherry lip balm. He blinked at the immediate mental image of Abby's lips, and before he could stop his brain, he was wondering if they tasted like cherry.

Shaking off the image, he sifted through the items again. No receipts.

"Anything?" The chief opened the passenger door and stuck his head into the car.

"Nothing." Ethan's foot struck an item on the floor. He reached down and picked up a bottle of sports drink, half full of orange liquid.

"Did you get the results of her blood alcohol test yet?"

"She was completely clean." Ethan stared at the dashboard. Seemed far away. He reached a foot toward the gas pedal. "Check out the position of the seat. I have to stretch for the pedals."

"How tall is Ms. Foster?"

"Five-foot-six."

The chief rounded the car and squatted next to the open door. "Maybe she put the seat back when she was trying to get out?"

"Possible but unlikely. I'll ask her." Ethan was thinking about Abby's memory gap. No doubt the chief was too.

"It's probably nothing." O'Connell stared at the orange liquid. "But let's get that tested."

Ethan extended his foot and touched the brake pedal with the toe of his boot. There was no way Abby could've driven her car with the seat in that position. The chief handed him an evidence bag. Ethan slid the bottle of sports drink inside and sealed the top. He climbed out of the car.

A mechanic in winter coveralls and a watch cap came out of the tiny corner office and walked across the garage. "Do you want me to do anything with the car?"

Ethan glanced at the chief. "Not yet. Can you just ignore it for now?"

The mechanic stamped his boots on the cold concrete and shoved greasy hands into his front pockets. "Sure."

"Thanks." Ethan closed the door of Abby's sedan. It had to be an accident. Why would anyone want to hurt a schoolteacher?

―――――――――――

Krista eyed the clear bottle Joe pulled from a narrow paper bag. Guilt twisted her insides. She shouldn't be doing this. She'd broken her promise to Derek—again. The beer had been bad enough, but at least it took some time and effort to get wasted on it. Empty bottles lined the counter like schoolkids in a fire drill. What was wrong with her? Other single mothers managed. They didn't wallow in self-pity. Derek should be enough motivation to get up in the morning. Unfortunately, he wasn't, but if it weren't for her son, she'd probably have called it quits years ago.

"This is a whole lot better than the horse piss you were drinking last night." Joe poured an inch of vodka into a glass of ice and handed it to her.

She sipped. The fiery liquid burned a path down her throat and warmed her belly, loosening the knot of shame. Another couple of swallows wiped her disgrace away like an eraser. Her sadness floated, and the pain in her heart eased a little. She finished the shot.

Joe tossed his back and gave his head a shake. He refilled both glasses and tapped his against hers.

The look he gave her was full of expectation and lust and drove the heat simmering inside her lower. Krista drained her glass.

"Hey, babe." Joe leaned over her neck. His hands came around her body and cupped her breasts.

She didn't pretend he really liked her or that she felt anything for him. They were using each other. The loneliness of the last six months had eaten away at her until she'd felt hollow inside. She ate, worked, ate, slept, and then got up and did it all over again, day after day. Her life was the same shitty song stuck on repeat.

All she wanted was a little break.

Joe's hands slid under her shirt. His fingers found her nipples and pinched. If she wasn't half-numb from alcohol, it probably would've hurt. But Krista turned to him.

Yes, he was cruel. She could sense it under the amiable facade. But his body was warm, young, and hard under her hands. For the next hour or so, she could forget the crushing hopelessness that overshadowed every waking moment of her life. Misery was a physical ache, a bone-deep exhaustion no amount of sleep could cure.

"Come on." He grabbed her hand and pulled her toward the stairs.

Why not?

Derek was next door. A stab of jealousy pierced Krista's heart. Abby Foster would make a far better mother than Krista. But then, Abby hadn't gotten pregnant and tossed out of her parents' house at fifteen. Krista's parents had been right. She'd ruined her own life just to feel affection for a few hours.

The same as she was likely doing now, minus the affection. She was sliding farther over the edge. Eventually, there'd be no climbing out of the hole she was digging for herself.

Krista followed Joe upstairs. Excitement and fear quickened her pulse. A mean glint shone from his eyes. He ripped off her shirt with rough hands and shoved her pants down. Before Joe, she had no idea that pain and humiliation could be erotic, so satisfying. Being punished was exactly what her soul craved. She'd screwed up her life and Derek's both so badly. She'd suppressed the secret desire to hurt herself. She'd never had the courage to follow through. It was so easy to let Joe do it for her. Could she get any more fucked up?

"On your knees." Joe pushed her to the floor, moved behind her, and sank his fingers into her hair. He yanked her head back. Pain roared through her scalp as a moan escaped from her lips. Liquid heat raced deep through her belly.

The thin line between bliss and agony blurred. Pressing against him, she arched her back and welcomed the punishment.

———

Tires crunched on ice as Abby pulled away from the community mailbox. She pressed a button on her visor to raise her garage door, then turned into the narrow driveway of her one-bedroom unit. Pulling the car forward until the suspended tennis ball touched her windshield, she shifted into park. Good thing she drove a small sedan. The builder had been stingy with garage space.

She tucked her mail under her arm and pushed into her condo. Her hand swiped the wall switch. When light flooded the small laundry room, she reached back and closed the garage door. Stepping out of her low pumps, she left them in the corner and tugged her blouse out of her skirt. Walking barefoot into the kitchen, she rifled through the letters. Junk. Junk. Bill. She opened the cabinet and threw the ads and credit card offers into the paper recycling container. She tossed the electric bill into a basket on the counter.

She opened the freezer and selected a frozen dinner. The school board meeting had run into overtime, as usual. Her stomach rumbled as she popped the plastic film with a fork before sliding it into her microwave. She left the machine humming and headed down the hall to change out of her conservative suit. Hello, pajamas.

She walked into her dark bedroom. Abby turned the switch on the dresser lamp. Nothing happened. The bulb must have blown, but the hair on her nape prickled. She shook it off. She turned to return to the hall. Spare bulbs were in the linen closet.

Fabric rustled. Abby startled. A hand clamped over her mouth, and she was jerked against a large, hard body. Her heart slammed against her sternum. The smell of his leather gloves flooded her sinuses.

He breathed in her ear. "Hello, Abigail."

No! It was him.

Abby sat up to darkness, both familiar and terrifying. Sweat dripped into her eyes and soaked her yoga pants and sweater.

Her heart pumped in her chest like a piston. Her lungs tightened, her breath heaving in and out with an asthmatic wheeze.

Her pupils expanded. The shapes of furniture solidified. She was in her bedroom. Here and now. Not there and then.

She snapped on the bedside lamp. Light flooded the room. A glance at the clock told her she'd slept all afternoon. Darkness had fallen outside. But her house should be bright as day.

Soft voices murmured from the doorway that led into the hall. A scant amount of light eased through the door, ajar barely an inch, and slanted on the wood floor. Abby had left her door wide open. Who had been in her bedroom? Derek? It didn't seem likely.

Wooziness flooded her head as she swung her legs over the side of the bed, but her head settled in a few seconds. She stood, satisfied when the room remained still and steady. She padded to the doorway and stuck her head into the hall. Brooke's voice floated up the stairs.

Relief eased her breathing.

Abby withdrew to the bathroom, flipping on every light switch she passed. She started the shower and stripped off her sweaty clothes as the water warmed. She stepped under the spray, and hot water cascaded over her head and body. She soaped and shampooed, then stood with her back to the pounding heat until the water began to cool. Afterward, dressed in flannel pajama pants and a heavy sweatshirt, Abby emerged into the hall and opened the linen closet.

"There you are."

She jumped.

"I'm sorry if I startled you." Brooke put a hand on Abby's arm. She glanced down at the clean sheets in Abby's arms. "Rough nap?"

Abby pressed a hand to her forehead, where heaviness lurked. "Feels more like the flu than a concussion."

"Go downstairs." Brooke took the linens from her. "I'll get this."

"But—"

Brooke was already attacking the sheets on the bed. "There's soup in the kitchen," her friend called over her shoulder in a voice that allowed no argument.

Abby descended the stairs. In the living room, Derek and Brooke's fifteen-year-old son, Chris, were watching hockey and eating pizza. Zeus sat in front of the boys, an intense gaze riveted on Derek's slice as it moved from his plate to his mouth. Abby forgot about her fuzzy head for a second. Derek didn't relax with many people, but Brooke and her kids were the exceptions.

Derek's head swiveled. Relief passed over his face as he spied her stepping off the landing. He jumped to his feet and gestured to his spot on the sofa. "Here, sit down."

"I just got up." She was still tired, but the nausea had faded and her mouth was dry as chalk. Abby wandered into the kitchen. She filled a glass at the tap and downed the water in a few gulps. Her throat was still parched. She refilled. Drinking, she opened the fridge. A mammoth container of chicken soup sat on the top shelf. She ladled a portion into a bowl and stuck it in the microwave.

Brooke hustled into the room with Abby's sheets tucked under one arm. "You know all your lights came on at four o'clock?"

"They're set on timers to make it look like someone is home all the time. I'll have to check the settings." The lie burned on its way out of Abby's dry lips. But how could she tell another adult that she was terrified of the dark? No one over the age of six would understand. "Is Haley with Luke?"

"Yes." Brooke opened the louvered closet door in the back of the kitchen and stuffed Abby's sheets into the washer. "He took her shopping."

"Brave man." Abby leaned a hip on the counter.

"He is." Smiling, Brooke added detergent. Water rushed into the washer. Her new beau had been good for Brooke in many ways. Her friend's tight wiring had loosened ever so slightly over the past couple of months. The fact that the serial killer who targeted her back in November had pled guilty to avoid the death penalty also helped. Neither Brooke nor her daughter would have to testify or relive their kidnappings during a trial.

"She still doesn't remember anything?" Abby drifted to a chair and lowered her tired muscles into the seat. Brooke's daughter had been drugged and unconscious through most of the ordeal.

"No." Brooke closed the closet door.

Abby traced a yellow flower on her placemat. "How does she cope?"

"The therapist helps." Brooke turned and leaned against the closed door. "Do you want her card?"

Abby recoiled. "No."

"She's helping me too." Brooke tilted her head. "I can tell you firsthand that burying your issues doesn't work in the long run. There's no shame in needing counseling, Abby."

"I never said there was." Abby turned to the window. Darkness pressed on the glass. Her image reflected back on her. Shivering, she reached up to close the blinds. "I'm fine."

Brooke's eyes were doubtful, but she dropped the topic. "How about some orange juice?"

"No. I just want water." Abby drained the second glass. She longed to tell Brooke about her past. Brooke was her best—make that only—friend. But Abby had been betrayed by people she'd known much longer. And frankly, talking about her past was just too painful. Before Friday's accident, she'd been working hard to shake off the paranoia that ruled her life. But how could she do that now?

The microwave dinged.

"Sit." Brooke waved Abby toward the table and brought her soup and crackers.

Abby inhaled the steam rising from the bowl. She dipped a spoon and took a tentative taste. Her stomach rumbled in approval. *Yay.* Her disturbing discussion with Brooke hadn't dulled her hunger. She forced herself to eat slowly.

Brooke washed a few glasses and wiped the counter. She checked under the lid of a pizza box sitting on the stove. "There are two slices left if you want one."

"I'll stick with soup." Abby spooned the last of the broth into her mouth and pushed the bowl away. "That was really good. Thanks. Did you make it?"

"Don't be silly. I have many skills, but cooking isn't among them." Brooke laughed. "Luke did. Do you want more?"

"Thank him for me." Abby sat back, sipping her water. "I think I'd better let that bowl settle." She glanced at the clock. It was almost seven p.m. She hadn't eaten since breakfast yesterday.

Brooke dropped into the opposite chair. She propped an elbow on the table and rested her chin in her palm. "How about I stay over tonight?"

"That's not necessary. I feel a lot better now." Abby set the glass on the table. "But thanks."

"Are you sure?" Brooke frowned. "It's no trouble. I'm worried about you."

"You don't live far away. I can call if I need you."

"Call for any reason at all, even if you just need to talk."

"I will." But that wasn't likely. Despite the fresh drama in her life, Abby preferred to keep her past buried. After all, the whole reason she'd come to Westbury was to hide.

CHAPTER EIGHT

Morning was still dark when Derek crept along the hall, his ears tuned to the snoring emanating from his mom's closed door. Joe was a heavy sleeper, but Derek didn't want to take any chances. Except for overnight and school, he'd spent most of Sunday and Monday at Abby's. So far, he'd successfully avoided Joe, and continued invisibility still seemed like the best plan.

On the top landing, he stepped over a creaky board. Joe choked on a snore. Derek froze, holding still until the rhythmic rumbling continued. At the bottom of the steps, his socks hit the dented wood floor.

Empty beer bottles littered the coffee table. Cigarette butts overflowed the ashtray. Derek ignored both. Such was life when Mom was in boyfriend mode. He went into the kitchen and stopped. His mom sat at the table, smoking a cigarette. Derek brightened. Mom being up this early was a good sign.

"Hey," she said softly. Her eyes were bloodshot, her skin pasty. Her sweatshirt and jeans looked baggy. She glanced at the clock. "Early for you to be up."

"Mom, it's a school day. It's Tuesday." Derek filled a glass of water and handed it to her.

A confused wrinkle formed between her brows. Then shame washed across her face. A floorboard creaked overhead. Mom glanced at the ceiling. Apprehension tightened her face. When the house remained quiet, she breathed and tucked a strand of hair behind her ear. "How about I make you breakfast?"

Derek opened the refrigerator. The milk and juice were gone. Butter and eggs occupied the top shelf right above a twelve-pack, but frying an egg was too noisy. They'd wake Joe.

"Nah. I'm gonna go or I'll miss my bus." He eased the fridge door closed. Hanging from a magnet, his last math test fluttered, the giant C circled. Mom had been proud that afternoon last month. She'd been working then, waitressing at the fast-food place on the interstate. Her last guy, Steve, had skipped out in July after Mom got fired and the money ran out. For six great months, she'd been boyfriend-free.

Then she'd met Joe.

"OK. Then I'm going to go back to bed for a while. I'm not feeling very well." She dropped the cigarette butt into an empty beer bottle and stood. She pressed a palm to her forehead. "I have the dinner shift tonight. Want me to make macaroni and cheese tonight before I go to work?"

"Sure," Derek answered. He figured his chances were fifty-fifty on the mac and cheese, probably lower that she'd make it to work.

She passed him, pressing a kiss on the side of his head. "I love you."

"Love you too."

Mom shuffled up the stairs.

With a last, lingering look at his math test, Derek slipped into his sneakers and jacket, then slipped his fingers through the top loop of his backpack. The front door opened with a small squeak. Cold air rushed through the opening. Freedom.

A hand grabbed him by the arm and jerked him back inside. Pain shot up his arm as it was twisted above his shoulder.

"Where've you been, kid?" Joe stared down at him. He was a tall guy, and Derek was downright puny. Joe's lean body shivered in his boxers and a gray T-shirt. A combination of day-old smoke and beer, his breath smelled like something had crawled in his mouth and died—last week. Joe stuck his head out the door and scanned the street as if he were looking for something.

Or someone.

"Around." Determined to keep his cool, Derek tried to shrug, but Joe's grip was too tight. How had Joe sneaked up on him? Derek had sharp ears and quick feet, his reflexes honed by a lifetime at the bottom of the food chain.

Maybe Joe had practice in sneaking around too.

Not good.

"Hey." With a rough shake, Joe lifted Derek to his toes and shut the door with a bare foot. "I asked you a question. I expect an answer."

His skin was pale with a grayish, dry hue the color of ash, and his pupils were permanently dilated. Alcohol wasn't Joe's only vice. Despite his unhealthy pallor, his grip was strong. "Why are you sneaking out?"

Derek wasn't sure which was worse, the fear streaking through his empty belly or the humiliation of knowing he was as helpless and scared as a kindergartener. Was he ever going to grow? Would he ever not be vulnerable to anyone who felt like picking on him?

"S-school." Derek's breath rattled with his words.

Joe's gaze dropped to the backpack hanging from Derek's hand. Light gleamed off his bald head. His bloodshot eyes narrowed in a mean glint. "Let's get one thing clear. I'm not here. OK? Anyone asks about me, you lie. Got it?"

Derek nodded, fear loosening his neck muscles to bobblehead.

"Now that we understand each other." Joe released his grip.

Derek's heels hit the floor hard, the sudden impact slamming his molars together with a jarring snap.

Joe scratched his belly through his T-shirt. "I guess you'd better get going. Wouldn't want you to get into any trouble."

The veiled threat sent fresh panic sprinting through his veins. Derek turned and bolted out into the stinging cold. His lip trembled and his eyes brimmed with tears as he stumbled down the porch steps. Sunlight glared off the icy lawn. Derek blinked against the brightness as he crunched through the crusty snow to the sidewalk, thighs shaking, breath catching. Snow melted and seeped into his sneakers. A tremor coursed through him.

Joe was different from the other losers his mom had picked up. This guy was dangerous to more than her wallet and pride. Was he an ex-con? A wanted criminal? A drug dealer?

A wind gust pushed against his back, hurrying him along. Derek hunched his shoulders against the cold, against the frustration, against the humiliation that was his life.

This had to end.

The longer Joe stayed, the more danger he posed to Derek and his mom. He pictured the needle marks on Joe's arm. No doubt about it. The guy had to go. Derek's mom had enough trouble. The last thing she needed was some guy getting her hooked on hard drugs. But how could Derek get rid of him?

He rounded the corner. The wind shifted to smack him square in the face. He put his head down and trudged forward.

"Hey, look. It's the little faggot."

Derek's head snapped up.

Trevor and Trent were Derek's twin enemies. In the same grade as Derek, they looked like they'd been nursed on steroids instead of a bottle. The high school football coaches already had their eyes on the pair of them. They rarely took the bus. Usually, their dad dropped them at school. Still, Derek remained vigilant on most mornings, except this one. The interaction with Joe had sidetracked him. Kids at the bottom of the food chain couldn't afford to get distracted.

A mean grin split Trent's square face. "Get him."

Derek's feet pivoted without any instruction. He slung his backpack over both shoulders in flight as he sprinted down the block. Heavy footsteps pounded the sidewalk behind him. The twins couldn't outrun him. They were born linebackers, not running backs. They knew it, and Derek knew it. Like all predators, they still enjoyed the chase.

Derek turned onto a lawn and vaulted over a fence into old Mr. Sheridan's backyard, the neighbor who lived behind Abby. The nosy old man took great pride in his yard and remained on constant vigil against kids or dogs trekking on his precious grass.

Derek ducked behind a fat tree.

A door opened. "Hey, you kids. Get the hell off my lawn," Mr. Sheridan shouted.

"Come on. Forget him. We're gonna miss the bus, and Mom'll be pissed." Footsteps crunched away.

Derek waited a few seconds for Mr. Sheridan's door to close before slinking out of his hiding spot. Thinking invisible thoughts, he crept from the cranky old guy's property, circled around the block, and approached the bus stop from the other side. The twins were facing the other way, probably keeping watch for him. Once he was on the bus, he'd be fine. The twins were assholes, but they wouldn't risk getting in trouble at school. Rumor had it their dad was always looking for a reason to beat the shit out of them. An engine rumbled. Derek looked ahead. A block away, the school bus was pulling away from the curb.

"Wait," he yelled, holding up a hand and breaking into a run. But the bus drove away. It disappeared into the glaring sunrise with the bright white reflection of sun on metal. A tear leaked out of Derek's eye. He wished it was from the frigid wind. One more late arrival to school was another chance for the social worker to take notice of him. Slogging forward toward the main road and the long walk toward the high school, his spine and backpack sagged under the weight of his load.

Sometimes invisibility had its drawbacks.

———————————

The morning sun blazed with deceptive strength in the clear winter sky. Ethan flipped up his collar against the brutal wind. A gust sent snow dust blowing across the frozen pasture. He rolled the barn door open. The snort of a horse greeted him.

He'd missed that sound. Closing the door behind him, he crossed to the roan's stall. The pony greeted him with an eager nose. Four days of rock-star treatment had brought out the roan's giant-puppy disposition. Twin plumes of steam puffed from its nostrils, like the breath of a miniature dragon. He rubbed the scrawny neck with a gloved hand. Clearly enjoying the attention, the pony leaned against him. Warmth unfurled in Ethan's chest. He fished a carrot from his pocket. The pony ate it and sniffed Ethan's pockets for more.

He gave the roan's head a gentle nudge. "Sorry, this one's for your buddy."

"Morning." Cam emerged from the other stall. "Can you give me a hand? I can't get a rope on him."

"Sure." Ethan went into the stall. The horse was in the back, head in the corner, hindquarters—and sharp hooves—facing Ethan. The horse's ears twitched. Ethan stepped sideways, so he was in the animal's field of vision. Startling a flight animal in close quarters wasn't a good idea.

The animal turned its head toward Ethan and blew air from its nostrils. Ethan moved slowly, extending a hand, reading the animal's body language until he was at the horse's head. He snapped the rope to the halter and walked out of the stall. The skittish bay followed, tentatively stepping its front feet into the aisle and stopping.

"Easy there, big boy." Ethan stopped, patiently waiting for the horse to settle. The bay blew hard and gave Cam a nervous eye roll.

"Thanks." Cam took Ethan's place at the horse's head. "The farrier will be here in a few minutes. Poor guy's feet haven't been trimmed in so long, his hooves are curling up in front."

"Maybe his attitude will change when he can walk right." Ethan dug the second carrot out of his pocket. After a cautious sniff, the bay crunched it down. "Where's Bryce?"

"Lumberyard." Cam removed the bay's blanket in slow motion and hung it over the stall door. Picking up a soft brush, he swept it over the horse's side. With proper nutrition, the scraggly coat would shed out into healthy fur over the next month or so. "We're going to start repairs on the pasture fence today."

"Cold day for fixing fences."

Cam sighed. "Yes, it is, but these guys have been cooped up too long, and we have to go back to school soon."

"Thanks." Ethan rubbed the bay's neck. "You and Bryce were a big help this weekend."

Cam glanced over. "I know we were a pain in your ass in high school, but we're not kids anymore. You can depend on us."

"You weren't a pain in the ass." Ethan examined the rub mark on the bay's nose. It was scabbing over nicely.

Cam snorted. "Yes, we were."

"OK, you were, but it wasn't your fault." At sixteen, his younger brothers hadn't been emotionally equipped to deal with their father's sudden death. Ethan had worked hard to get them both through high school and into college.

The next five minutes passed in silence as Cam picked out the horse's hooves and spread the blanket back over the bony body. "You're welcome to help with the fence today."

"As appealing as that sounds, I have to work." Ethan had more questions for Abby Foster today. Warmth spread through his chest. He should not be looking forward to interviewing her with this much enthusiasm.

"Sure you do."

"I actually do." Ethan gestured to his uniform with both hands.

Cam secured the blanket straps. He brushed past Ethan and entered the roan's stall. The animal shoved its nose deep into his brother's coat pocket. Giving the pony's forelock a playful tousle, Cam ducked out of reach. "You already ate it, greedball."

"That guy has a great disposition." Ethan braced himself as the bay horse rubbed its head up and down his body. "He'll get adopted no problem."

Ethan gave the bay a worried look. That one would be hard to place. "Yeah. The pony's like a big dog."

"He is." The thought of big dogs brought Abby and Zeus to Ethan's mind. How was she feeling four days after the accident? Had she remembered anything? "We're not keeping them."

Cam held up a hand in surrender. "I know. No time. No money."

The farrier arrived, and Ethan handed the horse off to him with a final pat. "I'm going to take off then. See you later."

He stopped at the house to wash the horse smell from his hands. He reached for his truck key on the rack. The hook was empty. He glanced out the window. His pickup was gone. The shiny red MINI Cooper Cam and Bryce shared mocked Ethan from the driveway. Of course Bryce had taken his truck. There was no way to stuff lumber into a car the size of a mailbox.

Ethan glanced at the time on his cell phone. He couldn't wait any longer. He grabbed his brothers' keys and folded his body into the driver's seat of the subcompact. The MINI Cooper's three-hamster engine whined as he pressed the gas pedal.

He was cruising past Abby's neighborhood when he spotted a figure walking next to the snowplow berm. It was a kid. An unwieldy backpack sagged from his shoulders. Ethan slowed. The kid turned, and Ethan recognized the boy who lived next door to Abby.

Stopping, Ethan lowered the passenger window. "Hey, Derek."

Derek backed a step. He tripped on a clump of snow and nearly fell into the dirty roadside slush. His eyes darted to the horizon, as if he wished he was there.

"Cold morning for a walk," Ethan said.

"I missed the bus."

"That sucks. Can I give you a ride?" Ethan pressed the unlock button on the door.

The kid hesitated. He scanned the MINI Cooper.

Ethan had a feeling if he'd been driving his police cruiser the answer would have been an emphatic "no." He checked the dashboard clock. "I can still get you there before the first bell."

Derek sniffed and gave a reluctant nod. "Yeah, thanks." He slid into the passenger seat and jammed the backpack between his feet.

"No biggie." Ethan pulled out onto the road. "I don't like to be late."

No response.

The MINI's engine sounded like an electric weed-whacker as Ethan accelerated. "What do you think of the car?"

Derek shrugged. The kid spoke zero words during the seven-minute ride. Ethan dropped him off in front of the main entrance. "Have a good day."

"Thanks for the ride," Derek mumbled. Swinging his pack over one shoulder, he darted for the door.

Ethan wasn't offended. Most kids didn't talk to cops. But Derek's reluctance seemed excessive. He reminded himself he'd intended to check the kid's history. A few minutes later, he parked in the station lot and went inside. As he hung up his coat, the chief waved him over. Rubbing his cold hands, Ethan walked back to O'Connell's office. The chief sat behind his desk. Abby Foster's open case file stared up from the blotter.

"You were going to follow up with Abby Foster today?" O'Connell removed his reading glasses and rubbed the bridge of his nose.

"Yes." Ethan dropped into one of the two chairs facing the desk. "I don't see any reason she can't have her personal stuff back. I went through everything. There's nothing out of the ordinary there."

The chief leaned back in his chair. "I want you to bring her into the station."

"Why?" Ethan's insides clenched.

"The report on her Gatorade came in."

"That was fast." Incredibly fast for the overwhelmed county lab.

The chief shrugged. "The lab tech's daughter is a big horse nut. I might have traded some riding lessons with Rachel to move this up in the queue." O'Connell's fiancée was a former international equestrian champion. He scratched his cauliflower ear, a reminder of his collegiate wrestling days. "If someone tried to kill Abby Foster, I wanted to know about it before the responsible party could follow up." The rough-looking police chief was a total marshmallow when women and children were threatened, a fact everyone knew but no one mentioned.

"Well?"

The chief's phone rang. As he picked up the receiver, he tossed the file across the desk. It landed on the oak with a *thwack*.

Ethan opened the manila cover, but he didn't need to read the words. The sharp, angry edge in O'Connell's light blue eyes told Ethan that the report contained bad news.

CHAPTER NINE

"Ready to go?"

Abby looked up from the geometry quizzes she was stuffing into her briefcase. Brooke hustled into the classroom. She was wearing her long parka. Her briefcase and purse were slung over one shoulder.

"Almost." Abby zipped the case. "I appreciate the ride."

"I'm just dropping you off at the car rental agency. It's not a big deal." Brooke smiled. "You're my friend."

"You've helped me a lot this week."

Brooke waved her comment off. "One trip to the store and a ride to work this morning? I wish you'd let me do more. How do you feel?"

"Fine. I should have come in yesterday." But she'd slept most of Sunday and was still so tired on Monday, she'd ended up calling in sick.

"No, you shouldn't have." Brooke gave her a *that's ridiculous* eye roll. "The doctor said to rest."

"I don't understand how I can have a concussion. I don't even have a headache." Abby shrugged into her puffy down jacket, which didn't coordinate with her long skirt and knee-high leather dress boots. But her wool coat had washed downstream, and she wasn't going looking for it.

"It's been a few days." Brooke stepped aside while Abby pulled her classroom door closed.

"Well, in an hour I'll have a rental car. Then I won't have to bother you anymore."

"I told you, I don't mind," Brooke said. "Have you heard from your insurance company?"

"They said they'll have an adjuster out soon. I'm waiting to hear. " Abby dropped her keys in the old purse she'd pulled out of the back of her closet. Her pocket buzzed. She fished for the new cell phone Brooke had taken her to buy on Sunday afternoon.

"I can't believe you don't like smartphones," Brooke said.

"I'm not a tech person." Abby didn't recognize the caller, but the exchange was local. Hope sparked. She'd only given the new number to a handful of people, and her insurance agent was one of them.

"Hello."

"Ms. Foster?" The voice was male and familiar enough to send a tingle into Abby's nerve endings. Ethan. *Stop it! He isn't calling for a date.*

"Yes?" she answered.

"This is Officer Hale." He paused. "Ethan."

With the phone pressed to her ear, she followed Brooke down the hall.

"Can you come to the police station?" The cop's serious tone ruffled her on-edge nerves.

"Now?" Abby halted. Brooke stopped and faced her. Her head tilted with concern as she analyzed Abby's face.

"Now would be good," the cop said.

Anxiety snuffed out Abby's hope like wet fingers on a candle wick. "Is something wrong?"

"It would be better to discuss it in person." His voice went flat. "Do you need a ride? I could come get you."

"Hold on a second." Heart scurrying, Abby covered the receiver and turned to Brooke. "Ethan wants me to go to the station."

"Did he say why?" Brooke's head tilted.

"No." Abby shook her head.

Brooke pursed her lips. Her eyes narrowed as she pulled her keys from her coat pocket. "I'll drive you."

Abby removed her hand from the mouthpiece. "I don't need a ride. I'll be there soon." Her voice was steady, but unease rattled in her stomach.

"Thanks." Ethan ended the call.

Abby removed the phone from her ear and stared at the blank display.

"Relax." Brooke wrapped an arm around Abby's shoulders and steered her toward the exit. "He probably just has a couple more questions."

"Maybe, but it sounded serious." Abby slid the phone into her jacket pocket. They stopped to zip up and pushed through the metal doors. "And urgent."

The snowbank-bordered parking lot was spotted with icy patches. Wind kicked snow dust across the asphalt.

"It'll be all right." Brooke tugged on a pair of gloves. "Oh my God. I can't remember a January this cold and windy in years."

Abby flipped up her collar and shoved her hands into her pockets. A gust blew her hair around her face. Not willing to expose a hand, she ignored it. Rock salt crunched underfoot as they trudged across the pavement and got into Brooke's small SUV. The leather car seat froze Abby's butt, and she longed for the knee-length coat the creek had stolen. Remembering the icy creek, her body shuddered hard. Why did the police need to see her so urgently? And why at the station? The last time Ethan had questions, he'd come to her house.

She gnawed on her chapped lip for the ten-minute drive into town. The car had barely begun to warm as Brooke turned into the parking lot of the small brick police station.

"Abby, look at me." Brooke shifted into park and turned a level gaze on Abby. "These are good men. I've no doubt they are trying to help you. You can trust them."

Abby nodded but couldn't bring herself to agree. Just because the police were *supposed* to help people didn't make it so. "Thanks for the ride. I can walk to the car rental agency from here when I'm done. It's only six blocks or so."

"If you think I'm abandoning you here, you're crazy." Brooke pulled her keys from the ignition. "Let's go."

Abby opened her mouth to protest. Going it alone was an instinct, a reflex honed by years of neglect. The wind made her teeth ache, and she pressed her lips together. When that cold water had closed over her head, she'd regretted being a loner. She'd moved to Pennsylvania for a complete do-over of her life, and that included having real friends—like Brooke. But pushing people away was a hard habit to break.

Inside, Brooke unbuttoned her parka. Abby kept her jacket zipped to her chin. The puffy fabric was one more barrier between her and the bad news she sensed was coming.

A somber Ethan greeted them in the small lobby. "Please come back to the chief's office."

Brooke touched Abby's forearm. "Do you want me to stay out here or come with you?"

Putting her independent nature aside, Abby remembered the last time she'd been at the mercy of a policeman. "Please come."

Brooke looked to Ethan.

"That's fine with me." He shrugged. "In that case we'll use the conference room."

Abby's knees felt stupidly loose as she followed him down a short hallway. Brooke rounded the oval laminate table and dropped into an office chair on the far side. Abby chose the chair next to her friend, which also gave her a view of the doorway and an unobstructed exit. A laptop computer occupied the center of the table.

"I'll get the chief," Ethan said as he ducked out.

A beefy man with muscular shoulders that nearly spanned the width of the doorway entered. He nodded to Brooke. "Hi, Brooke."

"Hi, Mike. This is my friend Abby Foster." Brooke emphasized the *friend*. Abby glanced sideways. She'd known the police, particularly Ethan, often assisted Brooke with her self-defense classes, but Abby had no idea her friend was on a first-name basis with the police chief.

Mike held out a hand toward Abby. "Police Chief Mike O'Connell. You can call me Mike. Most people do."

Abby half-stood and shook it.

His red hair grayed at the temples, and his nose had a previously smashed look. But as tough as his exterior appeared, his eyes were a soft shade of sympathetic and worried blue. He sat opposite Brooke. Ethan closed the door and took the seat across from Abby.

Brooke cocked her head. "What's going on?"

Ethan's mouth flattened out. He met Abby's eyes. "When the chief and I went through your car, we found your seat adjusted to its farthest position from the dashboard. I could barely reach the pedals. There's no way you could have driven the car like that. Now it's possible you moved the seat accidentally while you were trying to get out of the car."

Impatient, Abby interrupted. "You told me all this the other day."

Ethan frowned. "We also found your half-empty sports drink bottle in the car."

"I drink Gatorade before and after I run," Abby explained. Why did it matter how she hydrated for a workout? But next to her, Brooke tensed.

The police chief's gaze flickered to Brooke for a second. His expression went grimmer as his attention refocused on Abby. "On a hunch, we had the contents tested." He softened his voice. "Your Gatorade came back positive for GHB."

"What?" Brooke's upper body shot forward. "That's impossible."

"What's GHB?" Abby asked.

Brooke turned to her, anger radiating from her eyes. "GHB is like Rohypnol."

Shock swept over Abby. "Are you saying I was roofied? Like in *The Hangover*?" Who would do that to her? And why? She'd been at work, not a wild Vegas bachelor party.

Ethan grimaced. "Sort of. Rohypnol or roofies are a different drug. Street names for gamma-hydroxybutyrate or GHB are 'grievous bodily harm' and 'salty water,' among others. But the effects are similar."

The chief nodded. "In small amounts, GHB is a steroid alternative used by bodybuilders to enlarge their muscles. In larger doses it's a sedative. It's usually a clear liquid, generally odorless but salty. Typically, it's slipped into alcoholic drinks in bars or parties, but a sports drink already has a salty taste that would also easily mask the GHB. We used to see more Rohypnol, but GHB is gaining popularity. Probably because it can be cooked up at home with floor stripper and drain cleaner."

Disbelief hollowed Abby's chest, as if someone had squeezed her dry. "And someone put this in my sports drink." Her voice sounded as flat and empty as her chest. So much for starting her life over.

"Yes. Immediate signs of GHB ingestion are lack of inhibitions, loss of muscle coordination, nausea, sedation, and amnesia. The next day, symptoms might mimic a hangover or flu. Nausea, vomiting, or increased sweating are common as your body recovers from GHB poisoning."

Brooke leaped to her feet and paced the narrow space behind the chairs. "I should have thought of drugs. Damn it. You had textbook symptoms all weekend."

The chief shook his head. "Brooke, you know that, out of context, those symptoms can be confused with a concussion or virus. None of us suspected this. If Abby had been out at a bar or party and woken up with the same symptoms, you would have pegged it right away."

Brooke took two rapid steps and pivoted. "Who would do that to Abby and why?"

"That's what we're going to find out," the chief said. "According to the report, it's a good thing you only drank half the bottle. If you'd have finished it, you wouldn't have woken up and gotten out of the car."

Panic gripped Abby's insides. She put a hand to her stomach. "I drank paint thinner and drain cleaner. Those are poisonous. Are there any permanent effects? Do I need to go back to the hospital?"

Brooke stopped her pacing and dropped to the edge of her chair, facing Abby. "No. People do die from GHB ingestion, but not this long afterward. You're fine. The body processes the drug quickly. After twelve hours there's no sign of it, though you might feel like crap for a couple of days, which you did. In fact, it's way too late for a lab test to find any trace of it in your blood by now."

"You should see your doctor, though." The chief's voice went tight. "You're missing two hours. Do you think there's a possibility that you were raped?"

Abby stared at the salt-streaked leather toes of her boots. Too many horrific thoughts raced through her mind. She couldn't process all the sickening possibilities. Two hours was a long time. What else had the person responsible done to her? *Had* she been raped? She hadn't had sex in so long, surely her body would have noticed. There would have been signs of sexual activity, right?

The muffled ring of a telephone sounded through the closed door, but her body was silent. She remembered her trip to the ER. Other than the bump on the head, she'd had a few bruises from her escape from the vehicle. Most of those had seemed to be in logical places, considering she'd somersaulted in the empty car and shimmied out a window.

Abby's cheeks heated. She stared down at her clenched hands as she forced an answer through a constricted throat. "I don't think so. I was wearing multiple layers of running clothes, and they all seemed undisturbed. But let's be honest. It's been four days. There's no way to be a hundred percent sure, is there?" She lifted her chin, looking from Brooke's furious expression to the controlled police chief and finally settling on Ethan. Anger, compassion, and frustration played over his face. "But we do know for sure that someone poisoned me, drove me out to the creek, put me in the driver's seat, and rolled my car into the water."

And that was more than enough to freak her out.

"That's our working hypothesis." Ethan didn't blink. His jaw was clamped, the cords of his neck as tight as bridge cables.

His visible tension was nothing compared to the fear boiling inside Abby. "Someone tried to kill me."

Again.

CHAPTER TEN

The accident file was officially relabeled ATTEMPTED HOMICIDE.

Ethan watched Abby process the news and arrive at the conclusion he and the chief had already drawn. Pity and anger churned in his gut.

Abby was silent. Disbelief and shock glazed her eyes. Her hands clenched into tight fists on her knees, and her gaze strayed to the door, as if she couldn't wait to get out of the chief's office. Which was the opposite reaction he'd expect from a normal person who'd just discovered she'd almost been a murder victim.

"What else are you doing?" Brooke's eyes pinned him to the wall. "What about the school's security cameras?"

Ethan nodded. "I reviewed all the school's security tapes. Unfortunately, the cameras don't cover the entire parking lot, only the building exits, the main halls, and a few other strategic spots. We have footage of Abby leaving the building along with kids and teachers. I'm going to ask you both to review a few screenshots and see if you notice anything out of the ordinary."

Abby rearranged her face into a composed mask. Too composed. Why wasn't she freaking out? Wouldn't most women be crying if they'd thought they might have been raped?

She cleared her throat and straightened her spine. She might be reining in her emotions, but Ethan could see the distress deep in her eyes. "Can I use this computer? I need to check on the status of an inmate at Greenville."

"Oooo-kay," Ethan said, his turn to be stunned. "Want to tell us what's going on?"

She gave him a nearly imperceptible shake of her head. Her face was bloodless, the skin on her face stretched tight. "After."

Ethan opened the laptop, booted it up, and established a secure Internet connection. Brooke was on her feet again and pacing the tiny strip of floor behind her chair. He slid the computer across the table, turning it to face Abby. Then he got up and walked around to look over her shoulder as she pulled up the website for the Victim Information and Notification Everyday system, otherwise known as VINE, which was a nationwide database to help victims keep tabs on prison inmates. She typed into a few blanks. Her speed with the site suggested practice. She didn't have to look up any of the inmate information either.

Abby pressed SEND. She interlocked her fingers while the computer chugged. Her knuckles paled under the pressure.

INMATE NOT FOUND.

"No. It has to be a mistake," she whispered to herself. She typed in the number again.

INMATE NOT FOUND.

The air whooshed out of her in one huge exhale. Her face whitened, and her brown eyes went dark with shock. Ethan pulled her chair away from the table and put a hand between her shoulder blades. He guided her head down. "Breathe."

"It can't be right. There has to be a mistake." She bent forward, hanging her face in front of her knees. "He had three more years before he was even eligible for parole."

The chief leaned back in his chair and rubbed his jaw. Brooke stared in alarmed silence. Ethan kept his hand on Abby's back. Her spine trembled under his palm. He wanted to wrap his arms around her but doubted she could handle it.

He moved his hand in a gentle circle. "Who, Abby? Who were you looking for?"

"Zeke Faulkner. The man who kidnapped me three years ago." Abby spoke to the carpet.

Ethan's heart dropped into his gut. He barely held back the *what?* that was screaming through his head.

Abby sat up. "I met Faulkner at my gym. He asked me out, but I said no. There was something creepy about him. I came home from work one night. He was waiting in the bedroom closet. I didn't see his face, but I knew it was him. He wore very distinctive cologne, and I recognized his voice. He knocked me out. When I woke up, I was in a hole in the ground. It turned out to be an abandoned well."

"How long did he keep you?" And what did he do to her while he had her prisoner? Ethan dropped his hand to her forearm. He needed to keep touching her, to maintain a connection. Without it he feared she'd withdraw again. She didn't protest.

"Faulkner never came back. The school reported me missing when I didn't show up for work. Several people had seen him following me around the gym. When the police started looking for him, they found out he was already in jail. He'd been picked up after a bar fight the same night he grabbed me. They didn't find me for ten days. The farm was in the Pine Barrens. Luckily, there was a small amount of water in the bottom of the well or I would have dehydrated."

"Faulkner went to prison?" Ethan asked.

"Yes." Her voice was distant and disconnected. "They found my hair in his trunk, and he'd left DNA on a cigarette butt near the window he used to gain entry into my house. Faulkner pled not guilty, but he didn't take the stand. With all the physical evidence, the trial was short, and he was sentenced to eight years.

But the prosecutor told me he wouldn't likely get parole until he'd served at least five."

"Eight years for kidnapping?" Ethan said through clenched molars. "That's ridiculous." But Ethan knew the sentences for violent crimes were often horrifyingly short due to prison overcrowding, tight budgets, and other lame, horseshit-type reasons.

"I'll double-check with the warden." The chief stood. "Brooke, can you come with me? Ethan, get that slideshow going."

Brooke followed the chief out of the conference room.

Ethan flexed his jaw, which ached from grinding his teeth. "While we're waiting for the chief, I'd like you to watch some video segments to see if there's anyone at the school who shouldn't be there."

"All right." Abby brought her knees up to her chin and hugged her shins. Her gray skirt was long enough to cover her to the ankles of her black leather boots. Her brown eyes, usually warm, were desolate and vulnerable.

"Can you think of anyone else who has a grudge against you? Anyone else who would want to hurt you?"

A slight hesitation. "No." She was still hiding something. How bad could it be? She'd already told them a horrific story. What could possibly be worse than that? Ethan's stomach soured. She'd been kidnapped three years ago, and someone had tried to kill her last Friday. The sky was the limit on surprises after those events.

Abby's curled body was stiffer than his dress blues. He opened the laptop. He doubted she would see anything, but the distraction might be helpful. Besides, she looked like she was withdrawing, and Ethan wanted to keep her engaged.

Her gaze fixed on the screen, her expression unreadable.

Most people would be losing it if they'd learned they'd been poisoned, but Abby had gotten more composed after hearing the news. She hadn't even flinched at the possibility that she'd been raped.

What. The. Hell?

Ethan tapped on the touchpad to wake the hibernating computer and clicked on the media player. The open file was paused. He clicked PLAY, and the segment rolled.

With bleak eyes, she watched the exodus of students and teachers. What was she thinking? "Let me know if you see anyone out of place or someone you don't recognize."

She slid further down in the chair and hugged her legs harder. "OK." Staring at the screen, Abby pressed her knuckle against her mouth.

She'd only lived in Westbury for two years. Ethan needed to know everything about her life prior to the move. "Any chance you have an angry ex?"

"No." She didn't take her eyes off the computer screen. "I haven't dated anyone since I moved here."

"Social media accounts?" he asked in case he'd missed her pages in his Internet search. The last young woman attacked in Westbury had broadcast her every activity on the Internet.

"None."

Ethan had thought maybe if they were alone, she'd talk to him. He was obviously wrong, and her one-word answers weren't going to help him solve his case. If anyone had a chance to get some information, it was Brooke. Ethan hoped the chief was making that point to Brooke right now. But how could Ethan get Abby to trust him?

"How about family?"

She blinked. The corner of her mouth trembled, but she smoothed out her expression with a sniff. "There's no one."

"No one?" As soon as the surprised words left his mouth, Ethan silently cursed his lack of tact.

"My mother died shortly after the trial," she said in a monotone voice. "I have no siblings, and I haven't seen my father in years. He wasn't a big part of my childhood."

"I'm sorry." Ethan tilted his head and tried to catch her gaze. Her eyes flickered to his and returned to the computer with a frightening lack of emotion. He'd seen her with her young neighbor and her dog. She wasn't the cold, controlled person next to him.

What was going on behind that guarded expression? Why was she wearing it? Ethan had to find a way to break through the brick wall she'd constructed. She needed to share whatever secret she was holding back. What he didn't know could get her killed.

The chief appeared in the doorway. "The warden just confirmed that Zeke Faulkner was released from prison two weeks ago."

Abby opened her eyes to total darkness. Her head pulsed with pain. She blinked. Was she blind? She reached up and felt her eyelids with the pads of her fingers. Either something was wrong with her eyes, or the room was totally dark. She touched her forehead and scalp. When she probed behind her left ear, agony blasted in her skull like a bullhorn. Her stomach heaved. Riding the wave of nausea, she curled on her side and breathed through her nose.

The pain eased back to a dull throb. She lay still and listened. A faint scratch sounded on her left, so soft that she turned her head and strained her hearing to catch a repeat. But all she could hear was the muffled sound of wind from above.

She felt the floor around her. Dirt. Her palm slapped a puddle she sincerely hoped was water. Was she in a shed or basement? With slow and deliberate motions so as not to jar her aching brain, she lifted her head then rose to a sitting position. She raised her hands overhead but encountered no ceiling. With one arm still lifted to shield her head, she eased to her feet. She wobbled. Several moments passed until her legs steadied. She reached high over her head. Still she could feel no ceiling. She turned in a circle, arms outstretched.

Sliding her feet across the ground, she shuffled forward. In two steps, her hands hit a rough surface. Her fingers probed. The material was dry and crumbly. Some sort of rough stone.

Where was she? How long had she been here?

Long enough for her hearing to sharpen. A buzz sounded behind her. Following the sound, her head jerked around. An insect brushed against her face. Abby swiped at it, recoiling and banging her elbow on the wall.

She turned around and shuffled carefully in the other direction, each foot sliding forward to make sure the ground topography didn't change. Two shuffles forward and her fingers hit another wall. She waved her hands horizontally. The wall curved. Her hole was cylindrical and barely wider than her arm span.

Something on her body jingled. Her fingers searched for the source. Straps crisscrossed her torso. She traced their presence around her chest, waist, and the top of each thigh. Cold metal rings hung from the ensemble.

A harness? Oh my God. Rappelling gear.

Even though everything was black, she looked up on reflex. He had lowered her into a hole in the ground. A well?

She stretched her hands high. Nothing was above. She'd been lowered deep into the bowels of the earth. Her eyes probed the darkness above. Fear crawled through her belly. Where was she? Where did the man go who'd taken her? And when was he coming back?

Abby sank into the cold leather of Brooke's passenger seat and tried to shake off the memory of her kidnapping.

"Are you all right?" Brooke settled behind the wheel.

"Yeah."

She gave Abby a flat-lipped, sad smile. "Mike wanted me to ask you again if you think there's any chance you were raped."

"I don't think so." Panic, intensified by her flashback, bubbled into Abby's throat. "There's really no way to know for sure, is there? It's been four days. But my instincts and all the facts we do have say no." She was going to hold onto that for now because at this moment she couldn't deal with the alternative.

"I'm so sorry." Brooke reached over and squeezed her hand. "You're probably right, but you might want to see your doctor."

Fortunately she was on birth control pills. But what about sexually transmitted diseases? She'd been healthy and hadn't bothered to find a new doctor since she'd moved. Except for her house and job, she hadn't done many of the things people did when they were putting down roots. In the back of her mind, had she known this new start was temporary and that eventually she'd have to find another place to hide? Tears burned the corners of her eyes. One escaped, sliding down her cheek.

She buried the thoughts, like so many others. She had to get home. Dig in. Hide from reality. It was what she did best.

Brooke started the engine. "Let's collect Zeus and some of your things and go back to my house."

99

"No." Abby swiped a thumb under her eye. "I won't endanger you or your family. Your kids have been through enough."

"You're not safe alone. How about I stay with you?"

Abby shook her head. "Your kids need you. I have Zeus. I'll be fine. The police chief said he'd have someone ride by my house frequently." Besides, Abby needed time alone.

What was she going to do?

Brooke smiled. "I know Mike and Ethan. They'll do their best to keep you under surveillance."

"You have that much faith in them?" Abby leaned her forehead against the cool glass. She had no idea how she'd been poisoned. A patrol car driving by her house wasn't that reassuring.

"I do. Ethan saved your life."

"I know." In her head she knew she should trust him, and her heart agreed. Every time he was with her, it thumped a little faster. But her instincts, honed by a lifetime of betrayal and disappointment, weren't controlled so rationally.

Brooke turned onto Main Street. "You still want to rent a car?"

"Yes." Abby didn't want to be stranded with no way to run should fleeing become necessary. The thought of leaving Westbury filled her with sadness.

They stopped at the shopping center that housed the car rental agency. Abby selected a midsize gray sedan, the kind of car no one noticed.

"I'm going to call you in a couple of hours." Brooke hugged her good-bye in the parking lot.

Abby got into the sedan. She drove home in silence, her brain too overwhelmed for music. Her eye on the rearview mirror confirmed that Brooke followed her all the way home. Abby turned down her street. A police cruiser already sat at the curb. Ethan was at the wheel. Brooke waved, smiled, and drove off.

"I didn't expect you here so quickly." Abby locked the sedan with the fob. Truthfully, she was relieved to see him.

He got out of the vehicle and walked with her to the front door. Zeus barked at the window as Abby opened the door.

Ethan followed her into the foyer. "Do you always leave all the lights on?"

"I don't like the dark." Abby tossed her keys in the bowl on the desk. "Not anymore."

Anger flared in Ethan's eyes, then softened. "It's no wonder."

Zeus rubbed on her legs. "Good boy." She patted his head and stumbled under the force of a head butt.

Ethan caught her elbow. "The whining is ridiculous."

"I know." Abby pushed the dog backward and scratched his head until he settled. "He loves me."

"Wait here. I'll check the house." Ethan walked toward the closet.

Abby hung her jacket on a coat tree by the front door. "OK, but if anyone were here, Zeus would know about it."

"Humor me." Ethan checked the first floor and went upstairs. She heard his footsteps overhead, moving from room to room. A few minutes later, his boots clunked back down the steps. "Where's the door to the garage?"

Abby led him through the kitchen and pointed. She reached for the phone. Even though three years had passed, the number for the prosecutor's office that had handled her kidnapping case was burned into her brain like a brand. Two minutes later, Abby hung up with an appointment. She dialed the school and left a message that she'd be out for the rest of the week. She never missed work. In fact, she hadn't used a single sick day the whole year. But there was no way she could focus on teaching until she got some answers, and she'd been on her way home from school when someone had tried to kill her. She could endanger her students.

Someone tried to kill me. The truth hit her with shocking intensity. What were the chances? About the same as being struck by lightning twice? Getting bitten by two sharks?

She'd never be safe. Never.

Hands shaking, she started the teakettle. A knock at the back door startled her. Zeus barked, and the furious wag of his thin tail suggested friend not foe. With one hand pressed to the base of her neck, Abby moved the curtain and peeked out the window. Derek stood on the back stoop, his hands shoved into his pockets, his shoulders hunched in defeat. Bracing her spine and gathering her control, Abby let him in. The dog went through his wagging and whining routine. Derek dropped to a knee. Zeus wiped slobber all over the boy's jacket.

"Where's the cop?" Derek got to his feet. His gaze pinged around the room.

"He's checking the house," Abby said. What would Derek think of the GHB poisoning or her kidnapping? Should she tell him? As much as she hated to frighten him, she had to be straight with him. Being at her house could put him in danger. "The police think my accident wasn't an accident."

Derek's eyes stopped roaming and snapped to meet hers. "Someone messed with your car."

"Something like that."

His eyes widened. "Seriously?"

"Seriously." She didn't provide the details. It was enough that he was informed about the risk. Maybe he should stay away from her for a while. But what about his mom's latest? "You need to be careful."

He gave her a *no kidding* shrug.

"Maybe you shouldn't hang around here for a couple of days. I don't know when or where it happened. It might not be safe here."

"Safety isn't a guarantee anywhere." The look in his eyes was as weary as Abby felt.

The stamp of boots signaled Ethan's return from the garage. He stopped short. "Hey, Derek."

"Hey." Derek didn't bolt, but his sneakers pointed toward the door as if he wanted to run.

"I was checking to make sure Abby's house was all clear." Ethan unzipped his coat. He caught Abby's gaze. "I didn't find any sign of an attempted break-in."

Which meant her Gatorade had probably been tampered with at school. Goose bumps swept across Abby's exposed skin, and she was relieved that she wouldn't have to go back to work this week. The thought that her house hadn't been violated was comforting, though.

"Are you going to be home tonight?" Ethan asked Derek.

Derek sniffed. "Yeah. Probably."

"Would you mind keeping a lookout?" Ethan took off his jacket and tossed it over the back of a chair. "There'll be a cop here, but you know what's normal and what's not for the neighborhood. If you see anything suspicious, please call me." He dug a business card out of his chest pocket and held it out.

Derek hesitated. Indecision stiffened his stance. He plucked the card from Ethan's two fingers.

"I can do that," the boy said, his back straightening.

Ethan nodded. "Thanks, man. I really appreciate it."

"No problem." Derek turned to Abby. "You still want me to take Zeus for his walk?"

"I'm sure he'd love that." Abby smiled. "But be careful."

"Always." Derek snapped the leash onto Zeus's collar, and the two headed out of the kitchen. Abby heard the front door open and close.

She turned to Ethan. "He's usually shy. How did you charm him?"

"You think I'm charming?" A wicked glint shone in Ethan's eyes.

Yes. "I didn't say that." Abby blushed. "I was talking about Derek."

"I know. I'm sorry." He gave her a sheepish grin. "I spotted him walking to school this morning and gave him a ride. No big deal."

"He got into your police car?" Abby asked. Derek would walk to the coast before he willingly got into a cop car.

"No." Ethan sighed. "I was driving my brothers' car. It's a MINI Cooper, probably the least intimidating vehicle on the face of the earth. It's a bright red shoebox outfitted with a lawnmower engine."

"Thank you. Derek needs more people he can trust."

Ethan shifted his weight. "What's his story?"

Abby went into evasive maneuvers. She couldn't forget that Ethan was a cop. There were things he couldn't know. Things that could make Derek vulnerable. "Single mom. She has to work a lot." OK, well that wasn't a total lie. When Krista was working, she *did* work a lot, mostly to make up her late bills from her bi-annual man and booze binge. "They've had some rough times."

"Where's his dad?"

"Neither Krista nor Derek has ever mentioned him."

"He seems like a good kid. He was going to walk to school

today. That's a long haul in this cold. Most kids would've gone home and skipped it."

"He's very diligent about school." Abby's chest warmed. Her tutoring had helped, as if that one small bright spot in Derek's life mitigated a small part of the horror that overshadowed hers.

On the stove, the kettle whistled. Abby reached for it. "Tea?"

"No, thanks." Ethan leaned a hip against the counter. "What does Derek's mom do?"

"She's a waitress." Time for a subject change. "If you didn't find any sign that someone broke into the garage, how did my Gatorade get poisoned?"

"We'll have to assume for now that the GHB was put into your drink while it sat in your car in the school parking lot."

"That's not much better."

"No. It isn't. It means whoever did it knew your routine. He planned for you to drink the Gatorade on your way to the park. He must have followed you." Ethan stopped there, but his eyes said more.

Abby shuddered. Whoever had tried to kill her had been watching her long enough to predict her activity.

She poured steaming water into her mug. "After the kidnapping, I couldn't stay in the same house where I'd been attacked. I didn't even want to stay in the same area. I needed a fresh start. Now I'm thinking I'll never be able to get away from it."

"I can't imagine what you went through," Ethan said. "And I'm pissed off that he got out of jail early. If he's the one behind this, we'll get him. What I can't figure out is why he'd risk his freedom for revenge."

"We're talking about a man who kidnapped me because I wouldn't go on a date with him. That's not exactly rational behavior.

He spent a couple of years in prison because of me. I can't imagine how angry he is now." Helplessness filled Abby's chest. God, she despised feeling vulnerable. Deep inside her a switch flipped. She couldn't take it anymore. Regardless of the risk, this time was going to be different. She was taking offensive action. No more running and hiding.

The decision empowered her. Yes, she was still scared. She would be foolish not to be. But she wasn't going to sit around and wait for another attack or give other people control over her future. She was taking charge.

Ethan's jaw tightened. "We'll take it one step at a time."

"First I need to find out how and why he got released." Abby tossed her tea bag and added a spoonful of sugar to her drink. "The prosecutor who handled my case died of a heart attack a few months ago. I have an appointment with his replacement tomorrow. I want to know what happened. I was registered to receive a notification if Faulkner was released." Abby wrapped her hands around her mug and sipped. The hot liquid warmed her belly but couldn't cut through the chill in her veins. "Obviously, that didn't happen."

She turned toward the table, but Ethan blocked her path. Her tiny kitchen wasn't designed for entertaining. He made no move to get out of her way. "I think you should let me handle it."

Abby shook her head. "I can't. For my own sanity, I have to be proactive. I won't hide." Not anymore.

Ethan nodded. "I don't like it, but I understand."

Their gazes met. His acceptance soldered the connection between them. He wasn't going to demand she cede control.

Respect flared bright blue in his gaze. "How did you get an appointment that fast?"

"I convinced the secretary that the new prosecutor wouldn't like to hear about my case on the news." Not that Abby would ever go to the media. The last thing she wanted was publicity. But her bluff had worked like magic.

"I'm sure that's true." Ethan stepped closer. "I'd like to drive you."

Abby leaned away, but her heels hit the cabinets. "That's not necessary."

His lean body crowded her. "I know. But it's my day off, and I don't want to spend it worrying about you."

"You would worry?" The heat in Abby's stomach spread. She should want to run and hide from Ethan. Instead, he made her blood sing through her veins. Desire flared in his eyes, mesmerizing her.

"Yes." Ethan took her mug from her hands and set it on the counter. His irises darkened as he squared his body off with hers. "I would. All day. Just because I understand and respect your need to be involved in your case, I still want to protect you."

"Um. OK then." Abby's trapped heart skittered. "I have to leave by seven."

"I'm an early riser." A car engine sounded outside. "That'll be Pete," he said against her cheek. His minty breath wafted over her face. "He's going to watch your house tonight." Ethan pressed a kiss to her temple, near the stamp-size Band-Aid that covered the healing cut. The contact of his lips sent tingles radiating through Abby's body. Her eyes drifted closed, and her hand strayed to Ethan's chest. Her fingers splayed, touching as much of him as possible with one hand. Under the uniform shirt, his muscles were hard under her palm. He smelled of peppermint, and his lips lingered a few seconds longer than she expected, but disappointment washed through her when he lifted his mouth from her skin. "Be careful, Abby. Call me if anything scares you."

"I will."

"Pete will come in to introduce himself." He pulled away and searched her face. "He's a good cop. You can trust him."

Abby nodded. She believed him. Why? What was different about Ethan?

He grabbed his jacket and walked out of the kitchen.

Swaying slightly, Abby put a steadying hand on the counter next to her. Wow. She touched her cheek. He hadn't even kissed her on the mouth and she was practically swooning like a schoolgirl. What would he taste like?

The front door opened. Zeus and Derek trooped in. Abby walked to the front window. Outside, Ethan was talking to a short, stout, older cop. Ethan looked at the window as if he sensed her presence. His gaze burned through the chill that hovered near the glass.

Uh-oh. Her hand fluttered to her throat. There was no mistaking that look. He wanted her. She wondered if the rest of his muscles were as solid as his chest. Abby shut down her imagination before it ran with the idea.

This was not the time.

Ethan turned toward his car, while the older cop started up the walk. She wished it were Ethan watching over her through the night.

After Derek went home, she let the dog out one last time. Across the backyard, Mr. Sheridan waved at her and walked up to the fence. Abby grabbed her jacket, stomped into a pair of boots, and went out to see what her cranky old neighbor wanted.

"Bad storm coming."

"I know." Abby clutched the lapels of her jacket together. "Do you need anything?"

"No, but thanks for asking." Mr. Sheridan rubbed his gnarled hands together. "Not many people know how to be neighborly these days. I got extra rock salt in the shed if you need some."

"Thanks."

Mr. Sheridan jerked a thumb toward Derek's house. "The Tanner kid was in your yard again."

"I know." Abby smiled. "It's all right. He walks the dog for me."

"Long as it's all right with you." Mr. Sheridan thought everyone under the age of twenty was a "hoodlum" with intentions of robbery or vandalism, but he meant well.

"Thanks for keeping an eye out."

"The weather keeps me in more than I'd like, but I try." He shrugged. "You take care. Good night."

"Good night." Abby called Zeus and went back inside. She shed her outerwear and checked all her locks before going up to her bedroom. The door to the walk-in closet was open from Ethan's search. She turned on the light and went inside. A small fireproof safe hunkered in the far back corner. Abby picked it up and carried it into the bedroom. Inside was her plan-of-last-resort. Spinning the combination to the correct numbers, she lifted the top. Tucked in a neoprene holster was her mom's 9mm Glock. She ignored the envelope full of cash and the prepaid, unregistered cell phone that remained in the box.

Abby gripped the weapon in her right hand. The weight and feel was simultaneously comfortable and eerie. She hadn't handled the gun since her mom overdosed. The kidnapping and trial had proved to be too much for Mom's already precarious emotional state.

But she hadn't left Abby without a legacy. Some women passed beauty tips down to their daughters. They instructed them in the art of applying mascara and lipstick. Others taught their girls to cook, leaving recipes as their lasting gift to their families.

Abby's mom had taught her daughter to put a cluster of bullets into a torso-shaped target at twenty feet.

CHAPTER ELEVEN

Zeke parked his Camaro behind the Dumpster and hurried toward his room. His get-out-of-jail-free card had been a lucky break. But were a couple of years long enough for a certain client to forget about money spent and not earned? Too bad his release had been so public. It was hard to stay under the radar when he'd been in the paper. The list of affected inmates had been long, though. Maybe no one had noticed his name among the many.

He opened the door and stepped inside. The room was a bare-bones rat hole complete with bolted-down remotes and mystery stains on the carpet. But it was only temporary housing. Once the settlement from the county came through, Zeke could pay off his outstanding debt and move far, far away from New Jersey. He tossed his jacket on the bed and shivered. Enough wind blew through the window jambs to move the faded curtains.

Florida sounded good. Yeah. He was heading south. No more freezing his nuts off.

He cranked the thermostat on the wall to seventy-five. The unit on the wall shuddered, rattled, and wheezed out a pathetic cough of lukewarm air. Zeke knew the room temperature would barely budge.

The attorney he'd met with said the county would settle. His conviction had been based on tainted evidence, which was why it had been overturned. They'd fucked up, and they knew it. They wouldn't want the expense of a huge lawsuit they couldn't win.

It was only a matter of when and how much.

Zeke headed for the bathroom. The room was a friggin' freezer, but the hot water heater worked just fine.

He stopped short at the gun muzzle in his face and the pair of dead eyes focused on him. "Hello, Zeke."

Guess his client hadn't forgotten. Zeke cursed himself. Lawsuit or not, he should have left for Florida the day he was released. Poor was better than broken kneecaps, missing fingertips, or worse.

"I can get the money." Zeke backed up, hands in the air. He was going to be OK. Right? A dead man couldn't repay debts, and money was the key to the universe. But the guy with the dead eyes was scary. "I'll even pay interest."

"Zeke, close the curtains."

Zeke back-stepped and drew the heavy drapes across the window. Thick blackout fabric completely blocked the sunlight, showing his willingness to cooperate in good faith. "There. No one can see in."

"Perfect," Dead-eyes said. "This is a very private conversation."

———

Ryland picked up his buzzing phone.

"I've handled the first issue," Kenneth said in a matter-of-fact voice. "Moving on to number two."

"Thank you, Kenneth." Pleased, Ryland ended the call. He swiveled to stare out the glass wall of his office. The afternoon sun sparkled on the choppy sea with deceptive brightness. The sand below looked warm and inviting. But whitecaps dancing across the Atlantic exposed the truth. A frigid arctic wind turned the beach brutally cold.

Unfortunately, Kenneth's phone call had been the highlight of his day. Completing the cessation of his last illegal business venture was proving to be even more difficult than he'd anticipated.

His intercom beeped. "Mr. Medina to see you, sir."

"Send him in." Ryland turned back to his office, to his work, and greeted one of his oldest business associates. He stood and extended a hand across his desk.

"Paul, always good to see you." The lie slid out of Ryland's mouth as easily as the sun disguised the frigid conditions on the beach. "Scotch?"

"Yes." Paul inclined his head a fraction of an inch. "On the rocks. Thank you."

Ryland went to the small bar in the corner. He filled two tumblers with ice and poured a generous shot of amber liquid in each.

Like Ryland, Paul Medina had aged since they'd both started out. Gray peppered Paul's black hair, and his skin bore the craggy evidence of his enthusiasm for golf. Ryland studied his guest. Did his own eyes reflect the same detached brutality? Did others meet his gaze and flinch at the knowledge that no shred of mercy lived within?

Probably. God knew Ryland had earned his hardness with deeds that would cause nightmares in a compassionate human being.

"I didn't know you were in town." Ryland settled in his seat. "Don't you usually stay in Miami until March?"

"I fly in now and then to keep tabs on the business." Paul sat in one of the leather-and-chrome guest chairs and crossed his legs. He steepled his fingers and looked at Ryland over them. "You can't trust anyone completely."

Paul's implication was clear, as was his disinterest in small talk, which suited Ryland just fine. He'd had enough bullshit as well.

Ryland leaned back in his chair. "What brings you to my office today, Paul? Surely you didn't fly in from Miami just to talk about our grandchildren."

"No. As I said, the trip is about business." Paul's black eyes flashed with annoyance. "Did you really think you could simply cease taking shipments?"

Ryland chose his words carefully because checking Paul for a wire would have been a direct insult.

"You had adequate notice."

"And I warned you that there would be repercussions if you proceeded with your plan," Paul snapped.

Ryland waved a hand. "You had plenty of time to find other avenues of distribution."

"You cannot leave a hole in the delivery process." Paul's tone went colder than the ice cubes in his scotch. "And what about your sons? Don't they deserve the same opportunities that made us what we are today?"

No. They deserved more. Ryland swallowed the words. His sons had never been part of that end of the company. They didn't even know it existed. He'd groomed them to take over as CEO and CFO of the legitimate company.

"I made myself clear last year, Paul." Ryland didn't change his position. He remained comfortably reclined. "You knew this would be coming."

"There are many others who depend on your company's role in the industry. You've left us with a hole we cannot fill."

"That isn't true," Ryland said. "There are plenty eager to step into place."

"But trust hasn't been established. The risks are too great to open the doors to new partners. You won't reconsider?"

Ryland didn't blink. "No."

Paul stood. He set his glass on the desk with a final *clunk.* "Remember, Ryland. I'm not the only one you betray, just as you are not the only one at risk."

CHAPTER TWELVE

Abby watched the scrub pines flow past the truck window. After the trial and her mother's death, she'd sworn she'd never come back here.

"This is where you lived before you moved to Westbury?" Ethan exited the Atlantic City Expressway and followed the sign toward Harris, where the county prosecutor's office was located.

"Yes. I had a townhouse not far from here." The well Faulkner had kept Abby in wasn't far away either. Anxiety tumbled in her belly.

Harris, New Jersey, was one of the lesser-populated sections of the state. Located fifteen miles west of Atlantic City on the southeastern edge of the Pine Barrens, it was exactly what that name suggested: mostly barren and full of pine trees.

"Did you grow up here too?"

"Yes."

"Was it always just you and your mom?"

Abby sighed. Her reluctance didn't deter Ethan at all. "My father wasn't around much. He'd pop in for an occasional check-in and give my mother money. Other than that, he didn't want anything to do with my life." She was about to say she couldn't miss what she never had, but knew Ethan would see through her bravado. Abby had never experienced a loving father, but she had friends with real dads, fathers who threatened their dates and danced with them at their weddings.

"I'm sorry. Were you close to your mom?"

"She wasn't naturally maternal, but she tried." Abby had never doubted her mother loved her, even if she often seemed disconnected. Mom wasn't the most affectionate person on the planet, but she'd taught Abby to shoot in grade school, and Mom would have fought to the death to protect her daughter. "She suffered from depression. Sometimes she drank too much. I think she loved my father, and the fact that it was a one-way street took its toll. She never dated. Not once." Abby rested her head on the glass of the passenger window. Talk about an overshare. Why did she tell him that? What was it about him that lowered her defenses?

Following a command from the GPS, Ethan turned left. He drove in silence for a few minutes. "Did I tell you I live with my mother?"

She lifted her head and looked at him. Was this a you-showed-me-yours-so-now-I'll-show-you-mine thing? And why did the mutual sharing bother her even more than her own too-much-information slip? It was as if they were bonding. "No."

A wry, close-lipped smile crossed his face. "I do. My father had a heart attack and died at fifty. I was a New York City cop at the time. My younger twin brothers were still in high school, and my mom has rheumatoid arthritis. It was either move home or make her sell the farm. She loves that farm."

"You gave up your career for your family?"

"Not really. I'm still a cop." Ethan squirmed.

"New York City and Westbury are barely on the same planet."

"True." Ethan laughed. "But it turned out all right in the end. Cam and Bryce had a hard time accepting Dad's death. We all did. Grieving together was the best therapy."

"How are your brothers now?" Abby asked. The loss of her mother was still a hard lump in the center of her chest. She'd done her grieving alone.

"They're doing great. They go back to college tomorrow." Ethan followed another directional prompt from his cell phone, turned into the municipal complex, and parked in front of the prosecutor's office. "Are you ready?"

No. The unexpected intimacy formed between them during the long drive had left a bittersweet taste in her mouth. Their tenuous bond felt fragile and tender. A connection so sweet shouldn't be soured by the news that waited for her in the prosecutor's office.

But such was her life. Beautiful sunny days were always followed by a storm.

"Yes." Abby opened her door and stepped out onto the asphalt. A freezing wind whipped across the open space. So much for the temperature being milder near the coast. She zipped her down jacket. At least there wasn't any snow on the ground.

Ethan walked at her side. His busy blue eyes scanned the parking lot as he steered her toward the building. Dressed in jeans, boots, and a leather bomber jacket as black as his hair, his casual attire didn't camouflage his cop nature.

Inside, Abby gave her name to the receptionist. She rubbed her hands together to warm them and dropped into a chair. Despite the cold, nervous sweat dripped between her shoulder blades. She took off her jacket and draped it over her arm. Ethan took the upholstered chair next to her. He took her hands between his, which were absurdly hot considering how cold it was outside.

"Ms. Foster, Mr. Whitaker will see you now." In addition to the prosecutor being replaced, the leggy brunette receptionist was new. She crossed the room and opened her boss's door. Porcelain skin, even white teeth, and dark red lips lent her a vampire-like sexuality. Where was the older woman who ran the office for the last prosecutor?

Abby stood. Next to her, Ethan put his hand on the small of her back. Warmth seeped through her blouse and steadied her as they entered the office. Behind a scarred desk, a tall blond man in his late forties smoothed his tie and stood as they approached.

"Dan Whitaker." He held out a hand.

Abby shook it and introduced Ethan.

From his shined shoes to his *GQ* hair, the new chief prosecutor was way too perfect to be honest.

At Whitaker's gesture, Abby sank into the worn leather wing chair opposite his desk. Ethan dropped his hand from her back and took the other chair. She instantly missed the contact. Her hand drifted to her collarbone as she waited for Whitaker to explain his lack of communication. Three years ago she'd spent hours sitting in this same seat being prepared to give testimony, but this afternoon the once-familiar space felt like foreign territory.

And Whitaker felt like the enemy.

Which was ridiculous. The man hadn't spoken yet, and even though they'd never met, they were on the same side.

Determined to conceal the panic crawling up her throat, she set her hands on her lap and intertwined her fingers to anchor them. No amount of willpower could stop the sweat that seeped through her pores.

"Are you sure I can't get you anything, Ms. Foster?" At Abby's mute nod, the receptionist pivoted on a narrow heel and withdrew.

Whitaker rounded his desk and posed on its edge, looking

down at the seated Abby and Ethan. Superior body positioning. Well done. Score one for the new prosecutor.

Whitaker gave Abby a solemn stare. "I'd like to offer my apologies. You should have been informed about Faulkner's release. We've had quite a bit of staff turnover. I looked into the matter. Your new telephone number wasn't in our records."

"What about the VINE system?" Ethan asked. "The whole purpose of automating the victim notification system was to eliminate human error."

Whitaker shrugged. "Any system that size can have an occasional glitch."

Glitch? That's all she was to this man? An unfortunate computer error?

Anger locked Abby's breath in her chest. She struggled to inhale enough air to respond. "I don't understand. Faulkner wasn't supposed to be eligible for parole yet. What happened?"

Whitaker crossed his arms in front of his chest. Silver cufflinks shimmered. "A few months ago, a state lab technician was convicted of tampering with evidence. A clerk from this office was also implicated. Every defendant whose evidence one of those two individuals handled filed a challenge to his conviction. Unfortunately, this included your case."

And explained why the prosecutor's office had cleaned house. Whether or not they were truly responsible, someone had to pay the public-image piper.

Except for a slight, polite frown, Whitaker's flawless face remained devoid of expression. Either he didn't really care or his facial muscles had been Botoxed into submission.

Whitaker's predecessor would never have blindsided her like this. Mark Bailey had kept her apprised of everything. Light glinted off Whitaker's gelled hair as he leaned closer, reaching to rest a manicured hand on Abby's shoulder. Unable to retreat any further in the high-backed chair, Abby gritted her teeth. His touch felt metaphorically slimy. She'd need a decontamination shower to get rid of the taint.

"Does anyone know where Faulkner is?" Ethan glared at Whitaker's hand.

The prosecutor put it back on his thigh. "Faulkner wasn't paroled. He was released. His conviction was overturned. Without the physical evidence, we decided there was no point in retrying his case."

"So he isn't required to report in to anyone," Ethan finished in a dead tone.

"Right," Whitaker said. "After all, you never saw his face. You only recognized his voice. He never admitted his guilt. It isn't likely a jury will convict a man based solely on the sound of his voice."

Abby couldn't process the news. "But there was other evidence. . . ."

"Not enough for a conviction." Whitaker blinked.

Abby's stomach heaved. One hand shot up to cover her mouth. Whitaker slid backward on the edge of his desk, his mask cracking with revulsion for an instant.

She swallowed, sucked a deep breath in through her nose, and let it out through pursed lips. The cut on her temple stung. She touched the bandage.

"Are there any records of family or last known address?" Ethan asked.

Whitaker's voice turned sour. "I can't give out personal information. Nor can I allow you to harass Faulkner, even if you are a police officer. You are out of your jurisdiction, Officer Hale, and legally, Faulkner is now an innocent man. His conviction was wiped away as if it never happened."

Abby took another deep breath. *Oh God.* He really was out. And not just out, but free to do as he liked. No check-ins with a parole officer. No reporting requirements. Nothing. He could be anywhere. Faulkner had accomplished what Abby was unable to do. He'd wiped his slate clean.

Ethan got up and moved to stand behind her chair, positioning himself eye to eye with Whitaker. "Someone tried to kill Ms. Foster last Friday."

Ethan rested both hands on her shoulders. The weight of them anchored her. She reached across her body and put her hand on top of his.

Apprehension flickered in the prosecutor's eyes. "I don't see what that has to do with Mr. Faulkner's release."

Abby opened her mouth to protest, but no words came out. What could she say? The only retort readily available in her brain was, *Seriously, are you an idiot?* Voicing it wouldn't gain them any cooperation. Not that they were getting much now, but animosity from the prosecutor's office wouldn't help matters.

Ethan squeezed her shoulders in a silent *I got this* assurance. "It seems convenient that he was released a few weeks before Ms. Foster was attacked."

"Or it's just a coincidence." Whitaker lowered his honed body into the chair and picked up a file from the bin on his desk. Their interview was over. "There are lawsuits pending against the county because of the situation. I can't discuss it any further."

Ethan's fingers tightened. "I don't believe in coincidences."

Ethan barely kept up as Abby bolted from the heated building into the chill of the parking lot. The heels of her boots echoed on the pavement. A bus drove past. Lingering exhaust fumes smelled harsh after their meeting with Whitaker, as if the air was tainted by his message that Abby wasn't worth the effort of retrying her kidnapper.

She stumbled. Ethan caught her by the elbow. He wrapped an arm around her waist, slowing her down as they approached his truck.

"Easy." He opened the door and helped her into the passenger seat. Her hands were trembling, and tears welled up in her eyes. Ethan rounded the truck and slid into the driver's seat. Starting the engine, he blasted the heat and aimed the vents at Abby.

She fumbled with her purse, opening it and pulling out a travel packet of tissues. "I'm sorry."

"You have no reason to apologize." Ethan quelled the desire to go back into Whitaker's office and knock a couple of his perfect teeth out. *What a dick.*

Abby blotted her eyes and nose. She covered her eyes with one hand and slumped against the armrest.

Ethan swiveled in his seat. He lifted her hand from her face. Her eyes blazed with raw despair. "You've been kidnapped twice and poisoned once. You escaped from a car submerged in a frozen river and found out a former assailant has been prematurely released. Instead of feeling sorry for yourself, you look for answers. You are one of the toughest people I know."

"This last week has felt like I'm skiing on ice, just barely scraping enough traction to get through the next turn." She sniffed and exhaled through pursed lips, clearly seeking composure. Abby needed to be in control. He wondered how many times in her life had she been at someone else's mercy.

He leaned across the console and wrapped his arms around her. She leaned against him, silent and still for a few minutes.

The cab warmed, and Abby stopped trembling. With a deep breath, she sat up. "We need to find Faulkner."

Ethan's thoughts echoed Abby's, but he wanted to shield her from this new threat as much as he wanted to solve her case. "Are you sure you're up for it right now? I could take you home and come back another day."

"No." She stretched taller in the seat, as if her decision to continue moving forward was holding her up. "We're here, and I don't want to waste time. I need to know what he's been doing since he was released. If he's guilty of poisoning me, he'll run."

"OK. I'll call the chief." Ethan shifted back to his own seat. "He has connections. If Whitaker won't help us, Chief O'Connell will."

Ethan drove to a convenience store on the highway and bought two bottles of water while they waited. Ten minutes later the chief called back with an address.

"Faulkner's mother lives in Somer's Point." Ethan plugged the address into the GPS on his cell phone. Somer's Point was the last town before the bridge to the barrier islands that comprised the Jersey Shore, the family resort not to be confused with the *Jersey Shore* television show filmed in Seaside Heights sixty miles to the north.

Twenty minutes later, Ethan pulled up in front of a boxy rancher the size of a doublewide. The entire lot was barely big enough to play full-court basketball. Instead of a lawn, the yard was covered in a thick layer of smooth, round beige pebbles.

"Let me check it out first. Lock the doors." But one look at Abby's face told him she wasn't happy with his plan. "Was his mother at the trial?"

Comprehension dawned on her face. "Yes."

124

"I hate to take the chance she'd recognize you and refuse to speak to us."

"You're right." Abby slumped.

"In fact, she might even see you from the door." Ethan rooted around behind the seat of his truck for a baseball cap. He handed it to her. "You can trust me, Abby."

She pulled the cap low on her forehead and slid down in the seat a few inches. A second of silence passed before she answered. "I know."

But did she? Her mother was depressed. Her father was a no-show. Had Abby ever had *anyone* she could fully trust?

Ethan got out of the truck. He yanked the zipper of his jacket up to his chin. Though it rarely snowed at the Jersey Shore and the temperature was milder than his mountain hometown, the wind barreling down the street was cold, damp, and thick with salt. Ethan scoped out the property as he walked toward the house. The stone-filled lawn surrounded the house. If anyone came running out the back door, Ethan would hear footsteps crunching in pebbles. Plastic flowers and cement gnomes lined the concrete walk. The only car in the driveway was an older model four-door Buick. A handicapped parking pass hung from the rearview mirror. The carport was empty except for a tan tarp piled on the cement like a snakeskin. After a quick look around the corner of the house, Ethan knocked on the door.

An old woman answered. She opened the door but kept the chain fastened. Her skin bore the permanent sun damage of a lifelong beach lover, as wrinkled and brown as distressed leather.

"Mrs. Faulkner?"

Her eyes narrowed. "Who wants to know?"

"My name is Ethan Hale, ma'am." Ethan gave her a respectful nod. "I'm wondering if you've seen your son, Zeke."

"Are you one of his friends?"

Ethan contemplated lying, but he wasn't very good at it, and the gaze leveled at him through the gap in the door was shrewd. "No, ma'am."

"Then you can come in." She shut the door. Ethan heard the chain sliding free. The door opened wide.

So Zeke's mom wasn't happy with him.

Mrs. Faulkner's five-foot-nothing, ninety-pound frame was dressed from head to toe in pink velour. She could have been anywhere from fifty to eighty years old, but since Zeke was only twenty-eight, he placed her in the lower end of that age bracket.

Ethan stepped into the foyer. A living and dining room combination fronted the house, with a large picture window that overlooked the street. Figurines of cats cluttered every available surface. The house smelled like a combination of boiled cabbage and mildew. "So, have you seen Zeke?"

Mrs. Faulkner leaned on a walker. "Exactly who are you?"

Ethan produced his wallet and badge from his back pocket. "I'm a Pennsylvania police officer, and I'd like to speak with Zeke about a case I'm working on."

"What's he done now?" With a glance at his badge, she pulled a crumpled tissue from the pocket of her fleece zip-up and wiped under her nose.

"We don't know that he's done anything." Ethan folded his wallet and returned it to his jeans. "I just want to ask him a couple of questions."

She snorted. "Whatever you think he did, he probably did it.

That boy could never stay out of trouble for a whole day, let alone two weeks."

"Have you seen him?" Ethan asked.

"I saw Zeke about ten minutes after he got out of prison," she huffed, and bitterness soured her expression. "He cleaned out my rainy day fund and was gone in another ten."

"I'm sorry."

"No need. You didn't raise the worthless son of a bitch." Turning, Mrs. Faulkner pointed her walker toward a yellow kitchen. She clunked and shuffled down the short hall and eased into a metal-and-vinyl chair, either the effort or the pain of her son's betrayal exhausting her. "Zeke comes by his worthlessness naturally. His father was also a waste of the life God gave him."

"Do you have any idea where he went?" Ethan asked.

"He didn't say outright, but Zeke isn't the sweetest cookie in the batch. He was talking about contaminated evidence and how this fancy lawyer was going to sue the county for false imprisonment. Zeke said he's going to be set for life." Mrs. Faulkner rolled her eyes as she shuffled through some pamphlets on the laminate counter. "Big ideas. Small brain. That's Zeke." She grabbed a pen and wrote on the back of a postcard advertisement. "Here are the three most likely places."

She'd listed three cheesy local motels.

Ethan folded the note and stuck it in his pocket. "I'm surprised he didn't try to stay with you."

"My guess would be he's gorging on hookers, another habit he had in common with his daddy."

Ouch. "Other than the lawsuit, did he mention the old case at all?"

The loose skin of Mrs. Faulkner's neck flapped turkey-like as she shook her head. "No, but he was acting nervous."

"In what way?"

"In a way that made me suspect he left some people hanging when he went to prison and is afraid they'll be looking for him now that he's out."

"Do you think there's any chance he was innocent?" Not that Ethan thought for a second that Faulkner had been wrongly convicted. But what kind of a case did he present to his mother?

She snorted. "The one thing I know for sure about Zeke is that he sure as hell isn't innocent. He never said he did it, but he didn't deny it either. Not to me. His feeling was that his actual guilt or innocence was irrelevant. What mattered was that the county had to *prove* he did it, and they screwed up."

"Does he have a car?"

"Yup. 1990 Camaro. White."

Ethan spotted a photo on the fridge. Zeke was standing in front of the house with a couple of other men about the same age. He looked younger than he did in his mug shot. But then, no one took a good mug shot. "Who are those men with Zeke?"

"My sister's boys. Zeke's cousins are all nice young men. They have jobs and wives. My sister has three grandkids." Mrs. Faulkner heaved a disappointed sigh, rich with all life's milestones she would never reach.

Ethan stowed his pity. He couldn't help Mrs. Faulkner. Some people couldn't be changed. Zeke sounded like one of them. "Can I borrow the photo?"

"You can have it." Mrs. Faulkner reached back, snatched the picture off the fridge, and handed it to Ethan. Anger animated her features. "When you find Zeke, call me. He owes me three thousand dollars."

Steam followed Krista out of the shower. She wrapped her body in a towel, covering the bruise on her breast from last night. That wasn't the worst of what he'd done to her last night. In place of the usual exhaustive misery weighing her down, the aches in her body were real. The evidence of Joe's abuse mottled her body like purple camouflage.

Shame inched across her clean skin, making her feel like she needed to get back in the shower and scrub a hundred more times. But the darkness within her wanted to do it all over again.

What was she doing? Too drunk to drive, let alone wait tables, she'd called in sick to work last night. Her boss wouldn't put up with many missed shifts. This had to end. She should send Joe packing.

But God, the pain was more addictive than booze.

In the bedroom, a naked Joe was lounging on her bed. She turned away from him. "I have to go to work."

"First you have some work to do here."

"Didn't you get enough last night?" She tried to laugh off her fear. "I have an early shift."

"I never get enough." Joe's young, hard body moved fast. In a second, he had her pinned against the wall. "I have a present for you."

He held a small pipe in one hand. A tiny smoking chunk of bluish crystal sat in the bowl. That explained the strange smell coming from the basement last night. Krista's stomach heaved. The remnants of last night's beer and bile burned a path up her chest and into her mouth.

No. She couldn't let this happen. Her own life wasn't worth fighting Joe, but Derek's was another story. She was already up for shittiest mother of the year. Meth addict was not a title she wanted to add to her résumé.

She pushed his hand away. "I don't do that."

"Come on. You'll love it." He wrapped a hand in her hair and towed her to the bed. Still sore from the night before, her scalp screamed. He released her, and she stumbled onto the mattress. The scarf he'd used last night was still in the covers. One look at it sent fear skittering through Krista's bowels. She cringed and inched in reverse until her back hit the wall. Joe followed her, crawling across the bed like a big cat, a predator cornering a helpless mouse. On his knees, he pressed his body up against hers, pinning her with his hips. He wrapped the scarf around her throat and pulled the silky fabric tight.

Krista choked as he cut off her breath. The pressure around her neck increased. Lights danced in her vision. She pulled sideways, but his body held her against the wall. His erection ground into her stomach.

He was enjoying every second of her distress. She'd learned that about him. He liked to dish out pain and humiliation as much as she liked to receive it.

He put the pipe to her lips. "Just take a little hit."

She shook her head.

"I said do it." Twisting the fabric around his hand, Joe tightened the scarf then suddenly released it. Krista gasped, inhaling the smoke deep into her starved lungs. Coughing, she exhaled and sucked in a lungful of air.

"That's my girl." Joe put the pipe to her mouth again.

Krista gasped as the smoke filled her lungs. Euphoria flooded her. Her fears and pain melted. Joe whipped off her towel and shoved her hard against the wall. She slumped against him, her muscles as limp as her resolve.

Pleasure overwhelmed her. It flowed through her veins and penetrated deep into her body. Her thoughts went liquid, her despair vanished, and her determination to send Joe packing floated away.

───────────────

Abby kept the ball cap on her head as they pulled up in front of the first motel on the list. The U-shaped building of about three dozen rooms sat on a poorly maintained four-lane highway. There was an office at the end. Across the parking lot, Dumpsters butted up against the last unit. A strip of scraggly pine trees obscured whatever was behind the property.

She didn't want Zeke to run if he saw her. Ethan had filled her in on his conversation with Zeke's mother, and nothing indicated Zeke intended to go after Abby. Had he tried to kill her? If it wasn't Zeke, then the *who* and *why* of her attack became even more frightening questions. As if the sight of Zeke Faulkner didn't make her bowels cramp every time she looked at the mug shot Ethan had brought along.

Through the glass doors, a burly bald man sat on a high stool watching a tiny television on the counter.

Ethan drove by the office slowly, then parked outside next to the only other car in the lot, which probably belonged to the guy behind the desk. There was no sign of Faulkner's Camaro.

Abby scanned the motel. "Looks empty."

Ethan shifted into park. "I'll go in and see if I can find anything out from the clerk."

"Wait." She scrutinized his trimmed black hair and cleanly shaven jaw. Though his casual sweater was one size too large and bulky, it still didn't completely conceal the bulge at his right hip. But it was his shrewd eyes that gave him away. "You look like a cop."

"I am a cop."

Abby looked back at the guy in the office. "He has tattoos on his face."

Ethan raised a hand, palm up. "Hey, I don't judge people by the way they look."

"But he might." She took off the cap and fluffed her hair. "Let me go in."

"It's not safe," Ethan protested, those sharp eyes narrowing.

"I thought you didn't judge people by their looks."

His eyes heated. "There are exceptions to every rule. Your safety is more important than political correctness or good manners."

"You'll be sitting right here, watching." Abby tilted her head toward the door. "I doubt that glass is bulletproof."

Ethan leaned back. His fingers drummed on his thigh. "OK, but I still don't like it."

Neither did Abby. But if she lost momentum, she might not be able to gather the courage to keep moving forward. Returning to her habitual prey-mode would be too easy. No more running. No more hiding. That was her new mantra.

"Here, you can show him this." Ethan handed her a snapshot. "Mrs. Faulkner gave it to me. No love lost there."

"I guess not." Faulkner grinned at the camera. The desire to rip the photo into shreds burned hot, but Abby made herself take it. She couldn't very well use the mug shot they'd brought along.

"Stay in front of the door, in my direct line of sight." Ethan pulled his handgun free of its holster and rested it across his leg.

Abby suppressed the fear rising in her esophagus. She needed to do this. She took a sip of water to wash the acid from her throat. Getting out of the pickup, she adjusted her jacket hem and pushed open the glass door. A bell tied to the inside handle jingled. The man looked up at her. Thick arms crossed his chest, mirroring Ethan's stubborn and reluctant posture. She'd made the right call. Ethan wouldn't have gotten anything out of this guy.

He scowled at her. The black scorpion inked on his temple wrinkled, making the tail wrapped around his left eye twitch.

How to proceed?

For starters, she should probably stop staring at his tattoo.

She blinked and gave him a weak smile. His scowl deepened. She guessed she didn't look like the usual clientele, and there was no way she could pull off the femme fatale thing, especially not dressed like she'd just stepped out of an L. L. Bean catalog. Could she be Faulkner's sister? No. No one would believe they were related. But good girls fell for bad boys all the time.

She pulled the snapshot of Faulkner out of her purse. "I'm looking for my boyfriend." She wanted to vomit as she said it. "He was supposed to call me. . . ." She let the words trickle off.

His gaze dropped to the photo. His facial expression didn't change, but recognition flickered in his eyes. "Haven't seen him."

Oh yes he had. After eight years of teaching high school, Abby could spot a liar from fifty feet away.

She squeezed her eyes. Moisture gathered in the corners. She tried to look desperate. Unfortunately, it wasn't much of a stretch. "I'm really worried about him. He would never ignore my calls."

Big man's nose twitched as if he was trying not to laugh out loud. Clearly, he had no trouble believing Faulkner would ignore a girlfriend's calls. Abby tried to look even more wretched. She sniffed. "Are you sure?"

He sighed and looked again. "He might look familiar."

"Oh my God, really? If you could remember where you've seen him, I'd be grateful." Abby put the photo back into her purse and pulled out three twenties. She slid the bills across the counter.

Big man didn't hesitate. He swiped the money and stuffed it into the chest pocket of his flannel shirt. "He's in room 27, but I haven't seen him today."

"Thank you so much." Abby smiled and walked out. She got back into the car, conflicting nerves roiling in her belly. "He's here. Number 27."

Ethan's brows lifted in surprise. "Nice work."

"Thanks." Her mission had been successful, but now she had to face Faulkner. Her heart stuttered for a couple of beats. She inhaled deeply and held the breath in her lungs for a few seconds before letting it slide out through her nose.

Ethan reached for her hand. "It's OK. I'm here. I won't let anything happen to you."

Damn it. Abby believed him.

CHAPTER THIRTEEN

Unit 27 was at the other end of the property. Ethan surveyed the empty parking lot. Were the other units occupied? He drove over but parked a few units away. In case Faulkner was inside, Ethan didn't want him to have a clear view of the truck—and Abby.

On reflex, Ethan checked the weapon at his hip. "His mother said he was driving an old white Camaro, so it looks like he's not here. I'll just knock on the door to make sure. I want you to stay in the car. Keep your head down and the doors locked."

Abby opened her mouth.

Ethan cut off her protest. "It's not safe." He touched her forearm. "Plus, if he sees you, he might run."

"You're right. I wasn't going to argue. I was going to say be careful. Honestly, I doubt I could face him again." She sighed. Relief or regret? Just coming down here and facing the prosecutor proved Abby's courage, but Ethan had no doubt fear pulsed through Abby. The man who had terrorized her was staying twenty feet away.

"You shouldn't have to." Ethan squeezed her hand. It was steady. Amazing. "Do you want me to drop you at the diner down the road while I talk to him?"

"No. He's probably not here anyway." She took her cell phone out of her purse. "I'll have 911 ready to dial, just in case."

"OK." Ethan unzipped his jacket for access to his gun and got out of the car. He pointed at the door locks and waited for the click.

A few hundred yards down the road, they'd passed a road crew patching potholes. The smell of burning tar carried on the cold air. He approached door number 27. Stepping up onto the concrete walkway that fronted the building, he passed into the shade of the roof overhang. Without the sunlight on his back, the temperature dropped to butt-numbing. He tried to peer through the window, but the curtains were drawn. Standing to one side, he tilted his head and listened for a minute. When he heard no sounds from inside the unit, he tapped on the door.

No response. Ethan knocked again. All he heard was the *swish* of traffic on the highway. A tractor-trailer clattered past.

"Zeke? Zeke Faulkner." He probably wasn't here. Ethan tried one last time. He pounded on the door with a fist. The weak latch gave. The door eased open an inch. Sweat broke out on Ethan's back, and the hair on his nape lifted in alert. He pulled his gun, stepped behind the jamb, and nudged the door with a fingertip. A foul and distinctive stench wafted out of the room.

Shit.

The room was dark. His eyes probed the shadows. Nothing other than the usual motel fixtures. A duffel bag sat on the dresser, open. A shape lay on the bed.

Leading with his weapon, Ethan side-stepped into the room. He swept the gun around, but the space was empty.

Except for what was left of Zeke Faulkner, but he was no longer a threat.

At least Ethan was pretty sure the body on the bed was Faulkner. From the smell and the color of his skin, he'd been dead at least a day. A clear plastic bag covered his face, secured at the neck with duct tape. Under the plastic, his face was distorted and purple. His eyes bulged, and his black tongue protruded. Ethan looked away from his face. The body was dressed in jeans, a T-shirt, and a black hoodie. The sleeves and the pants' legs were pulled up slightly. Plastic zip ties bound his hands and ankles. He'd fought enough for the binds to have cut into his flesh, but there was no other blood on his body. The room was clean for a violent murder scene. The lamps were upright. No other signs of a struggle.

Either Zeke had known his attacker, the killer had incapacitated him immediately, or there'd been more than one assailant.

Not touching anything, Ethan squatted and checked under the bed. The bathroom was empty too. The sunshine seemed brighter when he went back outside.

A frigid gust kicked a plastic bag across the parking lot. Ethan sucked in a great big lungful of not quite fresh air. After the death-stench in the motel room, he welcomed the harsh smell of burnt tar.

Abby sat up in the passenger seat. She took one look at his face and paled. She got out of the truck. "What happened?"

She rose on her toes and craned her neck to look over his shoulder.

"Don't." He moved in front of her to block her view. "He's dead."

Abby had enough baggage. She didn't need to carry the grotesque sight of a suffocated man in her head. Ethan pulled out his cell phone and called the local police.

Abby waited until he disconnected the call. "How?" Her gaze searched his face. She wrinkled her nose. "Fight, gunshot, overdose?"

Ethan stayed downwind. Nothing short of double showers would erase the smell from his skin. "Oh no. This was definitely murder."

By the setup of the scene, it was a particularly vicious, cold, and methodical killing. Actually, the word in Ethan's mind was *execution*.

———————————

Faulkner was dead. Murdered.

Abby sat sideways on the edge of the passenger seat. Her feet rested on the running board. Standing next to the open door of his pickup, Ethan called his boss and reported in. Every time the wind shifted, the putrid smell on him wafted toward her.

Ethan lowered his phone and shoved it in his jacket pocket. Frustration brightened his eyes.

"Who would kill him?" This morning, she'd been afraid of seeing Faulkner. Now she was more frightened. How would she ever know if he was the one who'd poisoned her?

"He wasn't exactly a pillar of the community," Ethan said. "I looked up his official arrest record yesterday. Besides his conviction for kidnapping you, his arrest record was long and distinguished: couple of misdemeanor possession charges for marijuana, drunk and disorderly, simple assault, resisting arrest, etcetera. Since getting out of prison two weeks ago, he got involved in a lawsuit against the county over the disallowed evidence in his trial, and he ripped off his own mother. Who knows what else he did?"

Sirens announced the arrival of the local police. Abby was grateful that Ethan handled them, showing his badge and explaining why they'd come to talk to Faulkner. Abby didn't have much of a statement, which suited her just fine.

Despite the freezing temperature, she kept the pickup door open and watched the activity. Several more cars arrived, including the medical examiner. Ethan moved amongst the cops, but he always seemed to have her in his view. His concern warmed her.

What did Faulkner's death mean? Was he involved with other criminal behavior? Did his murder have anything to do with her case? And now that he was dead, how would she ever find out what had happened?

Too many questions without answers reeled in her belly. The smell of melted tar added to her nausea.

She wasn't sure how much time passed, an hour, maybe two, before Ethan came back to her side. "We can leave. They'll call us if they need anything else, and the detective is going to send a copy of your kidnapping case file to me."

He slid into the driver's seat, rolled down the window, and blasted the heat. "I'm sorry about the smell."

Abby closed her door. "It's not that bad," she lied.

He snorted but didn't argue.

"Faulkner's car is behind the Dumpsters." He backed out of the parking space.

"Why would he put it there?"

"Maybe he didn't want anyone to know where he was, or maybe the guy who killed him moved the car so it would look like Faulkner wasn't in the room." Ethan drove out of the lot onto the highway. A mile down the road, he pulled into a gas station and parked next to the restroom. He grabbed a gym bag from behind his seat. "Lock the door. I'll be right back."

When he came out, he was wearing sweatpants and a snug T-shirt. He locked his odorous clothes and leather jacket in a storage bin in the pickup bed before getting behind the wheel. He smelled much, much better.

His next stop was a fast-food joint. He followed the arrows to the drive-through window. "What do you want?"

"How can you be hungry?"

He shrugged. "We missed lunch, and the drive home is two and a half hours." He ordered a burger, large fries, and a Coke.

The smell of hot grease drifted in the window. Abby's stomach growled. She leaned across the cab. "Make that two of everything."

They ate in the parking lot. Abby scarfed the burger down embarrassingly fast. Ethan took the Atlantic City Expressway headed west. He had the window cracked. The blasting heat couldn't counter the freezing air whipping around the cab.

Sipping the remains of her icy soda, she shuddered hard. "Can we close the window?"

"Are you sure?" Ethan glanced over. "I smell pretty bad."

"I don't smell it at all now, and you have to be freezing." Not that she minded what he was wearing. The snug T-shirt outlined defined biceps and shoulders but was hardly winter wear.

"The odor must be imbedded in my sinuses." He raised the window.

"Thanks."

The sign for the Route 206 exit passed by the window. Abby sat up straighter. The greasy food in her belly did a cartwheel.

"Get off here." The words were out before she could stop them. Why did she want to torture herself?

Ethan exited without questioning. She directed him through more turns onto a long dirt road. They passed rows of blueberry bushes, winter-barren and scraggly in the sandy soil. It had been summer then. If it had been winter, she would have died of exposure. Gravel and sand crunched under the tires as the road cut through a patch of woods and emerged into a clearing. In the center was a partially collapsed house.

A strange detachment filled Abby. "Can you drive around back?"

The pickup bumped along the weedy earth. Behind the house, Ethan drew a sharp breath as he parked the truck. Just ahead was the well where Faulkner had kept her prisoner. She stared out the windshield, her mind sucked back through the black hole of time. Fear enveloped her as if she were back in the well all over again. She could see nothing but darkness. The sound of wind was muffled overhead. Had she been more afraid of what Faulkner would do to her when he came back? Or that he never returned?

"Abby?"

She startled.

Ethan was shaking her arm. His worried gaze searched her face. "Are you all right?"

She couldn't answer. The air felt hot and thick. Her breathing quickened. Her hand found the door release, and she stumbled out of the truck. Cold air, ripe with the scent of pine, washed over her. She leaned on her knees, gulped, and stared at the remnants of the well. Tree trunks swirled around her at dizzying speed. "They filled it in."

The stone circle was still visible, but someone had dumped a few tons of dirt into the hole since her kidnapping.

"That's where he kept you?" Ethan was next to her.

"Yes. It was about thirty feet deep. He covered the top with a few sheets of plywood." She raised her head. The trees had stopped spinning. "I don't know why we're here."

Ethan moved closer. He grasped her elbow and pulled her body straight. His arm came around her body. How could he be so warm? The outside temperature was in the midthirties, and he was in short sleeves. Abby was zipped into a down jacket and freezing to her bones. Shivers wracked her body.

He guided her back to the truck. He got behind the wheel and slid across the bench seat. Wrapping both arms around her, he drew her into a full embrace. Heat blasted from the vents, but it was Ethan's body that provided Abby with the warmth she sought.

She rested her head against his shoulder. "There was a little bit of water in the bottom. That's what kept me alive, plus the warm nights. It was summer."

His arms tightened around her. Her usual reaction when panic struck was to withdraw, but with Ethan, she couldn't get close enough. The feeling overwhelmed the anxiety rushing through her veins. Nearly frantic to touch more of him, she unzipped her jacket and pressed her body to his. Ethan worked his hands around, stroking her back through her sweater. He scooted closer and drew her onto his lap, as if he knew exactly what she needed: full body contact.

Curled in his arms, her heart rate slowed, and her lungs stopped heaving. She lifted her head. "I'm sorry."

"Don't be." He rested his chin on the top of her head.

"I don't know what made me want to come here."

"Faulkner is behind you now. Maybe you needed to put this memory in your past as well." Ethan put a finger under her chin and tipped her face up. "Start looking toward your future."

"I thought that's what I was doing when I moved to Westbury."

His eyes darkened. "Burying your past isn't the same as accepting and moving past it."

"The future is a moving target right now." Abby licked her lips.

Ethan ducked his head. Soft and warm, his lips touched hers.

Despite her surprise, it was Abby who took the kiss deeper, opening her mouth and welcoming him inside.

"More." Her hands clutched at his arms. Heat shimmered along her skin and bloomed deep in her belly.

"Shh." The fingers on her chin opened, cupping her jaw and angling her face. His tongue slid past her lips and explored her mouth with a thorough gentleness she imagined being extended to the rest of her body.

Abby tipped her head back and let the desire wash through her. Her blood thickened, and her pulse throbbed in her ears. Her hands relaxed, sliding from his arms to splay across his muscular chest. Ethan lifted his head. His eyes had darkened from piercing blue to navy. He kissed her jaw and temple.

She pulled her head back. "I need to take this slow."

His eyes didn't like it.

"My last relationship didn't end well."

"I thought you didn't have an ex." Ethan perked up. "Could he be involved in this?"

"No," Abby said. "It was over before Faulkner kidnapped me. He was older, and I fell for him in the most embarrassingly cliché trying-to-replace-the-father-I-didn't-have way."

"Everyone makes mistakes." Ethan brushed a thumb along her jaw. "What happened?"

"He neglected to tell me he was married." Years later, Abby could still feel the sting. "I'm not sure what was worse, the humiliation of being duped or the betrayal of being lied to for several months."

"That sucks. What a jerk." Ethan cupped her jaw.

Realization hit Abby. She trusted him. When was the last time she had trusted anyone? Her mother had let Abby down.

Her father wanted nothing to do with her. Brooke was her best friend and hadn't been able to break through the instinctive wall of suspicion that surrounded Abby's heart.

But in less than a week, Ethan was on the inside looking out. Was she rushing things? Was her reaction mainly physical? There was no denying the desire raging in her body. Perhaps she should slow down on the emotional confidence.

Abby leaned into his palm. "How about you? Any deep, dark secrets in your past?"

He snorted. "I haven't even had a date in ages."

"Why not?" What she meant to ask was how he kept women away.

"For years I was too busy taking care of the family," he said. "But they don't need me all the time anymore. I'm out of practice. It's probably best we take this nice and slow. I don't want regrets for either one of us. But I really like you."

"Me too." With a smile she felt all the way to her heart, she slid off his lap and straightened her jacket. "Maybe you're right about me wanting to come here today. Maybe I needed to see it couldn't happen again. I can't believe he's dead."

"He can't ever hurt you again." Ethan adjusted his sweatpants.

Abby averted her eyes, but not before she got an eyeful that demonstrated how much Ethan wanted her too, at least physically. The attraction went both ways. Good to know. Now back to the case. "Do you think Faulkner was the one who poisoned me?"

Ethan looked thoughtful. "I don't know."

"And who killed him?"

"I don't know that either, but I'm going to do my best to find out." Ethan turned the truck around.

Abby grabbed the armrest as the pickup bounced over a rut in the gravel and dirt road. "Where do we go next?"

"Home. But early tomorrow, I'll make some calls. The Harris cops said they'd keep me updated on Faulkner's homicide investigation. The autopsy will probably happen in the next day or so. I also have a call in to the detective who handled your case, Roy Abrams. He's retired now, but I'm sure he remembers plenty."

"I'm sure he does." Abby swallowed. The flush on her skin chilled. "It was his fault I wasn't found for so long."

CHAPTER FOURTEEN

Ethan's hand jerked on the wheel. The truck hit a tree root and nearly bottomed out. He straightened the vehicle, and it slid back into the ruts in the dirt. "What?"

"Faulkner had the address of the farm." She jerked a thumb over her shoulder in the direction of the truck's rear window. "It was in his cell phone the whole time. The detective never checked it out."

"That doesn't sound right." Ethan's jaw clenched. "Cell phones are one of the first things any good cop checks out. People keep half their lives in their phones."

Abby shrugged. "Just because you're a good cop doesn't mean they all are."

"True." The large majority of his fellow cops were honest and hardworking, but as in any profession, a handful were either incompetent or corrupt. "Are you sure it wasn't a legal hang-up? Sometimes cops get a bad rap simply for doing their jobs. The legal system doesn't always make sense, but we have to work within it."

"Not only did he mess up the investigation, but he tried to cover it up. I found out later, by accident," Abby shot back. "Do cops always stick together? Even when one of them is wrong?"

"Sometimes," Ethan admitted. Cops tended to close ranks when one of their own was threatened. "We depend on each other. Doubts about the loyalty of a team member can get a cop killed in a high-stress situation. You need to know without question that your partner has your back."

But the revelation about her kidnapping explained why she was so distrustful of him at first.

Abby didn't respond. She rested her head against the window and closed her eyes. At first Ethan thought she didn't want to talk to him anymore, but her even breathing convinced him she was asleep. She stayed that way for the next two hours, waking as he exited the Northeast Extension of the PA Turnpike.

"I'm sorry." She yawned and stretched. "I didn't mean to sleep."

"No worries. You were tired."

They'd left the dog at Brooke's house in case their trip ran late. Ethan pulled into the driveway, and Abby ran in to fetch Zeus. Then she shoehorned the big dog into the small backseat of Ethan's pickup.

"Will you be all right alone tonight?" Ethan pulled out of Brooke's driveway and headed for the main road. Abby's development was closer to town. A few miles later they passed the high school. A figure walked on the side of the road, his dark gray jacket and black backpack blending into the early winter twilight.

"Is that Derek?" Ethan slowed the truck. Zeus whined and stuck his head over the front seat.

"Yes," Abby said. "He must have stayed after school and missed the late bus."

Ethan pulled over in front of the boy. In the rearview mirror, he saw the kid stop. His posture said he was considering whether or not to run. Abby lowered the window, stuck her head out, and waved. Derek jogged to catch up.

"You want a ride?" Ethan asked.

Derek shrugged. "Sure."

Abby opened the door, and Derek squeezed into the back with the giant dog. Instead of moving over, Zeus practically sat on Derek's lap. The kid didn't seem to mind.

Ethan pulled back into traffic. He was supposed to be simplifying his life, paring it down, limiting his responsibilities. So why did it seem he was picking up needy strays at an alarming pace?

His phone vibrated. Cam's mobile number.

Ethan answered. "What's up?"

"I hate to bug you, but I could use you back home." A loud *thud* sounded over the connection. "Like now."

"What was that?" Ethan asked.

"That was Bryce trying to get a rope on the bay horse," Cam explained. "He's sick. We called the vet, but neither of us has been able to even get in the stall with him."

Ethan rapped the phone against his temple. He did not need this. He was spread as thin as a sheet of paper over his responsibilities. Cam and Bryce were going back to school the next day, and Mom was headed to her sister's house. Normally, Ethan would be looking forward to a few weeks of post-holiday alone time, but not this week. "I'm on my way."

He hung up and turned to Abby. "There's a small emergency at home. Do you mind if we stop at my place?"

Abby shook her head. "Of course not."

Ethan looked at Derek in the mirror. "Derek?"

"Nope." The kid draped a companionable arm around Zeus's neck.

"Do you need to call your mom?" Ethan held his cell over his shoulder in offer.

"Nah. She's at work." Derek turned his attention to the dog.

"OK. Thanks." Ethan made a U-turn toward home. Tomorrow he was calling Ronnie and pressuring her to find a foster home for those horses.

———————————

Abby sat up straighter. Nerves quivered fresh. She was going to see Ethan's house and meet his family. The truck turned into a gravel driveway next to a weather-beaten mailbox. There were no other houses in sight. A football field away, a white farmhouse sprawled in front of a small compound of outbuildings. Behind the barn, a snow-covered corral and pasture spread out to woods in the distance.

She got out of the truck. She folded the front seat to give Derek and Zeus more room to climb out. Abby looked up at the house. Three wide steps led to a front porch. Despite the fact that Christmas had passed three weeks before, an evergreen wreath decorated with a huge red velvet ribbon hung on the door.

She glanced over at Derek, who chewed a bit of skin from the side of his thumbnail. He looked as nervous as she felt.

What had it been like to be raised in the country? Abby's ears prickled at the lonely sound of wind whistling across the open land. She imagined you could sit on your deck in complete silence in the middle of the day, quite unlike the suburbs, where the sounds of lawn equipment and kids punctuated the weekends.

"Oh good, the vet's here." A MINI Cooper, a midsize SUV, and a large white van were lined up in the yard. Ethan led the way into the barn. Abby and Derek hesitated at the door.

"It's OK. You can come in." Ethan wiggled his fingers in a *come along* gesture. The most trusting of them, Zeus, followed him first.

Three men and a woman were gathered around a half door. The woman was striking. Even in her bulky winter gear, she was tall and thin, her long black hair partially covered with a watch cap. She turned to Ethan, and her mouth opened in a warm smile. An unexpected shaft of jealousy speared Abby. She tamped it down. She and Ethan had shared one kiss, one desperate embrace born as much from her loneliness and raging emotions as her desire. She had no claims to him.

Abby blinked away to study the two younger men, also tall and slim, with the same black hair and bright blue eyes as Ethan. His brothers. Which made the remaining man the vet.

"Abby, Derek, these are my brothers, Bryce and Cam." Ethan gestured. Cam was clean-cut, while Bryce wore his long hair in a ponytail. Other than their hairstyles, their features were identical. Twins?

"This is Doc White." The vet was to people what Zeus was to dogs. The huge white-haired man, dressed in winter coveralls, nodded at them.

Ethan's open hand shifted to the gorgeous woman. "And my cousin, Ronnie."

Cousin? Abby perked up. The relief that swept through her was as unexpected as her earlier prick of jealousy. One kiss. That's all it had been, and it likely meant more to her than Ethan, since she'd been the one melting down.

"Nice to meet you." Ronnie walked over and shook their hands. A patch on her jacket identified her as a humane society police officer.

Next to Derek's shoulder, a reddish nose poked over the nearest stall and snorted. A pony head followed, barely reaching over the half door.

Derek's eyes brightened. "Can I pet him?"

"Sure." Ethan rubbed the pony's nose. "This little guy is as friendly as a puppy."

"What's his name?" Derek mimicked Ethan, stroking the pony between its soft brown eyes. Zeus put his front paws on the stall door. Mutual sniffs were exchanged. The dog wagged his tail. The pony pricked its ears.

Ethan frowned. "He doesn't have a name. These horses aren't ours. We're fostering them for the humane society."

Abby glanced over the stall door. The blanket didn't cover the bony neck. She didn't know much, OK anything, about horses, but she recognized a starving animal when she saw it.

The vet cleared his throat, and Ethan's attention moved to the next stall, where Abby assumed the sick horse was kept.

"Bryce, why don't you take Abby and Derek into the house? It's cold out here," Ethan said.

Bryce raised a brow and pointedly looked at Abby. "Really? With Mom?"

Ethan sighed. "Just tell her they're hungry. That ought to keep her busy."

Bryce laughed. "Come on up to the house." He waved toward the exit.

Abby glanced over her shoulder. Ethan approached the stall door. He plucked a rope from a wall hook and walked inside without hesitating. A few seconds later, he emerged with a horse on the other end of the lead. The nylon was slack with no tension. The horse stopped and gave the vet a nervous eye roll. Without looking back, Ethan left the rope loose and took a step. The horse shifted forward and followed. Ethan turned. The horse stopped, stretching its nose toward his face. For a minute, they seemed to be sharing breaths—or thoughts. Ethan raised a hand and rested it on the thin neck. The horse sighed. Its head lowered as its spine relaxed.

Goose bumps rose on Abby's arm. She knew how the horse felt. Ethan had the same effect on her.

"Amazing." The vet straightened and moved toward the animal. "You still have the touch, my friend."

Ethan moved his hand, rubbing a spot at the base of the horse's neck. "He just needs someone to trust."

"Don't we all," said the vet.

As Abby left the barn, she could hear Ethan and the vet discussing possible infections and feeding issues.

She closed the big wooden door quietly and hurried to catch up with Bryce and Derek. Twilight was settling over the snowy yard in shades of gray and white. Bryce opened the back door. Abby, Derek, and Zeus followed him inside. They hung their coats on hooks in the mudroom. A short hallway opened into a spacious living room. Two overstuffed sofas and a recliner clustered around a stone fireplace. A flat-screen TV hung on the wall, and a Christmas tree glittered in the corner. The room was furnished for comfort, not aesthetics. Abby wanted to start a fire, take off her shoes, and curl up with a good book and a glass of wine. A big glass.

An old tomcat stood at the entrance to the kitchen.

"Oh look, a cat," Abby said.

"Oh shit! Where?" Bryce whirled.

"It's OK. Zeus likes cats," Abby said.

"It's not the cat I'm worried about." Bryce lunged, but before he could snag the big dog's collar, Zeus shuffled up to the cat, sniffed, and wagged his tail. The scraggly feline arched its back and hissed in its best impression of the dead cat from *Pet Sematary*.

Zeus cocked his head and backed up a step. With an ear-splitting yowl, the cat attacked, jumping forward at lightning speed and swiping at the dog's gigantic nose with one taloned paw. Zeus yelped. He shook his massive, loose-lipped head, sending gobs of spit and drops of blood flying through the air.

"Sweetums, stop that!" Bryce changed direction, heading for the cat, but Sweetums was on the offensive. Zeus backed up at warp speed through the living room, upending an end table in his path. The cat chased the retreating canine across the debris.

"Oh dear. Come here, Sweetums. Bad cat." A slim blonde woman hustled through the doorway just as Zeus backed into and over the cheerfully decorated Christmas tree. The six-foot artificial evergreen went over with a creak and crash. The sound of glass bulbs breaking and lights popping filled the room, accompanied by more high-pitched howling from the dog and hissing and spitting from Sweetums. The woman swooped up the cat and tucked it under one arm.

Abby was unable to move. Shock and embarrassment rendered her motionless. Her larynx froze in horror. Then she heard an unbelievable sound. Ethan's mother was laughing, and it wasn't just a giggle, it was a full belly roar.

Bryce grabbed Zeus's collar. He sighed. "Abby, Derek, this is my mom, Lorraine Hale."

"Mrs. Hale, I'm so sorry," Abby stuttered.

"Please call me Lorraine, and you have no reason to apologize." Lorraine laughed so hard that she dropped the cat. Sweetums climbed a nearby bookshelf.

"Where's the video camera when you need it?" Lorraine slapped her knee and lowered her body to the living room chair. Tears streamed down her face, and she snorted indelicately.

"That would've taken the grand prize." She sniffed and tried to catch her breath.

Derek and Bryce stared at the carnage of broken ornaments, overturned furniture, and the felled tree with identical expressions of disbelief.

Cam came in from the mudroom. "What the hell happened in here?"

"Zeus met Sweetums," Bryce said.

"I take it Sweetums was his charming self?" Cam asked dryly.

"The gracious host, as always." Bryce let go of the dog. Zeus tucked his tail between his muscular legs. Strands of tinsel hung from his ears, and blood dripped from his nose onto the hardwood floor.

"You know, I think you were right, boys. It's past time to take down the tree." Lorraine took a ragged breath and stood up, extending her hand to Abby. "I'm the one who should be apologizing. Your poor dog! He's terrified. Sweetums can be territorial."

From his elevated perch, Sweetums stared down at the dog and humans below with pure feline disdain.

Zeus whimpered.

"He won't bite, will he?" Lorraine contemplated the giant canine.

"Oh no. Zeus is very gentle. He wouldn't have hurt the cat."

"I wish I could say the same for Sweetums." Lorraine held her hand out for Zeus to sniff. His tail rose a few inches, and just the tip wagged. "You just ignore that mean old cat. Let's get you in the kitchen and wash that scratch."

Lorraine herded Zeus toward a doorway. She gave out orders with a glance over her shoulder. "Cam, get the vacuum. Bryce, haul that tree back to the basement. Derek, would you mind helping?"

"No, ma'am," Derek answered.

Abby followed Lorraine into a large country kitchen. A long trestle table occupied half the space. Worn cabinets formed an L along the remaining walls. Pots and pans, their copper bottoms discolored from age and use, hung from a circular rack. Lorraine's kitchen was no fancy entertainment space. It was a workroom.

Abby's finger trailed along the scrubbed-smooth table. "I'm sorry about the mess."

"Don't give it another thought. I raised three boys. This old house has seen it all." Lorraine pulled a first aid kit from the kitchen drawer. She dabbed some antiseptic ointment on Zeus's nose. The dog stood quietly for her. "He's a very nice dog. I imagine he can be fierce if he wants to be, though."

"Yes, I guess he could."

Lorraine packed away the first aid kit and moved to the freezer. "Do you and Derek like spaghetti and meatballs?"

"Oh, we can't trouble you for dinner," Abby protested.

"Nonsense. I'm cooking anyway." Lorraine gave Abby an appraising stare. "In fact, you should stay in our guest room tonight."

"What?"

"Well, Ethan's going to be tied up with the horse for quite a while, and you really shouldn't be alone, should you?"

Shame filled Abby. "What did Ethan tell you about me?"

"Honey, I've been on the committee of the Methodist church for more than thirty years. Ethan doesn't have to tell me anything about what goes on in this town." Lorraine put an arm on her shoulder.

Abby had no words.

"Why don't you go out to the barn and let Ethan know you'll be staying." Lorraine steered Abby toward the back door.

"Yes, ma'am." Abby zipped her coat. Wait. Had she even agreed?

CHAPTER FIFTEEN

Ethan leaned his forearms on the half door. Inside the stall, the bay horse dozed, head low. But the animal's sleep was restless. Its hips shifted restlessly as it transferred weight from one rear hoof to the other.

The barn door opened. Cold night air—and Abby—rushed in. A healthy pink flush colored her cheeks. The change was welcome after the despair she'd emitted at the sight of the filled-in well that afternoon.

"Dinner will be ready soon." Her warm brown eyes peered out from beneath a black knit cap pulled low on her forehead. Too-large gloves flapped on her delicate hands. Both were his, extra sets kept in the mudroom. At the sight of her in his outerwear, his heart did a touchdown dance.

He was an idiot. And he was beginning to think he was an idiot in big trouble. Every time she blinked those big brown eyes at him he remembered their kiss, and he wanted to do it again. This time without all the despair. He wanted her edgy with desire instead. "What are we having?"

"Spaghetti and meatballs." She sidled up next to him and peeked into the stall. "How is he?"

"The vet thinks he'll be OK. Probably an infection of some sort—not a surprise considering where the poor guy lived." He told her about the rescue.

"The poor thing."

"Ronnie says she's seen worse pull through." But the horse's lethargy worried him.

"Can you come in to eat, or do you need to stay out here?" She turned.

Ethan glanced at the bay. "I don't want to leave him just yet in case he has a reaction to the medication. Cam or Bryce can come down after dinner and take a turn."

"You must be hungry," she said.

"I am." Ethan dipped his head and caught her mouth. The kiss was soft and sweet. "That'll tide me over."

Her eyes darkened, and Ethan's pulse kicked into second gear.

"Did I mention your mother invited me to stay in your guest room tonight?"

"Invited?" Ethan raised a disbelieving brow.

"Well, suggested." Abby's mouth pursed. "OK, *insisted* is probably a better word."

"Don't feel bad." Ethan grinned and threw an arm around her shoulders. "My mom can twist a conversation until you don't know what's happening. Let me guess, you were nodding your head and had no idea what you were agreeing to?"

Abby blushed. "I'm sorry. I should have said no. I should have checked with you. Do you mind?"

Ethan grinned. "No. It's fine as long as she didn't bully you into it."

"Bully me?" Abby said. "Your mom is one of the sweetest people I've ever met."

"Yes, that's one of the many weapons in her arsenal." Ethan brushed his mouth against hers again.

Abby laughed. Pleasure filled Ethan's chest at the sound. He could overlook his family's idiosyncrasies if his mom and brothers could make Abby smile.

"It's a great idea. After dinner I'll run Derek home, and you can pick up a change of clothes." He brushed his lips against hers again then lifted his head. "Is Derek OK?"

Abby's smile turned fake. "Sure."

"I get the feeling his home life isn't the best."

"Not everyone lives the American dream."

"Yeah. I know that," Ethan said. "I looked him up in the system the other day." Derek had been in the foster system a few years ago.

Abby stiffened. "Krista cleaned herself up."

"Is she clean now?" Ethan hated asking the hard questions, but Derek's safety had to take precedence.

Abby's eyes glittered with moisture. "Does his file say anything about the two older boys who beat him and tried to molest him while he was in foster care?" Her voice turned tight and angry.

"No." Ethan blew out a hard breath. "Poor kid."

"Yeah." Abby sniffed. "The system is a big roulette wheel."

The tone of her voice set off an alarm inside Ethan. "Were you ever in it?"

Abby rolled a piece of hay between her fingers. "Once, for a couple of weeks when I was seven. My mother had been drinking, and a neighbor called social services. Scariest time of my life."

Ethan's insides clenched with pity. "What happened?"

"Nothing really. The parents pretty much left me alone. Other than providing meals, they didn't do much for any of the kids. It was the other foster children who scared me. The oldest was a girl of about fourteen. She stole my doll on the first night and made it clear she'd hurt me if I breathed a word of it. She didn't need to threaten me. Like most of the others, I was already conditioned to keep my mouth shut."

The image of a frightened seven-year-old Abby sent Ethan's empty gut into another spasm.

"I'm sorry."

"Mom sobered up and got me back." Her voice steadied. "It never happened again."

"Did she drink often?"

Abby lifted a noncommittal shoulder. "No. Mostly after a rare visit from my father. He was the love of her life, but he was already married and refused to leave his wife and kids."

Ethan pulled her closer. They stood in silence for a few minutes, then her body relaxed and her head dropped onto his shoulder. Warmth filled Ethan, the cold of the barn forgotten. He kissed the top of her head. "You should go eat."

She lifted her head, rose onto her toes, and gave him a soft kiss. "I can wait for you."

Ethan liked the sound of that. Too much. Somewhere in the back of his mind he remembered vowing to simplify his life, but it seemed he was doing the exact opposite. Abby and Derek were working their way into his heart. And he'd taken in two horses he needed about as much as frostbite.

While he teased Abby about his mother's interference, he was glad she'd taken the initiative. Faulkner was dead, but Ethan couldn't shake the anxiety that gripped him when he thought about Abby's case.

Maybe it was Faulkner who'd tried to kill her. But why? What did he have to gain? Risking freedom for revenge didn't make sense when the man was already involved in a lawsuit that could score him cash.

Despite Abby's claim that Abrams screwed up her case, Ethan hoped retired detective Roy Abrams had some ideas. Because if it hadn't been Faulkner who poisoned her, then who wanted Abby dead?

Shivering on his front porch, Derek turned the knob. The front door was locked. Weird. Mom never locked up until Derek was home. And when she was lost in her current boyfriend, it was usually Derek who locked the house up for the night.

He fished his key from his front pocket. The rumble of the garage door startled him. He peered around a porch post. Joe carried a black lawn and leaf bag out of the garage.

Huh. Tomorrow wasn't trash day. Apprehension trickled down Derek's spine.

The garage door rolled closed. Joe hefted the bag down the driveway. He tossed it into the bed of his truck, got into the vehicle, and drove away. Strange.

Derek went into the house. "Mom?"

He followed the sound of the fridge opening and closing to the kitchen. His mom was popping the top off a beer. He could tell by the glassy shine in her eyes that it wasn't her first.

"What's Joe doing?" he asked.

Fear broke through the haze in Mom's gaze. "I don't know. He said he had to run an errand, and he'd be right back." She picked the edge of the beer label and glanced at the door.

"No work tonight?"

She worked a tiny strip of label and turned the bottle, peeling the paper away in a long strip like an apple skin. "Maybe tomorrow." She raised the bottle to her lips and drank.

Derek knew better than to press the issue. If she felt overwhelmed, she'd only drink more. She took her beer into the family room. Derek checked the pantry. She hadn't gone shopping. Good thing he'd filled up on spaghetti and meatballs at Ethan's house.

A stab of envy hit him in his full belly. Ethan had cool brothers and a mom who would never drink until she forgot to feed him. Mrs. Hale wouldn't tolerate the likes of Joe either. Ethan was winning Abby over too, with the same quiet way that he charmed that horse.

Derek pictured Joe again. What had been in that trash bag?

He went to the living room and peered through the window at the street. Joe wasn't back yet. Derek hurried back through the house to the door in the laundry room that led into the garage. His gaze swept over the piles of rusted junk. Nothing unusual.

Derek traced his steps into the house. The basement door was under the stairwell in the living room. He opened the door and flipped on the light. A strange smell drifted up the steps. Derek started down, the meatballs and tomato sauce tumbling through his belly. His sneakers squeaked on the wooden treads.

He scanned the unfinished cellar. Boxes of discarded crap still dominated the room, but the windows had been covered with towels. In the far corner, the clutter had been shoved out of the way. The items that sat on a discarded table brought the taste of Italian seasonings into Derek's throat: a scale, a hot plate, and rubber gloves.

An engine rumbled from the street. Derek bolted back up the steps. He didn't stop until he was locked in his bathroom. The situation had just gone from a yellow caution to red alert.

There was only one reason Joe would have a scale and a hot plate in the basement. He was cooking meth.

Derek leaned over the toilet and heaved up his spaghetti and meatballs. With the food's exit from his body, every ounce of contentedness from the evening was replaced with terror.

Derek flushed the toilet, turned on the faucet, and splashed cold water on his face. As he brushed his teeth, possible outcomes ripped through his mind, each one a nightmare scenario. Was his mom using yet? Given her weaknesses, it was only a matter of time.

What should he do?

The card Ethan had given him poked his thigh through the thin fabric of his front pocket. Derek memorized the number, ripped up the card, and flushed it down the toilet. No point in giving Joe a good reason to kill him.

But there was no way Derek could maintain his current air of invisibility.

He had to stop Joe before he blew up the house and Derek and his mom both ended up dead. But how?

CHAPTER SIXTEEN

Late-morning sunlight slanted over the dormant grass of the backyard. Looking out the kitchen window of his one-story house, Roy Abrams chugged his third cup of coffee. His rise-at-dawn habit had gradually faded over the past year, but this was fucking ridiculous. Even though he'd slept until ten o'clock, he was still achy and stupid from another restless night. It wasn't his conscience that kept him awake. He had to get up and take a weak-ass leak every two hours. Some days he felt like he was ninety instead of fifty-seven. Maybe being a cop had aged him prematurely.

Getting old sucked.

In the summer, he spent his days on the water. The sea air and physical exertion wore him out until his body passed out at the end of the day. But in the winter, he had nothing to do but scratch his own ass.

If the housing market in Jersey hadn't tanked, he'd have moved to Florida when he retired. He should have squeezed just a little more cash out of that last deal. When the payee coughed up that much dough without any attempt at negotiation, Roy knew he'd set his price too low.

But on the other hand, dead men couldn't spend a nickel.

Rays of sunlight splashed over his pride and joy, an eighteen-foot Grady-White fishing boat with a center console and a 150-horsepower four-stroke outboard engine. The trailer took up a quarter of his small rear yard, but what the hell else was he going to do with the space? His next-door neighbor had a swing set for his grandkids, three loud and whiny toddlers the older couple babysat regularly. Roy didn't have grandchildren. Both his marriages had failed before kids had even been considered. Thank God.

A sudden wind gust sliced across the yard. The cover on his boat flapped. One of the cords must have loosened. This winter had been brutally cold and windy. Roy went to the closet and pulled out a coat. Shrugging into it, he fished in the pockets for a hat and a pair of gloves, then went out the back door in the laundry room.

God damn, it was cold. He hunched his shoulders and tucked his chin behind the neck of his jacket. Bits of crusted snow crunched under his sneakers. The cold blasted through his jeans before he'd crossed the twenty feet of brown grass that comprised his backyard.

A cursory inspection revealed a snapped bungee cord. Roy ducked into the shed for a new one. A few deft movements later, the cover was secure and his boat was protected. He ran a hand across the gleaming white fiberglass hull.

Yes, he'd splurged. But he deserved the best. He'd gone through hell for the money to buy this boat. His moment of genius had bought him a shitload of grief.

But that was all in the past. He had years left to enjoy the fruits of his nasty labor. He sure as hell couldn't have afforded the Grady-White on his pension alone. Damn it. He'd put his life on the line for decades. He deserved something nice for his retirement.

He gave the hull a final caress and headed back to the house and a hot cup of coffee. Maybe he'd drive down to the bakery for fresh doughnuts. Back in the laundry room, the heat stung his cold-raw face. He stripped off his outdoor gear. Rubbing his hands together and blowing into his fists, he went into the kitchen.

He picked up the glass carafe, side-stepped to the sink, and dumped the half inch of lukewarm coffee. He rinsed the pot and refilled the machine.

Fabric whispered. Roy froze. His shoulder blades itched, and his bowels cramped. His long career as a cop gave him extra senses, and right now they were telling him he wasn't alone.

His gaze shifted to the blur of a figure in the shiny chrome of the toaster. He eyed the knife block, but it was out of reach. The glass coffeepot was the only weapon at hand. Roy's fingers tightened on the handle. The figure moved. Roy started to whirl around, but a body slammed into his back. The coffeepot was knocked from his hand. Glass shattered on tile. A cord whipped around his neck. Thin and flexible, it cut off his next breath like a blade.

He grabbed for his throat and tried to work his fingers under the cord. But even as he struggled, he knew it was pointless. His attacker was bigger and stronger and had the element of surprise on his side.

Plus, the confidence in the grip suggested this wasn't his first time. Pain bloomed like a Roman candle on the Fourth of July, overwhelming Roy's senses.

His sight dimmed. The cord sliced deeper into his flesh. He gave his life one more last-ditch effort. He reached up and tried to claw for his assailant's eyes. The guy shifted backward to avoid Roy's hands. A knee slammed into his back, but he barely felt the kidney slam as he was hauled into a backbend. Agony exploded in his neck as the cord tightened more, cutting into his windpipe.

His lungs screamed, and his sight dimmed. His last vision was the sunlight glimmering on the ill-gotten boat in his yard.

What awaited him, heaven or hell?

———————

Abby tiptoed into the kitchen in her socks. One hand held Zeus's collar. Her boots dangled from the other. Sweetums was not in sight. Abby checked the top of the fridge and under the kitchen table before releasing the dog. Zeus headed for the large bowl of water Lorraine had placed on the floor. Abby poured some of the dog food she'd brought into a bowl. While the dog ate, she crossed to the window.

Behind the house, sunrise gleamed on the frozen yard and white-patched barn roof.

Where was Ethan?

They'd had dinner together. He'd driven her home to pack a bag and drop off Derek. Then she'd gone to bed in the guest room, and he'd returned to the barn to check on the horse.

"Good morning." Lorraine buzzed into the kitchen in a floor-length robe. "I'll have coffee on in a minute."

"No rush," Abby said.

"Sure there is. No sense in wasting daylight." Lorraine started the fire under a huge griddle. She grabbed a dozen eggs from the refrigerator. A full pound of bacon went into the two-burner pan. She went to the bottom of the staircase in the hall. "Boys! Breakfast in ten."

Footsteps thudded on the steps. Cam and Bryce walked in.

"Cam, please start coffee. Bryce, you're on scrambled eggs." Lorraine gave orders in a sweet voice that her sons jumped to obey. "Where's Ethan?"

"Not in his room." Cam filled the coffeemaker.

Abby pulled her boots on. "I'm going to take Zeus out."

Lorraine moved bacon slices in the hot pan. "I imagine Ethan is out in the barn. Would you tell him to come in for breakfast?"

"Yes, ma'am." Abby donned her coat and Ethan's hat and gloves in the mudroom. Zeus cowered against her legs. Abby spied Sweetums glaring down at the dog from the space between the laundry cabinets and the ceiling.

She opened the back door, and Zeus trotted out into the snowy yard, relief evident in the spring in his step. Typically, he was a slow mover.

Her breath fogged in front of her as she rolled the heavy door open just enough to squeeze through. The barn wasn't much warmer. The pony greeted her with a happy snort. Abby patted his nose as she walked by. She looked over the half door.

The horse was curled on its side in the middle of the stall. In the corner beyond, Ethan slept sitting up, hat pulled low on his brow, arms crossed over his chest, hands tucked into his armpits.

Had he been there all night?

At the sight of Abby, the horse heaved to its feet. It turned its head and nosed Ethan. His eyes opened. He touched the animal's forehead. "How're you feeling?"

The horse snorted. Ethan brushed at the front of his jacket and laughed. "That good, huh?"

He stood and stretched. His black hair was mussed, his jaw was shadowed, and his blue eyes were heavy with compassion and lack of sleep. He was the sexiest man she'd ever seen.

Inside her boots, Abby's toes curled. "Good morning."

He turned. His blue eyes brightened, and his mouth curled in a sexy smile. "Morning."

"Breakfast is almost ready."

"Great. I'm starving."

"Did you stay out here all night?"

He rubbed the horse's neck and let himself out of the stall. "Nah. Just from two to six. Cam and Bryce each took a shift."

She nodded toward the horse. "He looks better this morning."

"He does." Ethan exhaled. "I'd kiss you, but I haven't brushed my teeth."

Abby popped up on her toes and planted a kiss on his mouth. "I don't care."

He wrapped his arms around her waist and pulled her to his chest. His stubble scraped her cheek. The hug was more about comfort and companionship than sex and felt more intimate. He released her. "How did you sleep?"

"Great." Better than she had for years, which was strange. She'd left her light on, but the rest of the house had been dark. It hadn't bothered her. Was that because she hadn't been alone? Or because Faulkner was dead and that chapter of her life was finally closed? She wouldn't ever have to worry about what would happen after he was paroled.

Ethan gave the horses a small amount of hay, and they left the barn.

Abby glanced back at the closed door. "Will he be all right alone today?"

Cam was driving Lorraine to the airport in Scranton for her Florida-bound flight. Later that afternoon, he and Bryce were driving back to school. Abby and Ethan were headed back to Jersey to talk to retired detective Roy Abrams.

"Yeah. I'll give him his medicine before we leave, and Ronnie is sending one of her staff over to babysit while we're gone."

Breakfast was noisy and fast. The three men ate more food in one meal than Abby and her mother had consumed in a week.

Two hours later, Abby and Ethan were on the way to see Roy Abrams in Greenland, New Jersey, a shore town fifty miles north of Atlantic City.

"Does he know we're coming?" Abby asked.

"No," Ethan said. "After what you told me yesterday, I thought it might be best if we just dropped in on him. The cop who gave me his address said if it's too cold to fish, Roy should be home."

"What else did the Harris cop say?" Abby plucked an animal hair from her jeans.

"They don't have much to say yet. There were a few defensive bruises on Faulkner, but his struggle couldn't have lasted long. He died of suffocation. No sign that the room was broken into, but the lock was old and outdated. A toddler could've picked it. They'll call me when they have the full autopsy report."

"Faulkner wasn't a genius, but he was cagey and physically strong." Abby sipped coffee from a travel mug. "How did someone overpower him that easily?" Faulkner had tossed her over his shoulder as if she were a bag of mulch. She doubted he'd allowed his muscles to deteriorate in prison.

"I don't know." Ethan exited the Garden State Parkway. "Hopefully the medical examiner will figure that out."

He followed the voice on his GPS and turned into a retirement community of nearly identical one-story homes. A boat and trailer dominated the rear yard of Roy Abrams's house and distinguished it from his neighbors' cookie-cutter units.

Ethan parked at the curb. "How were things between you and Detective Abrams? Do you want to wait in the car?"

"No. I'll come in." Abby unsnapped her seat belt. "I didn't really talk to Abrams that much. He interviewed me after I was pulled out of the well, but I spent more time at the prosecutor's office prepping for the trial. Abrams avoided me, probably because he'd messed up so badly. The missing address issue didn't come out until later."

"You never had a confrontation with him?"

"No." She stared at the house that belonged to the man whose incompetence nearly killed her. Coffee and anxiety stirred up acid in her gut. No butterflies for her. Tension flapped in her stomach like the wings of a giant luna moth. "I won't hide anymore, Ethan."

"OK then. Let's go." Ethan gave her hand a quick squeeze before opening his door. "Maybe guilt will loosen his tongue."

They headed up the walk. Abby squinted against sunbeams reflecting off the freshly waxed paint of a Cadillac. "His car looks new."

"The boat does too." Ethan put his hand on the small of her back. She didn't need steering, and the possessive gesture sent those nerves in her belly flying in a whole different direction.

Ethan knocked on the door. The sound of footsteps sounded through the door, but the door didn't open.

He pressed the doorbell but nothing happened. "Must be broken. It sounds like he's in the back of the house. Maybe he can't hear well." He jogged off the cement stoop.

Abby followed him around to the rear yard. Ethan climbed three concrete steps to the back door. He raised his hand to knock. The door flew open. An arm jutted out, striking Ethan in the jaw and knocking him off the step. Abby skidded to a stop next to Ethan on the brown grass.

The man on the stoop was tall and slim, wearing a black hoodie pulled over his head and a black bandana over his face. His eyes were gray and cold as stainless steel. He took a step toward Ethan, stunned on the grass. Abby reached down and pulled Ethan's gun from the holster. She pointed it at the man with both hands, snapping into correct shooting form as if her mother was still alive and shouting instructions in her ear.

The man changed course and headed for the back of the yard at a dead run.

Ethan leaped to his feet. His shocked gaze landed on Abby, then his gun in her hand. She handed him the weapon.

"Wait here." He took off after the intruder.

"Like hell." Abby stuck close to him as he sprinted after the fleeing man. There was no way she was waiting by herself. There could be more than one intruder, and Ethan had the gun. The intruder disappeared over the chain-link fence that led into the neighbor's yard.

"Hey," Ethan yelled and pulled ahead. He vaulted over the fence. Landing, he yelled something back at her.

But Abby couldn't make out the words. She stopped to climb the fence. Her jacket caught on a metal loop. Why hadn't she learned to hurdle on the track team? Ethan drew ahead.

Once on open land, though, Abby caught up. The guy they were chasing set a brutal pace, and they didn't gain any ground. He disappeared down an alley lined on both sides with some type of evergreen shrubs. The greenery blocked visibility. They stopped. Breathing hard, Ethan shot her a *what the hell* glare and pushed her behind him as he peered around the corner. An engine started.

Ethan sprinted down the alley. Abby followed. They emerged just in time to see a dark sedan disappear around a corner two blocks away. Ethan took off after it, cutting through a service alley. Abby kept pace. The sedan halted at a stop sign.

"Stop!" Ethan darted out in front of the vehicle, took an official looking stance, and pointed his gun at the windshield. Confusion and then frustration played over his face. He lowered the gun.

A little old lady sat behind the wheel, complete with a puffy white hairdo and thick trifocals. Ethan tapped on her window and flashed his badge. When she lowered it, he glanced in the backseat. "We're chasing a fugitive. Would you please open the trunk, ma'am."

"Of course." She complied. The trunk bounced up. Gun at the ready, Ethan peered inside.

"I'm sorry to bother you, ma'am." He tipped his head.

"It's no problem, Officer." She gave him a serious nod. "I hope you catch him."

Ethan moved out of the street. She drove away, bumping over the curb and scraping the undercarriage of the sedan on the concrete.

"I thought out-of-state cops didn't have jurisdiction." Abby joined him on the sidewalk.

"We don't, but her glasses were so thick, I doubt she could see my badge at all."

"Tricky."

"Desperate." Ethan bent double and wheezed. "Did you get the make or model of the car?"

"No." Abby shook her head. "Dark blue four-door. That's all I saw. At least that's what I thought I saw. Maybe that wasn't even him. Maybe that was her."

Ethan scrubbed his face with both hands. He coughed and squinted at her with suspicion. "You're barely winded."

"I shouldn't be winded at all. I've missed my last few runs." Abby leaned forward and stretched her hamstrings. He was still staring at her. "I can run a marathon in under three hours."

"You run marathons?" Walking in a circle, Ethan holstered his gun. He pulled out his phone, called 911, and reported the incident. "The car was a four-door, dark blue. No, I don't know the make or model."

He ended the call and turned to Abby. "So, you handle a gun like a trained law enforcement officer. You run sub-three-hour marathons. What else don't I know about you?"

"I don't know." Abby followed him as he turned back toward Roy Abrams's house. "A lot of things, I guess."

His question was a reminder that they barely knew each other. Though the familiarity between them was hard to ignore.

"We have to work on that." He broke into a loose jog.

Oh.

Abby's heartbeat sped up when it should have been slowing down.

As they hustled back to Abrams's house, Ethan scanned their surroundings and stayed just ahead of her. Crossing the rear yard, Ethan went to the back door. He knocked. No answer.

"Did he already break in, or did we stop him?" she asked. But the little hairs on the back of her neck were tingling. Something was wrong here. She could feel it. Despite the heat generated by her body from the run, goose bumps rose on her arms.

Ethan walked up to the back window. He cupped his hand over his eyes. "He was already inside."

"Shouldn't we see if he's still alive?" Abby stepped toward the window.

Ethan caught her by the upper arms. "Don't."

But she'd already caught sight of the body on the floor. She barely recognized the retired detective with a discolored face, bulging eyeballs, and a swollen, protruding tongue. Her thigh muscles trembled. Her stomach heaved.

Ethan grabbed her elbow and lowered her to the concrete step. "Is that him?"

"Yes." Sirens sounded in the distance. Abby rested her forehead on her bent knees. Nothing would remove that image from her head.

There was no question. Roy Abrams was dead.

CHAPTER SEVENTEEN

Ryland's phone buzzed in his pocket. Equal parts apprehension and irritation washed through him. All he wanted to do was watch his grandson's school concert. Was that too much to ask? He checked the screen. Kenneth.

Apparently it was.

"Excuse me," Ryland whispered in Marlene's ear.

Sitting in the folding metal chair next to him, she frowned at his vibrating cell. Her hair was a soft brown, and except for the lines of disapproval currently creasing her face, her skin was remarkably smooth for her age. He patted her toned thigh. Outfitted in a slim skirt and matching jacket, her body put younger women to shame. Of course, he paid for the best in personal training and a few well-timed surgical enhancements to keep her looking her best. Nothing drastic, just a few touch-ups, regular injections, and beauty treatments

"Only a moment. I promise," he whispered. "It's ten in the morning on a workday." Her flashing eyes said she knew this but didn't have to like it.

He appreciated her temper. Marlene was no pushover, a contributing factor to the length of their marriage and one of the reasons Ryland had given up his extramarital indulgences. His young-blonde habit was over. He regretted many of the decisions he'd made as a younger man. His business wasn't the only part of his life getting a remodel.

She turned back to the stage, where a grade-schooler played a poignant classical piece on the piano. Their seven-year-old grandson waited in the wings. The private school his grandchildren attended cultivated the entire student, from math to the arts, a far cry from the urban Catholic school Ryland had attended, where more emphasis was placed on rules and rulers than academics.

Ryland stepped into the hall. A bulletin board of gap-toothed smiles faced him. He turned away from the innocent faces and answered the call. His gaze paused on construction paper snowflakes, decorated with glitter and pasted at random intervals on the pale blue cinder-block wall.

"Step two is complete." In a hallway filled with childish grins and art projects, Kenneth's chilly voice felt like a stain, dirty and permanent, as if the very nature of the call—and Ryland's mistakes—leaked from the phone and dripped onto the waxed linoleum like blood from a wound.

"And step three?"

"I'm heading west in the morning," Kenneth said. "I'll be in Pennsylvania before lunch."

"Excellent." Ryland ended the call. He reentered the auditorium just as his grandson left the stage. He'd missed the performance. He eased into the metal folding chair. Marlene's dark eyes flashed with disapproval. A fiercely protective mother bear in her own children's lives, she'd transferred her maternal instincts to her grandchildren. She'd be angry with him for days.

As if he wasn't angry with himself. He'd missed much of his children's early years. Now his grandchildren seemed to be growing up even faster, as if the frenetic pace of life was contagious. As if the shortage of years left in his lifespan made each existing one seem more fleeting.

Disappointment rose in his chest. His business intruded upon his personal life at every opportunity. He straightened, more determined than ever to make sure the sins of his past weren't inherited by his children.

———————

Ethan pressed an ice pack to his jaw. "He was tall and thin, in damned good shape, shoes were black but soft-soled. I never got close enough to get a specific height, but he had to be taller than me. He was wearing a black hoodie and jeans." Standing on the back patio of Roy Abrams's house, Ethan filled Detective Marshall of the Greenland Police Department in on the story from the beginning, starting with the attempt on Abby's life, through Faulkner's murder, to this morning's discovery of Roy Abrams. It took a while.

Marshall frowned. "That's not much of a description to go on."

"No. It isn't," Ethan agreed. If only he could've caught the guy . . .

"Could you pick him out of a lineup?"

"No. I never got a look at his face. Bandana."

"Fuck me." Marshall took copious, angry notes. Decades of stress lines and a double chin aged the detective. He could have been seventy but was likely closer to fifty-five, just old enough to live in this retirement community. "I have a dead retired police detective whose death is probably tied to the murder of a recently released kidnapper and his three-year-old crime in Harris, plus your attempted murder in PA. And a cop eyewitness who didn't get a good look at the killer."

"It does suck," Ethan commiserated. "I've been chasing this case for a week. I'm as frustrated as you are."

"It's a jurisdictional nightmare." Marshall stabbed his notebook. "I retire in three fucking months. I don't need this shit."

"Neither did she."

Marshall's gaze flickered to Abby, who had already given her statement and was sitting on a tree stump next to the boat. His face softened, and he sighed from the pit of a belly that could have been gestating twins. "I guess not."

Abby was pale, and Ethan wished she hadn't gotten a look at Abrams. Strangulation made for an ugly corpse, not that dead bodies were ever pretty, but the whole protruding purple tongue deal was just nasty.

Marshall looked past Abby at the boat that towered over her. "Awfully expensive boat for a retired cop."

"The Cadillac in the drive looks new too," Ethan said.

"Fuck me." Marshall tapped his forehead with the notebook. "I guess we have to add a possible dirty cop to this cluster."

"Looks like." Ethan felt like he was stuck in the bottom of a giant hole that kept getting deeper and deeper. Eventually, there'd be no way in hell he'd ever climb out.

"Course, just because he might have been dirty and somebody killed him doesn't necessarily mean both of those factors are related to each other or to her."

Ethan looked at him.

"You're right. Fuck me." Marshall stuffed his notebook into his chest pocket. "I'll call you when I have preliminary autopsy findings or if anything else interesting turns up."

"Appreciate that," Ethan said. "I'll do the same."

Ethan's boots crunched across the dry lawn. He'd offered to put Abby in his truck with the heat on, but she hadn't wanted to be in the front of the property, in full sight of the neighborhood gawkers. In a fifty-five-and-over development, the residents had an abundance of free time.

Her face was bloodless, her eyes still horrified.

Here in the backyard, she also didn't have to watch the medical examiner's staff wheel out the black-bagged body.

He crouched in front of Abby and took her gloved hands in his. "We can go."

"OK." She sniffed and stood, steadier than he expected. But then, she was tougher than her slim body and delicate features suggested.

They walked around front. Onlookers, bundled into their heaviest gear, gathered in driveways. Ethan shielded Abby with his body as they walked to his truck. He pulled away from the curb. "Are you all right?"

"Yes." She picked up a bottle of water in the console cup holder and sipped. "So I guess it wasn't Faulkner."

"I don't know." Ethan drove toward the Garden State Parkway. "My question is, why are they both dead? Did they know something about your case? And who has something to hide?" Taking the northbound entrance ramp, he glanced at Abby. "Are you sure it was Abrams's fault that you weren't found?"

Abby's eyes snapped to his. "That's what the prosecutor said."

"And he's dead too, right?"

"Yes." Abby chewed on her thumbnail. "You can't think his death is related too. Whitaker said he had a heart attack."

"Who the hell knows at this point." Ethan lifted his phone and dialed the detective in Harris who was handling Faulkner's homicide. The call went to voicemail. He left a message asking for a return call, then called Chief O'Connell. The file on Abby's kidnapping hadn't arrived at the Westbury police station yet.

"You're sure he'll give them to you?" Abby asked.

"I don't see why not." Ethan accelerated to merge into traffic. "We're on the same side."

"Won't he want to protect Abrams's reputation?"

"Maybe. Maybe not. I didn't get the feeling that Abrams was that well liked."

Abby's fingers tapped on her thigh. "What else can we do?"

"I don't know," Ethan said. "Nothing makes sense."

"I'll need to stop at my place."

"We can do that tomorrow." Ethan was in no rush to leave her alone.

"Eventually I have to go home," Abby said.

"As soon as it's safe." Ethan's gut twisted. He didn't want her to go home, and it wasn't just because she was still in danger. He liked being around her. He liked talking to her. He liked kissing her.

And there were a thousand other things he could think of that he wanted to do with her.

Midday traffic was light. They made the drive back to Westbury in a few hours, arriving just in time to feed the horses. Abby went with him into the house.

Ronnie's assistant, a college-aged brunette, was in the kitchen drinking a cup of coffee. Zeus was sleeping at her feet. The dog heaved to his feet and greeted them with messy snorts.

"How's the bay look?" Ethan asked.

"Better. The vet stopped by an hour ago. Fever's down. Doc thinks he's on the right track." She put her mug in the sink and grabbed her coat from the back of the kitchen chair.

"Thanks for your help," Ethan called after her.

"You're welcome." Her long brown ponytail swished as she bounced out the door with the energy of a kid.

Watching her, Ethan could feel every hour of sleep he hadn't gotten over the past few nights. Long hours of driving and standing out in the weather hadn't helped. His bones ached with cold exhaustion.

"I'm going to feed the horses."

"Would your mom mind if I rummaged around the kitchen for dinner?" Abby asked.

"Not at all." Ethan headed for the back door. "There're usually leftovers in the freezer."

With the drop of sunlight came the raw damp of night. Moisture on the air suggested precipitation was on the way. The bay did look better. He greeted Ethan and nosed his hay with interest. The roan attacked his meal. By the time Ethan returned to the house, his hands were stiff and frozen. Zeus was at the door. Ethan held the door open. While the dog did his business in the yard, Ethan toed off his boots and left them by the back door. His hands and face burned as he stripped off his gloves and coat in the mudroom. Zeus woofed, and Ethan let him back inside.

The microwave dinged as they entered the kitchen. The scent of something bread-like baking wafted across the room. Ethan's stomach growled. He headed for the sink and scrubbed his hands. The warm water thawed his frozen skin.

"I found a container of some sort of stew in the freezer." Abby lifted a bowl from the microwave and stirred its contents. "And I threw some biscuits in the oven."

"You made biscuits?" Ethan shivered. The chill had followed him into the house.

"It's not hard." She smiled. "The horse is all right?"

"Yeah. He looks good."

"Are you going to sleep in the barn tonight?"

"No." Ethan's tone was pointed.

Abby froze.

And the knowledge that they were alone in the house buzzed between them.

"I'm going to start a fire." Ethan went into the living room. Nothing short of flames was going to thaw him out completely. Logs, kindling, and newspaper were stacked on the hearth. In a few minutes, a small blaze crackled. He held his hands out to the fire. Heat soaked into his skin.

Abby carried a tray loaded with bowls of beef stew, a basket of biscuits, and a bottle of wine. Ethan cleared the coffee table.

"My mother makes a mean beef stew." And why was he talking about his mother? Ethan stirred the logs then joined Abby on the sofa.

"It smells fabulous." Abby poured a glass of red wine and handed it to him. "I hope you don't mind. I helped myself to the wine rack."

"You can have anything you want." And he meant anything. The wine and beef warmed Ethan from the inside out. He leaned back on the sofa, content.

Abby set aside her glass. The food and fire had brought color back into her face. Firelight played across her smooth skin. Ethan moved closer. He wrapped an arm around her shoulders. A few strands of hair drifted across his hand. He twirled them with a finger.

She tilted her head to look up at him. Her brown eyes were soft from the wine, but wariness still lurked in their depths.

Ethan lifted her chin with a finger. "Abby, you know you can trust me. I would never hurt you."

"I know." She smiled. "I'm an excellent poker player, and my favorite color is blue."

"What?"

"This afternoon you said you wanted to know more about me."

"I do." Longing unfurled in Ethan's chest. He wanted to know everything about her. "Tell me more."

She pressed a finger to his lips. "I think we've done enough talking today."

Ethan dropped his head. He caught her lips in a tender kiss. She opened for him, her mouth tasting of wine. He worked his way from her mouth to her jaw and trailed kisses into the hollow of her neck. Her soft sigh quickened his heartbeat. Under his lips, her pulse throbbed. He returned to her mouth, licking his way inside. His palm trailed up her arm, past her shoulder, and cupped the back of her head. His fingers trembled as they threaded through her silky blonde hair.

Slow and steady. Do this right.

But his heartbeat had moved from his chest to his groin, and it called Abby's name with every throb.

"Ethan," she breathed. Her hands clutched his shoulders, her fingers squeezing in urgency.

She was wearing a thick sweater over her jeans. Ethan's free hand slipped under the hem and splayed on the smooth skin of her belly. She pressed closer. Ethan moved his hand up to cover her breast through her bra. "Are you sure?"

A small noise of frustration escaped her lips. She leaned away and made direct, undeniable eye contact. She reached out and grabbed the hem of his shirt, lifting it over his head and dropping it on the floor. Her gaze roamed over him. Her pupils were dilated, and she was breathing hard. "I'm sure."

CHAPTER EIGHTEEN

Abby couldn't believe she'd just done that. She'd always dated older men and had let them take the lead. Could she have been more of a stereotypical fatherless woman? It didn't matter now. Apparently those days were over.

She let her gaze roam over Ethan's naked torso. Definitely not an older man. He was a male in his prime. His chest was broad and nicely muscled, with just a dusting of dark hair that swirled down a defined stomach in a thin line into his jeans. She reached out and traced his pectoral with a fingertip and smiled in blatant approval.

Ethan's face split in a sexy grin. "I like the way this is headed, but you're entirely overdressed."

"Maybe." Abby sat up. She lifted the hem of her sweater a few inches. "I do get cold, though." She stopped, teasing him.

Desire gleamed in Ethan's eyes. Power flooded Abby.

"There are better ways to stay warm." Ethan edged closer. "You know, the more clothes you wear, the more I want to take them off you, like unwrapping a fancy present on Christmas morning." He reached for her sweater with greedy hands.

Sliding just out of reach, Abby stopped him. With a playful shove, she pushed him back onto the sofa cushion. Then she stood, turning to face him.

With slow, deliberate movements, she lifted the hem of her sweater, moving it up her torso, revealing the bare skin of her belly one inch at a time. Ethan's eyes were riveted on the moving fabric. When she reached her breasts, she hesitated just for a second then pulled the sweater over her head and dropped it from one fingertip.

Ethan sucked in a harsh breath. "Abby . . . You're playing with fire." His tone held both promise and warning.

Thank goodness she'd worn a decent bra. It wasn't anything fancy, just simple white with a pretty lace edge. But the way Ethan was staring at her made her feel like this year's *Sports Illustrated* swimsuit issue cover model.

How would he react if . . .

She unzipped her jeans.

He licked his lips. The playful light in his eyes shifted to raw hunger as she slowly slid the denim over her hips, revealing the white lace panties that matched her bra. She stepped out of her pants, flipping them to the side with a flirty kick.

Ethan's breath caught. The sound that rumbled from his chest didn't remotely resemble a laugh. His groan was primitive male hunger. He reached for her.

Abby backed up a step. "Patience."

"You're killing me," he moaned.

But Abby had never been so turned on. And Ethan hadn't touched her body with anything but his eyes.

She played with the front clasp on her bra for a few tantalizing seconds before flicking it open. Her breasts spilled out. The straps slid down her arms.

"Oh Jesus." Ethan sat up. His hands were on her waist, holding her in place. He leaned forward and kissed the smooth skin just above her navel. His lips trailed to her hip bone. His tongue played with the lace. Abby's nerve endings rose. Every touch of his mouth sent a tiny current of pleasure right to her core. But she wanted this night to last. Forever if possible. She tried to back away.

"Oh no you don't." With one movement, he swept her feet out from under her. "That's enough teasing. I'm only a man. I can only take so much."

Abby tumbled into his arms. "Oh."

"I want you." Primal need roared from his eyes, and the brilliant blue darkened and sharpened with desire.

He shifted, laying her down on the couch and stretching out next to her. Their bodies pressed together. Heat shimmered from his skin in waves like a sultry day in August. She definitely wasn't cold now. Her blood heated and flowed through her body as slow and thick as warm honey. The man had hot hands. Those heated palms kept moving. Callused fingertips trailed up and down along her ribs, alerting the skin on her sides that something good was going to happen to the rest of her body. *My God, the way this man could make her feel with a simple caress was amazing.* Her bones turned to liquid whenever he touched her.

He lowered his head, and she felt his warm breath wash over her face before his mouth even made contact, and she trembled slightly. He kissed her cheek then her temple, right along the nearly faded bruise. When his lips brushed a sensitive spot on her neck, her head automatically fell to the side to give him more room. Her body leaned into his all on its own, quivering in anticipation.

His fingertips stroked her collarbone and hovered over her breast. "Are you sure you're ready for this? Maybe we should wait."

"What?" Abby moaned softly. "No."

Ethan lifted his head to grin down at her. One look at the mischievous glint in his eyes and she knew she'd lost. Or won.

She wasn't sure yet because her brain was now the consistency of oatmeal, but a little voice in the back of her head told her that despite her earlier striptease, now she was the one being thoroughly, expertly seduced.

"Oh, forget it. You win. I can't hold out any longer." Ethan dipped his head and caught her nipple in his mouth.

Abby arched back as every brush of his lips on her breast sent warm waves of want rolling through her. Tension built as his hands and lips traveled the length of her torso, not leaving an inch of skin untended. His legs intertwined with hers.

Wait. She ran a foot up his hard calf. "When did you take your pants off?"

"A minute ago." He stroked a hand up her thigh.

"How did I miss that?" Abby asked. "Are you some kind of magician?"

"You tell me." His hand was between her legs. What happened to her panties? Oh, who cared? His fingers were nimble all right. They stroked and circled, building her pleasure in overlapping waves, until Abby could barely breathe. She pried a hand off his shoulder, where her nails had left marks in his skin.

"I'm sorry. I scratched you." She took him in her hand.

"I know," he hissed. "It's so hot."

She stroked him from base to tip. He twitched in her palm. "You find me scratching you a turn-on?"

His body stiffened. "You losing control is a total turn-on."

"Like this?" Her hand dipped and cupped.

"Jesus." His erection jumped toward her.

She wrapped one leg over the back of his thigh. "Ethan, now."

"Yes. Now would be good." He lifted his head. Their gazes met. Unexpectedly nervous, Abby swallowed hard to ease the fluttering of her stomach. What was wrong with her? She was no virgin. But something in the back of her mind suspected this was going to be a whole new experience. Her blood had certainly never surged through her veins at this temperature. Nor had every nerve ending in her body ever stood at attention quite like this. Never had a man looked at her as if he couldn't take his next breath without her.

Her entire body was waiting, anticipating, strung as taut as a tightrope.

Because she also knew to her very soul that sex with Ethan would be more than physical pleasure. They were joining more than their bodies tonight. The last week, they'd been dancing around this moment, this culmination of vulnerability and trust.

"Hold on." Ethan reached for the floor. He came up with his jeans and fished in the pocket one-handed. He pulled out a foil packet and ripped it open with his teeth. A second later, he settled between Abby's legs. Wow. The man had magic hands.

He slid inside her, filling her with an aching slowness. The internal stroke set a new bundle of nerves alight. Abby arched backward as pleasure speared her. But Ethan seated himself deeply inside her and held completely still. In the firelight, sweat glimmered on his skin.

"What, now you're in no rush?" she panted.

"I want this to last as long as possible." Ethan rested his forehead against hers. "I feel like . . ." He seated himself deeply in her.

"Like what?" Unable to resist another stroke of pleasure, Abby's hips rocked. It wasn't enough. She needed him to move, to finish what he'd started.

"Like I've been waiting for this my whole life."

Her heart stammered.

"But I can't do it." Ethan pulled back and slid in hard again.

Abby's body tensed. His admission sent a fresh burst of heat through her. Pleasure coiled, tighter and tighter with each thrust of his body. She wrapped her legs around his waist and bowed backward.

"No. Don't close your eyes." Ethan thrust faster. "I want to see you."

They locked gazes. Tiny dots swirled in Abby's vision as her body soared and crashed. Energy pulsed through her body. Ethan's eyes went dark and lost as he followed her over. Breathing hard, he dropped his forehead to hers. Abby could feel his heart thundering against her breasts, mimicking her own racing pulse.

They lay still for several minutes. The fire crackled. Wood shifted. Zeus snored.

Abby gave his shoulder a tap. "You're heavy."

"Oh, sorry." Ethan lifted his upper body off Abby. "So, you didn't answer my question."

"Which one?"

"Am I a magician?"

Abby laughed. "You're a regular Houdini."

Ethan woke to a dark and empty bedroom. He swept a hand over the indent in the mattress next to him. The sheets were cool. Where was Abby? He threw back the covers and stepped into a pair of sweatpants. The hardwood was chilly under his bare feet.

He went downstairs and turned into the kitchen. Abby was standing at the window, but with all the lights blazing, she wouldn't be able to see much except her own reflection. She was dressed in flannel pajamas and a heavy, floor-length robe. The dog at her feet stretched and sighed heavily.

Ethan stepped up behind her. He reached out to touch her shoulder, but her stiff posture stopped him. Their reflections were both visible in the window, but she was so lost in whatever she was seeing in her own head, she didn't notice him. "Can't sleep?"

She gasped and blinked, one hand rising to her throat as she whirled to face him. The fingers of her other hand clenched the edge of the countertop behind her. "I didn't hear you."

"I'm sorry I scared you." Ethan paused. Something was off. This wasn't the same playful, in-charge woman who'd thoroughly seduced him. Instead of confidence, fear and helplessness shone in her eyes. An internal alarm went off inside Ethan. "What's wrong?"

"Nothing." She leaned backward, putting more space between them, but there was no way Ethan was letting her pull away from him. He took two steps forward, bringing their bodies into contact. Her eyes misted.

"Bullshit." He searched her face.

Her gaze shifted to the window. Her eyes closed. Her shoulders slumped. "I thought that maybe now that Faulkner was dead, it would go away."

"You thought what would go away?"

"But tonight I was just as afraid as always, maybe even more."

Ethan drew her closer. He stroked her back through her thick robe. "What are you afraid of?"

With a defeated sigh, she leaned her head into his chest. Ethan's arms slid around her.

"The dark. I sleep with the lights on." She lifted her head. "And

I'm not talking about a nightlight. At home I usually keep every light in the house on all night. They're set on timers. Even if I'm not home, it's as bright as an operating room in there all the time."

Ethan stiffened. "You said it was dark in that well."

She nodded. "He'd nailed plywood across the opening. I couldn't even tell if it was night or day."

Ethan's gut twisted. She'd spent ten days in a dark hole in the ground drinking out of a puddle to stay alive. How could anyone do that to another human being? How could anyone take a beautiful woman and treat her worse than an animal? If Faulkner wasn't dead, Ethan would kill the bastard all over again. He ached to take away all her pain. But that wasn't possible. The best he could do was help her through the night.

"Come back to bed," he whispered into her hair.

"I can't sleep in the dark."

"Abby, we can light up the house like the Meadowlands. All I care about is having you in my bed." He took her hand and tugged her toward the stairs. He flipped wall switches as they walked down the hall. In the bedroom, he turned on the lights on both nightstands and the overhead fixture in the bathroom. He made sure the blinds were closed tightly. Not that there were any houses nearby, but so that Abby wouldn't be staring at the black windows all night long.

She stood in the middle of the room. Looking lost. Adrift. He went to her, wrapping his arms around her and holding her close.

Pressing her cheek to his chest, she shuddered. "Make love to me, Ethan."

"Are you sure?" he asked. Terrified women weren't really his thing. "I'm perfectly happy just to hold you all night."

"I need you." Her voice cracked.

Those three words stirred his heart in a way he couldn't articulate. The thought that only he could get her through the night was powerful. The need to chase away her fear coursed through him. With a gentle smile, he slipped the robe from her shoulders and let it fall to the floor. Then he slowly unbuttoned her pajama top. When he spread the fabric apart and looked at her, she blushed from head to toe, pink heat spreading across her pale skin and wiping away her pallor.

He voiced his male approval. "You are amazing. Why on earth do you hide under baggy clothes?"

"Because hiding is what I do best."

Ethan silently cursed his stupid comment. "I didn't mean—"

She put a finger to his lips. "It's OK. It's not your fault, and I'm working on it. No more hiding for me. But I could use some help."

Ethan couldn't form the words to express the feeling in his heart. He'd have to show her instead.

One hand splayed at the base of her spine, nudging her hips closer, letting her feel the evidence of his desire. "See what you do to me?"

Her answering moan sent more of his blood racing south. He skimmed her rib cage until his hand gently brushed her breast. One fingertip circled her nipple in a feather-light caress.

"You have the most beautiful body." He pressed his lips against her throat and trailed his mouth down her chest. Her torso bent backward over his arm.

He stripped the pajamas from her body, like he wanted to strip her fears away, leaving every inch of her bared to him. He stroked and caressed, kissed and tasted until her muscles went lax. When a heavy sigh left her lips, Ethan scooped her up and laid her on his bed. Shedding his pants, he stretched out beside

193

her. His eyes roamed her flushed skin. Her nipples were pebbled from his tongue, her lips swollen from his kisses.

"I'll tell you what." He brushed his lips across her jaw. "I am loving this whole lights-on thing. I can see every inch of you, and you are perfect."

She smiled, desire seeping through the sadness.

He was in no hurry. His hands moved lazily across her skin. His mouth took hers deeply over and over. His tongue stroked thoroughly, showing her just how much he cared about her.

Earlier their lovemaking had been playful, with a touch of frantic need. This was tenderness defined. He slipped a hand between her legs.

She opened for him. "I need you, Ethan. Hurry."

Never had his body felt this primitive, basic urge that was now consuming him. He rolled toward her. Ah, *shoot*. Condom.

He reached into the nightstand drawer for a packet. There. He had it on in a second. He stretched out on top of her. She wrapped around him as he slid into her heat.

Her body arched off the bed. "Ethan." His name escaped her lips as a plea.

Were those tears on her face?

"Shh. I know. I'm right here." He rocked inside her, claiming her as his, promising with his body to be part of her, to keep her safe. Her body surged up to meet his, trying to find his rhythm. "Just relax, Abby. I got this."

But her body tensed more, so he put aside his tender intentions and matched her rhythm instead. Speeding up his thrusts to bring her close to the release she desperately needed.

Her body went tense, and she clamped around him, tight as a vise. The aftershocks of her orgasm rolled around him and faded to a shimmer. Ethan let himself go. Abby's body went soft underneath him.

Levering his weight off her with an elbow, he kissed her head and brushed the tears from her face. Her eyes blinked up at him, a heady mix of gratitude and confusion.

Yeah. What just passed between them had rocked him too.

But Ethan wasn't confused. For once in his life he was absolutely sure about something. Abby had slid under his defenses.

CHAPTER NINETEEN

Abby opened her eyes to a beeping sound.

"I'm sorry I woke you." Ethan swiped his cell phone from the nightstand. "I have to work today. And I have the horses to take care of first."

The night's events flooded her brain in a collage of humiliating images. Never in her life had she been so needy. But despite the lack of sleep and the threat that remained to her life, her body felt lighter this morning. What did Ethan think?

Abby sat up, dragging the bedclothes up to cover her breasts. She smoothed the edge of the sheet between her fingers. "I'm sorry about last night."

Ethan lowered his cell. "Why would you be sorry?"

"I don't know what happened to make me lose it like that."

"You mean except for nearly being killed, finding two dead bodies, and realizing that the people involved in your case are being murdered?"

"The last time I broke down was after I was rescued." She flattened a wrinkle in the cotton. "I held it together while I was in the well. It wasn't until it was all over that I lost it."

"You were in survival mode," Ethan said.

Abby looked up. "I'm sorry I dumped all that on you."

"Don't be." Ethan pried her fingers off the linens. "Last night was amazing." He lifted her hand to kiss her knuckles. "You're an amazing woman. I've never met anyone as strong as you."

"I blubbered all over you."

"You can blubber on me anytime." Ethan pulled her to his chest. "Why don't you close your eyes for a while? You didn't get much sleep last night."

"No, I should get up. If you're working today, perhaps I should go home." But she didn't really want to be alone.

Ethan planted a kiss on her lips. "No way."

He turned his pillow vertically and propped up his sculpted torso. Watching his lean body move, Abby was reminded of what those muscles felt like under her hands.

"Do you want me to stay here and keep an eye on the horses?" Where else would she go? Not home. After the detective's murder, she wouldn't feel safe anywhere.

He scrolled through messages on his phone. "The chief messaged me. Some files came from the Harris Police Department. Plus Detective Marshall, that's the cop who's handling Roy Abrams's murder, wants you to look at some mug shots and see if anyone looks familiar."

"But I didn't see the killer's face."

Ethan shrugged. "You saw his eyes, and you said they were distinctive."

"Dead gray." Abby shuddered. "Like a fish, a shark."

"Gray isn't as common as brown, blue, or hazel. Maybe we'll get lucky."

"Is this just an excuse for me to sit at the police station all day?"

"Oh, look at the time." With an exaggerated glance at the clock, Ethan pushed back the covers and stepped into a pair of jeans thrown over a chair. He pulled a sweatshirt over his head. Picking up her robe, he handed it to her. "Not that I really want you to put it on, but I know you get cold."

Laughing, she got out of bed and wrapped the thick fabric around her.

"You can use the shower while I take care of the horses." Ethan tugged on socks. "There's an electronic tablet in the nightstand. You can take it with you today in case you get bored." He kissed her before leaving the room.

Abby grabbed her overnight bag from the dresser. Her body might feel relieved from last night's emotional purge, but her face looked like a truck had run over it. Then backed up and run over it again.

She splashed cold water on her swollen eyes while the water heated. As the hot spray poured over her shoulders, Abby remembered Ethan's hands and mouth on her body. Her skin flushed, and she didn't know whether to be happy or humiliated. He'd seen her at her worst, a rare moment of self-pity. She rarely allowed herself to wallow, but last night she'd wanted to stay in Ethan's arms. Her terror got the best of her, and she'd fled to the kitchen where she promptly turned on all the lights—which illuminated both the room and her failure in stark reality. The temptation to run and hide had nearly been unbearable.

She hadn't been there more than ten minutes when he found her. And what he gave her was so much more than sex. More than comfort and compassion, he refused to let her retreat into herself. He made it clear that whatever her issues, he wasn't letting go. She didn't have to go back to being alone. But could she do it? Her entire life had taught her that all relationships eventually ended in disappointment or betrayal. Or both. Even her mother had let her down in the end, abandoning her daughter through suicide. Could she let Ethan in? The thought of losing him created a hollow space behind her breastbone.

Abby dressed in fresh jeans and a turtleneck. She opened Ethan's nightstand and took out the tablet. Thin and light, it fit easily into her purse. Abby went to the kitchen. Pale light washed the room in shades of gray. No Zeus, but an empty bowl sat on the floor. Ethan must have fed him and taken the dog out with him. He'd also made coffee. Shouldn't he be back? She went to the window. An overcast sky hung low over the barn. The forecast was for a couple of inches of snow later in the day.

She grabbed her jacket and borrowed a hat and gloves in the mudroom. One sniff of the morning air verified that a storm was on the way. The barn door was partway open. She went inside, inhaling the comforting smell of hay and dust and large animal bodies. Zeus greeted her with his typical snort and trotted out of the barn to lift his leg on a nearby pine tree.

"Ethan?"

"In here." His voice carried from the second stall.

Abby gave the pony a pat on the way by. The bay horse was in the middle of its stall. Its blanket had slipped sideways and tangled around its legs. Ethan reached for a strap, but the horse shifted sideways.

"Is everything all right?"

"No. I have to cut these straps, but he won't hold still." Ethan went back to the head and shushed the animal until it calmed again. "If I give you the number, can you call my cousin Ronnie?"

"Why don't I just cut the straps for you?" Abby opened the stall door and eased inside. The horse eyed her but didn't move.

"I don't want you to get hurt."

"He seems to be calm as long as you're at his head." Abby moved forward.

Ethan considered. "OK, but come up here by his shoulder and let him sniff you. Watch his ears and his eyes. Rolling eyes, tense posture, or pinned ears means he's not happy. And no sudden movements."

But the bay stood while Abby took Ethan's pocketknife and cut the nylon straps. The blanket dropped to the ground. Ethan moved the horse away. Abby collected the ruined blanket and left the stall.

Ethan joined her. He closed the half door and fastened the sliding bolt. Then he turned and kissed her. "Thanks."

"Anytime." She nodded toward the bay. "He looks a lot better today."

"He does. No fever. His appetite is back, and he's not quite as skittish." He steered her out of the barn.

"Hold it right there."

Abby looked up, right into the barrel of a shotgun.

Ethan froze.

Mr. Smith, the old bastard who'd starved his horses.

Ten feet in front of Abby, the wiry old man pointed a shotgun at her head. His arthritic hands were steadier than Ethan would have expected. Behind him, a rickety truck and rusted horse trailer were parked in the barnyard.

Panic scrambled in Ethan's chest. He'd been worried about Abby's past. He hadn't considered his job could put her at risk. He pushed her behind him. His hand clenched in front of his hip, but his gun was in the house. "Put the gun down, Mr. Smith."

"Those are my horses. I've come to take them back." Mr. Smith jerked the barrel toward the house. "You all get out of the way so no one gets hurt."

Ethan didn't budge. "Put the gun down, Mr. Smith."

Smith peered around him. A mean glint shone from his eyes as he focused on Abby. "Get out of my way, or I'll hurt her."

Ethan's blood chilled. He made sure Abby was completely behind him, but now what? Without taking his eyes off Smith, Ethan spoke to Abby. "Call 911."

"If she moves, I'll shoot." Smith's eyes sharpened. "At this range, the buckshot will definitely get you, but I might get lucky. Some of it might hit her too."

A load of buckshot at this range would blow a hole in Ethan the size of a potato. Since his body armor was in the house with his weapon, using his body to shield Abby was the only strategy that came to mind. It wasn't much of a plan, but he couldn't risk any shot getting past him to hurt Abby.

Something big and tan moved in Ethan's peripheral vision. With a short bark, Zeus barreled at Smith. The gun swung toward the dog. Ethan lunged forward, grabbing the barrel and shoving it toward the ground. He ripped the weapon from Smith's hands just as Zeus's bulk hit the old man dead center and took him to the ground.

Smith rolled onto his belly and covered his head with his hands. "Get him off me!"

Standing on the man's back, Zeus growled. The dog's inch-long fangs were millimeters from the back of his neck. A string of saliva dripped from the dog's curled lips and landed on Smith's jacket collar.

"Easy, Zeus." Ethan moved forward, unsure of the dog's intent.

Abby was beside him. "Good boy. Come here."

Except for a flicker of his ear, Zeus ignored her. Under the huge canine, Smith whimpered. If Ethan was sure the dog wouldn't break the guy's neck, he would enjoy the sight of Smith getting some animal payback.

"Zeus." Abby deepened her tone. "Come!"

The dog eased off Smith's body with a reluctant sigh, but his eyes kept focus on the prone man even as Abby took hold of his collar and tugged him farther away.

"Don't move, Mr. Smith," Ethan said. He had no doubt if Smith so much as blinked, Zeus would be on him, and there wasn't a thing Abby would be able to do to stop him.

Ethan moved in. In a few deft movements, he had Smith's arms behind his back. Abby called 911.

"I didn't see that coming." Ethan used his knee to pin the man to the ground. "My handcuffs are in the house. Could you grab them for me?"

Abby put Zeus in the house before the on-duty police officer came to collect Smith. Back outside, she handed Ethan the cuffs with shaking hands.

Ethan secured Smith's hands behind his back with a metallic *snap*. "Are you all right?"

She nodded. "We can't seem to catch a break."

"No, we can't. I'm sorry. I never considered that I could put you in danger." Ethan stood. Nausea rolled through him. Fear for his own life didn't even come close to the panic at the thought of Abby taking a load of buckshot.

"It's not your fault. I know better than anyone that life doesn't come with any guarantees."

They waited in silence for the approach of sirens in the quiet winter morning, and Ethan struggled to process the fact that his job had nearly gotten Abby killed.

Krista opened the basement door. The harsh chemical smell that assaulted her nose told her she was right about where Joe got his meth. He was making it in her house. If she wasn't a total waste of space, she'd have noticed.

"Joe?" She gripped the banister. Her balance was off, and her fingers felt even weaker than her knees. The wooden basement steps creaked under her socks. She finally caught a couple hours of sleep this morning after spending the night wide-eyed and twitching.

Still, she couldn't wait until Joe came back so she could do it again. The first time he'd made her. The second she'd gone to him. Like she was doing now. Nothing had ever chased away her sadness before, made her feel like her problems had flown away. The downside was that it didn't last.

Had he left any down here?

She flipped on the light switch. The cellar was messy. Piled randomly on top of one another, boxes and discarded furniture cluttered the slab. She stepped off the stairs. The concrete was ice-cold and unyielding under her feet.

The far corner had been cleaned of debris, and Joe had covered the windows with towels. A scale, a hot plate, and rubber gloves sat on a low table. A nearby box contained a strange mix of household chemicals. Empty cold medicine boxes littered the floor.

She didn't know anything about making meth, only that it

was dangerous, but right now she didn't care. The sadness was coming back, the ache that turned her inside out and made her think about doing something to end it for good.

Wait.

What was that?

She stepped closer. Panic skidded through her belly.

"Krista?" Joe's boots thudded on the steps. "What are you doing?"

"I-I was looking for some more." She jerked her eyes off what she instinctively knew she shouldn't have seen.

"You have to wait until I give it to you." His voice sharpened. He tilted his head.

Krista's heart went trapped-rabbit.

Joe's gaze traveled behind her. "You shouldn't have come down here, Krista."

Nausea rose in her throat. Her stomach heaved, and last night's alcohol bubbled sour into her mouth. Joe came closer. He raised a hand and backhanded her across the face. Pain exploded through her cheek. Her legs folded, and she crumpled to the cement.

"Greedy bitch." Joe stood over her. "I have to punish you for disobeying."

"I promise I won't say anything."

"Oh, you won't say anything." Joe wrapped his hand in her hair and dragged her to her feet.

"Ow," Krista cried.

Joe turned, anger gleaming from his dilated eyes. He'd been using without her. "You'll do what you're told, you fucking bitch."

Fear slid through her bowels. He pulled a gun from the back of his pants and shoved the muzzle into her mouth. The metal tasted oily and sharp. "I will blow the back of your head onto the cinder blocks if you make one more sound. Do you understand?"

Krista's head nodded like there weren't any bones in her neck.

Joe took the muzzle from her mouth and ran it down her breasts to her crotch. "I wish I had time to punish you properly."

Terror vibrated in her chest. Krista bit her tongue to hold back a moan.

"I have some cleaning up to do." He stroked her cheek with the gun. The sight scraped her skin. "I wish I had time so we could have some fun. Or at least I could. But I have a delivery to make. Then you and I are going somewhere."

No! She couldn't leave. When would Derek be home? She thought it was afternoon, but time had been floaty that morning. School got out at three.

"Oh, you don't like that idea?" Joe's mouth split in a nasty grin.

"N-no." She shook her head. The vibrating fear had amplified to trembles that shook her skeleton from her heels to her head.

"Well, I can't leave you here. You know too much now." Joe's brows lowered as he considered something. "Would you rather wait until the kid gets home? Then he can come with us."

A chill sprinted through Krista's blood. The best thing she could do for Derek was get Joe out of the house. She shook her head again. "No. I'll go with you."

"That's what I thought." Joe produced a pair of handcuffs from one of the boxes. "I brought these especially for you. I'd intended to use them more for recreation. Hopefully we'll have time for that later." Light from the bare bulb on the ceiling joist glinted off silver. Joe snapped one cuff on her wrist. He dragged her to the wall and snapped the other ring around a pipe.

Joe opened an empty box and started loading it. "I won't be much longer. I promise. Then it's just you and me, baby."

"Anything?" Ethan walked into the chief's office and perched on the edge of a chair.

The chief took off a pair of frameless reading glasses and rubbed his eyes. "No. She didn't recognize anyone. I tried to get some more information out of her, but she isn't the easiest victim to interview."

Ethan pictured Abby's frustrated middle-of-the-night tears, and the calm that had followed the release of three years of pent-up emotion. "She doesn't like to talk about it."

"I guess not." Mike leaned forward. He placed his elbows on his desk and pointed at the file with his reading glasses. "The case files on her kidnapping are awfully thin. Not much more information here than in the system. The hard evidence is in here, but most of that was compromised."

"You think the Harris cops are holding out on us."

"I doubt it. Sure, the scandal of a dirty cop wouldn't help a department already skewered by the press. The prosecutor came in and cleaned house. I doubt he wants his new department soiled by an old crime." The chief leaned back in his chair. He knew all about dirt and scandal. Westbury had its own political scandal of murder and deceit a few months back, and the fallout had almost cost the chief his life. Since then, the townspeople had elevated him to hero status. His support hefted a lot of weight. "But I think it's more likely that Abrams didn't put all of his notes in the file."

"No sense incriminating himself."

"Exactly." The chief dropped his glasses on the blotter and rubbed his neck. "Stick close to her, Ethan."

"I'd already planned on it."

The chief nodded. "I thought so."

"Do you have a problem with that?"

"I don't want anything to happen to her, and there's no indication she's anything but a victim." Chief O'Connell scraped a beefy hand across his ruddy face. The sound of beard stubble rasped. "You have my full support." The chief gave him a wry frown. "It's not like I can throw stones."

The chief and his fiancée, who was the center of a big murder case, were getting married in a few weeks.

"Thanks." Ethan stood. Even though it didn't affect his decision to protect Abby, it was good to know the chief had his back. Not that Ethan expected anything else.

"Is she cooperating?" the chief asked.

"Yeah, but I don't know for how long." Ethan voiced his fear. "What if this drags out? What if she wants to go back to living like a normal person?"

"I don't know." The chief closed the file. "Let's take it one day at a time for now. Tonight, you keep her safe. We'll address tomorrow in the morning."

Ethan collected Abby and Zeus from the conference room. The lack of sleep from the night before and a day spent looking at photos on the computer showed in her eyes. "You want takeout or something from my mother's vast stores of leftovers?"

"Either is fine." Abby stood and let him steer her out of the building. "I need some fresh clothes and dog food. I'd also like to pick up the rental car."

"You could just return it." He climbed into his truck.

"I'd rather keep it for now," Abby said. "Hopefully, this will all be over soon."

"Maybe," Ethan agreed. Optimism was a good sign. Unless she wanted the car because she was planning to go somewhere without him. Wait. Why read into her response? Last night they'd crossed a line. Their relationship was no longer professional or casual. She'd let him see her most terrifying secrets. She'd let him in. She'd trusted him. Surely she wouldn't break that trust now. Not after what had passed between them.

He drove to Abby's house. Night had descended on the small neighborhood. Abby's house was dark.

Ethan made a U-turn and parked at the curb. "Are you ready?"

Her face was pale, her eyes wide with alarm. Was she afraid to go in?

"What's wrong?" He touched her arm. She jumped.

"Are you all right?" he asked.

Eyes glazed, she shook her head. "The lights aren't on."

Ethan followed her gaze to the dark house. "Should they be?"

"Yes. They're set on timers."

"That's right. You told me that last night." The hair on Ethan's neck quivered. He glanced at the surrounding houses. "It looks like the whole neighborhood is down. Probably a blown transformer."

Why hadn't he noticed? Moonlight reflecting off the snow-covered ground brightened the evening and camouflaged the lack of electricity.

"I'll check it out. You stay in the car and lock the doors."

"No." She grabbed the door handle and opened the door. "I can't wait here by myself in the dark."

Oh. He squeezed her hand. "OK, we'll stay together."

There was as much determination as fear in Abby's face. Her gloved hands shook, and in the gray moonlight, her face was as pale as the icy sidewalk. She was working hard to control her terror, but her body looked like the wind whipping off the street could knock her over.

She got out of the car. Zeus whined. "You stay here." She closed the door, leaving the dog in the truck.

"You really think anyone would mess with him?" Ethan asked.

"Probably not."

"He'd know if anything was wrong before we would." Zeus was also big enough to eat an intruder in a few juicy bites.

Abby shook her head. "I can't predict how he'll react. He's agitated." She swallowed. "Plus, you said dogs can be poisoned or shot."

"Yes, I did." And he was a dumbass for pointing that out to her. She didn't need any more worries. "All right, but stay behind me and do exactly what I say."

She nodded, but Ethan didn't have much confidence in her agreement. He'd asked her to stay behind at Roy Abrams's house too, and look what that request had gotten him. She'd followed him to chase down a killer.

He tucked her behind him and walked toward the front door, heartbeats pounding in his ears. Abby's breaths were too rapid and shallow.

"Breathe," he whispered, putting a hand on her arm. Her body trembled.

She drew in a long, shaky breath, and then gave him a short nod. Ethan released her elbow and tuned his ears to the night sounds as they climbed the concrete steps to the front porch. The house was silent.

Ethan held out a hand. "Keys."

Abby fished in her pocket and dumped her keychain into

his open palm. As Ethan took it, he closed his fingers around hers and gave her a reassuring squeeze. Their gazes met. Emotion flashed in her eyes. She blinked it away and nodded toward the door.

Right. Get your head out of your ass and back in the game.

Ethan unlocked the door and eased it open. Nothing but quiet greeted them.

"I'm going to check the house," he said.

"All right." Abby's teeth were chattering.

Leading with the flashlight, Ethan led the way into the living room. The room was warm, so the electricity hadn't been out for long. He checked the house room-by-room, looking under every piece of furniture and checking every closet. Lastly, he passed through the kitchen and utility room into a garage too narrow to park anything in but the most compact of cars. Ethan gave the room a quick sweep of his flashlight beam. The space was fairly neat, except for an array of plastic bottles. Either Abby liked to shoot for the recycling container and had terrible aim or the big bucket had been knocked over. But there wasn't anyone skulking behind Abby's bike or trash can.

He returned to the living room. Abby had pulled a couple of camp lanterns from her closet, and the room was awash in their soft glow. She was on her cell phone.

"Everything looks fine."

She ended her call. "The outage is isolated to this neighborhood. The power company is already working on it. A tree took out a transformer."

"I'll get Zeus and your bag. Why don't you start gathering what you want to take with you?"

But Abby followed him out onto the porch. Ethan realized with a tightening of his chest that she couldn't stay in the mostly dark house by herself. He opened the truck door and flipped the front seat forward. The dog barreled out. Ethan made a grab for his leash, but the massive canine moved faster than he expected.

"Here, boy," Abby called.

Zeus dodged his mistress like a cutting horse. He stopped on the lawn. Nose scenting the air, he swiveled his head left and stared down the narrow strip of yard that separated Abby's house from the hovel next door. The dog's feet dug into the snow as he sprinted in the new direction. Snow flew from under his paws.

Ethan and Abby jogged after him.

They turned the corner. The dog was sniffing the ground. He stood up on his hind legs and pawed at the small garage window.

Abby grabbed for the dog's collar and tugged him away from the house. Zeus obeyed, but he stood at Abby's side on full alert, legs stiff, huge muscles tensed, hackles lifted.

Ethan swept the beam of his flashlight on the window.

"What do you see?" Abby asked.

"Scratches on the sill. Not sure if they're from the dog's claws or something else." He turned back toward her. "I'll need a ladder to get a better look."

But the dog's reaction was pretty clear. Someone had tried to break into Abby's house.

Ethan glanced around the neighborhood. Shadows gathered beneath trees, shrubs, and sheds. He'd already checked the house for intruders. "Let's get back inside."

The dog sniffed. His head and tail were on alert. Tension radiated from his body.

"Let's walk through the house so you can see if anything is missing or disturbed."

"OK." Abby nodded.

But Zeus ripped the leash from her hands and bolted for the

back of the house. Abby and Ethan ran after him. The dog scrambled across the kitchen floor and hurled his front paws at the door that led into the garage.

Ethan grabbed the dog's leash and hauled him back to Abby's side. "Stay here," he said to both of them.

He went through the door and swept his beam across the concrete floor again. He didn't think it was possible that he'd missed a person in the garage, but he didn't like the dog's reaction one bit.

Skirting the recycling waste, his gaze went to the window to his left, the one that Zeus had zeroed in on outside. Even from ten feet away, he could see marks on the sill. He glanced down to maneuver through the littered floor and froze. The bottles at his feet contained a small amount of pale green liquid. The plastic was swollen and misshapen, not from being physically crushed, but from interior pressure.

Oh shit.

CHAPTER TWENTY

Abby stood in the middle of the kitchen as Ethan disappeared into the garage. Zeus whined but didn't strain against the leash. Fear bubbled into her throat. Moonlight filtered through the blinds and slanted across the table. The exterior of her laptop gleamed dull silver. She wanted to sit down and turn on the computer, but she couldn't move. Fear paralyzed every muscle in her body.

She strained her eyes to see into the shadows. Outside the front window, a branch rubbed against the glass. There was no other noise. The house was silent. No hum of the refrigerator. No rattle of the heater. Silence rubbed her nerves like a rasp, and the darkness pressed in on her.

Just like the last time she'd been trapped in the dark.

Zeus leaned on her leg and whined again, no doubt picking up on her distress. This was stupid. If there was anyone in the house, Zeus would know about it. As sweet as his disposition was, his breeding could not be denied. His ancestors had been guard dogs for thousands of years. No one was getting in on his watch.

There was no reason for her current panic. But if there were scratches on her window, then maybe someone *did* try to get inside yesterday. Whoever might have been in her house was long gone. The dog was settling, and Ethan had already done the under-the-beds-and-in-the-closets check.

The dog bumped her hip with his nose. Abby couldn't even move to stroke his head. Her brain circuits were as dead as the electrical lines running through her house.

Despair swelled. It wasn't fair. As hard as she'd tried to put the past behind her, it continued to give chase, snapping at her heels like the hounds of her own private hell.

The lights turned on, flooding the room with brightness. Next to the laptop, her printer beeped. The light on the cordless phone charger blinked. From the kitchen, she heard the hum of the refrigerator shifting into operation. Beyond, the heater clanked and groaned.

As the house came to life, relief flooded Abby. She grabbed her overnight bag and ran upstairs, flicking lights on all the way to her bedroom. She opened the bag, tossed her dirty clothes in the hamper, and grabbed clean clothes for another couple of days. In the closet, she accessed her safe and removed her mother's Glock. She'd been lucky she'd been able to reach Ethan's gun when the detective's murderer had confronted them. They both could have been killed. The memory sent fear sliding through her belly.

She tucked the handgun into the side pocket of the suitcase. On second thought, she also grabbed the cash and untraceable cell, stuffed both in her suitcase, and zipped it closed.

"Abby, we have to get out of here," Ethan yelled from downstairs.

She pulled her bag from the bed and carried it down the steps. Ethan grabbed it from her hand and pulled her toward the front door. The grim set of his mouth warned her that the news wasn't good.

"What is it?" She snagged her purse from the desk.

"Just come." He bent down and picked up Zeus's dragging leash from the floor. "Please. I'll explain once we're outside."

Abby tucked her laptop under her arm and followed him. Ethan didn't stop until they were in the street.

He turned to face her. Temper flashed across his face. "Someone broke into your garage through the window." He paused. His breath blew out in an angry foggy huff. "And left what appear to be homemade explosive devices on the floor."

"Homemade explosive devices?" Abby's head whirled. "You mean bombs?"

He pressed buttons on his cell. "Yes. I'm calling in the bomb squad."

"Someone tried to blow up my house?"

"Maybe. These look like bottle bombs, which are usually made with household products that have a chemical reaction when combined. Mostly kids use them to blow up mailboxes. People have lost fingers or been blinded by the liquid that disseminates upon detonation." He swept a hand through his black hair.

"But you don't know what's inside these bottles?"

"No."

"So I can't go back into my house?"

"Sorry, not until the building has been cleared. We'll have to clear out your immediate neighbors too."

"I don't understand." Abby put a palm to her forehead.

"Movement can make them explode," Ethan explained. "So if you had gone into the garage and started picking up bottles or tripped over one . . ."

"Chain reaction."

"Yes," he said.

"I'm going to move the rental car."

"I'll do it." Ethan set down her luggage and took her keys from her hand. He backed the sedan into the street and parked it two houses down. Abby walked over. She put her suitcase in the trunk and Zeus in the back, then dumped her purse and computer in the passenger seat.

She turned and scanned Derek's house. Krista's car sat in the driveway. No truck. But a light glowed upstairs in Derek's window. "Derek is home."

Ethan's lips flattened out. "Get in the car with Zeus and lock the doors. I'll go knock on the door."

Derek didn't answer Ethan's knock. The boy was probably afraid. Abby grabbed her phone and called his house. He answered on the second ring, and she gave him a quick explanation. A minute later, light spilled onto the cement as Derek opened the front door, jacket and sneakers in hand. Ethan hustled the boy down the driveway.

Abby got out of the truck. "Is your mom home?"

Stooping down to slide his sneakers onto his feet, Derek shook his head.

Two official county police vehicles parked behind Ethan's cruiser, lights swirling. Derek sidled behind Abby as the cops got out and spoke to Ethan.

"It's all right," Abby said.

But the despair that washed over Derek's face disagreed.

Abby's stomach clenched. "What's wrong?"

A tear slipped out of Derek's eyes and caught the moonlight. He gave his head a fast shake.

"You need to tell me if it's important, Derek."

He sniffed. "It's Joe."

"Your mom's boyfriend? The bald guy?"

"Yeah." Derek took three rapid breaths as if hyperventilation was imminent. "I think he's cooking meth in the basement."

"Why do you say that?"

"Stuff I saw down there. Chemicals. Equipment."

"I need to tell Ethan."

"I know." Derek looked away.

Abby waved at Ethan.

Ethan walked over. "They're going to start clearing out all your immediate neighbors."

"Derek says his mother's boyfriend brought some suspicious stuff into their basement."

Ethan's posture sharpened. "Is he there now?"

Derek shook his head.

"Do you know where he went?" Ethan asked.

"No."

"When did he leave?"

"I don't know," Derek said, his voice cracking. "They were gone when I got home."

Dread pooled in Abby's belly.

"Where's your mom, Derek?" Ethan asked.

Derek's shoulders shook. His silence sent another wave of unease rippling through Abby. Derek feared two things. That something would happen to his mom because of her addiction and that he'd end up back in the foster care system. Tonight, his worst fears could be realized.

Ethan and Abby exchanged a look. Ethan's face was grim.

"When did you see her last, Derek?" Abby asked gently.

"This morning. Before I went to school."

Abby whipped out her cell. "I'll call the restaurant where she works and see if they've seen her."

But as she dialed the number she already knew they hadn't seen Krista.

━━━━━━━━━

Krista's head lolled. The hit Joe had given her earlier was wearing thin, but her mind was still fuzzy and cluttered. She blinked hard. The cab of Joe's pickup came into focus. A whir and clang startled her. She looked beyond the inside of the truck. A two-car garage. An old sedan was parked next to her.

"Rise and shine." The door opened. Joe grabbed her by the hair. Pain made a vague stab at her tingly and numb scalp. She pressed her hands to her head. She stumbled out of the truck and fell. Her knees hit the concrete. "Where are we?"

"We have new digs." His movements were jerky, his eyes chemical-bright. "Get up."

Krista pulled her wobbly legs under her and followed him. She'd learned doing what she was told didn't eliminate the pain but lessened the severity of her punishment.

She'd also learned she didn't really have a death wish. She wanted to see her son again.

Not that it mattered much. There was no way Joe was letting her go alive. She'd seen too much.

Joe released her hair and shoved her ahead of him. They went through a doorway and into a kitchen. Krista's feet slipped. She looked down. The floor was smeared with red.

Blood.

The scream burst from her throat.

Joe's slap cut it off. "Shut the fuck up."

218

Her head snapped back. Already dizzy, she fell backward. Her head hit the floor. As her vision went dark, she looked into a pair of dead eyes.

———

Hours later, Ethan sat in the chief's office waiting for his boss to finish his call. Ethan crumpled up his sandwich wrapper and tossed it in the trash can. Abby's turkey sandwich was still in the bag, unopened.

"You should try to eat," he prompted.

She shook her head. "I'm not hungry."

"It's going to be a long night," Ethan said.

"I know." Her gaze went to the closed door. In the conference room next door, the police artist was working with Derek to get a composite sketch of Joe. Hopefully, his description would be detailed enough to get a lead on Joe's identity.

The chief hung up his desk phone. "Joe wasn't just making meth in Derek's basement."

Ethan's gaze snapped up. He lowered the cheesesteak he'd been about to bite. "But Derek said he had an assortment of chemicals, a scale, and a hot plate down there."

"He did." The chief's gaze shifted to Abby. "All this is preliminary. Verification will have to wait until the lab tests come back, but the evidence team found traces of meth production, in addition to the necessary household ingredients and equipment to make the chemical bombs and the GHB that poisoned Abby. It looks like Joe is a well-rounded amateur chemist."

Abby's hands tightened on the arm of the chair. "Krista's boyfriend poisoned me?"

"That's our working hypothesis," the chief said. "They found fingerprints. They're running them now."

She dropped her forehead into her fingertips.

"We should be able to get an ID on this guy." Ethan set his sandwich aside. The man who tried to kill Abby—twice—had been living right next to her this whole time. "With all that going on, I doubt this is his first crime."

Abby lifted her head. "Why would Krista's boyfriend try to kill me?"

"When did she start dating this guy?" Ethan asked.

"About a week before . . ." She stopped. Her skin faded from white to whiter.

Ethan reached for her hand. Her fingers were cold and didn't return his squeeze. "Just enough time to learn your schedule and figure out how to administer the GHB."

"But why?" Abby rubbed her temples. "It doesn't make sense."

"We won't know that until we identify him." Ethan touched her forearm.

Someone knocked then opened the door. The police artist stuck his head into the office. "We're finished."

He handed the sketch to the chief, who turned it to Abby. "Does he look familiar?"

She studied the picture. "I'm not sure. I only saw him once in the dark and once from a distance."

"But you don't know him from anywhere else?" Ethan asked.

"No." She shook her head.

The chief studied the drawing. "What about height, weight, or body type?"

Ethan leaned over and looked at the picture. "Derek said the guy is a little bigger than me. Similar build. So, estimate six-two, one-ninety." "Let's get this distributed." The chief handed the sketch back to the artist. "I want to find this guy."

Abby picked up her water bottle and stood. "I'm going to see how Derek is doing."

Ethan followed her. Theories rumbled through his head. Joe was a serial killer. Doubtful. The methods of attempted murder didn't seem to fit a serial killer. He kept the possibility in the back of his head, but the attempts on Abby seemed too impersonal.

They went into the conference room. Derek was stuffing the end of a foot-long meatball sub into his mouth.

Abby sat next to him. "Are you all right?"

The kid had been nervous when they'd first brought him to the station, but he'd relaxed during the long stint with the artist.

"Do you know where your mom met Joe?" Abby set her water on the table and picked at the label.

"The restaurant bar, I think." Derek sucked on the straw of his Coke. "He came home with her from work."

But did Joe target Abby before or after he picked up Krista? Did he spot Abby and decide to kill her? Or did he pick up Krista because she lived next to Abby?

The latter made the most sense. Krista was a means to get close to Abby. Living right next door, Joe was able to watch Abby without seeming suspicious. No doubt Krista knew things about Abby as well. They'd been neighbors for two years.

Abby was awfully tight-lipped on Krista's personal life. But Ethan had made a call to social services. A couple of years ago, Derek was taken away because Krista was an alcoholic. She'd gotten sober and done the AA thing and gotten him back.

Had she stayed sober?

Nancy, the chief's secretary, popped her head through the doorway. "Ethan, the woman from social services is here."

Ethan looked past Nancy. A middle-aged woman in a cheap pant suit stood in the lobby by the desk. Guilt, undeserved but strong, slammed through Ethan's gut.

Derek dropped his Coke. His eyes widened in disbelief, then horror. He stared at Ethan, betrayal seeping from every pore.

The blade between Ethan's ribs twisted.

A tear welled in Derek's eye. "How could you?"

CHAPTER TWENTY-ONE

"What?" Abby leaped to her feet. She whirled to face Ethan.

He couldn't. He wouldn't betray Derek like this.

But he had. Guilt crawled across his face as he watched Derek's reaction.

"You have to trust me, Derek." Ethan's voice was tight, the words dry as dust as he spit them out. "It's only temporary."

Abby couldn't speak to him, not without losing it and upsetting Derek even more. She smoothed her features and sat back down next to Derek.

"It'll be OK." She fished in her purse for her cell phone. In the bottom of her bag was the charger. She'd been carrying it around since she'd been staying with Ethan. She pressed both into Derek's hands. "Quick. Put these in your pocket. I have another one. I'll text you with the number."

He nodded. She could tell he couldn't speak, and he was trying hard not to cry.

"They're going to find your mom really quick." She tried to hug him, but he pulled away, wiping at his face with the sleeve of his sweatshirt.

The rest happened too fast for Abby to process.

An older woman came into the conference room. With a plain brown pant suit and square-heeled shoes, she could have been a schoolteacher. "I'm Martha Jenkins, Derek. I'm going to take you to a foster home now."

Abby got up and rounded the table to stand in front of the social worker. "Where are you taking him?"

"And you are?" Martha gave her a tired smile.

"Derek's neighbor, Abby Foster."

"I can't give you the address, Ms. Foster," Martha said. "I'm sorry."

Then she took Derek away. He went without a single look back. His shoulders fell forward as if his entire body deflated.

Abby sank into a chair, shock weakening her legs. Panic churned behind her breastbone.

"I'm sorry." Ethan came in and closed the door behind him. "I had no idea they'd be so fast. I was going to warn him."

"How could you?" Abby's hands trembled. Emotions bubbled in her chest, the pressure building to pain.

Hands on his hips, Ethan paced the small space with short, frustrated steps. "What was I supposed to do?"

"Not call social services."

"Where would he go?" Ethan scraped a frustrated hand through his hair. "You think any judge in his right mind would let you take him? Someone is trying to kill you. Derek would be in danger. Joe was probably in Derek's house because of you. Did you think of that?"

Realization sank in Abby's belly, turning and churning like acid. This was her fault. Joe had sought Krista to get close to Abby. To watch her. To plan his attack. To kill her. Abby had put Derek in danger just by living next door and being friendly. Her entire selfish plan to have a normal life had ruined Derek's future. Not only had her past followed her, the violence was contagious, spreading to the few people she'd befriended like a deadly virus.

An exhausting sense of helplessness washed through her. What was she going to do? "I'll go to the family services office tomorrow and fill out the paperwork. When Joe is caught, maybe they'll let me take Derek."

"Maybe." But Ethan's tone wasn't promising.

"I have to do something." Abby's head fell forward into her hands. "This is his worst nightmare. I told you what happened to him last time he was in the system."

"I told Martha. She said she was placing him with good people."

Abby didn't respond. Martha couldn't know everything that went on in every foster home. She probably managed more kids than she could possibly handle.

Ethan stopped pacing. He turned around and clasped his hands behind his back, taking the stance of a confident soldier. "Look, Abby, I didn't have any choice. The rules are clear."

"It's a broken system."

"It's the only one we have, and it's there as a safety net to protect kids. His mother has been aiding and abetting a criminal." Ethan took two steps and dropped into a chair as if his legs had given out.

"Krista has no idea what Joe is." Abby sighed.

Ethan leaned forward. "And why is that? Why would she pick up a strange man at a bar and bring him into her home when she has a child to protect?"

Abby didn't answer. There wasn't anything to say. She knew Krista's faults. Abby's mom hadn't brought strange men home. Instead she'd stayed in bed for days at a time. The symptoms were different, but the disease was the same.

"She's an alcoholic. Her AA sponsor hasn't seen her in weeks." Ethan had obviously done his homework. He knew about Krista's alcoholism and the terms under which she'd retained custody of Derek.

"She tries." But Abby's voice sounded as small and weak as her argument.

"Sometimes trying isn't enough."

No kidding.

A knock sounded, and the door opened. The chief stood in the doorway. His eyes were sad and frustrated. "Ethan, can I see you in my office?"

Ethan left the room.

She had to do something. She couldn't let this go on. Krista was with a killer, maybe willingly, maybe not. Either way her life was at stake. There was also the chance that Joe would go after his only other link to his crimes: Derek.

What was he feeling right now? Memories of her own brush with foster care swamped Abby: the fear, the loneliness, the desolation, along with the knowledge that you were at the mercy of strangers. Derek's experience had been far worse than hers. Was he all right?

Abby knew what she had to do. There was one man who had the power to make this all go away, a man Abby had sworn she'd never contact again. That he'd use illegal means was a given, but Abby was done with following the rules. The legal system had done nothing but turn its back on her all her life.

She wished she could tell Ethan where she was going, but he was too honest, too good of a cop to ignore the law, and she was too desperate to obey it. But sorrow for what could have been between them filled her heart as she reached for her purse.

An arctic wind blew across the parking lot. The rented sedan sat in the last row of spots. She'd brought it from her house so it wouldn't get blown up. She got in the car and started the engine. She had to stop Joe and learn why he was trying to kill her. To save Derek and his mother, Abby would sell her soul. It was a good thing she was acquainted with the devil.

She turned onto Main Street and headed toward the highway. Fifteen miles away, she made a stop for a triple espresso and a huge chocolate bar. She paused to text Derek the number of her disposable cell. He didn't respond. What was he doing right now? How was the foster home? Were the people nice? How many other children lived there?

Willing her exhaustion away, she sipped her espresso and popped a large piece of chocolate into her mouth. She doubted the caffeine and sugar would be enough to fortify her for the next call she needed to make. She glanced at the clock on her dashboard.

In less than three hours, she'd be in Atlantic City.

Ethan perched on the edge of the credenza.

The chief stared at him from over the top of his reading glasses. A file was open on his desk, and he'd scrawled a half page of notes on a yellow legal pad. "Ethan, there was nothing you could do to keep Derek out of the system."

"I know." Ethan crossed his arms over his chest. "But I feel like a real shit."

"You could have saved the kid's life. His mother's boyfriend is bad news. Derek is lucky to be alive."

"They got a hit on the prints already?"

The chief pulled a paper from under the legal pad. "Joe's real name is Joseph Torres. He's from Atlantic City. On top of a list of small-time charges, he's been arrested twice for felony drug dealing and once for murder. Charges were dropped all three times. Twice witnesses recanted their statements. The murder witness conveniently disappeared. So did the evidence."

"Shit." Ethan rubbed his forehead. "Atlantic City is awfully close to where Abby used to live. And where she was kidnapped."

"Agreed," the chief said. "This isn't a coincidence."

Ethan got up to pace the four-by-eight space in front of the chief's credenza. "This must be tied to Abby's original kidnapping case. But how?" Nothing made sense. "What if Faulkner's kidnapping of Abby wasn't random?"

"You mean she was targeted for some other reason?"

"Yes."

The chief pulled off his reading glasses. "Do you think there's something she hasn't told you?"

Ethan considered. He put aside his heart and the pain a lie of that magnitude would cause it. Would she keep important information about her case from him? She wanted to find the truth as badly as he did. "She seemed as frustrated and confused as me about the case. I really don't think she's intentionally holding anything back. But it's possible there's something from her past she doesn't realize is important to the case."

The chief circled a note on his legal pad. "Why would an Atlantic City drug dealer be interested in a schoolteacher?"

Ethan had nothing. "And why did he take Derek's mother with him?"

The chief dropped his glasses on his paper-strewn desk. "She knows too much to let her go. This guy has a history of eliminating witnesses."

"He did a half-assed cleanup job. He had to know we'd find the residue in the basement. Why did he leave it there?"

The chief pinched the bridge of his flattened nose. "Maybe he was going to come back to do the nitty-gritty cleaning, but things didn't work out the way he planned. Or maybe he's just a dumbass. He could have found much easier, cleaner ways to kill her."

Ethan's stomach flip-flopped. "Or he's so used to getting away with his crimes, he doesn't bother to clean up."

"Either way, Derek's mother is in deep trouble. He won't let her go."

They'd put out an alert for a blue pickup with occupants that met Joe and Krista's description. But the vehicle was generic, and Joe had a full day's lead.

Ethan pushed to his feet. "I'll go break the news to Abby." A fistful of dread lodged behind his sternum at the thought of facing her.

"She's upset, but she knows you didn't have a choice," the chief said. "She'll come around."

But Ethan didn't share the chief's confidence. The look in Abby's eyes had been pure horror, and he'd caused it. He braced himself before going back into the conference room. He opened the door. "Abby . . ."

The conference room was empty.

Maybe she'd gone to the restroom. But Ethan's stomach was flipping out. It knew. He knocked on the door anyway. When no one answered, he went inside and checked both stalls.

"Abby?" His voice echoed on the tile. Empty.

Ethan did a quick run through the rest of the station, which took a minute.

He rushed into the chief's office. "She's gone."

The chief closed his eyes, and a *give me strength* expression crossed his face. "Where do you think she went?"

"I don't know."

"Would she try to find the foster home?" the chief asked.

Ethan shook his head. "As much as she'd like to get Derek out of there, she wouldn't put him in danger. As long as Joe is loose, there's a risk he's following Abby."

Who was now alone and vulnerable. Ethan paced, panic outpacing his strides in the confined space. He had to find her before Joe. But how?

"Put out a BOLO on her rental car."

But law enforcement was spread thinly over the rural region. State, county, and local police hadn't spotted Joe, and Ethan was certain the killer hadn't left the area.

An image of Abby sitting in the conference room and surfing the Internet on Ethan's electronic tablet popped into his head.

"Wait." He dug his smartphone out of his pocket. "My tablet is in her purse. It has a GPS chip. If she still has it and the battery hasn't died, I can locate her though the find-my-device app."

Please, let it still be in her purse.

Ethan opened the app on his phone and tapped through the menu. His heart thudded as the program searched. A live road map appeared on the screen. His tablet was a small green dot on the highway. "I've got her."

"Where is she?"

"Headed south on the Northeast Extension." Toward Atlantic City. Ethan's confidence in Abby's honesty took a nosedive. After all that had passed between them, how could she lie?

CHAPTER TWENTY-TWO

"I'm sorry. Would you please repeat that, Kenneth?" Ryland went to the sideboard and poured scotch into a tumbler. His doctor wanted him to give up alcohol. What was the point of living longer if a man couldn't enjoy anything?

"Homemade explosive devices, Mr. Valentine," Kenneth repeated.

"Messy way to kill a person." Ryland sipped his scotch. The aged amber liquid slid down his throat with a smooth, smoky burn. "Unreliable too."

"Obviously." Kenneth's tone dripped with disgust. He detested shoddy work.

Ryland despised unanswered questions. "Do we know who or why?"

"No, sir. But I will shortly," Kenneth said. "The only witness is a child. He's been taken into custody."

As much violence as Ryland had seen and perpetrated in his scratch-and-claw fight to the top of life's dog pile, harm to children left a bad aftertaste. But a witness could be a problem.

"Do you know where he is?" Ryland settled at the desk in his study. He eased his conscience with a deep swallow of scotch.

"Yes." Kenneth's voice turned grave, and Ryland wondered if Kenneth had ever drawn a line. Or had the atrocities he'd witnessed at a tender age left him completely numb to humanity, devoid of compassion? "I'm sitting outside the house now."

Ryland ended the call. He turned to face the bank of windows that encompassed the wall of his study. His home was on the Point. On one side, a deck and pool area led onto a private beach. On the other, patio seating and a hot tub overlooked the harbor. The windows in his office had a stunning view of Little Egg Harbor Inlet. Tonight the water was busy. Whitecaps churned and black water undulated. Small green buoy lights bobbed and blinked in the darkness. With each pulse of dancing light, the ocean warned him.

A storm was gathering force.

Ryland clicked on the flat-screen that hung on his wall and tuned to the weather channel. Needing quiet, he muted the volume. A wall of green marched up the coast. The forecast hadn't changed. No coastal advisory had been issued. The weather would be nasty, but it wasn't time to board up the windows. Ryland shut off the TV and turned back to his scotch.

"Ryland!" Marlene's voice interrupted his musing. His wife must have returned from her girls' night out.

Pocketing his phone, he left his office. In the center of a two-story glass atrium, the stairway curved to the lower floor. Marlene was in the living room. Still dressed from her dinner and show, she looked every bit the elegant wife of a successful businessman. Pride warmed him. He'd done the right thing by preserving his marriage. Once, he'd been tempted to throw it all away for a pretty blonde. Thank goodness he'd come to his senses. His sons, his reputation, all would have suffered if he'd succumbed to his affair. He'd have become a walking cliché, one more man who thought buying a younger wife would somehow stop the passage of time.

He had plenty of associates who left their children's mothers and accumulated trophy wives. The same men got manicures and facial treatments. Botox and plastic surgery left them ridiculous caricatures of themselves.

Ryland was old-fashioned that way. Beauty treatments were for women. Period.

A man earned respect through power and money. Unless referring to his wife or girlfriend, *pretty* didn't enter into the masculine equation for success.

"How was your evening?" He buzzed her smooth cheek with his lips, careful not to muss her still-perfect makeup. After decades of marriage, he'd never seen her without her "face" on, as she referred to her morning beauty routine. It pleased him that she cared to make herself attractive for him and that even now she was still willing in the bedroom.

"We had a lovely time."

"The show?"

Marlene had attended a concert at a rival casino.

She shrugged. "Disappointing. We left early and had more wine instead."

That explained the sparkle in her eyes.

He eyed her shapely calves. Maybe tonight . . .

Marlene caught his look. Was that a frown?

Ryland shifted closer. "What's wrong?"

She pulled back. Coy? Marlene liked to play games. She kept him on his toes. "Nothing."

"Would you like a nightcap?"

Marlene crossed her legs. Her skirt rose on her thigh. "Yes, please."

She was going to make him work for it. As usual. Ryland got up and crossed the hardwood to the bar in the corner. He refreshed his scotch and mixed Marlene a martini. One thing about his wife, she had never been "easy." Her philosophy was that when a man worked for something, he appreciated it more.

Ryland gave her credit. Her methods worked. Young women could take lessons in catching and keeping a man from his wife. He'd strayed over the years, but he always came back. He handed her the martini, and she sipped delicately and licked her lips.

Ryland's cell phone vibrated in his pocket.

His wife raised a *now?* eyebrow.

"I'll turn it off." Ryland pulled the phone out. His thumb went to the OFF button. A number popped onto the screen, and the call went to voicemail. He froze.

"I'm sorry. I have to make a call." He stood.

Marlene's eyes sparked with anger. "Work will be the end of you. At your age, you should be relaxing, not working until you drop."

At his age?

Well, didn't that take the wind out of his metaphorical sails. His erection deflated like a punctured bike tire.

A *whoops* look crossed her face. She knew that insinuating that he was too old to take care of business was one step over the line. "I'm sorry. I didn't mean that the way it sounded. I simply want you to enjoy the life you worked so hard to create."

"It's quite all right, my dear." He patted her thigh. "I'm not as young as I used to be. Perhaps you're right. I should be easing back on my responsibilities."

As Ryland walked out of the living room, in the corner of his eye, he saw his wife toss her martini back.

He was going to have to face facts. He was old. And his new plan did include passing the family business down to his sons. After he'd cleaned up the last few entrails, of course.

He went back into his study, closed the door behind him, and pressed CALL BACK.

Tension gripped his muscles as the ring sounded in his ear. This call followed Kenneth's too closely for it to be a coincidence.

———————

Abby left the rental car in the parking garage attached to the casino. The cold damp was welcome. Despite the triple espresso and chocolate, her head was fuzzy and her eyes sticky with exhaustion. But then it was two a.m. Not that you could tell from the casino, designed to camouflage the time of day. Were there any windows on the casino level? Probably not. Management wanted people inside, with the clanging bells and flashing lights urging them to lay down their chips. Views of a pretty beach would draw customers away from the tables. Casinos wanted people inside, handing over their money on the pie-in-the-sky chance of hitting it big—something that wasn't going to happen. The odds were always with the house.

She walked past the opening to the gaming floor. For a winter night, business was good, but weekends were usually busy. Even in the off-season, people within driving distance sought Atlantic City as a weekend getaway. Take in a show, have a nice dinner, gamble, and then maybe spend the following afternoon shopping the outlet stores.

She turned down a wide hallway and passed a bank of silver-fronted elevators. She emerged into the hotel lobby. Black marble floors gleamed. Overhead, chandeliers sparkled. At this hour, the view out the glass doors was all dark night and bright lights. In the morning, the landscape couldn't hide under the cover of darkness. Under her glitz and glamour makeup of shiny surfaces and bright lights, Atlantic City was an expensive whore, ready and willing to take your money for a wild ride and give you the boot when your wallet was empty.

Abby's boots clicked on the marble as she went straight to the concierge desk. The African American man behind the counter was dressed in a black suit and impeccably starched white shirt. All part of the classy image the casino was trying to project. "May I help you?"

"Abigail Foster. I'm here to see Mr. Valentine. He's expecting me." Abby was suddenly aware of her own ragged appearance. With the stress and rattled nerves of the evening, her jeans and turtleneck had passed fresh hours ago. Appearances were valued by some people. Ryland Valentine was one of them. A more put-together look would have served her well for this meeting.

But it was too late now. She'd passed the jumping-off point when she'd made that call from the car.

"Yes, Miss Foster." The concierge turned and called over his shoulder, "Randolph?"

A large, hard-looking man stepped out of a doorway behind the counter. The bulge under his jacket and the earpiece looped over one ear identified him as security. "This way, Miss Foster."

Abby followed his hand gesture to a hallway off the opposite side of the lobby. He walked a step behind her and to her right. They stopped in front of a private elevator. A swipe of his card key opened the doors. He waited for Abby to board first. She stood to the side, as far away from him as she could get in the small space. He swiped his card again and pressed the very last button. The car shot upward with a smooth launch and glided to a stop ten seconds later. Abby's stomach kept dropping for a few more nauseating seconds.

As the doors slid open, fresh sweat damped Abby's lower back. What had she done?

Ethan turned his truck into the parking garage of the Valentine Casino. He'd pushed his pickup hard all the way down the Atlantic City Expressway to catch up with Abby. He popped a handful of antacids into his mouth and chewed. The extra bold venti, and Abby's inability to trust him, burned all the way up his esophagus.

With a fist to his on-fire solar plexus, he watched her park her rental car two aisles over. Laughing and talking, a trio of middle-aged women crossed in front of his pickup, their voices echoing in the concrete structure. Abby got out and walked toward the casino elevators with purposeful strides. She knew where she was going, he realized with another stab to his pride.

It was no coincidence that she'd headed for Atlantic City, where Joe Torres lived. She knew a lot more than she'd told Ethan.

He followed at a discreet distance. Fortunately, he'd changed out of his uniform before chasing after her. His jeans and boots blended with the varied dress of the casino's patrons. He waited outside the elevator until her car stopped on the lobby floor. Then he jumped in the next one that opened. On the main floor, he spotted her at the end of the long hallway that led to the hotel registration desk. Stopping on the other side of the lobby, he peered through a tall potted fern.

Abby was talking to the concierge. Ethan drew back when the security goon escorted her down a private hallway behind the desk. How the hell was Ethan going to follow her?

Three young couples in cocktail attire walked from the direction of the gaming floor and crossed the lobby. A slender brunette stopped, put a hand on her man's shoulder, and slipped off her sky-high heels. The relief that relaxed her face was close to orgasmic. Hooking two fingers in the skinny straps, she padded barefoot to the elevator banks.

Ethan skirted the lobby and studied a display of brochures next to the concierge desk. Picking up a pamphlet on the historic town of Smithville, he glanced casually down the private hall. The goon card-swiped a key slot and escorted Abby onto an elevator.

Damn. How would he follow her?

"Excuse me, sir."

Ethan turned. The two guys standing behind him were twin mountains of brawn. Ethan eyed bulges under their jackets. Armed mountains of brawn. The little earpieces with the wires down the sleeves indicated they were part of the staff, whatever that meant. The fact that they were official employees of the casino didn't give Ethan any warm or fuzzy feelings of security.

"You were following the lady." Number One had a head the size and shape of a microwave oven. The flat-top buzz didn't help.

"What lady?" Ethan lied.

Number One took a step back and mumbled something into his wrist. Thing Two didn't budge.

Number One nodded toward the hall behind the counter. "Please come with us, sir." Despite the "please" and "sir," it wasn't a request.

Ethan was tempted to show his badge and talk his way out of the situation, but he held his tongue. If he were lucky, these guys would lead him to Abby.

Number Two led the way. At the end of the narrow hall, he swiped their way onto the same elevator that had transported Abby. Ethan got on without being told. Though hardly small, standing between his linebacker escorts, Ethan felt like the water boy.

The elevator climbed to the top floor. Whoever Abby was meeting was a VIP. The doors opened with barely a swish of the rubber seals.

Number One nudged Ethan's shoulder. He stepped off the elevator. His shoes sunk into ocean-deep pile carpeting. Valentine Entertainment Group was written in gold letters on the facing wall. Except for the landing, the floor was dark. Guess the execs didn't work 24-7. They went through a set of glass doors and turned right. From an office at the end of a hall, a light beckoned.

This was going to get interesting.

CHAPTER TWENTY-THREE

Abby's footsteps were silent on the plush carpet. The entire first floor of her house would fit in Ryland Valentine's penthouse office. Everything was clean-lined and luxurious. It was the kind of space that politely whispered money rather than screamed it. She'd only been here once. The other times she and Ryland had met, he'd come to her.

Ryland's expansive mahogany desk sat on a raised platform that was more throne than workspace. He stood as she entered. He was thinner than the last time she'd seen him. The small paunch was gone. He was paler too, his hair fading from elegant silver to white. Though an inch or two over six feet tall, the slight stoop he'd acquired made him seem shorter. Age was catching up to him. No one, not even the powerful head of Valentine Entertainment Group, could outrun time.

"My dear." Ryland rounded his desk and held both of his hands out to her. Over a sad smile, his eyes shone with a mixture of heartache and regret, the two emotions she most associated with him. She didn't run to him with open arms. They hadn't parted on the best of terms.

His face sagged with displeasure at her rebuff. "Thank you, Randolph. You may leave us."

Randolph gave Abby a doubtful glance, but Ryland nodded. The security guard closed the door as he exited.

Abby glanced away from Ryland. Behind him, a wall of glass

overlooked the Atlantic Ocean. The forecasted storm hadn't arrived yet, but heavy white chop on the dark water told her nasty weather was blowing up the coast.

She blinked away from the mesmerizing seascape.

He walked to her side. "Let me get you a drink. Wine?"

She sidestepped out of reach. "Just water, please."

Her head was already foggy. Too much espresso instead of food and sleep.

Without touching her, he herded her toward the other side of the room, where a long, low sofa and two boxy chairs formed a conversation area. "You look tired. Have you eaten?"

"No, but I'm not hungry." The muscles of her thighs trembled. Anxiety or exhaustion? Both, she decided, plus the jitters from her caffeine overload.

"Well, I am." Ryland steered her toward the couch. He picked up a phone from an end table and murmured instructions into the receiver.

As she sank into the black leather, blood rushed in her ears and drowned out the sound of Ryland's voice. What was she doing here? Saving Derek and his mother, she hoped. But at what cost? It felt like she was offering herself up on a silver platter. Perhaps she should have ordered an apple for her mouth.

Ryland went to a sideboard and poured water from a carafe into a crystal tumbler. He handed it to her and sat on the sofa next to her. He leaned forward, forearms on his knees, fingers intertwined, studying her.

"What's going on, Ryland?"

He turned slightly until he was partially facing her. "What do you mean?"

"Someone is out to get me."

"That sounds paranoid."

"It isn't paranoid if it's true."

"You make a good point." Ryland leaned back. His expression turned pensive. He was deciding how much to tell her.

Anger burned through Abby's exhaustion. His all-powerful, controlling attitude always ticked her off. Reining in her temper, she waited. She'd learned one thing from Ryland. Silence was a powerful negotiating tool.

"I know about the recent attempts on your life. Honestly, I don't know why you are being targeted. But I am looking into the matter as we speak."

"Do you know who is trying to hurt me?"

"No." A slight shift in his eyes gave him away. Oh yeah. He definitely knew more than he was willing to say.

"But you have suspicions?"

"Maybe." Ryland got up and walked to the bar. He poured himself a short glass of scotch and returned to his seat. Buying time, no doubt, while he carefully phrased his thoughts. "I am in the process of ceasing my activity in a certain trade. My business associates are unhappy with my decision."

Ryland was the master of vaguely specific statements.

Abby sat up straighter. "You're going straight?"

"As an arrow, as the saying goes." Ryland's mouth flattened in a tight smile. "I've been moving in that direction for several years."

"How many years?"

"A little over three."

So he'd started backing off the illegal operations right before . . . oh my God. The truth was a metaphorical smack to the back of Abby's head. "Right before I was kidnapped."

"Yes."

"Do you think it was related?" Abby's mind whirled. "Do

you think Faulkner was hired by one of your partners? It would explain why he never took the stand."

Ryland scratched his chin. "I don't think so. No one ever claimed responsibility, made threats, or contacted me with ransom terms. Messages not delivered aren't very effective as methods of persuasion."

"So you didn't think it was about you."

"Three years ago, I couldn't see how your kidnapping could've been related to my business." Ryland sipped his scotch. "Though it's possible Faulkner was supposed to deliver the message and didn't follow through. Still, if one of my enemies was behind your capture, the ball Faulkner dropped would've been picked up and carried by someone else."

A knock sounded on the door.

"Come in," Ryland commanded.

A waiter in a black suit carried a tray. He set it on the table and removed the silver domes from dishes of cheese, crackers, and fruit. A plate of finger sandwiches, a pot of coffee, and a bottle of red wine rounded out the snack.

Ryland waited for the server to exit. Then he waved at the food. "Please eat something. You're exhausted. You'll be able to think clearer with food in your body."

He was right. Abby reached for a slice of cheese.

Ryland's intercom buzzed. He picked up the phone. Scowling, his gaze snapped to Abby's face.

"Bring him in." Anger radiated from his eyes as he got to his feet. "You shouldn't have."

Abby's mouth went dry. The nibble of aged cheddar turned to dust. With effort, she swallowed and set the rest of the cheese on a cocktail napkin.

The office doors opened. Flanked by two extra-large security guards, Ethan walked in. His gaze moved from Abby to Ryland and back again.

Bitterness tightened Ethan's features as he stared down at her. "Was it all a lie?"

———————————

Tiny ice pellets pinged off Derek's face. Heaving his backpack over the sill, he climbed out the first-story window onto the roof. Nothing terrible had happened at the foster house yet, but the time to leave was now. Once somebody—or worse, two some-bodies—had a good hold on another kid, it was damned hard to get away.

There were three other kids staying here. One was little, but the other two were about Derek's age. He knew better than any-one that age wasn't a good indicator of innocence.

He'd thought Ethan was different, but the cop had turned him in, which proved that Derek really couldn't trust anyone. Except maybe Abby. She'd been as shocked and pissed off as Derek at the cop's betrayal.

But Abby couldn't help him now. She had enough of her own troubles. Joe had tried to kill her—twice—and Derek's mom had made it possible. It was partially Derek's fault. He should have called the cops on Joe when he saw the chemicals and equipment in the basement. He'd thought Joe was making meth, but the re-ality was so much worse. As usual, Derek had been a big coward. And look what he'd gotten for being a chicken. He'd ended up in foster care anyway.

Maybe he deserved to suffer, but it wouldn't be here.

He eased the window closed. A freezing wet wind blowing through the house would be sure to wake everyone in the house up fast. Derek needed the biggest lead he could get. The best scenario would be if he wasn't missed until morning.

He inched his way to the edge of the roof. His sneakers slid on wet shingles. He spread his arms and regained his balance. *Whew.* Close one. Ignoring the ten-foot drop to the ground, he wiped his face and eyed his next move. Without the sleet, the low branch of a mature oak tree was an easy leap. Slippery surfaces would make his escape more of a challenge. But there was no going back now. Derek jumped. His rubber soles skidded on the slick bark. He threw his upper body forward. His stomach hit the fat branch and knocked the wind from him. As his lungs struggled for air, his hands scrambled for a hold. He teetered for a moment, and then his body stilled. He swung a leg up and over. The movement of his body shook water droplets from the bare limbs overhead. They rained down on him in an icy shower.

Straddling the branch, he scanned the house behind him. All seemed quiet. The windows were still dark.

Satisfied his exit hadn't woken anyone, he inched his way to the trunk and shimmied to the ground. The impact jarred his frozen bones. The sleet was light but steady. His jacket and sneakers would be soaked before long.

Nothing he could do about that. The bad weather had its benefits. Derek scanned the sky. Thick cloud cover kept the neighborhood nice and dark. This place was a little farther outside of town than Derek's house. The lots were bigger, the homes more spread out.

He jogged around the side of the property. Overgrown evergreen bushes lined the edges of the driveway. No one would see him from the house once he ran into the shadows. He breathed a sigh of relief and slowed to a walk once he reached his goal. He reached the end of the drive and turned left on the street.

A hand slapped over his mouth as someone grabbed him from behind. He was jerked backward against a tall, hard body. An arm wrapped around his ribs and lifted him off his feet. Derek kicked, panic giving his movements a frenzied randomness. One sneaker caught his assailant on the leg. The blow had no effect. The guy didn't flinch or grunt. Nothing. Derek was tossed into the backseat of a dark sedan with no more difficulty than handling a bag of groceries. The door slammed. The locks came down.

Derek was trapped.

———

Ignoring the security guards and the older man in the expensive suit, Ethan's eyes locked on Abby, sitting on a leather sofa. On the table in front of her, a tray of food and an unopened bottle of wine made a casual and intimate late-night meal. Jealousy burned a path through Ethan's chest and spread through his limbs until his entire body felt like it was on fire.

"I didn't lie about anything," she said in a quiet voice.

"Right." Bitterness tasted like bile in Ethan's throat.

The old guy in the fancy suit stepped in between them. Was this Abby's *older man*?

"I don't know who you are, but you will explain yourself immediately. It's late. Abby is exhausted, and I'm running out of patience."

Ethan jerked his attention to the suit. He looked familiar. In his midsixties, he was frail-thin, not fit-thin. His eyes were a soulless black. Despite his aged state, the old man was a killer, pure and simple. This was a man who would flinch at nothing. Violent, heartless deeds had left their imprint in his eyes.

This was the older man Abby had had an affair with? The guy practically had *mobster* tattooed on his forehead.

The guard who'd emptied Ethan's pockets in the elevator walked to the table and set his badge and gun on the glass. "This is Officer Ethan Hale."

The old man spoke to Abby. "You brought a policeman here?"

The cold anger in his tone sent a sliver of fear through Ethan's anger. He couldn't let the old man hurt Abby, even if she had betrayed his trust. "No. She had no idea I followed her."

The old man nodded. One member of the security team faded to stand against the wall. The other exited, Ethan assumed to take a post on the other side of the door.

The old man held out a hand to Ethan. "Ryland Valentine."

Holy freaking shit.

No wonder he looked familiar. Tycoon. Mobster. Whatever label you wanted to hang on him, Ryland Valentine was a serious BFD. Sporadic racketeering, drug dealing, and murder investigations on Ryland magically melted like ice cubes in August. Maybe his fancy suit was coated with Teflon. Ethan had never seen him in person, and the last time Ryland had been in the media spotlight was several years ago. He'd been heavier. Ethan supposed aging was the one thing Ryland couldn't buy or bully his way out of.

And Abby had been one of his . . . ? Ethan tried to block the mental image as he stared her down. "I can't believe you didn't tell me about him."

"I've never told anyone about him." Abby closed her eyes for two seconds. When she opened them, she looked to Valentine. "I changed my mind. I'd love a scotch."

Valentine went to a small bar and poured her a generous shot of amber liquid from a decanter. He didn't offer Ethan a drink.

She took a sip and a deep breath. "My relationship with Ryland isn't public information."

"I'm hardly the public," Ethan said. Had anything between them been real? Or had he been duped? "But seriously, isn't he a little old for you?"

Her jaw dropped. "You think . . . ?"

Ethan ground his molars. "Was it the money or the power?"

Ryland barked out a surprised laugh. He returned to the bar, refreshed his drink, and poured another. He handed Ethan the tumbler. "Now I understand."

What. The. Hell?

Easing into a white leather chair, he raised his glass to Abby. "Do you want to tell him or should I?"

Her brows drew together. "Is it all right with you?"

Ryland lifted a hand. "Go ahead. Your Officer Hale isn't a threat to me."

Ethan wasn't following the conversation, but for some reason he resented not being considered a threat.

Abby held her glass in both hands. Her eyes met Ethan's. "Ryland is my father."

CHAPTER TWENTY-FOUR

Abby waited for Ethan's reaction. His gaze darted back and forth between her and her father.

Ryland set his glass down on the table. "We don't look much alike. Abby looks exactly like her mother." His eyes softened. "She was beautiful and blonde as well."

"I came here to ask for Ryland's help." Abby took another tiny sip of scotch. The liquid warmed her throat and stilled the turmoil in her belly.

"You shouldn't have taken off like that." Ethan still looked shell-shocked by her news.

Abby didn't apologize. "I'm desperate. Ryland can do things you can't. He doesn't always play by the rules." The jab at Ethan left a foul taste in her mouth. She washed it away with scotch.

"That's not fair." Ethan's jaw jutted. "I didn't have any choice."

"I know," Abby admitted. "But the fact stands that Derek is in foster care, it's my fault, and you can't help."

"I'm doing everything I can, including wasting time chasing you to Atlantic City."

Ryland snapped to attention. "Derek? Foster care. Do you have a child?"

"No. Derek is my neighbor's son. The man who tried to kill me twice started a relationship with Derek's mother so that he could watch me. He was stalking me from the house next door."

Abby shivered. Sleeping had been difficult before. How would she ever close her eyes again? "I think he took my neighbor with him when he ran. I'm worried he'll hurt her or go after Derek. They've seen his face. They can identify him. If he's arrested and tried, they could testify against him."

"We no longer need Derek or his mother to establish his identity." Ethan put his glass down and paced the carpet in front of the coffee table. "His fingerprints were in the system. We know who he is."

Abby sat up. "Who?"

Ethan addressed Ryland. "Do you know Joe Torres?"

"No." Ryland motioned to the silent man by the door. The guard nodded and slipped out of the office. "We will know everything about him shortly."

Abby rolled her glass between her palms. Light swirled gold in the scant amount of liquid left in her glass. "Did Torres kill Faulkner and Detective Abrams? If so, then why? If not, then who did?"

"Other than being established criminals, is there any relationship between Torres and Faulkner?" Ethan pivoted, took three steps, and turned again. He swept both hands through his hair. Frustration pulsed from his ever-moving body. "Since Abby has never heard of either of them, did the same person hire them both to kill her?"

Ryland's man came back into the room. Ryland got up and met him at the door. The guard murmured in his boss's ear. Ryland turned back to Abby and Ethan. "Excuse me. I have to make a call."

The only sound in the room was the soft scuff of Ethan's boots in the carpet.

Abby tossed back the remaining mouthful of scotch. Her

empty tumbler clinked as she set it on the glass table. The liquor melted her inhibitions. She raised her chin and followed Ethan's lean body as he stalked back and forth across the office. "I'm sorry I took off."

Ethan stopped. "I'm sorry I didn't warn you and Derek about social services."

"I know you had to call them." Fear ate through the scotch. Was Derek OK? Where was Krista? "Besides identifying Torres, is there any other news?"

Ethan glanced at his phone and shook his head. "The chief will message me if anything happens."

Their eyes met, and Abby wanted nothing more than to hurl herself into his arms. But more than a few feet of carpet separated them now. Would he forgive her for her outburst about Derek? For not telling him about her father? For running to Atlantic City? For a man like Ethan, her lack of trust would hurt the most. As it should. When she'd left, Abby hadn't seen any other choice. But now that he'd followed her, she realized she'd been wrong.

Horribly, nauseatingly wrong.

Ryland walked briskly back into the room. "Torres is a local lowlife, much like Faulkner. Given their proximity, it's possible they were both hired by the same party."

"Do you have any idea who that could be?" Abby asked.

"No," Ryland lied. His body language had shifted from casual to take-charge. He had a plan and wasn't including Abby or Ethan in it. Not a surprise. "What will you do now?"

"Go back to Westbury and try to find Torres and Krista." Ethan nodded toward his badge and gun, still lying on the table. "May I?"

"Of course," Ryland said. "You are both exhausted. You

should grab a few hours of sleep and a meal before you drive back." He turned to Abby. "And you shouldn't drive back alone. It isn't safe." Dark eyes flickered to Ethan for a second. "I'll put a car and driver at your disposal or have your rental car driven to your house. Your choice."

Abby was too damned tired to be annoyed with Ryland's orders. She put a hand to the dull throb in her forehead. She should have opted for another espresso instead of scotch. The effect of the single shot had been amplified by her empty belly. "Maybe some food would help wake me up."

"I could eat," Ethan admitted, pressing a hand to his stomach.

"A suite is at your disposal." Ryland walked to Abby. He held out a hand. She took it and allowed him to help her to her feet. He wrapped her in a one-armed hug. "I'm glad you came to me."

"Thank you." She leaned into him for a second. When she was a child, she would have given anything to have received this affection from him. Why was he offering it now? What had changed?

The suite was on the same floor. The huge living room and dining room combination was decorated in the same contemporary style as Ryland's office. Multiple bedrooms and a kitchenette opened off the main space.

"The kitchen is stocked with beverages and snacks. Room service will bring you whatever you like." The guard exited.

And they were alone.

Abby dropped her coat and purse on a chair and walked across the room. She stared out the wall of glass at the turbulent ocean that stretched into the darkness.

"Ryland is up to something," Ethan said.

"I know," Abby agreed. "Whatever it is, there isn't anything we can do to stop him, and he won't do anything to hurt me."

"You trust him?"

"To tell the truth? No. But I don't think he'd deliberately hurt me." Abby put a hand on the window. The glass was cold under her palm. "My experiences with Ryland were mostly full of disappointment and neglect, but no fear."

"You should have told me you were his daughter."

"I didn't want anyone to know," she said. "Everyone knows what he is."

Possible indictments used to make the news every few years. Though lately, Ryland had kept a low profile.

"How old were you when you found out?" he asked.

"I've always known he was my father, but I was never allowed to say. Plus, it wasn't until I was older that I realized the full implications of what it meant." The pain welled up as fresh as when she was a child. "He and my mother always claimed it was for my own safety, but that was only part of it. He has a wife and two sons, and he didn't want to destroy his perfect family by admitting he had an illegitimate child." Abby paused for a shaky breath.

"I'm sorry," Ethan said.

"When I was a child, he'd visit us a few times a year. He gave her money, always cash. I'd get a small present, but he kept his distance. He'd spend the night, and she would stay in bed for days afterward."

"She loved him?"

"Until the kidnapping." Abby choked on her next breath. She swallowed her bitterness. "When I was kidnapped, my mother went to him and asked him to find me. He refused to intervene, and the police botched the case. Mom never spoke to him again. She overdosed a month after the trial. The stress was too much."

"I'm sorry." Ethan's voice was hoarse.

Abby shrugged. "Maybe he was right. Maybe I'd have been a target all my life if my paternity was public knowledge. Maybe someone found out I'm his daughter and is trying to kill me because of something to do with his business." How much could she share? "Ryland is shedding the illegal portions of his portfolio. He implied his business partners in those ventures are unhappy with him."

"Do you have any idea who his enemies are?"

"No. He's never shared anything about his life with me. I've only been to this casino once. After my mother overdosed, I told him I never wanted to see him again." Abby leaned her forehead on the cool glass. She could see Ethan's reflection in the window. His posture was tense, his hands fisted at his sides. "He is one of the reasons I moved away. I wanted to start over. I wanted to forget he was my father." She closed her eyes. "Ryland is a powerful man who chose to let me suffer rather than take the chance his affair with my mother would be revealed."

Ethan moved closer, silently eliminating the distance between them.

"You don't know how much I didn't want to come here and ask him for help." Ryland's old betrayal still burned deep in Abby's soul. "When I was a child and they took me to a foster home, I kept waiting for him to come and get me. I thought he'd swoop in and take me home, make me a part of his other family. He never did."

"What do you think he's doing?" Ethan asked.

Even though they weren't touching, she could sense his body behind her. More than anything, she wanted him to touch her. Her desire transcended sexuality. She wanted the intimacy they'd shared, the soul-deep bond she'd never felt for another person.

And she needed to give him the trust he deserved, the piece of her she'd held back.

"I don't know. I hope he's looking for Torres and Krista. He might be cleaning up his business now, but I'm sure he still has plenty of contacts on the wrong side of the law. If anyone can find a criminal, it's Ryland."

Ethan put a tentative hand on her arm. She leaned into him, and his arms came around her.

"I shouldn't have blamed you." Unshed tears stung the corners of Abby's eyes.

"It's all right. I should have warned Derek, but I wanted him to finish with the artist. I was afraid if he knew he was going into a foster home, we'd lose an important piece of evidence that could help find his mother." Ethan turned her to face him. His eyes were misty. "I was trying to help him."

"I know. I lost it when that woman took Derek away." Abby trembled. "I know exactly how scared and alone he felt when she put him in the back of the car." Exhaustion and emotions buckled her knees.

Ethan scooped her into his arms and carried her to the closest bedroom. He set her on the bed. He tossed his jacket across the bottom of the bed, placed his gun on the nightstand, and stretched out next to her. "I don't know how to convince you that you really can trust me. I would never do anything to hurt you. I drove half the night because I was insane with fear that something was going to happen to you."

Abby slipped off her boots. "My heart trusts you, but my head has been conditioned not to trust anyone." She leaned against his chest and closed her eyes.

"Next time, talk to me, all right?" Ethan rested his chin on the top of her head. "No running off alone. Promise?"

"Promise. I'm so glad you're here." Abby nestled closer, grateful for his presence.

He rolled to his side and draped an arm over her.

She welcomed the reassuring weight of it. "Don't let me sleep more than a half hour, OK?"

"Just a quick power nap." Ethan lifted his upper body. He set the alarm on his phone, turned up the ringer volume, and settled back into place.

But his phone rang less than a minute later. Abby read the display as he levered up on one elbow and reached for it.

WESTBURY POLICE DEPT.

"Hale." Ethan held the phone a few inches from his ear so Abby could hear.

"Where are you?" Static sounded over the chief's voice.

"Still in Atlantic City." Ethan sat up. "Why?"

The chief raised his voice. "Derek is gone."

Ryland let himself into his private suite. Closing the door behind him, he punched Kenneth's number into his cell phone. The boy Abby had referred to had to be the same one that Kenneth was pursuing. Plus, Kenneth needed to find out who employed Joe Torres.

Was it Paul Medina? Was Paul angry enough over Ryland's exit from the drug business to kill Abby as a warning to Ryland that the rest of his family could suffer the same fate unless he continued to provide distribution for Paul's product?

He knew the answer without further consideration. Anger had nothing to do with it. Money was at stake. Huge piles of it.

At one time, Ryland would have been more than willing to do anything to rake in more of it.

But he'd changed these last few years. The physical frailties that accompanied aging had humbled him. As had the knowledge that he had far more years behind him than stretched out on the road ahead.

Kenneth's phone rang, but he didn't pick up.

What was he doing? Fuck. Ryland should have made it clear the child wasn't to be harmed when Kenneth called last time. Maybe Ryland hadn't changed as much as he'd thought. He was still a selfish man, willing to let another child suffer so that Ryland's own family could be safe.

Ryland pressed END without leaving a message. When Kenneth saw that he missed the call, he would return it. Ryland checked the time on his phone display. It would take three hours for another man to reach Kenneth's location. By then it might be too late.

He walked to the window and stared out at the roiling sea. His internal sensors were alarming. Something was going down. Something bad. The coming storm wasn't the biggest threat on the horizon.

———————

"What?" The cobwebs in Ethan's brain were swept away by the chief's statement.

"The foster parents heard a car engine outside. They checked on all the kids. Derek was gone. There was water on the floor under his window. They think he jumped from the roof to a nearby tree and then someone picked him up on the road. Where's Abby?"

"She's with me."

"Then she didn't pick him up," the chief said.

"No."

Ethan's gaze went to the window. Sheets of rain obscured the view of the ocean. "Is it raining there?"

"No. Sleeting and cold," the chief said. "I hate to think of a kid out in this weather. We're organizing a search, and we've notified county and state law enforcement."

"Any leads on Torres or Derek's mom?" Guilt tore into Ethan. Abby had feared Derek would run away if he was sent into foster care again. Damn it. He should have listened to her. He should have broken the rules and found a place to hide the kid.

"No," the chief answered. "And now I have to divert manpower from the case to look for Derek."

Ethan told him about Ryland Valentine and his relationship to Abby.

The chief swore softly. "When are you coming back?"

"We're leaving in a couple minutes." Ethan ended the call. Abby was already up and moving. She went into the living room and grabbed her purse. From its depths she produced a cell phone. She dialed and waited, sweeping a hand across her forehead. "He's not answering."

"He has your phone, right?"

"Right."

"You have my electronic tablet in your purse. I found you by tracking it." Ethan stood up, hope energizing his limbs. He put his gun back into its hip holster. "Even if you don't have the app downloaded, we can try to track the phone's location."

"My phone doesn't have GPS."

And hope took a swan dive over the deep end. "What?"

"I always use cheap prepaid phones without GPS." She held up her new cell phone.

"Why?"

"Because I don't want the wrong people to be able to track me." She picked up the hotel phone and ordered coffee to-go. She retreated to the bathroom. Ethan heard the water running and the toilet flush. He took his turn next. When he came out, a waiter was setting a tray with travel mugs of coffee and a cardboard box on a table. He exited, closing the door behind him.

Ryland was talking to Abby in the living area. Of course, his staff would have let him know the second they called for coffee. Abby's face was pale, her eyes too wide.

Ethan walked over to see what dear old dad was up to.

Ryland stopped talking. "This is a private matter."

Abby shook her head. "No. If it's important, you can tell us both. If it's not, then we're leaving."

Ryland's eyes debated. "All right. There is one more piece of information you should have. When you were kidnapped, Detective Abrams was not incompetent as you were led to believe. He was corrupt. He knew exactly where you were. He withheld that information until I paid him a hundred thousand dollars."

Face. Palm.

Ethan should have connected those dots. "That's where he got the money for the boat and the new car."

"Yes." Fury burned in Ryland eyes.

"Did you have anything to do with his death?" Ethan asked.

Ignoring Ethan's question, Ryland turned to Abby. "I owe you an apology. I shouldn't have refused your mother when she asked me to find you. I should have done it myself, but I didn't think it was related to me at all."

Other than the victim was his daughter. Ethan held back the words. There was no need to emphasize Ryland's neglect.

"What about now?" Ethan slid into his jacket.

Ryland looked away. "I'm not sure."

That wasn't helpful.

"We have to go." Abby picked up her coat and purse. "Thank you for being honest."

Ryland bowed out. "I had my staff put a box of sandwiches together. If you can't sleep, food will be better than nothing."

Ethan had his doubts about Ryland's honesty. The furtive look in his eyes said he was still holding something back.

He and Abby didn't speak until they were in his truck. The casino had cameras pretty much everywhere. He started the engine.

"Emotionally, I can't even process all that he's told me. I feel like the last three years have been a lie. I thought my kidnapping was random. Now I find out it might have been one of my father's business associates. Maybe he did keep me a secret all my life to protect me. I always thought that was bullshit, but now, I don't know." Abby set their coffees in the center console. "I'm tired of secrets and conspiracies."

"Are you OK?"

"I'll deal with it all later. Right now we have to find Derek. Then get back to the search for Torres and Krista."

"Does Derek have anywhere he feels safe?"

"Besides my house?" The irony in Abby's question was all too clear. "No."

"Where did he go last time?"

"The woods, but it was summer." Abby sipped her coffee.

"He's a smart kid." Ethan drove out of the garage into a steady, soaking rain. "I think he'll hole up somewhere out of the weather."

"If he can."

An hour later they drove across the Benjamin Franklin Bridge and went north on the Schuylkill Expressway. The rain changed to sleet, and Ethan was forced to slow the truck as patches of black ice spread across the road. At this speed, it would be morning before they got home.

The sleet intensified, mixing with snowflakes as they headed north. It was definitely not summer, and Derek didn't have a warm coat or boots. If the boy was outside, exposure was only a matter of time.

CHAPTER TWENTY-FIVE

Derek shivered in the backseat.

The tall man turned up the heat. "Where are you going, Derek?"

"Dunno. Far as I can get." Derek shrank into the cold leather. Water dripped from his hair onto his nose. The guy knew his name. That wasn't a good sign. He scanned the passing scenery for landmarks and recognized a billboard for a local ski hill. They were heading back toward town.

"Shitty walk in this weather." The man turned on the defroster. "My name is Kenneth. I'm looking for the man who took your mother. I could use your help."

"Are you with the police?"

"No." They passed under a streetlight. In the rearview mirror, Kenneth caught Derek's gaze. Kenneth's eyes were flat gray, no color, no expression. Dead eyes. "You can think of me as the opposite of the police."

A killer going after a killer? Derek tried to sort out facts, but the events of the past few days felt like pieces to different puzzles all mixed together. "What do you want with Joe?"

"His whole name is Joe Torres. Does it matter why I wish to find him?" Kenneth's words were carefully articulated, as if English wasn't his original language. The faint trace of a weird foreign accent gave his words an odd ring. "You want your mother back, right?"

The question felt dangerous, but so did not answering. "Yes."

"Then we should work together." Except being with Kenneth made Derek's intestines want to tie themselves into knots. There was something inhuman about him. Derek's instincts told him to run far, far away. Not that his instincts were doing him any good locked in a car doing fifty miles an hour. Kenneth had to stop the car eventually, though. The needle on the gas gauge was leaning into the red.

Derek considered the hard body that had picked him up like a newborn kitten. The guy was lean and mean in a way that didn't suggest a membership at the local Y. Derek would need a cagey plan to get away from Kenneth. Pure speed wasn't going to cut it. "Where are we going?"

"I'm going to be straight with you, Derek. Joe freelances as a contract killer. My boss believes he was hired to kill Miss Foster."

Derek cringed. A hit man had been living in his house. He didn't doubt Kenneth's claim. That was the first real fact to snap into place. Joe had picked up his mom just so he could get close to Abby, and Derek hadn't done a thing about it. His mom and Abby were both in danger because he'd been too afraid, too selfish, too cowardly to rat out Joe.

The car passed by the high school. His neighborhood was a couple of miles away. Before he worried about where he was going, he had to shake creepy Kenneth.

"If my boss is right, I doubt Torres is leaving with the job unfinished," Kenneth said. "He's hanging around here somewhere. I bet you know your neighborhood better than anybody. Are there any good places to hide?"

"Not really." Derek wasn't so sure Joe would stick that close. Abby hadn't been home much. She'd been with Ethan. If Derek wanted to find her, he'd hang in the woods behind

Ethan's place. But Derek wasn't going to explain his theory to Kenneth.

"Unless she is at the policeman's house," Kenneth said.

Derek's empty stomach cramped. He and Kenneth were thinking the same thoughts, which creeped Derek out even more. They passed the Food Rite shopping center. Kenneth turned into the gas station and pulled up to a pump. On the other side of the cement island, an older guy was taking the gas nozzle out of his pickup.

Kenneth's phone rang. He got out of the car. Pressing the phone to his ear, he locked the doors and gave Derek a pointed look through the window before going inside the convenience store.

Ethan's farm was in the opposite direction. How many miles? Derek had only been there once. Would he even be able to find it in the dark? Whatever. Escape first, make new plan second. Derek opened the backpack at his feet. He took the phone Abby had given him out of the front pouch and slid it into his inside jacket pocket. He'd have to leave everything else behind.

Pickup guy screwed his gas cap back on and got into his truck. In the store, Kenneth was getting cash out of his wallet, his phone jammed between his shoulder and ear. Derek pried off the dome light cover and took out the lightbulb. He hit the unlock button and pulled the door lever. It didn't open. Stupid childproof locks. Sliding over the seat, he slipped out the driver's door, which faced away from Kenneth and toward the cement island. The engine of the pickup on the other side of the pumps turned over. In a crouch, Derek ran around the far side of the truck, climbed into the bed, and pulled a tarp over him. The sound of sleet pinging on metal covered the scrape of his clothing.

They pulled away from the gas station. Derek resisted the temptation to check to see if Kenneth was coming after him. He kept his head down and thought invisible thoughts.

———

"Have you found the boy?" Ryland held his breath. Rain hammered his office window and blurred his view of the tumultuous water beyond.

"Yes," Kenneth said.

Ryland heard voices in the background. "Where are you?"

"A gas station." Fabric rustled on Kenneth's end of the line.

Ryland refocused. "Where is he?"

"He is with me."

"The boy and his mother are not to be harmed," Ryland instructed.

"Now you tell me." Static interspersed Kenneth's words. Either the storm or his rural location was interfering with reception.

Shit. Ryland's heart double-tapped.

"The boy is fine," Kenneth clarified. "But it would have been preferable to have that information earlier this evening. Things might have gone differently."

"I agree." A chill slid into Ryland's belly.

"Fuck." Wind whistled through the open line, muffling Kenneth's exclamation.

What now? Ryland focused beyond the raindrops, on the black water and the blinking green light bobbing in the distance.

"The kid gave me the slip." Respect colored Kenneth's voice, then regret. "I should have expected as much. He's no coddled child. At his age, I certainly wouldn't have given up so easily."

"Can you find him again?"

"Maybe. I think Derek and I have much in common, including our present goals." A car engine started as Kenneth spoke. "I will continue to look for him."

"Abby is on her way back to Westbury to find the boy."

"So Abby is looking for the child, who is looking for his mother, who is with the man trying to kill Abby." Kenneth summed up the mayhem.

"Yes. And you still have no idea who is behind the current attacks and why."

"That is correct," Kenneth admitted. "But rest assured. I will find out the truth."

Ryland had a few ideas. If Abby was being targeted because of him, there were only a few people who would dare take that initiative. He ended the call with Kenneth and dialed another number.

The line rang three times before Paul Medina answered. "What can I do for you, Ryland?"

"We need to meet."

"I agree," Paul said. "We have unfinished business to discuss."

They settled on a time and place. Ryland ended the call and turned back to his window. He anchored his emotions to the shifting buoy on the water and gathered his resolve. In thirty years, his daughter had asked one thing of him. He couldn't fail her the way he had in the past. She deserved better. She was his child. Unless she wanted to continue to keep her existence a secret, he no longer saw the point. Hiding her hadn't protected her from his enemies. Yes, it had kept Ryland's life clean and shielded his family from living with an ugly scandal, but that was no longer enough. Of course, he'd had other reasons for keeping Abby's paternity a secret.

He would have to tell his sons and his wife. If the attempts on Abby's life were a warning, the rest of his family could also be at risk.

Watching the water, Ryland breathed deeply. Would the boys forgive him? How would Marlene react? And when would he stop causing other people pain? He'd been a selfish man over the years. Unfortunately, everyone close to him was paying the price for his sins.

CHAPTER TWENTY-SIX

Abby stared down at the ruined sneakers and stained jacket hanging from the peg on the garage wall. "They're Derek's."

Ethan turned to the homeowner, a thin man in his fifties. "What did you say was stolen, Mr. Hanes?"

"Coat, boots, gloves, and a hat. That wet stuff was left right there." Mr. Hanes rubbed his bald head. "Boys' size twelve. My son's just about outgrown the boots and coat. If I hadn't seen the clip about the missing kid, I would've thought maybe one of his friends borrowed the coat or he lost it. I certainly wouldn't have bothered calling the police."

"We appreciate that you did, Mr. Hanes." Ethan put Derek's jacket and shoes in a paper bag. "Did you want to press charges?"

"Hell no." Mr. Hanes hooked his thumbs in the front pockets of his jeans. "I wish I'd seen the kid. I would've brought him in and fed him. I hate to think of him out in this storm."

"Us too," Ethan agreed. "Any idea how he got in?"

"I got home late from a job in Philly. All I can think is he followed my truck into the garage last night, helped himself to the gear, and went out the side door. He must have been gone before daybreak. I didn't see him when I came out to get my wallet this morning. There really isn't anywhere to hide in here. If only I'd noticed the missing coat then. Maybe you could've found him."

"Thank you for calling us, Mr. Hanes." Ethan shook his hand.

Abby and Ethan left the garage through the overhead door. The afternoon light was dimming as they walked down the driveway. They climbed into Ethan's truck parked at the curb. The sandwich Ethan had forced her to eat for lunch balled up inside her stomach.

Pulling away from the house, Ethan reached for her hand. His glove squeezed hers. "At least he's dressed warmly now."

"Small favors." Frustration pounded in Abby's temples. "Where is he?"

"He's on foot. He can't have gotten that far."

"He managed to get back into town from the foster home." Abby took off her gloves and held her hands to the heat vents. "That's a few miles from here."

"Long walk in that sleet last night. Another mile and he'd have been back in your neighborhood." Ethan drove toward Main Street. "This is all residential housing. Lots of opportunities for unlocked sheds and basements."

"But it's not just Derek we're missing. Krista and Joe are nowhere to be found either." Abby flexed her fingers. "How can three people disappear in a town this small?"

"This might be a small town by population but not geographically. Law enforcement is spread thin over a good-size chunk of land. There are a lot of heavily wooded areas, abandoned buildings, hunting cabins. We have every available resource working this case." He glanced sideways and caught her gaze for a second. "We will find him." Determination strengthened his words—Daniel Day-Lewis, *The Last of the Mohicans*-style.

But Abby wasn't so sure. "There are so many awful possibilities."

"Don't think about it." Ethan pulled up to a stop sign. "We have to stay positive."

But the worst-case scenarios were stuck in her head. "Derek's been gone all day. What if Joe found him? What if Joe decided to cut his losses and get out of town? He could have already killed Krista and Derek."

"He probably took Krista as insurance, a hostage in case he needs a bargaining chip. Why would he kill her?"

"If he's already a few hundred miles away, she could be dead wood he's tired of dragging around," Abby said. "Also, she and Derek can both testify against him."

"True, but we have enough physical evidence that the case wouldn't rely completely on their testimony."

"You think Joe is that smart?"

"Hard to say. Some criminals are pretty savvy about the law and how to avoid prosecution. Others are complete dumbasses. He left a lot of evidence behind, including fingerprints. He's either a dumbass, or he's cocky. He's been able to skate off charges in the past."

"Derek loves the comic book store." Abby pointed ahead. "Let's stop and see if the owner has seen him."

"OK." Ethan parked at a meter. They got out of the car and trudged up the sidewalk. Abby flipped a hood over her head. The sleet had given way to light rain during the day. The temperature, which had hovered just above freezing, was dropping. Tonight was going to be treacherous. Search teams were finishing up their current rounds and heading in until daybreak. There'd been no sign of Derek. The chief didn't want rescue volunteers killed during the search.

An electronic beep announced their entry into the store.

The fortyish guy at the register was too old to wear skinny jeans. "Hey, I was just closing."

"We won't be more than a minute," Abby said. She dug out the snapshot of Derek and showed it to the clerk. "Have you seen him?"

"Yeah, I know that kid." The overhead light winked on his tongue stud. Ew. "He comes in here once in a while."

"When was the last time you saw him?" Ethan asked.

The clerk shrugged. "Dunno. Last week maybe."

"Thanks." Ethan handed him a card. "Call me if you see him."

The clerk's eyes widened. "Is he in trouble?"

"No," Abby said. "He's missing."

"Shit. That sucks." The clerk shoved Ethan's card in his front pocket. "I'll call you if I see him."

"Thanks." Abby followed Ethan outside. Sleet pelted her face. "Now what?"

Ethan squinted and hunched his shoulders against the wind. "Now we go home."

"I want to drive through my neighborhood one more time." Pain zinged through Abby's frozen toes with every step.

"OK." Ethan took her elbow and steered her toward his truck. "Ronnie said she can stay at my place all night if we need her."

Abby's house was close to the center of town. Even at a crawl, the drive didn't take long. Ethan turned down her street. The cloud cover was thick enough to bring an early twilight.

Ethan drove around the surrounding blocks. There was no sign of Derek, or anyone else. He parked in her driveway. "Do you want to grab anything from your house?"

Abby opened the car door. "I want to check the shed out back."

"You think he might be in there?"

"Probably not, but I have to check. As you said, Mr. Hanes's house is only about a mile from here." She got out and trudged around the house. Tamping down the illogical grain of hope budding inside her, she opened the gate and walked across the yard toward the big wooden shed that took up the rear corner of her property. She opened the door. Her hope deflated as she wrestled the door from the wind. It was empty. She turned back toward the house.

"Wait." Ethan called her back with a low voice. "Look at the ground but don't react."

In the half-frozen slush, a line of footprints led away from the shed.

Water dripped from Derek's nose. He shook ice crystals from his hat and peered through Mr. Sheridan's shed window. Fifty feet away, Abby and Ethan were checking out her shed, the place he'd been hiding all day.

That was close.

Ethan went into the building for a minute. Abby looked sad as she closed the door. Watching her, Derek's chest hurt. If she'd been alone, he wouldn't have run. But Ethan would send him back to the foster home. Cold and wet was way better than . . .

Nope. Not going there again. Though he probably wouldn't. This was his second bolt-and-run. He'd probably end up in juvenile detention if he got caught this time—one more reason for him not to get caught.

Derek coughed. Even with the dry coat and boots he'd stolen from the owner of the pickup that had assisted in his escape, he had never been this cold in his life. He couldn't feel his feet or his hands. Really, he couldn't feel 90 percent of his body. He felt bad about taking stuff that wasn't his. He'd try to return it someday. But for once, luck had been with him last night. The boots were a little big, but better than his waterlogged sneakers. When he'd sneaked out the side door before dawn, to his surprise, he'd found himself not far from home.

Kenneth's words wouldn't get out of Derek's head.

I doubt Torres is leaving with the job unfinished. He's hanging around here somewhere. I bet you know your neighborhood better than anybody. Are there any good places to hide?

Where would Joe go? If Kenneth was right, Joe would stay close to places he was likely to find Abby.

Derek had headed home. Abby's shed was a better hiding place in the summer. But where could he go? It was too cold to walk far, and the ice storm nixed any ideas of hiding in the woods. And he couldn't leave, not with his mom missing. For all her faults, she wouldn't leave without him. Joe must have made her. But where were they?

Ethan and Abby turned back to her house. Derek fought the urge to yell out to her. He pressed a hand to his empty belly. He was so hungry, his stomach felt like it was eating itself.

The corners of his eyes burned with tears. He didn't want to spend the night in Mr. Sheridan's shed. Not that his neighbor would find Derek. As nosy as Mr. Sheridan was, he couldn't see Derek way back here, not through the precipitation. And at seventy-six, Mr. Sheridan wasn't coming outside in an ice storm. Derek looked at the back of his neighbor's house.

Weird.

All the blinds were drawn. Mr. Sheridan liked to watch the neighborhood activity. He loved catching kids doing something, anything that might get them into trouble.

Derek's empty belly roiled. A piece of sleet melted, ran into his collar, and rolled down his spine.

He pushed the shed door open and went out into Mr. Sheridan's yard. The maple tree's limbs overhead were coated in ice, and the freezing rain had built up a shiny layer on the brick walkway too. Something was definitely wrong. Mr. Sheridan should have put rock salt on his stoop. He always tossed it by the cupful from the back door.

Derek crept to the window, but he couldn't see anything. He tiptoed to the half-glass back door and put his eye to the crack between the blind and the doorframe. He could see a thin slice of Mr. Sheridan's kitchen.

What was that? Derek squinted. *Oh no.* Sticking through the doorway, Derek could see legs clad in muddy brown polyester pants. Mr. Sheridan was lying on the floor. A shadow crossed the room, the figure moving way too fast to be old Mr. Sheridan. Derek turned, ducked, and pressed his back to the door. He glanced over at the back of Abby's house. Were she and Ethan still there? Calling Abby meant Ethan would send him back to foster care, but Derek didn't care. Mr. Sheridan was hurt inside, and the sick feeling in Derek's gut told him maybe Joe was in there too. Was Derek's mom?

He pulled Abby's phone from his pocket and turned it on. His thumbs shot out a quick text. He zipped the cell back into his pocket. Should he go back to the shed or try to get another peek inside?

The door opened, and a hand yanked Derek inside.

"I've been looking for you." The veins in Joe's neck popped, and his eyes were black and buggy. He grabbed Derek by the front of his jacket and tossed him into the wall.

Derek's head and shoulders bounced off the sheetrock. Pain rolled through his head. He slid to the floor and fell to his side. Putting his hands under him, his gloves slipped in something wet. He turned his palms over. Red liquid coated the gray nylon. Blood. The edges of Derek's vision blurred. His heart rattled in his chest as he pushed his upper body off of the floor and looked right into Mr. Sheridan's dead eyes.

He scrambled to his feet. Joe got a hold of the back of Derek's jacket and hauled him across the kitchen. Derek skidded in the smeared blood and tripped over Mr. Sheridan's arm. His hollow stomach heaved. Acid bubbled into his mouth.

There was so much blood. . . .

Joe dragged him into the living room.

Derek's heart skipped. His mom was lying on the floor, arms out-flung as if someone had tossed her there. Her eyes were closed, her body limp. Her jeans and sweater bagged on her thin frame. Was she unconscious? *Please don't be dead.* He started toward her.

"Stand still." Joe yanked him backward.

Trembling, Derek wrapped his arms around his chest. On the outside, he was standing still and silent. On the inside, he was running and screaming.

A shove on his shoulder spun him around. Joe had a knife in his hand. Derek's bladder almost gave out. Joe picked up a roll of duct tape. Yanking some loose, he slapped a piece over Derek's mouth. Light glistened on the blade as Joe gestured toward a straight-back chair. "Sit."

Derek shuffled over on shaky legs and dropped onto the seat. He strained as Joe taped his wrists to the armrests. Next, he secured Derek's ankles to the chair legs.

"Fucking hold still." Joe backhanded him across the face.

Pain rocked Derek's cheekbone. Blood filled his mouth. Dazed, he looked beyond Joe, at his mom. From this angle he could see her chest rise and fall. The movement seemed slow and shallow. A darkening bruise and swelling colored the side of her jaw. She was alive, but for how long? They'd seen too much. Joe wouldn't let them go.

"Eventually the bitch has to come back." Joe went to the window and moved the blinds an inch. "Oh, there she is." He turned. A crazy grin split his face. "She's hiding behind the shed, and it looks like she's all alone."

Panic tumbled through Derek's chest. Ethan had been with Abby before. Where was he now? Had he left? He and his mom couldn't do a thing.

With his text, Derek had called Abby right to Joe.

She couldn't face Joe alone. He'd kill her. Derek pulled at the tape binding him to the chair. He'd strained hard enough when Joe was securing the binds that the tape wasn't super tight. He rocked his forearms back and forth. His skin burned as the adhesive moved. The silver tape didn't break, but it did stretch just a little. Could he loosen it enough to slide his arm out?

"What are you doing?" Joe roared. He cocked his fist and punched Derek in the side of the head.

Derek's head snapped back, and agony rocked his temple. He couldn't hold back a whimper.

"Shut up. Christ, I hate kids." Joe pressed the point of his knife into Derek's cheek. "If I didn't need your sniveling, sneaky little ass, I'd slit your throat right now."

Blood and tears dripped down Derek's face. Joe's eyes brightened. He was getting off on Derek's suffering and fear.

Out of the corner of his eye, Derek saw his mom stir. One arm moved a couple of inches. Her eyes opened and blinked several times. Focusing on Derek, they widened with alarm and anger. She rolled to her stomach and belly-crawled toward Joe.

"Don't you hurt my son!" Her shout was raspy. On her hands and knees, she grabbed his ankle.

"You're awake." Joe turned on her. A kick to the head sent her sprawling. "Move again and I'll cut out his tongue."

She cringed, falling back, her muscles giving out from hopelessness or weakness, maybe both.

He ran the knifepoint along Derek's jaw. Derek's face burned as the blade made a shallow slice.

"Fuck. Maybe I'll just do it for fun." Joe ripped the tape from Derek's mouth.

His mother screamed and launched herself at Joe. He kicked her again, his boot making solid contact with the side of her face. She flopped backward, unmoving.

Eyes glittering with excitement, Joe bent over Derek. With one hand, he grabbed Derek's jaw and wrenched his mouth open. In his other, he clenched the knife.

CHAPTER TWENTY-SEVEN

"Don't point." Ethan concentrated on acting casual. "Don't stare at the ground either. He might be watching."

"And you think he'll run?" Abby kept her voice soft.

Ethan barely heard her over the sound of sleet pinging off the shed roof. "Don't you? Those prints are fresh. Obviously, he saw us and took off."

Abby frowned.

Ethan read her mind. "It's not you he doesn't trust. It's me. I'm the one who sent him to foster care."

"You didn't have a choice."

"You and I know that, but Derek is twelve." Regret hardened Ethan's heart. "I just wish he would have trusted me."

Abby's purse buzzed. She reached into the outer pocket and pulled out her cell phone. "It's a text. Oh my God. It's my number. It must be Derek."

Ethan took two steps and stood beside her. "What does it say?"

She pulled off a glove with her teeth and pressed OPEN. "Mr. Sheridan's house."

"Who's Mr. Sheridan?" Ethan tracked Abby's gaze to the split-level catty-corner to her yard. The footprints in the slush pointed right at the fence between the properties.

Abby's mouth twisted into a thoughtful frown. "Mr. Sheridan doesn't close his blinds. He likes to see what's going on all the time."

Every window on the back of the house was covered.

"Are you sure?"

"He is getting old and a little forgetful, but he's still the busiest busybody on the block." Abby sent Derek a return text. WHERE R U?

"Let's not take any chances. His house would be the perfect place to watch for you." Ethan whipped out his phone and called for backup. "They're on the way, but there's a pileup on Route Six. Plus, the roads are covered in ice. It's going to be a little while." He pocketed his phone. "Did he respond?"

"No."

"I'm going to check it out."

Abby was already moving toward the back of her yard.

Ethan grabbed her by the arm. "You wait here."

She shook her head and reached into her purse. She pulled out a frigging Glock.

"Where the hell did you get that?"

"It was my mother's." Abby checked the clip like a pro. "It was pretty much all she left me. She wasn't much of a jewelry girl."

"Do you have a concealed carry permit?" Yeah, that sounded lame.

"No." Abby gave him a *that's ridiculous* roll of her eyes. "It's a good thing it isn't concealed. Are you coming?"

"Can you shoot that? It looks big for you." But Ethan remembered her practiced stance when she'd pointed his gun at Detective Abrams's killer.

"I can shoot it just fine. My mother believed in reliability and stopping power. Weapons aren't supposed to be delicate." Abby tossed her purse in the shed. Tucking the gun in her coat pocket, she put a toe in the fence and climbed over.

"Have you ever shot at a person?" Ethan wasn't sure he

wanted the answer to his question. Abby had been full of surprises. She wasn't the fragile flower he'd thought. Damaged, yes. Delicate, no.

"No."

"It's a lot different than firing at a paper target."

Abby deadpanned him from the other side of the fence. "I'll do anything to keep that man from hurting Derek."

Damn it. He'd have to arrest her and handcuff her to something heavy to keep her away. Ethan vaulted the chain-link and took the lead. "Stay behind me and do exactly what I say."

He tugged Abby in back of the neighbor's shed. "I want you to stay here just while I take a look around."

Abby opened her mouth to argue. Ethan put a finger to her lips and shook his head. "You need to keep watch. In case I don't come back, someone has to be able to tell the police what happens." He pointed up the side of the property. "From here you can see the road. The street light is on. If Joe makes a run for it, you'll know."

Abby's mouth flattened. "I don't like it."

"I know, but please do it anyway."

"I'll give you five minutes." She glanced up at the sky and shivered. Night had descended in full. Heavy cloud cover and driving rain blocked any possible moonlight.

"Are you all right? It's dark."

"I'll be fine," she said, clearly lying through her clenched teeth.

But there wasn't anything Ethan could do about the darkness. To contact Abby, Derek was risking being returned to the foster home. He could be in big trouble. "I'll be back as fast as I can."

Ethan jogged across Mr. Sheridan's rear yard. His boots slipped. Sleet, rain, and snow pelted the exposed skin of his face.

Crouching below window height, he made a quick circuit of the house. Coming around to the back again, he tripped. There was something solid under his feet. He scraped away three inches of shitty wet snow. Bulkhead doors. Ethan gave the handle a light tug. No lock?

Rusted hinges yielded with a slow groan. Ethan pulled a flashlight from his pocket and shined the beam down the stairs before descending. The cellar was empty except for the usual basement fixtures: washer, dryer, furnace, boxes of old junk.

Ethan crossed the slab. Wooden steps led up into the house. At the top of the stairs, he put his eye to the crack under the door. A short hall opened into a room. Shadows moved. More than one person.

A woman screamed.

———————

Abby checked the time on her phone. Nerves jittered in her belly. Six minutes had passed since Ethan disappeared into the basement, and she'd had no response from Derek.

A muffled female scream carried across the freezing rain. Krista? Had to be. Mr. Sheridan lived alone.

Abby ran toward the back of the house. Ethan had gone into the basement more than five minutes ago. Was he all right? Was Derek inside too?

Even up close, she couldn't see in the windows. She crept up to the back door. Wait. She peered through a tiny crack between the window frame and the blind. With the limited view, she could see the feet and lower legs of someone lying on the floor. Something red was smeared on the pale gray tile. The shoes were black, bulky, and looked orthopedic. Mr. Sheridan. Was he alive?

Abby strained for the sound of approaching sirens but heard nothing but freezing rain and sleet filtering through foliage and pinging off every surface. Heart thumping, she approached the bulkhead doors where Ethan had disappeared a few minutes before.

She put one foot on the first step and bent over to see into the space. The basement was dark. Way darker than the yard. Her eyes had adjusted to the lack of light outside. But down there . . .

Inside the sleeves of her winter coat, goose bumps crawled up Abby's arms as she stared into the black hole. Dark and below ground. Like the well. Like a grave.

Leading with his gun, Ethan eased the basement door open. The house was small. A short hallway opened into a living room.

"Whoever you are, get your ass in here or I'll slice the kid's tongue out."

Ethan's stomach dropped. He stepped around the corner and took in the scene with a wave of nausea. Derek was taped to a chair, his body sideways to Ethan. Tears and blood dripped down the side of the boy's face. Joe was on Derek's other side, using the kid's body as a shield. Joe had the kid's mouth pried open with one hand, the glistening knife poised with the other. Ethan couldn't shoot. Not without hitting Derek.

In his peripheral vision, Ethan could see Krista lying on the floor. She wasn't moving.

"Put the knife down, Joe," Ethan said.

"No fucking way." Joe's hands shook. His eyes were the unnatural black of a meth addict. "You put your gun down or the kid never talks again." Joe demonstrated his willingness with a poke at

Derek's tongue. The boy's whimper was distorted by the hard grip on his lower jaw. Blood trickled from the corner of his mouth.

But if Ethan put down his gun, what would stop Joe from doing anything he wanted to Derek? Absolutely nothing.

Ethan needed to stall. Surely backup would be here any minute. "I'll lower the gun if you take the knife away from his face."

"Fuck you."

"I think what we have here is a stalemate."

"Bullshit. You can't shoot me without hitting the kid, and you know it." Joe's eyes gleamed. He was enjoying the power and control. "Drop the gun or I start cutting bits of the kid off."

A thin line of blood trickled from the edge of Derek's mouth. Ethan's body tensed.

"Don't come any closer." Joe slid the knife out of Derek's mouth. More blood welled. The blade must have sliced the boy's tongue. Joe lifted the kid's jaw, stretching his neck out and positioning the sharp edge of the weapon along the jugular vein.

Ethan didn't move.

"Drop the gun and kick it over here."

Shit. Shit. Shit.

Terror had cranked Derek's eyes wide open.

But Ethan knew that dropping his gun meant they were helpless. "I can't do that, Joe." The situation had gone from bad to worst-case scenario. Where was his backup? And what were they going to do when they got here? Joe was an alarming mix of cunning and meth-addict crazy. "Look, why don't you let the kid go? I'll let you have me instead."

"As long as I have this kid, I have you. But I'm sure you called for backup. Two hostages are better than one." Joe grinned and nicked Derek's neck.

CHAPTER TWENTY-EIGHT

Don't think about it. People could be dying. No time for a panic attack.

But Abby's belly cramped and her pulse went into overdrive as she stepped down again. The steps were wooden and rickety. The third tread squeaked. Abby moved to the side to minimize any more sound. Descending to the bottom, Abby squinted into the darkness. Six steps led to the basement floor. Her boots scuffed on the dusty cement. The scant gray light from the open door ended two feet in front of her. Her next step would take her into total darkness.

Murmured voices drew Abby into the basement shadows. She shook ice crystals from her jacket and pushed her dripping hood off her head. Her outerwear was waterproof. The beads of moisture running between her shoulder blades and pooling at the base of her spine were pure sweat. Her eyes adjusted to the reduced light. A large angular shape loomed on the other side of the room. She shuffled across the slab. Stairs.

Abby crept up. At the top, the door was open. Staying low, she peered over the top step. At the end of a short, dim corridor, Ethan's back was to her. He was pointing his gun forward. Eight or so feet in front of him, she could see Derek in a chair and Joe using the boy as a shield. Derek's face and mouth were bleeding, his neck and light gray jacket wet and red. Anger and pity burned in Abby's chest as Joe made a shallow cut in the boy's neck.

A low moan came from Derek.

And suddenly Abby wasn't afraid for herself anymore. Nothing that could happen to her could be worse than Joe hurting Derek.

"Put the gun down, cop," Joe said.

No! A fresh burst of fear coursed through Abby.

Ethan and Joe were at a standoff, but Joe would win because Ethan's heart must be twisting as hard as Abby's at the sight of the bleeding, terrified child. Once Ethan put his gun down, he'd be in danger too.

"Come on, Joe. Take me instead of the kid," Ethan offered.

Oh my God. Not Ethan. He'd taught her to trust, to be a part of a relationship rather than a separate and lost soul. She couldn't let anything happen to him.

She loved him.

Joe shook his head. "Do I look stupid? There's no way I'm taking a cop hostage."

The answer brought calm to Abby's trembling limbs. Joe didn't want Ethan. Joe wanted Abby. She could feel it in the marrow of her bones. There was only one solution to the problem, something Joe wouldn't be able to turn down—her. She was a twofer: contract completion and get-out-of-jail-free card.

Abby tucked the gun securely in the back of her jeans and pulled her wet jacket down over it. Then she walked out of the basement, hands up, palms facing Joe in a submissive position. "You don't really want him, do you, Joe?"

"Look who it is, the bitch who wouldn't die." Joe's eyes brightened. "You have more lives than a fucking cat."

"Abby, what are you doing?" Ethan yelled. "Get out of here."

She ignored him and kept her eyes focused on Joe. "I'll make you a deal. I'll trade me for them. It's your only chance of getting out of here, and you know it. The police will be here in a couple of minutes."

Hope gleamed in Joe's eyes.

Abby pressed forward another step. "Come on. Let's go. You and I can drive out of here right now. Everyone else stays."

Joe froze with indecision. Sweat dripped from his temple down his cheek.

"Minutes, Joe. They'll be here in minutes." Abby willed her voice not to shake. Fear shook her bones. Not for herself. That had passed. No, now she was afraid he wouldn't take her offer. That he had a death wish and he'd want stay here and engage in a go-out-in-a-blaze-of-glory type shoot-out with the police.

But along with the drug high, hope shone through his dilated eyes. Joe didn't have a death wish. He wanted an out.

"What do you think is going to happen if you stay here?" She inched forward. "I'm the one you've wanted all along, right?"

Joe licked his lips. Could he taste his freedom? Abby hoped so. As much as she didn't want to go with him, she needed to get him away from Derek and Ethan. She couldn't bear it if anything happened to either of them. She seemed doomed to attract killers anyway. Even if she escaped this one, another was sure to follow. She should never have formed any personal relationships. The danger to Ethan, Derek, and Krista was all her fault.

She moved around Ethan, staying too far away for him to reach her and make her stop.

"Abby, don't do this," Ethan said.

She stopped a few feet in front of Joe. "What do you say?"

The answer was in the ready-to-roll set of Joe's body. "Turn around."

Abby pivoted, giving him her back. She met Ethan's gaze

across the room. Her own terror was reflected back at her. He silently pleaded with her. But the decision was made.

Joe moved faster than she anticipated. In an instant, he was behind her. One hand grabbed her shoulder. The sharp edge of the knife pressed into the skin of her neck. She arched backward to keep the blade off her neck and the gun in her waistband from touching Joe.

"Don't come after us. I'll slit her throat." Joe steered her away.

"You're going to kill her anyway," Ethan said.

"True," Joe admitted. "But I'll kill her right now as opposed to later."

Abby stumbled over something. Without moving her chin, she cast her gaze downward. Mr. Sheridan lay on the kitchen floor. Blood covered his clothing from a gaping wound in his neck. The sight made it very clear what the knife at her neck could do with a small movement. Guilt swamped her, weakening her spine. Mr. Sheridan's death was all her fault too.

"In there," Joe prompted.

Abby opened the door in front of her. It led into the two-car garage. Joe's blue pickup was parked next to Mr. Sheridan's four-door Mercury. Joe handed keys to Abby over her shoulder. "You drive."

He pressed a button on the wall. With a whirring noise, the garage door rattled up. Joe pushed her into the passenger side. Lowering the knife to point at her belly, he forced her to scoot across the bench seat of the truck.

OK. This was bad. He had a knife pointed at her side, but she was armed too. And wouldn't that come as a surprise to Joe? Unfortunately, there was no way she could pull her gun in her current position. She reached for the seat belt.

"No seat belt for you." Joe flicked the knife across her side.

The point ripped through her insulated jacket. "No crashing the car on purpose." He fastened his own belt.

Still, he couldn't stab her while she was driving. He'd wait until he was safe before eliminating his hostage. Eventually, they'd stop. All Abby needed was a few feet of space. If she could just get out of arm's reach, she could shoot him.

"Go!" He poked her in the ribs. Pain burned her side as the knifepoint sank into her skin. Blood trickled warm down her hip.

Abby backed out of the garage into the street. Shifting into drive, she hit the gas too hard. The tires spun. Joe gave her another tiny jab. Blood, wet and warm, soaked her jeans. "Take it easy."

She eased up on the accelerator. The truck rolled forward, and she drove out of the development. The neighborhood was a gray, wet misery.

"Make a right." Joe turned on the heater. Warm air blew from the vents, but Abby's bones shivered.

She made a slow turn onto the country road that led away from town. The asphalt was covered in a thin sheet of freezing rain. Ice clumped on the wipers. She turned on the defrosters.

"Not too fast." Joe swiveled his head around to look behind them. "We don't want to attract any attention."

Sirens wailed, but Abby was driving away from them.

"My luck has finally changed." Joe opened the glove compartment. Abby's gut went colder than the slush on the windshield. He pulled out a gun.

Ethan's lungs seized as the door closed behind Abby and Joe.

No! She was gone. He had to go after her.

A whimper from Derek shook Ethan out of his daze. How badly was the kid hurt?

"You have to find her." Derek's shaky words were slurred, and speech was clearly painful.

Sirens wailed thin in the distance.

"I know." Ethan's gaze jerked to Krista, unconscious on the floor. Her chest was rising and falling. "Help is on the way."

Derek nodded, jerking his head toward the door. "Please. Go."

Ethan ran to the garage. He grabbed a set of keys on a wall peg and jumped in the big sedan. Taking Mr. Sheridan's car was faster than running back to Abby's house for the pickup. He stopped at the exit of the development. Which way?

Away from the sirens, he decided, and turned right. The mixed precipitation had turned to 100 percent freezing rain. The visibility was as shitty as the traction. The road surface was black and slick as an oil patch. Ethan could feel the ice slide under the tires, but he pushed the car anyway.

They couldn't have gotten far.

A blue spot in the distance gave him hope. He accelerated.

Please, let her not be dead.

Ethan drew closer. An SUV. Not Abby.

Where was she?

———

Once Abby had put a few miles between Joe and the people she loved, fear for her own safety gathered fresh in her throat. She was alone with a killer, a man who'd already tried to kill her twice.

"Slow down." Joe pointed to an intersection ahead. "Turn left up there."

"Why do you want to kill me?" Abby glanced over.

"You don't get to ask the questions." Joe slid the knife into a sheath at his belt and rested the gun casually across his thigh. The muzzle wasn't pointed at her. What were her options? "This time I'm making sure you are a hundred percent dead. A bullet won't look like an accident, but it's fast and efficient. I followed you until you pulled over, then waited for you to pass out. I drove your car to the creek. You were out cold when I pushed your car into the water. I had to hike two miles back to my vehicle in that fucking sleet storm. There's no way you should have been able to escape. I put enough juice in your bottle to put you under for hours."

"I saved half for after my run."

"Well, fuck me. I didn't think of that." Joe scratched his chin. "You escaped my chemical bombs too. No matter. No screwing around this time."

"What if I pay you to not kill me?" she asked.

"There are some people you don't turn on. What you're going to do right now is shut the fuck up. I got you. No more lucking out for you. I'm going to do this once and for all." Joe sounded relaxed and confident. Since they'd turned off the main road a few miles back, he'd stopped looking through the back window every ten seconds.

There went that idea. Back to finding a way to escape. She could crash the car. But Joe was wearing his seat belt. She wasn't. Driving into a tree would likely be worse for her than him. Slamming on the brakes wouldn't work on the icy road.

"Make a left," he said.

Abby turned. The truck fishtailed, but she straightened it out. A mile later, the road curved to the right. Just ahead, the Packman Creek bubbled on the other side of a narrow strip of grass. She'd woken up in the creek just a couple of miles downstream from here. Abby eased through the next turn with more care. She did not want to end up in the creek again.

Or did she?

She shivered at the memory of being submerged in the frigid water. She might not get so lucky a second time. Drowning was a definite possibility. But could anything be worse than whatever Joe had in mind? If she went to their final, private destination, she was facing a bullet to the head.

Joe sat up and started scanning the area with a critical eye. Was he looking for a place to kill her and dump her body? His fingers twitched on the gun. He checked the load. "Pull over here."

His gun was in his hand. Hers was at her back. Could she get it out while climbing out of the car before Joe shot her? Doubtful.

Her gaze slipped to the churning creek. A slim possibility of escape was better than none at all.

She jerked the wheel. The car skidded on an angle toward the bank of the creek. A bump sent her flopping over the steering wheel.

"What the fuck?" Joe dropped his gun and grabbed for the armrest. The truck bounced and bumped down the snowy bank and hit the water harder than Abby anticipated. The airbag exploded in her face. Her left arm buckled. Pain snapped through her elbow like a bolt of electricity.

Next to her, Joe coughed. "Shit. You stupid bitch."

Dust hovered in the moist air. He turned in his seat and punched her in the face. Pain burst through her cheekbone. She blinked at the blackness creeping across her visual field. Passing out meant death.

Water chilled Abby's ankles. Joe opened his window and released his seat belt. He bent double, sticking his hand in the eight inches of water on the floorboards and feeling around. He sat up and shook water from the barrel of his gun.

Abby's heart seized. This time, she wouldn't escape death.

The car rocked hard, and Joe fell sideways. Metal groaned.

"Fuck it." He hoisted himself up on the edge of the window, slid out, and fell backward with a splash.

Abby pushed at the button on her door. Nothing happened. She tried again, but the window didn't budge. The wires must have shorted out.

She scooted across the bench seat. A white-hot wave of pain shot up her left arm. She looked down. Nausea rolled through her. Her elbow was not supposed to bend in that direction. The creek lapped over her knees and froze her thighs.

Abby's vision tunneled. The pickup spun, the force of the current dragging the truck farther toward the center of the creek. The cab tilted, and gravity pulled Abby away from the open window. Water closed over her head and stole her breath.

CHAPTER TWENTY-NINE

Ethan stopped the car and K-turned to reverse his direction. With only a couple of minutes lead time, there was no way Abby and Joe had gotten any farther ahead. Ethan had pushed the Marquis to a crazy speed on the icy road.

They must have turned off onto a back road. But which one? Where would Joe want to go?

Joe was from Atlantic City. How well did he know Westbury? Not well, would be Ethan's guess. How would a stranger find his way using back roads?

Ethan cruised through an intersection. Wait. He braked. This was the road that led to the Packman Creek. He turned. Joe couldn't know every road in the area, but he'd definitely scoped this one out when he'd planned to kill Abby the first time. Ethan spun the wheel. The Mercury skidded, the ass end of the vehicle swinging forward. He steered into the skid. The car straightened, and he sped forward.

He slowed at a sharp curve in the road.

There! Just ahead, a blue pickup was door-deep and sinking in the raging creek. Wet from head to toe, Joe was stumbling up the bank. His knees gave out, and he fell face-first into the shallow water. Ethan called for backup as he hit the brakes. The car slid. The pedal vibrated under his foot as the antilock system kicked in. He parked and leaped from his vehicle. He sprinted to the water's edge.

The well-being of Joe Torres wasn't a blip on Ethan's radar.

Where was Abby?

She must be trapped in the nearly submerged pickup. Ethan plunged into the creek. The frigid water shocked his body as it lapped up his thighs.

A splash caught his attention. Ethan spun. Joe was on one knee, gun in hand. Ethan drew his weapon. Too late. The first bullet caught him in the chest. The impact spun him around. He dropped to his knees. He lifted his gun. Before he could aim or shoot, the second bullet knocked him off his feet and into the icy creek.

Abby . . .

Abby surfaced and sucked in a painful breath. The truck rested on its side. Cradling her injured limb close, she stood on the steering column and pushed her shoulders out the passenger window. A toehold on the dashboard sent her body up and out the opening. She landed on her back in the creek. The current was strong enough to move a pickup. Could she make it to shore?

What choice did she have?

She paddled with one arm, angling toward the bank as if caught in a riptide. Her feet dragged on the bottom.

A gunshot rang out over the roar of the flooded creek. Abby lurched to her feet and spun toward the sound. A few yards from her, Joe was pointing his gun at Ethan, standing twenty feet away. Abby spread her feet for balance against the thigh-deep current. She fumbled with the tight bottom hem of her jacket. Shoving the fabric up, she grabbed her gun and brought it around.

Joe fired again. Ethan recoiled from the bullet's impact. He slid under the water.

Abby screamed, "No!"

Joe turned toward her and brought his gun around. Abby squeezed the trigger three times in rapid succession. Joe fell backward, crashing through the sheets of thin ice at the water's edge. His head sank beneath the surface.

Abby rushed toward Ethan. The freezing water slowed her steps. She spotted him floating just under the surface in two feet of water. She grabbed the back of his jacket and rolled him over. His eyes opened, and he coughed. Abby's heart resumed beating as she used her good arm to drag him to the shoreline, then collapsed on the muddy riverbank. Ethan's breaths rasped. Abby knelt by his side and cradled his head on her lap. He was too heavy for her to pull all the way out of the frigid water. His skin was pale gray, and his eyes lost focus.

"Stay with me," she pleaded, her heart aching. He couldn't die.

Sirens approached. A minute later, two patrol cars and an SUV roared onto the scene.

"Please don't die." Abby cupped Ethan's face. Why had it taken her so long to open her heart? "I love you."

Please, let it not be too late.

CHAPTER THIRTY

The tiny surgical waiting room was cold and the plastic chair hard. Abby shivered. An X-ray had revealed her elbow was fractured, but all the bones were in the right place. Her arm was casted at a ninety-degree angle. She'd been warmed up and released. Brooke had brought her dry clothes and a heavy sweatshirt, but she'd had to cut the left sleeve off for Abby to put it on. A blanket draped around her shoulders, and her arm was elevated on a pillow. Brooke wanted to take her home, but even though the ER doctor had said that Ethan's injuries weren't life-threatening, Abby didn't want to leave until he was out of surgery.

Chief O'Connell appeared in the doorway. "Any word?"

"No," Abby said. "How's Derek?"

"The plastic surgeon is working on him now." The chief lowered his bulk into the chair next to Abby.

Though the cuts on Derek's face were small, the ER doctor hadn't wanted him to have any facial scars as permanent reminders of his trauma.

Abby shifted her position but couldn't get comfortable. "Maybe I should run down and check on him."

"Derek wouldn't know you were there. They sedated him to work on his tongue." The chief swallowed.

Abby's stomach turned.

"Yeah. The idea gives me the willies too." The big man

shuddered. "Brooke is with him. Did Joe Torres say why he was after you?"

"No," Abby said. And he certainly wasn't going to talk in the morgue.

The chief didn't say anything, but Abby could feel the tension rolling off of him. He wasn't comfortable with the loose ends Joe's death left hanging.

Movement in the doorway startled Abby, but it wasn't the surgeon. Ethan's mother, Lorraine, hurried into the room. She hugged the chief. "It was sweet of you to send a car for me. I would've been fine driving. The weather is clearing."

"It was no trouble." The chief blushed.

"Have you heard from the surgeon?" Lorraine asked. "When you called you said they thought Ethan would be fine."

"He will be." The chief pinched the bridge of his nose. "Thank God he was wearing his Kevlar vest."

One of Joe's bullets had hit Ethan dead center in the chest. If he hadn't been wearing his body armor, Ethan would be dead. The other shot had struck him in the shoulder, and blood loss had been minimized by the water temperature.

Lorraine turned to Abby with open arms. "Oh dear. I don't want to hurt you." Lorraine frowned at Abby's cast and gave her good arm a gentle squeeze.

"How did you get here so quickly?" Abby asked. Ethan had only been brought to the hospital a few hours ago.

"I almost didn't make it. I ended up on a crack-of-dawn flight to New York. I took a train from there and got in this afternoon." Lorraine tilted her head.

But? "I thought you were in Florida for another couple of weeks."

"Ethan called me yesterday and asked me if I'd come home

early." Worry lines fanned out from the corners of Lorraine's eyes. "He said he'd applied to be Derek's foster parent and asked if I would mind coming home to help out with him. Of course I didn't mind, though the weather made getting here a challenge."

Ethan's words echoed in Abby's head. *Trust me, Derek. It's only temporary.* Had he already filed when he'd said that?

Abby closed her eyes and rested her head against the wall. Derek was a child, and a damaged one at that. His inability to trust Ethan was understandable. But Abby . . . Even after all he'd done for her, she hadn't trusted him either.

Would she ever be normal?

"He didn't tell you in case it fell through." Lorraine took the chair on Abby's opposite side. "He didn't want Derek to be disappointed."

Emotions clogged Abby's throat. "Derek would have appreciated the fact that he was trying."

"The good news is that we have a temporary approval. Derek can come home with us when he's released."

"Oh, thank God." Abby let a small bit of tension escape. "You don't know how relieved Derek will be."

Lorraine leaned closer. "How is his mother?"

"I don't know." Abby looked to Chief O'Connell.

"She has a concussion. Her physical injuries aren't life-threatening, but she was pretty messed up when the EMTs brought her in." He shrugged. "My guess is that she'll go right from here to a rehab facility. She won't be getting Derek back for a long time."

"Well, he can stay with us for good." Lorraine nodded emphatically. "Does your arm hurt much?"

Yes. "It's not too bad," Abby said.

"If you want to go home, I'll call you the second the surgeon comes out," the chief offered.

Abby lifted her head. "No. I'm all right." Despite the pills the ER doctor had given her, pain pulsed through Abby's elbow with every beat of her heart. And she knew from experience that nothing was going to make her feel warm for the next couple of days.

She would not be able to rest until she'd seen Ethan with her own eyes.

Or so she thought.

"Abby." A pat on her hand startled Abby awake. She blinked and rubbed her eyes. She must have dozed off. Lorraine stood in front of her. A green-scrubbed surgeon was walking out of the waiting room, obviously just finished giving an update on Ethan's condition. Chief O'Connell was standing by the door.

"He's out of surgery and awake." Lorraine hugged her purse to her side. "They're putting him in the same room as Derek. We can see them both in a few minutes if you'd like."

"Yes." Abby wobbled as she stood. "Is he OK?"

"He's fine." The chief put a hand under her good elbow. "The bullet didn't hit anything vital. They took it out and stitched him up."

The three walked down the hall and into the elevator. Ethan was already settled when they reached the room.

Lorraine zoomed in and brushed his hair away from his face. "You shouldn't scare your old mother like that."

"Where's Abby?" Ethan's voice was hoarse.

"Right behind me." Lorraine poured water into a cup from a plastic pitcher on his tray. She held it close to his mouth so he could drink through the straw. Ethan's eyes shifted over his mom's shoulder to Abby.

"I'm going to get a cup of coffee." Lorraine stepped out of the way. Her eyes were wet as she walked past Abby.

"I'll go with you." Chief O'Connell joined her in the hall.

Abby stepped up to the bed.

Ethan reached for her hand. "I thought I'd lost you."

"That makes two of us." Abby leaned down and placed a soft kiss on his lips. She rested her forehead against his for a few seconds, then whispered in his ear, "I love you."

"I know. I heard you in the creek." Ethan kissed her back. "I love you too."

"I don't doubt it." Abby sighed against his cheek. "You're not the one with enough baggage to fill a freight train."

He squeezed her hand. "I love you and every pound of baggage that comes with you."

A tear slid down Abby's cheek. "Thank God. I thought I'd messed up."

"You risked your life to save me and Derek," Ethan said. "Sure, I was furious when you did it, but only because I couldn't stand the thought of Joe hurting you. Did you really think I'd fall out of love with you for an overabundance of courage?"

The relief that flowed through Abby's veins was better than the pain medication. She kissed him again. "I should have known better. No more doubts. Ever."

"I should hope not." He eyed her cast. "Now, what happened? Tell me everything."

"Broke my elbow."

"What happened to Joe Torres?"

"He's dead." Abby's stomach turned. "I shot him." She still couldn't believe she'd sighted and fired without a single hesitation.

Her reaction had been a reflex. Joe was trying to kill Ethan. Abby stopped him. No thought involved.

Ethan squeezed her hand. "You saved me."

"Now we're even." Exhaustion flooded Abby as she touched his hand and watched his chest rise and fall. Ethan looked better than fine. He was breathing and warm and alive. The moment when Joe had shot him would be imprinted on her mind forever. "I feel like I should have more remorse. I killed a man."

No doubt the guilt would come with time.

"He tried to kill you multiple times. He shot me. He cut up Derek's face. There's no reason for you to feel any guilt." Ethan blinked. "The nurse said they're putting Derek in here with me. How is he?"

"I haven't seen him since they brought us in, but Chief O'Connell said they were having a plastic surgeon stitch him up, and Brooke is with him."

"We're right here." Brooke walked into the room. Behind her, a nurse was pushing Derek in a wheelchair. Bandages covered the cuts on his cheek and jaw. His eyes were glassy as the nurse helped him into bed.

He smiled at Abby and winced.

"I wouldn't try talking just yet." The nurse adjusted the bedrail and handed him the remote.

"There will be unlimited ice cream and popsicles for the next few weeks." Brooke stood by Derek's bed. "But he's going to heal just fine."

Abby released Ethan's hand and went over to give Derek a one-armed hug. He leaned his head on her shoulder. She straightened and blotted a tear leaking from her eye. His gaze searched hers, fear lingering under the sedative's glaze. Did he want to know about his mother? Abby leaned closer and whispered, "Your mom's OK, but we can't see her right now."

He nodded, his body sagging with relief. Abby knew exactly how he felt. Tiny trembles started in her legs.

"Honestly, Abby, you look worse than he does," Brooke said.

"She's coming home with me." Lorraine came back in the room and put an arm around Abby's waist.

"I can go back to my house," Abby protested even though the last thing she wanted was to be alone.

"Nonsense. Your dog is already at my house—Ronnie is there with him—and you're hardly in any condition to drive." Lorraine gave her a gentle squeeze. "And what if you don't feel well during the night? I think Ethan will rest more easily if you're with me, won't you?" Lorraine gave Ethan a pointed look.

"Definitely." Ethan gave her a drugged half smile.

Lorraine's hug was so comforting, Abby didn't even mind that she was squeezing the small cuts Joe had made with his knife.

Abby kissed Derek on the top of his head. Ethan got a kiss on the lips that made her heart ache.

Ethan wiped a tear from Abby's cheek with his thumb. "Derek and I will be fine here. Right, Derek?"

The boy nodded.

"Go get some rest," Ethan pleaded.

"All right." Abby let Lorraine and the chief lead her to the ER lobby. The main doors had locked hours ago. Outside, the sleet had stopped and the temperature had risen above freezing. But the wind sent a shiver through Abby's bones. Chief O'Connell brought his SUV to the hospital entrance and drove them out to the farm. In the house, Lorraine tried to absorb Zeus's enthusiastic greeting.

Ethan's cousin Ronnie was in the kitchen. She was dressed in jeans, boots, and a sweater. Ronnie might be off duty, but she'd included her sidearm in her casual attire. "How is everything?"

Lorraine buzzed her niece on the cheek and filled her in. "Thanks for house-sitting."

Sweetums rubbed on Lorraine's leg and hissed at Abby. The dog cowered, which seemed to satisfy the cat. It jumped onto the bookshelf and stared down with a blend of disdain and superiority.

"Glad to help out, Aunt Lorraine. The horses and Zeus are fed." Ronnie leaned down to rub Zeus's head. "But your cat is evil. Isn't he, Zeus?"

The dog butted Abby's legs. She went down on one knee, hugged him with one arm, and buried her face in his massive neck for a minute.

"Are you staying?" the chief asked Ronnie.

"Yes," Ronnie said.

"Then I'm headed home." The chief left.

"I'm going to check the horses one last time. I'll take the dog out while I'm at it." Ronnie put on her coat. "Come on, Zeus."

Zeus followed her outside.

Abby swayed. "If you don't mind, I'm going to bed."

Lorraine walked Abby to the guest room. "Are you sure you don't need anything? Do you have your pain medicine?"

"I'm all set." Abby was unaccustomed to having anyone fuss over her, but Lorraine's concern gave her a warm spot in the middle of her chest.

"Good night then." Lorraine closed the door on her way out.

Every inch of Abby's body ached. She crawled into bed still dressed in the yoga pants and mangled sweatshirt she'd been wearing at the hospital.

It felt like she'd just closed her eyes when a noise startled her awake. Abby sat up. Even in the brightly lit room, it took a minute to orient herself.

Thump.

It was probably the cat. Abby sat up. Agony shattered her elbow. Her body was feverish-hot, her mouth dry as sand. A glance at the nightstand told her the pain meds had worn off. Doing her best not to jar her arm, she eased to her feet and walked gingerly to the door. The hallway and house beyond were dark. Abby felt for a light switch as she shuffled toward the kitchen. Where was it? Pain kept her nerves at bay, and frankly, she was too damned tired for her phobia to kick in.

Her hand swiped at the wall in the kitchen. The lights went on. A woman was standing in the middle of the room pointing a gun at Abby.

CHAPTER THIRTY-ONE

The dock creaked under Ryland's feet. The dark water of the bay rippled white all the way across the sound. On either side, boats bobbed. Metal clanged, and the tails of carefully secured sails and lines snapped in the wind. The storm had passed, but the cold front that had pushed the weather system up the coast left an arctic howl in its wake. He turned back to watch the dockyard. The wind sheared through Ryland's heavy overcoat with brute force.

Headlights swept across the pilings.

Paul was here. Had he come alone?

It had been their agreement, but Ryland knew from experience that promises didn't mean much when dealing with the likes of Paul Medina. A large sedan parked in the shadows. Ryland's vehicle was also parked far from the overhead lights. The darker the better.

Another gust shoved against his back, and he stiffened his spine against the push. Though Ryland hated the cold, a strong wind was his ally. He hadn't chosen the dock by accident. In case Paul was looking to double-cross him and wearing a wire to their meeting, the sounds of wind and water would interfere with microphone reception, rendering a recording useless. Paul knew this as well and, with similar suspicions of Ryland, had agreed to the neutral meeting ground.

A dark figure emerged from the vehicle and walked toward him. A small orange glow bobbed with his steps. Coming to a stop a few feet from Ryland, Paul didn't complain about the cold either. Instead of a two-way street, trust was a dead end in their relationship.

Paul nodded in greeting. He pulled his cigar from between his teeth. "Cigar?"

"No. Thank you." Ryland was in no mood for social niceties.

Paul sensed his all-business inclination. "Have you given any further thought to my proposal? I have only your interests in mind."

"Was it you? Did you try to kill her?" Ryland bit off the words. A fresh gust whipped off the bay and tugged at his coat.

"First of all, I don't *try* to kill anyone." Paul let the implication hang in the air. He tapped his cigar over the water. The ashes took flight, the glow blinking out seconds after they left the burning tip. "Secondly, I have no idea who you're talking about."

"My daughter."

Paul's eyes gave nothing away. "You have a daughter?"

"You didn't know?" Ryland wished he could be on equal emotional footing in this conversation. But family was his one weakness, the only piece of his life he couldn't compartmentalize, even the daughter he'd neglected all these years.

"As much as I would like to, I can't know everything." Damn Paul. Never gave a fucking straight answer. He'd never admit anything. Was he telling the truth? Was Abby's existence really a surprise? Paul was a damned good liar. Men without consciences usually were. Ryland should know.

"None of us can," Ryland said. "We make the best choices with the information at our disposal."

Paul's eyes flickered. "You're sure you don't want to reconsider your decision about the business? As I told you the last time we spoke, there are other parties upset by your actions. Perhaps one of them learned of your daughter's existence. Threats to one's family are so disturbing."

"You're right. Perhaps I should reconsider all my options."

"That would be the best way to secure your family's future." Paul's eyes gleamed with victory—and greed. Unlike the casino and entertainment industry, drug-running was impervious to economic downturns. "I'll let the interested parties know. How soon will your decision be implemented?"

"Immediately."

Paul nodded with enthusiasm. "You've made a wise decision, my friend."

"We're hardly friends."

"Be that as it may, you can rest easier knowing your family is safe." Paul turned and started down the dock.

Ryland drew his gun, put the barrel to the back of Paul's head, and pulled the trigger twice. Paul collapsed and crumpled to the dock. He rolled to his side. His eyes were a blank slate. He hadn't even had a chance to register his shock.

"Yes, I can rest easy now that my family is safe." Ryland signaled. His men climbed from a nearby boat and collected the body. He handed them his gloves and the gun. Ignoring the sounds of wood creaking as one of his employees replaced a bloodstained board, Ryland turned back to the horizon. A few minutes later, the boat eased from its mooring and chugged into the bay. He followed the sight of the boat's running lights until the vessel disappeared in the darkness.

He stood for a moment and stared out over the choppy water. For all the turmoil evident on its surface, what happened in its murky depths remained a mystery. Sometimes she hoarded her secrets like gold. Other times she tossed them onto her shores as if unworthy of her efforts.

Ryland had no worries. His men knew how to make sure Paul never surfaced.

Once Paul knew about Abby, he had to die. There was no way Ryland would put her in harm's way again. Plus, the death would serve as notice to any other parties who were considering various ways to pressure him into submission.

Ryland would not tolerate threats to his family.

He walked down the dock and got into his car. Maybe Paul had forgotten how to take care of his own business, but Ryland remembered how things got done before he had men like Kenneth on his payroll. Sometimes if one wanted a task completed, it paid to do it oneself.

"Don't move."

Abby froze as instructed. She had to be hallucinating. She blinked hard, but the woman was still there. The gun-toting lady was in her midfifties, medium height with professionally styled dark hair and expensive clothes. She looked vaguely familiar.

The woman was giving Abby the same critical once-over.

"How did you get in here?" Abby asked.

The woman lifted a confident shoulder. "Every wife should learn to pick locks. You never know what your husband might be hiding."

Where was Zeus? He should have barked. Abby spotted him in the next room, lying on his side. "What did you do to my dog?"

The woman rolled her eyes. "I gave him a couple of my sleeping pills. *He'll* be fine. You should be more concerned for yourself."

"What do you want?"

"You. Dead. It looks like if I want it done, I have to do it myself." Her tone was disgusted. "Neither of the two men I hired could get it right."

"I don't understand."

"Of course you don't. That's all right. You don't have to be smart. You're blonde, and you're pretty." Marlene snickered at her own joke.

"Who are you?"

"My name is Marlene Valentine. If you weren't the illegitimate daughter of a whore, I'd be your stepmother."

Abby's lungs expelled all their air. She'd only seen Ryland's wife in photos. "What? Why do you want to kill me?"

"He's dying, you know." From the gleeful tone of her voice, the thought didn't distress Marlene. "He was diagnosed with cancer three years ago."

The truth hit Abby. "When I was kidnapped."

"You're not as dumb as you look." With every word, hatred poured out of Marlene's mouth. "After that moron Faulkner botched your killing, Ryland went into remission. I let it go. But the cancer is back, and this time it's going to take him. That means your reprieve is over too. He thinks I don't know, that I'm stupid. Well, honey, I know everything. And not just about the cancer. I know all about the girls over the years. Your slutty mother. You."

"I had nothing to do with any of that." Abby took a step back. "Trust me, being born wasn't my decision."

"No, but now you have the power to take something that rightfully belongs to my sons." Marlene pointed the gun at Abby. "I've invested thirty-five years of my life in that man. Do you know how many hours I spent on my knees making him happy?

I put up with him coming to my bed smelling of hookers and dancers. I took the risk that he didn't give me any horrible disease. And I did it all for my sons. They deserve to inherit his entire empire. They shouldn't have to share it with a whore's daughter."

"I want nothing from Ryland."

"Then why did you see him Friday night?"

"I thought he might know who was trying to kill me."

"He doesn't." A self-satisfied smirk twisted Marlene's mouth. "I'm way smarter than him."

Abby eased back another step.

"You're going with me." Marlene gestured toward the door with the gun. "You don't need a coat. You'll be dead before you get cold."

Abby walked barefoot across the tile. If she could get a little distance between them, she could break away. She went through the doorway that led to the living room and the front door and darted to the left.

"Get back here, you little bitch." Marlene came through the doorway after her.

Yowl.

"Ah!" Marlene screeched.

Abby spun around. Sweetums was doing his back-arched, hissing routine at Marlene. Her expensive slacks were shredded. Blood seeped through the silky material at her calves. She pointed the gun at the cat. Abby raised her arm and brought her cast down on Marlene's wrist. The gun clattered to the floor. Marlene spun and grabbed Abby's hair. The cat hissed again, and Marlene kicked at him.

"Freeze."

They did. A rumpled-looking Ronnie leveled a gun at Marlene. "Put your hands in the air."

Fury contorted Marlene's features, but she complied.

"Don't move," Ronnie ordered. She whipped out her phone and called for backup. "Abby, there are some plastic ties in the garage. Would you bring me a couple?"

"Sure." Abby turned.

Glass broke. Something thudded. Marlene dropped to the floor, a perfect hole in the center of her forehead.

"What the . . . ?" Ronnie dropped into a crouch. She grabbed Abby and hustled her into the kitchen. "Stay down."

Abby held her arm close to her body. Her body was oddly cold and her head light, but the white-hot pain in her arm kept her focused.

"Oh no." Ronnie's hand was on her back. "Put your head down."

"What's going on?" Lorraine yelled from the hall.

"That was a gunshot! Stay back there, Aunt Lorraine," Ronnie shouted back.

Sirens wailed in the distance as Abby put her forehead on her knees. An hour later, the property was swarming with cops: local, state, county. But there was no sign of the shooter.

CHAPTER THIRTY-TWO

One week later

Ethan walked out to the barn. He was still embarrassingly weak, and his tolerance for the cold made him long for a Florida beach. But even recuperating, he had too many responsibilities to go anywhere.

But he was OK with that. More OK than he'd been in a long time.

Derek had the roan pony in the aisle. He was carefully combing the tangles from his mane while the animal nosed through the kid's pockets for treats.

Ethan gave the roan's neck a rub. "How is he?"

Derek just nodded. He still wasn't talking much. His cuts were healing, but his inability to enunciate words correctly embarrassed him.

"I wanted to talk about a couple of things." Ethan eased into a conversation that would likely upset the kid. He'd get the bad news over with first, then more into what he hoped would make the boy happy. "Your mom is going into a rehab center. They're going to help her quit drinking and get her life back on track, but she's going to be gone for a while."

The comb paused then resumed the short strokes on the pony's mane.

"I was hoping you'd be OK with staying on the farm. I could use some help around here. You know my cousin Ronnie has been pestering the devil out of me to adopt these two horses." Ethan unzipped his jacket to adjust his sling. Not only was Mr. Smith prohibited from owning large animals, he was going to jail for his armed assault on Abby and Ethan.

Derek put the comb in the bucket by the wall and pulled out a soft brush. He went to work removing some caked dirt on the pony's foreleg.

"I've been telling her I couldn't do it. I just don't have the time to take care of them. But if you were here, maybe you could do most of the work."

Derek looked up. His eyes were wet. Was he happy or sad? Probably both. He jumped up and threw his arms around Ethan's neck. Pain blasted through Ethan's shoulder, but he didn't care.

Derek released him, looking at his shoulder. "Sorry." His *r*'s sounded like *w*'s. Having the speech pattern of a three-year-old was one of the reasons Derek wasn't going back to school just yet. Physically, he'd heal quickly, but his emotional recovery was going to take longer.

"No problem." Ethan grinned. "I take it that's a yes?"

The boy nodded hard.

"Then you get to name them. You should hurry up before Cam and Bryce get home this weekend. They think of the weirdest names for horses."

"Batman and Robin."

Ethan laughed. "I assume this little guy is Robin?"

Derek nodded.

"Batman and Robin are excellent names." Ethan shivered.

The cold didn't seem to bother Derek. A thick parka and insulated boots replaced his old, inadequate outerwear.

"Do you need any help with him?"

Derek shook his head. The last couple of days, he'd spent

long hours in the barn, basking in the healing powers of the animals.

The bay stuck his head out of his stall. Ethan went over to give his neck a rub. "How's Batman this morning?"

"Good." Derek was a natural with the skittish horse. They had a lot in common.

"I'm going back up to the house then." Though he was nervous about leaving the boy alone, Ethan knew Derek needed some space. The bond of trust between them needed to go both ways. Derek had promised not to run again, and Ethan believed him. "Abby's coming over soon."

"'Kay." Content, Derek went back to grooming the already-clean roan.

Ethan walked back to the house through a few inches of fresh snow. He left his boots and coat in the mudroom.

Abby parked in her driveway. The house next door was empty, the windows dark. A piece of yellow crime scene tape fluttered from the front porch. She unlocked her door and stepped into the foyer. Zeus greeted her with the usual enthusiasm. Despite the dog's warm welcome, her house no longer felt like her home. Every time she looked at Krista and Derek's house, memories swamped her.

She set her briefcase on the table and fed the dog. Exhaustion rolled through her. Returning to work right away had probably been a mistake. She put on a pot of coffee and perused the fridge. Nothing looked appealing. Coffee for now, then.

She sat down at the table and started grading papers. Three tests later, her eyes were crossing.

Zeus's head shot up. He headed for the front of the house with a deep *woof.* Her doorbell bonged, and his barking turned serious.

Cautious, Abby went to the living room window. A dark sedan was parked at the curb. She leaned close to the glass to get a view of her front porch. Shock woke her more than the caffeine. She opened the door. "Ryland. What are you doing here?"

He was the last person she expected to see. Marlene's death had set off a media firestorm. Though the police hadn't tied him to her murder, the press was happy to speculate on his guilt. Ryland had practically gone into seclusion.

A man, taller and somehow ominous, waited by the car.

"Abby. We need to talk." His face had aged ten years since she'd seen him just a week ago. Lines of grief, exhaustion, and worry creased his eyes.

She stood aside and pulled Zeus back by the collar so her father could enter. The big dog was a convenient barrier. Zeus snorted, punctuating several seconds of awkward silence.

"Do you want some coffee?" she asked.

"Yes, thank you." Ryland gave the dog a worried glance but followed her back to the kitchen. Zeus stretched out on the floor, his attention never wavering from the stranger.

"Good watchdog?"

"Very," Abby said.

Ryland nodded in approval and took a seat at the table. Abby poured coffee into a mug and handed it to him. She took the seat opposite him.

He set his cup down. "I'll be brief. I certainly don't want anyone to see me here and bring more unwanted attention to you, but there are some things you should know."

Abby waited, her own coffee untouched. Her nervous system,

primed from the violence of the past few weeks, dumped adrenaline into her bloodstream. Caffeine was no longer necessary.

Ryland struggled for words.

"Are you dying?"

"Yes." His mouth tightened into a grim line.

"How long?"

"Maybe a year, if I'm lucky." His gaze drifted to the window and back. He was lost, his confidence shattered. "I don't know exactly what to say to you. I was stupid and arrogant. I did exactly as I pleased for many years with no thought to the consequences. I didn't even know my own wife. She hated me. She hated you. And I was clueless."

Ryland sipped his coffee.

"She said she was afraid I'd sue for part of your estate. You know I don't want your money?"

"I know," Ryland said. "Neither did your mother. She took some only because she had to leave her job because of you."

Abby turned away.

"She didn't regret it, but she wasn't happy."

"I know." Abby didn't have a single memory of her mother smiling.

"Her sadness made her drink." Ryland frowned.

"Not all the time," Abby said. "She did her best."

"She did, but it wasn't enough. And that's my fault." Ryland straightened his shoulders as if he'd come to a decision. "I told you I kept you secret to keep you safe and because I was doing the honorable thing for my wife and sons. I lied."

"What?"

"I lied." Ryland's face drooped. "I couldn't tell anyone about you because of who your mother really was."

"I don't understand." Abby's coffee sloshed in her stomach. Instinct told her he was going to upset her world. "Mom was a waitress."

Ryland shook his head. "No. Your mother was a DEA agent. That's how we met. She was investigating me."

Abby gasped. Her mother had been a drug enforcement agent who slept with the drug dealer she was investigating.

"If anyone had found out about us . . . Let's just say the fall-out would have been bloody. You would have been at risk as well as my sons. Ultimately, that was why I decided to get out of those less legitimate business ventures. There was no way I wanted my sons involved in that industry."

No mention of Abby being involved, but then he'd made it clear he wanted nothing to do with her all her life.

"I've cleaned up my businesses over the last three years. There isn't anything illegal. My sons will be inheriting a one-hundred-percent legitimate company."

"Funded with drug money," Abby pointed out.

Ryland lifted an unconcerned shoulder. "The past is the past."

"Until it catches up with you," Abby said.

"Yes," Ryland agreed. "When you were kidnapped, I should have intervened. Your mother told the police detective about me. She was concerned that Faulkner was working for one of my business rivals. The detective blackmailed me when he should have been saving you. Roy Abrams knew where you were the entire time. Faulkner had marked your location with the GPS on his cell phone. The detective told Faulkner to keep quiet about your location, and he'd talk to the judge about minimizing his sentence." Coldness glittered in Ryland's eyes. "I should have been your father. I should have taken care of you. Instead I paid him to keep it all quiet."

Abby couldn't agree more. "Why now? Why come to my rescue?"

"Because I couldn't go to my grave while you had to wake up with the knowledge that the men who hurt you were still out there. I've been following you these last three years. You live half a life. I thought if everything connected to your kidnapping were wiped clean, then maybe you'd be free of the past. All I want is peace, for both of us."

"It's a little late for that."

"You can't imagine how sorry I am." Emotions whirled in his eyes.

But Abby had barely absorbed what he'd told her. She couldn't deal with Ryland's needs. "If you're looking for forgiveness, I'm not ready for that yet."

"I understand."

"Who killed Marlene?" Abby's gut knew, but she had to ask.

Just as Ryland had to ignore her question, though the uncharacteristic flash of sorrow in his eyes was answer enough. "Your brothers would like to meet you. Not just yet, though. They're dealing with their grief and a load of guilt. Their mother wanted to kill you for them."

"Not their fault."

"I know, and so do they. But it will likely take a while for them to accept."

Abby knew the feeling. "I'm not quite there yet either."

Her father had his wife killed for her betrayal. The police might never be able to prove he murdered her, but Abby knew the truth in her heart. How could she ever let a murderer into her tiny circle of trust?

"But they both want to know you." Ryland gave her a sad smile. "I shouldn't have kept you apart all these years."

How did she feel about meeting her half brothers? Surprisingly, pretty good. She'd thought she didn't have any family left.

She escorted Ryland to the door. After he left, she looked down at the dog. "Let's go see Ethan. I know it's weak, but I really can't be alone right now."

Zeus barked and wagged his tail. Fifteen minutes later, they drove up to the farmhouse and parked.

Lorraine had the door open before they knocked. "Ethan is in his room. Go on up. Dinner will be ready in twenty minutes. You'll stay."

It wasn't a question. Why did Ryland's orders annoy her, while Lorraine's gave her the warm and fuzzies?

———

With the remote in hand, Ethan reclined on his bed. He hadn't had much time to watch TV over the past few years. Since Abby insisted on living at her house and going back to work, he was left to entertain himself.

A knock sounded on his door.

"Come in."

Abby opened the door.

"Hey, beautiful."

She didn't say a word, but her expression was tense. He rolled smoothly to his feet. "What's wrong?"

Abby crossed the room. Ethan wrapped his arm around her and pulled her close. Burying her face in his good shoulder, he felt the tension ebb from her body. He rubbed her back and waited for her to tell him.

"Ryland came to see me." She let her father's revelations pour out.

"Holy. Shit." Ethan pulled her down to sit on the edge of the bed. Her mother being a former DEA agent explained why Abby handled a gun like a cop. "No wonder they kept their affair a secret."

"Maybe." Abby sighed. "I don't know that it matters much. Do you think Ryland had Abrams and Faulkner killed?"

"That would be my guess." Ethan nodded.

"I think he had Marlene killed too, because she betrayed him." Abby shuddered. "One thing I know for sure. It was better that I didn't grow up with him. He kills anyone who crosses him." Abby's eyes were misty when she looked at him. "Do you think the police will find any evidence?"

"I doubt it. I've talked to the investigators. Those kills were operating-room clean. Marlene's too. Ryland has alibis for all the killings, and the cops haven't uncovered any proof that he ordered the kills either." The cases might never be officially solved, but Ethan didn't see any loose ends. He hugged Abby to his side. "Do you want to see if I can find out more about your mother?"

"I don't know. Not right now. I've already learned my entire life wasn't what I thought it was. That's enough for the moment."

"Whatever you want." Ethan pulled back and examined her face. Exhausted lines fanned from her eyes, and her skin was still pale. Had she lost weight? "Have you been sleeping?"

"Not really," she admitted. "Even the lights don't seem to help. I'm wondering if I'll ever be able to be alone again."

"Give it a little time. It's only been a week." Ethan kissed her temple. "Did you see the therapist?"

"Yes. She doesn't want me to make any life changes right now, but I'm going to sell my house. I can't stand being alone, and I can't be there. The memories . . ."

"Move in here." Ethan laughed. "I guarantee you'll never be alone. This place is a zoo."

"I don't know," she said, but her eyes shed their lost look instantly.

"Please." He nuzzled her neck.

"What about Derek?"

His lips trailed lower. He pushed her hair off her shoulder to get a better angle on her neck. "You could help homeschool Derek."

"What about your mother?"

"I believe she just drafted her letter to the pope to have you sainted." His voice was dry.

"But we're not married. . . ."

"Then marry me." It wasn't a new thought. He'd already intended to marry her as soon as she was ready. The idea was a huge turn-on. He brushed the neckline of her sweater with his lips. Her skin smelled like peaches.

"I think that would be one of those life changes my therapist wouldn't like."

Ethan lifted his head. "Stop worrying. Move in here. We'll get married if and when you're ready. I love you. We've all been through hell. I think we can give ourselves a break and just do what feels right. At the moment, having you with me is what feels right."

"I love you too." A tear rolled down her cheek. "Well, I do sleep better when I'm with you."

Ethan wiped her tear away. "Who says you'll be getting any sleep?"

"I hardly think either of us is in any shape for that."

He kissed her, pouring out the emotions he couldn't put into words. "Speak for yourself. I'm sure I could manage. I'm very creative."

She laughed, the sound making Ethan's heart swell.

"You let me know when you're ready. I'm a patient man."

"Yes, you are." With a contented sigh, she kissed him back. "Don't worry. I won't keep you waiting long."

He nibbled his way down her neck. "Before you'll sleep with me or marry me?"

"Both." Abby's eyes shone with the happiness she'd deserved for a lifetime.

ACKNOWLEDGMENTS

As usual, thanks to my agent, Jill Marsal, for all her support, and everyone at Amazon Publishing, including my editor, JoVon Sotak, and the entire author team, especially technological goddess Jessica Poore. I am a very lucky writer to have such a fabulous team of people supporting me and my work.

Special thanks to Kiki Ebsen of the Healing Equine Ranch for sharing her incredible rescue horses with my family at a time when we needed their healing spirit, and to June Gunter for making that day possible. I can't believe it was a coincidence that I'd already begun this book and included rescue horses before the invitation to visit Violet and the other rescued equines.

ABOUT THE AUTHOR

Melinda Leigh abandoned her career in banking to raise her kids and never looked back. She started writing as a hobby and became addicted to creating characters and stories. Since then, she has won numerous writing awards for her paranormal romance and romantic-suspense fiction. Her debut novel, *She Can Run*, was a number-one bestseller in Kindle Romantic Suspense, a 2011 Best Book finalist (The Romance Reviews), and a nominee for the 2012 International Thriller Award for Best First Book. *Midnight Exposure* was a 2013 Daphne du Maurier Award finalist. When she isn't writing, Melinda is an avid martial artist: she holds a second-degree black belt in Kenpo karate and teaches women's self-defense. She lives in a messy house with her husband, two teenagers, a couple of dogs, and two rescue cats.

Made in United States
Orlando, FL
21 April 2023